HAWKE

By R.J. Lewis

This book is a work of fiction. Names, characters, place, events, and other elements portrayed herein are either the product of the author's imagination or used fictitiously. Any resemblance to real persons or events is coincidental.
The setting of this story is completely fake, derived purely from the imagination of the author.

For Hibba and Maya, who listened to my mumblings and psychotic rants and told me to relax.

Damn your positive attitudes.

I will not relax.

Prologue

Take care.
Take care of her.
I took it.
I took.
Don't trust.
Don't trust.
Don't...

one

Tyler

I blamed myself often for being responsible for Hawke's incarceration. If I had changed things that day – if I had gone out sooner rather than later – he never would have found himself behind bars.

I was thirteen, and it was a warm autumn day. The leaves had only just begun changing and the wind was cool. I was walking back from the deli, sandwich in my hand, moving in the direction of the clubhouse as my footsteps crunched softly on the leaves scattered along the sidewalk.

I remembered my heart feeling heavy, and I kept rubbing my chest, struggling to breathe through the pain.

It'd been exactly one year since my father had been killed, and I was besieged with sadness. I was still trying to figure out my place in the world without him there to guide me. I'd tried to be brave, but I wasn't strong like the others. I couldn't not cry, and I hated that I carried my emotions on my sleeve.

I didn't hear him creep up on me. I didn't know how long he'd been there until he finally spoke out.

"Hello Tyler."

I turned my head just as an officer (or cockroach as the club called them) pulled up beside me in his police vehicle. I recognized him and knew he wasn't a nice guy, but I couldn't remember his name. It was Brinsky or Hinsky, or something along those lines.

He was also corrupt as they come.

"How are you, honey?" he asked with an insincere smile.

"Fine," I answered simply.

"You wouldn't be heading down to that Warlord clubhouse?"

I shot him a wary look. "I am."

"Is that a smart idea, angel?"

"It's my home."

"Oh, but sweetheart," he said, cruelly, "it's not your home. You have a home somewhere else, don't you, with your whore of a mother. Is she still drinking herself to sleep every night? How is she doing these days now that your daddy is dead? You know he died real bad, don't you? And you know what happens to people when they die?"

I just stared at him.

He smirked. "They go all gross and shit. Maggots feast on their eyeballs, sucking up their juices. Don't look at me like that. I *know* what I'm talking about – I've *seen* it! That old man of yours? He's probably got 'em crawling out of his eye sockets and out of his nose and mouth, and probably out of every one of them bullet holes in his body. His skin's all decayed and shit, and I think his insides are gone right about now, but I'm not a wiz with decomposition, so what the fuck do I know?"

My stomach twisted, and my hands shook.

"I hear he suffered," he continued, smugly, "sort of like the way you'll suffer if you keep hanging around that bad crowd of devil worshippers. They'll whore you out too, you know. That's all they're good for, and I'm sure there's a market for little jail bait girls like you."

White hot rage flowed through me.

"It'd be sad seeing a pretty little girl like you used as a cum bucket. You still a virgin, or has that young hole been used –"

Without thinking, I threw my sandwich at him and it smacked into his face, causing him to press down on the brakes abruptly. The car came to a screeching stop, and I smiled maliciously at him as he wiped the ham and cheese off his face, leaving behind a slimy residue.

"Hawke says that men who talk too much are insecure cunts looking for something to prove," I told him. "He also said if they disrespect me, he'll cut their throats clean off their heads."

Cockroach was pissed. "You trailer trash bitch, I'll beat you."

"Yeah, well I don't see you stepping out of your car. Are you afraid to knowing who I am?"

He looked around the streets before he narrowed his eyes at me and said, "You think you're so special because your *president*" – sneer – "is by your side all the time? Well, Hawke's going down, girl. A little birdy told me he's going to prison, and when he's gone, I'm coming after you and you can join daddy in the grave and have maggots crawling out of your eyes together."

I swallowed the pain his words inflicted on me, determined not to show it. "Do you feel like a big bad man talking to me like that?"

"Shut your whoring mouth, little girl."

"You're so bent on talking to me but you can't handle what I have to say?"

"I said shut your fucking mouth."

"The girls around here complain about you," I went on, unconcerned that he was turning red. "They say you like it rough because you're trying to compensate for your tiny dick."

That wasn't true.

I had no idea what the girls said.

But having grown up around foul-mouthed men, their insults had rubbed off on me and I wasn't about to let him know his words had hurt that deep part in me; it was a part that was now envisioning my father being feasted on by maggots.

By now he wasn't just pissed, he was shaking from it. He opened the driver's side door, surprising me for a second because I didn't realize his seatbelt had been off the entire time. I turned, was about to run when he closed in on me and grabbed me by the hair. He threw me to the ground in one swing.

I went down awkwardly, my legs bent in a weird angle as I struggled moving, kicking wildly as he brought his face to mine, still gooey from my sandwich, and seethed, “You think you’re hot shit, don’t you, with your dirty little mouth?” His hands travelled down my body, grabbing at the spot between my legs and he gripped it hard, causing me to wince. He dug his fingers in that spot, violating me in a way nobody else had ever done.

Don’t cry. Don’t beg. Don’t show him you’re weak.

I struggled and he looked smug, overpowering me effortlessly while he continued his assault. He was big and strong, and his breath smelled like cigarettes as he puffed his breaths in my face, looking remarkably giddy that I was defenceless.

“Let me go,” I demanded, my voice low and firm.

“Why don’t you say that a little louder?” he retorted.

I didn’t. I repeated my words slower this time. “Let. Me. Go.”

He pulled at my hair, and strands ripped from my scalp, but I kept my lips closed, not letting him know how pained I felt. His eyes darkened at that.

“Oh, I get it now,” he mused. “You’re one of them quiet bitches, huh?”

I didn’t answer.

“I’ve had quiet little bitches like you for dinner, and you wanna know what quiet little bitches like you are like?” His mouth stretched in a wicked smile. “You scream *louder* than all the others.”

I sucked in a breath and spat in his face. He punched me in the eye and my head dropped back, slamming against the cement.

“You feel that pain? You’ll get used to it when I’m fucking your little body in half. Do you know what I’m like, little girl? Do you know the kind of shit I have gotten away with because of this fuckin' badge, bitch? I ain't scared of your stupid fucking club. Hell, I'll take your tiny little cunt right here –"

The roar of a motorcycle cut him off. My vision was spotted and I turned my head, vaguely seeing a Harley come bounding our way, turning as it passed us and stopping right in front of the police car. A massive figure quickly climbed off, followed by the black helmet.

Hawke.

Instantly, I felt safe.

Fury engulfed his features. He looked at me on the ground first, surveying the situation mutely before he slid his icy eyes to Cockroach.

Cockroach let go of my hair and casually stood up, dusting his pants clean as he said, "You need to watch your girls, teach them about assaulting an officer in broad daylight."

Hawke stared at him for a short moment, his plump lips closed, his dark eyes narrowed. Then he turned back to me.

"Was he followin' you, darlin'?" he asked me, his voice dangerously low.

"Yes," I answered.

"Did he disrespect you?"

"Yes," I repeated, cutting my glare at Cockroach. "He did."

"Did he hurt you?"

"Yes, he shoved me to the ground."

Just as I said that another chorus of bikes came speeding down the road, circling around the car and us and coming to a stop.

Another figure jumped off his bike and the helmet came straight off.

It was Hector, the younger version of Hawke.

"Oh, fuck me, it's Helinsky," he announced. "Stepping on Warlord territory again. This is the man I've been telling you about, brother. He's been cuttin' our girls up; took a swing at Gina the other night and left her bleeding in bed. Real sick fuck."

Hawke's face hardened as he looked back at me and then at the cop. "Was he tryin' to force you in the car, sweetheart?"

"No."

"Did he touch you?"

I let out another breath. "Yes." My face went red, and my lips trembled, both from anger and humiliation. "He" – *stuck his fingers inside me* – "was telling me I'm going to have maggots feasting on my eyes like Dad after I painted his face with my sandwich."

"You wasted your sandwich on his face?"

"I did."

"How much did that sandwich cost you?"

"Three dollars and seventy-five cents."

"You wasted almost four dollars on this piece of shit?"

I nodded.

"So how'd you end up on the ground with him hitting you?"

Cockroach opened his mouth. "She assaulted –"

"Shut up," Hawke cut in, keeping his eyes on me.

I brushed the hair from my face and sat up, shaking my head again to clear my vision. "I didn't *assault* him. I verbally *insulted* his dick by calling it tiny."

Snickers fell out of the mouths of all the others.

Hawke's lips curled up, and even sitting there on the ground and in pain, I felt flutters inside my chest. My heart didn't feel so heavy after that smile. He always made things alright, ever since my father died and he took me into the arms of the club.

He was my protector.

As Hawke moved to me, Helinsky walked backwards to his car; all the while he was smirking like he was untouchable.

"Hector," Hawke said as he stopped in front of me, "don't let the cockroach get too far."

Hector blocked the driver's side of the car with his body and Helinsky was forced to stop. He shot Hawke a look of confusion. "You can't touch me," he growled. "I'm a fucking cop! You can't touch a fucking cop!"

Ignoring him, Hawke kneeled down next to me and leaned his head in, his stubble brushing against my cheek before he whispered in my ear, "Did he touch you down there, Tyler? Because you're squeezin' your legs shut real tight and lookin' like a ghost."

I fought back the sudden tears that sprang to my eyes and slowly stiffened a nod.

I heard him growl deep in his throat. "You know what happens to somebody when they disrespect you, right?"

I nodded my head slowly again.

He looked down at the helmet in his hand and I noticed his grip tightening.

"I wouldn't normally do this, Tyler, but I'm really angry right now," he explained calmly, his nostrils flaring. "I'm trying to rein it in, but darling, I'm not doing too well."

I blinked and winced, covering the eye he'd punched.

"You alright?" Hawke asked me, concerned.

"I'm fine," I answered.

"Why are you touching your eye?"

"No reason."

His face darkened even more, and he looked frightening as he asked me, "He hit you there too?"

I blinked again, feeling my eye throb. "Hawke, don't do anything stupid."

His jaw tensed. "Too late. My mind was made up the second I saw you pinned beneath him."

"But –"

"Cover your ears," he instructed, "and close your eyes for me, Tyler."

My heart picked up as he took my hands into his massive ones and raised them to my ears. I looked up at him, and his face purposely softened for me. Then he brushed my cheek in a comforting way with his thumb before I shut my eyes.

Almost immediately I felt his body leave mine, and then Helinsky shouted something out and I couldn't help but open my eyes fleetingly just as Hawke raised his helmet and smashed it against his head. My insides seized and I shut my eyes again, squeezing them shut, sucking in air as that one second scene turned into a never ending reel inside my head.

Not a minute later, Hawke's hands wrapped around my shoulders. He stood me up and steered me away, pulling down my hands. As I began to turn my head back to see what was happening, he took me by the chin before I could and forced it forward.

"Keep your eyes forward," he told me.

He took me to his Harley and, as I heard the sounds of painful grunts and something hitting flesh, Hawke put another helmet over my head.

"Let's get you another sandwich, Ty," he said casually.

He jumped on his bike and I climbed on after him, my arms wrapped around his hard front, holding him tightly as I pressed my chest against his back.

He started the Harley and looped it around the car. I couldn't see Helinsky anymore. All the guys had crowded around him, fixedly watching whoever was grunting and pummelling him.

It didn't take me long to realize he would be dead.

Hawke had a police officer murdered in broad daylight.

two

Tyler

The problem with Hawke was you never knew what was going on inside his head. He could be smiling at you, laughing and enjoying a meal, never making you realize that he was also absorbed in his own head and plotting.

I'd catch it sometimes, that robotic smile and the faraway look in his eye.

He was currently giving me that look as we ate with my new ham sandwich at the biker owned deli. I didn't mind it, though, because I was barely eating and locked inside my head too. He had also made the kitchen wrap ice in a cloth, and I was currently pressing it against my eye.

"You okay?" he asked me sometime later, catching on that I hadn't eaten.

I turned my focus to him as he leaned back in his chair, his gaze soft as he studied me with a comforting smile. He'd gotten so tanned during the summer, and it complimented his short dark hair and made his cheekbones all the more pronounced. I liked to compare Hawke to a dark prince in a fairy tale; the bad seed luring you in with his devilishly sexy smile and deep voice. He had a way of making you feel normal in the chaos, like this reality wasn't archaic and filthy in nature, though deep inside you knew it was.

Usually I fell into that look on his face, but right now…I was petrified of something.

"Tyler," he pressed, his voice firmer.

"I peeked," I whispered to him.

His smile faded. "I told you to shut your eyes."

"Yeah, well, I peeked."

"And?"

"And you struck him with your helmet."

"And then?"

"Then I shut my eyes."

He nodded slowly. "I shouldn't have done that with you around. I could have let the boys take care of him but…"

"But what?"

He looked at me with a furrowed brow. "Your dad told me to look after you."

He stopped there, using a sentence under ten words to describe why he did what he did. I could tell he was done talking about it.

"He was a police officer," I said. "You have a rule in the club, and that's never to kill a police officer. That's a shit storm –"

"I know about my rules, Tyler. Don't reiterate them to me."

I dug my fingers into my sandwich, feeling all kinds of confused. It didn't make sense for him to do something so impulsive and stupid. This was a plotting man, and he'd effortlessly manoeuvred through worse situations than that.

A pretty blonde waitress stopped by, gathering our empty glasses and smiling at Hawke.

"You need anything, Hawke?" she asked him sweetly, and I knew by the tone in her voice it wasn't about the food.

He looked at her for longer than a pause. "Like what?" he responded harshly. "You tryin' to offer me your cunt while I'm sittin' here with a bruised up girl?"

Her smile faded. "I'm sorry."

He didn't tell her it was okay like he usually would. Hawke was sweet to women, but this time…he was furious. He stared at her hard and waited for her to leave. When she got the message, she hurried off, looking mortified.

My brows came together. Something was very wrong.

And then it occurred to me…

"Cockroach said you're going to prison," I blurted out, blinking back the emotion behind my eyes.

Hawke didn't reply.

"Are you going to prison, Hawke? Is that why you stopped caring?"

He rubbed at the scruff on his face and sighed. "Honestly, Tyler, prison is made for people like me."

"People like what?"

"You know what kind of person I am."

"You're a good person."

His eyes twinkled with amusement. "Good?"

"You helped me when Dad died."

"He died exactly a year ago today."

I swallowed thickly and nodded.

"And that's why you were alone today."

"Yeah," I barely pushed out.

He nodded once, and his face went flat. "I'm sorry you went through that, Tyler."

"It's not your fault. Cowards did him in when he was alone, and now I'm scared something bad will happen to you."

"It's not for you to worry about me going to prison. You need to worry about yourself, darlin'."

"But is it true?"

He paused, as if debating whether to tell me or not. Then he said quietly, "There's a warrant for my arrest. They're on to me about somethin'."

"Is it bad?"

"It's not somethin' I can get out of."

I wiped away the tears falling from my eyes. "You're going to go away, aren't you? That's why you did what you did to Cockroach, because you don't care anymore."

He frowned, turning his head to the entrance window, looking out in thought. "That bastard was hurting the girls, and he was lookin' for one driving up and down that road. I would have handled him either way. But…yeah, I'm goin' away."

"So leave. Find a place to escape to. Run away."

"No point runnin'. I'm tired, Tyler. I got the grim reaper looking over me, waiting. I got blood on my hands everywhere I go. Maybe…maybe this is what I need, what I *deserve* for all the things I've done."

No. No. No.

I felt raw and panicked all of a sudden. This wasn't happening. My life couldn't endure another loss. No, my wounds were too fresh.

I sucked in a breath. "When will you be back?"

He glanced at me, a sad smile forming. "Darlin', you'll have grandbabies by the time I ever see daylight. Best thing you can do is forget me."

three

Tyler

That night was uneventful. Hawke didn't spend it with girls, or with his brother, or with any of the guys. It was like they had no clue about the warrant, and later I'd find out they didn't.

He spent it alone outside the clubhouse, drinking a beer in a patio chair and staring up at the night sky. I couldn't stay back and let him have his peace. I went to him and joined him in the empty seat beside him. He didn't seem bothered by my presence.

"Can I have a sip?" I asked him.

He looked at me for a long moment, considering my question, and then he passed the bottle to me. I took a big swig, bigger than I should have, and it ended up going down the wrong hole. I coughed and sputtered, some of it dribbling out of my mouth.

He chuckled. "Fuckin' hell, Tyler. Too young for this shit."

I handed him back the beer. "Yeah, I'll give it a go in a couple more years."

"You're too sweet for this poison." He finished the bottle and threw it on the ground and suddenly laughed deep in his chest. "I'm twenty-four, and I'm going to spend the rest of my life behind bars. It's justice in a way, isn't it? I'm the bad guy in all of this. They're going to paint me as the devil, and I'm gonna go to prison filled with my enemies."

"You won't be safe?"

"I'm a capable guy."

My heart hurt. "Hawke –"

"This club is a ticking time bomb," he interrupted. "It's going to collapse one of these days, like all the others before us. I don't know how they're going to carry on without me looking after things, and I can't trust they'll keep you away from the dirty side of things. I wish you'd leave. Go to your mom or something."

"She'll just ignore me and I'll spend my days alone."

"This is fucked up, though, Tyler. Doesn't she care you're here and not with her?"

"No, she cares about her second daughter Tequila. Says it keeps her stomach warm."

"That shit will kill her."

"She's more dead to me than Dad is."

"Maybe she'll change." He couldn't even hide his scepticism.

I looked blankly ahead. "Mr Cosway in English says we try and adapt to our surroundings and we change along with it. It's a survival mechanism. Most change doesn't come deliberately, but by force. Mom's surroundings will never change. She'll stay sitting in her fancy house Dad bought her and drink until her kidneys stop working."

He let out another laugh, but it was dry as a bone. "When did you get so wise? You were always so carefree. Last year fucked you up, didn't it? His death stole your innocence."

"The cowards stole my father." I looked down at my hands, feeling emptier than ever. "And now the law's going to steal you."

His lips flattened. "I would have liked to have seen you grow, Tyler. Something tells me it would have been worth watching."

I would have liked it too. Hawke had been the spark during a really dark time in my life. I wasn't sure I'd have functioned at all without him there to guide me. And I cared deeply for him.

"You've been my good little sidekick, haven't you? Learned all there is to know about cars too, huh?"

"And how to shoot a gun," I replied, my chest warming at the memories.

"Your father would be proud how far you've come in just a year," Hawke said. "He loved you, you know that? He never said it but he did."

"Yeah."

He turned to the cooler beside his chair and pulled out another bottle. He was going to get roaring drunk, which was a very rare sight when it came to him. Being president, he was always in control.

It would be the first and last time I'd ever see him drink so hard.

"What do you want to do?" I asked him, trying to bring light to the conversation.

"Honestly?" he replied, craning his head up to the night sky. "I just wanna look at the stars one last time."

Dazedly, I watched him neck bottle after bottle, until his face couldn't hide the tension buried inside him. His chest moved slower and he curled his hands into fists, but he never reacted to whatever anger he felt just then.

Hawke was so good at bottling it in.

My heart stirred something awful. Devastation had rocked our club one year ago when my father was killed, and now it would never be the same without Hawke. I waited until he was so drunk he could barely move. Then I stood up and crawled into his lap, catching him by surprise.

"Distance, Ty," he slurred.

"Shut up," I retorted, resting my head against his chest, breathing him in. "Let me enjoy this, Hawke."

He exhaled and wrapped an arm around me, and I sighed in content, shutting my eyes as he gently ran his fingers through my hair. His woodsy scent wafted into my nose, giving me comfort. It was a scent I would always associate with safety.

"You take care of yourself," he whispered. "Ignore the club when they're throwing parties. Don't join in on the drugs, and don't let any pencil dick pressure you to get into your pants, alright? I'll order a hit on him from prison, I swear it. You save yourself until you're ready."

I smiled. "Don't worry."

Even drunk, he managed to carry me inside hours later. I remember being put down on a bed – his bed – before he meandered back out. I remember opening my eyes and watching him leave, his face grave, his body slow and tight.

I didn't know it then, but this was the last time I would see Hawke in person for two years.

*

He got arrested the next morning by the feds and was charged with first degree murder of some gangbanger that'd caused the club grief. The evidence was circumstantial, until the murder of Helinsky suddenly surfaced, and Hawke was charged with another murder. The sad part was he might have gotten away with the first, but the evidence for Helinsky was piled so high you couldn't look anywhere without hitting it – the one crucial bit being a video of Hawke riding away from the site Helinsky's body was dumped in.

The process was long and gruelling, but it was shorter than most cases with prosecutors aiming for a speedy trial. It took a year and a half for it all to be over, and then he was sentenced to prison for life, no parole.

The newspapers called Hawke a murderous outlaw who lacked compassion. To the world he was a monster; a sick, vile being, and the streets were safer without him. The Warlords rose to notoriety over the case, and business had to be done quietly.

It was a rough time for me. Hector had me staying at my mother's for most of the year just so the drug enforcement cockroaches that sat along the street out front of the clubhouse wouldn't have surveillance of an underage girl living with a group of bikers. Hector had to keep things running clean. Deals were far and few, and the clubhouse was spotless.

Mostly, he was trying to navigate the world being president, and it didn't come natural to him. He spent most of his time trying to figure out why Hawke had gone to prison in the first place when so many people had been on the payroll. He would soon discover someone had sold his brother out, but he never found out who.

Worse yet, Hawke wasn't safe in prison. He was surrounded by his enemies, and Hector was stressing. He'd bought a few guards off, and they'd created reasons to put Hawke in solitary to keep him out of reach of those with murderous intent, but it was always a temporary fix. Plus, it was maddening for Hawke. Solitary confinement was a prison within a prison and it tested someone's sanity, no matter how strong you were.

I didn't know that the entire time Hawke was in prison, Hector was conspiring to bust him out.

Until one morning he came bursting through the door and said, "Tyler, get the fuck up. We're going for a drive."

four

Hawke

"You want pussy?" the voice asked.

This was fucking ridiculous. Hawke stiffened and glared up at his brother. Did he seriously just ask that fucking question?

He had just vomited his body weight, his skin was slick with sweat, he was missing a finger and was still bleeding profusely seven hours after he had been broken out of a prison he had spent a year rotting in. So he was a fugitive too, which was fan-fucking-tastic. His brother deserved the "stupidest fucking brother of the year" reward for this grand fuck-up.

Hawke glanced around the room – a hovel motel room in some no hope part of a town he didn't even know the name of – and felt his rage levels climb.

"No, Hector," he hissed, meeting his brother's eye with a cold look. "I don't want pussy. I don't *care* about pussy. I don't want some nameless twat sitting on my lap. What I want is my fucking life back, and you destroyed every goddamn chance of that happening by pulling what you did."

Hector ripped his gaze away from his older brother. He moved to the stained chair opposite of him and collapsed into it. His entire body gave out and he let out a long exhale as he stared up at the ceiling.

"What was I supposed to do, Hawke?" he asked harshly. "You were surrounded by enemies and there was a price on your head. You were going to get killed in there. Everyone wanted you dead! You expected me to just let that happen? Do you know the devastation this club would feel if you died? It would have killed all of us."

Hawke didn't reply. Frankly, he was too delirious to. His hand was pulsing like a motherfucker; the pain was so acute, it was debilitating. Instead, he sank back into the nasty twin mattress and held his hand to his chest, shaking. He was bare chested, his lower half in baggy sweats. The man that busted him out was a crazy motherfucker, insisting on making him leave his jumpsuit behind to make the scene look like a grizzly attack in the middle of the wilderness. Authorities would soon find nothing but blood, his mangled prison outfit, and his fucking finger (and he wanted his fucking finger back with a passion because having nine fingers was already a pain in the ass).

Personally, Hawke didn't think it would work, but the bastard blew his finger away without even giving him the opportunity to speak. After that, he passed out, and the timeline from that van to this nasty motel room was murky. All he remembered was waking up to this shithole and staring holes at his pretty boy brother wearing a cut with the word PRESIDENT on the front – a word that he had proudly owned for years before the entire world decided it wanted to take a giant shit on him.

"Where's the guy you hired?" he asked, his voice weak.

"Why?" Hector smirked. "You wanna kill him?"

"No, I want to thank the sadistic fuck for busting me out."

Hector's smirk fell from his face. "*I'm* the one that hired him, and he's already gotten his payment and left."

"What the fuck is his name?"

"Marcus Borden, and that name's getting more and more known as we speak."

"He'd be useful to the club."

Hector chuckled dryly. "He wouldn't be interested."

"Why the hell not?"

"There's a lot to catch you up on. The year you've been in there, a lot has changed. The powers in New Raven have shifted, the gangs have been put to ground, and I know this

Borden guy has something to do with it. He's rising, and he's got a fucking past that's interesting and scary to say the least. I knew he'd get the job done and frankly, I wouldn't want a guy like him in the club at a time like this anyway."

Hawke sucked in a breath as a wave of pain hit him. His eyes briefly shut. "Keep him in our pocket, then."

"We will. Now get some sleep, man. You look like shit."

Hawke didn't want to sleep. His mind wouldn't let him, and his body was fighting the pain hard.

He tried to console himself that it was better than being back there, in a shithole, staring at four walls for so many hours, until he lost his damn mind and they started talking to him.

"What am I supposed to do now?" he asked sometime later. He could hear how tormented he sounded, and it didn't fit him. Not at all. He was a tough motherfucker, but this…this changed everything.

Hector shrugged. "Lay low until the heat is gone."

Feeling scornful, Hawke scoffed. "The heat will never be gone. You know the shit I've done. If the cockroaches even suspect I'm alive, they'll be crawling all over Warlord territory for eternity to cuff me all over again."

"Then you gotta be dead, Hawke."

Hawke frowned. "A dead man has no purpose," he whispered, more to himself than anyone.

It was one thing having no purpose in prison, but out of it too? No, that was unfathomable. Without purpose he was a fucking nobody. What would he do? Where would he go? What was the purpose to his life without his bike and club?

Another wave of pain spread throughout his large body. He broke into sweat and turned to his side, cradling his mangled hand to his chest. His teeth clenched tightly and his entire body went rigid as he rode it out through heavy breaths.

"When does the doctor get here?" he rasped out.

"On his way," Hector assured him.

The club had their very own surgeon on call. Gecko wasn't from town. He was completely off the grid and had no relations to the criminal underworld in the slightest. He was practically a ghost. He'd come around, put you back together again, and went on his own way thousands of dollars heavier. He was a master with his hands, so the money was worth it, but at the moment he was fucking late, and Hawke needed him hours ago.

The room began to spin. Hawke scrambled to the edge of the bed and dry heaved. An acidic taste invaded his mouth, and he spat it out on the green carpet below. He groaned, waiting for the pain to dwindle. When it did, he pressed his forehead against the mattress and gulped in deep breaths. Sometime later, the faint sound of a door opening caught his attention.

"Please tell me that's him," he grumbled. He needed some morphine. And sleeping pills. And a new fucking finger. Yeah, he needed a lot of fucking things right now.

"Hawke?" a soft voice sounded out. "Oh, my God."

He recognized the voice.

My god, it was the sweetest voice he'd ever heard.

His entire body stilled and then sagged into the mattress. "Tyler," he replied, steadily. "What are you doin' here, darlin'?"

"The club's throwing a party to get the cockroaches off our back," Hector cut in before she could respond. "You told me never to let her around a party at the clubhouse. She's been waiting in the car this whole time, and that's where I told her to stay." His words were laced with disapproval. "I never gave her permission to get out of it, either."

"It's too hot out there and the air conditioner isn't working," Hawke heard her snap back. "You left me to bake in there. I was going to die."

"You weren't going to die."

"You don't know that."

Hawke would have smiled if his lips were working. Ty had a sharp tongue on her. Almost two years apart hadn't changed her a bit, and fuck, he liked that.

Quiet footsteps approached. He tried to move his body to face her, but breathing alone was hard enough. He felt the mattress behind him sink only a little bit. A little bit because Tyler was tiny, and quiet too. God, she could be so quiet when she wanted to be. He'd found her under tables, or hiding in closets, eavesdropping in conversations and events she shouldn't have witnessed over the years since she was five years old. Now she was what, fifteen? A decade of this shit and she still hadn't learned her lesson, and what had she seen in the time he had been gone? Who had she spent most of her time with? He hoped it wasn't Hector. Fucking hell, if it was Hector then she was fucked. He was not the kind of role model to have around an impressionable chick.

The thought bothered him. *A lot.*

A cool hand touched his arm. "Hawke, you don't look good," she told him sadly. "There's blood everywhere. Are you dying?"

"It's nothin', Ty."

"It doesn't look like nothing."

"Well, it is. It's nothin'."

She let out a long breath, like she'd been holding it for a while. "You're going to die. People say that when they're going to die."

"He's not dying," Hector said, irritated. "This is Hawke we're talking about. He's just scratched up bad. Lost his finger."

"How did he lose a finger?"

"The guy that broke him out blew it away."

"Why would someone that was *breaking* him out shoot his finger off?"

"You wouldn't understand. This is grown up stuff, Tyler."

"I don't think you understand it yourself, Hector, and quit treating me like I'm ten years old. I'm more of an adult than you are most days."

Hector grew impatient. "Look, you really shouldn't be here. This shit makes you an accomplice. Go take a walk. As far as you know, Hawke is dead and you never saw him once. Now go."

Of course she ignored him. She grabbed at Hawke's shoulder and pulled him back. He barely budged. She used both her hands on the second try and sucked in a breath, rolling him on to his back with all her might. Hawke's vision blurred under the light, and then slowly spotted and cleared. A face was looking down at him and…

Holy fuck. He thought. Had he been in prison longer?

She couldn't have been fifteen. Could she?

A pair of deep brown eyes searched his as he scrambled to recognize the girl. No, it was definitely her. She looked like a fucking angel.

He smiled at the familiarity of her face: small and round, lips pressed in concentration, brows furrowed. She appeared far beyond her years, and her features now were so prominent and symmetrical; he knew she was going to be an incredibly beautiful woman one day. Hell, she was already there.

"Did you get my letters?" she asked him then.

"I got 'em," he answered.

She'd sent him over twelve letters in the course of one year, talking about anything and everything. He understood why she did it. Tyler was infatuated with him, always had been, even now she was staring at him with want in her eyes. Truth be told, he had liked getting those letters, had expected them even every time the fucks at the prison handed the mail out. He'd kept them too. Had stuffed them in his jumpsuit before the escape.

They were probably gone now.

"They treatin' you alright?" he then asked her.

She nodded once. "Now we can go back to fixing cars, and…shooting guns in the paddock. It'll be like before."

Emotion pulled him under for a moment, and he swallowed a hard lump in his throat. Fuck, she was so sweet, wasn't she? Excited over the things he used to take for granted.

"Things aren't just gonna go back to the way they were before," he explained quietly, wincing for a second as his hand continued to throb. "I can't come breezin' through the door, Tyler. I'm not gonna be around to protect you again, and you deserve a normal life. Your old man wanted that for you. You gotta promise you'll stay away. For real this time 'cause I know you've been around while I've been locked away. Be with your mom and take care of her."

Tyler's eyes hardened a fraction. "You know what Mom is like, and besides, I don't want to stay away. It's my home. It's yours too, and just because you lost it doesn't mean I should too."

"You're not safe there."

"Safe from *what* exactly? It's all in your head. I get it, you know. Dad made you give him a promise and now you're obsessed about it and not seeing right."

"Need I remind you what that officer would have done had I not showed up?"

"That's why there's Hector. He's looking after things and he's done a good job with keeping his eye on me. He did all year long, and he didn't once try marching me out the door."

A vein throbbed at his temple. Anger surged for a fleeting moment as he envisioned Hector teaching her about life, because what the fuck did Hector know about life?

"Tyler…" he started in warning.

She slowly backed away from him, scowling at his tone. "I think I'll go back to the car."

"Stay," he told her sternly. "You might die from the heat, remember?"

"I'd rather die from the heat than be told I don't belong in the club."

"I didn't say that."

"You didn't have to."

Goddammit, she was stubborn. Before she was far enough out of reach, he grabbed her by the arm with his good hand. He pulled her to him abruptly, causing her to fall on top of his bare chest. They both lost their breaths as their chests crashed against one another. Her face was half a foot away from his. He stared hard into her startled brown eyes, not letting the pain stabbing him everywhere show in his.

"Just because I'm technically dead that doesn't mean I can't keep an eye on you," he told her quietly. "I'm your ghost now, darlin', and you'd be surprised how much control a ghost can still have from the grave."

Her lips formed a frown and her eyes narrowed. "We'll see about that, Hawke Navarro."

Despite losing his finger, becoming a dead fugitive, and having no purpose in life, he let out a hard laugh. "I guess so, Tyler Wilson. I'm watching you."

With that, he let her go and shoved her back. She fell back on the mattress, air knocked out of her lungs, before growling in frustration and sliding off.

"I see he's gotten ruder in prison," she told Hector, straightening her non-existent pink shorts and tank top. "You should have busted him out before he turned into an asshole."

She scurried out of the room without a glance back. Hawke smiled wistfully, already wishing he was back at the clubhouse to make her life a living hell.

God, he wished for a lot of things, actually.

"She did miss you, you know," Hector spoke from the chair, staring at the door like he could see her through it. "She took it hard. Lost her old man and you a year apart. We did our best, and everyone loves her. She's a good girl."

Instantly, Hawke's smile vanished. He shifted his gaze to his brother, and a tight feeling emerged in his chest. All his brother cared about was pussy and beer. He was no fucking role model. It irked him that he would watch Ty grow, mostly because Hawke had a feeling Ty was different. She had been around violence all her life, and it never bothered her. She was such a fucking oddity, standing there in her pink girly clothes, her hair done up all the fucking time, barely blinking when a fight broke out and teeth were lost and blood was spilled.

"Tyler is going to turn into a beautiful woman in a couple of years," Hawke said sharply. "If you touch her, Hector, I will come for you, and I will kill you."

Hector's face dropped, and he looked stunned. They stared at each other for several moments, the tension between them growing thicker by the minute.

"Wow," Hector finally said, astonished. "That escalated fucking quickly."

"Tyler doesn't need to get treated like a whore by you."

"Why the fuck would I treat Tyler like a whore?"

"Because you have no respect for women."

"I like to fuck, so what?"

Hawke clenched his teeth. "She's not one of them."

"I care about Tyler," Hector retorted, firmly. "I don't look at her like that. She's like a sister to me."

Hawke tilted his head to the side, smelling his brother's bullshit from a mile away. "I haven't heard that line before."

"This is different than that last time. I'm serious –"

"Just don't do it."

Hector dragged his teeth over his bottom lip, something he did when he was pissed. "You see her for five seconds and suddenly you're all up in that? She's fucking grown up, Hawke, and when she's old enough, I can't be responsible for her choices."

Hawke's anger pounded into his skull as he sharply snapped, "She's off-limits and you fucking know why she needs to stay away."

"I know why, but she doesn't."

"She thinks it's only because of her old man, and she needs to keep thinkin' that way."

"Fine, but that reason isn't enough to keep her from the club. She's fucking home there, Hawke. She loves it."

"The club gives her exposure, makes people wanna look into her."

"They won't find shit."

"Just don't touch her."

"You can't demand those things Hawke without putting a claim on her!"

"Then I'm claiming her," Hawke said impulsively. "Nobody from the club is to ever touch her."

"And outside it?"

"Outside it is fine because I want her to move on to someone decent. Just nobody from the club."

Hector was stunned, but he didn't question it. He looked away from his older brother and leaned back in his chair. Neither of them spoke after that. It was always like this between them. Always unnatural. Never easy. They were two completely different people, fated as brothers but never with the bond to prove it. Hawke knew it had to be this way. His brother was too loose, and he didn't trust him with his decisions yet.

They were a doomed duo.

When the doctor finally arrived, Hector excused himself. Made some excuse about needing to make phone calls, but Hawke knew it was bullshit.

Tyler reappeared minutes later and sat on the corner of the bed as Gecko went to work. The bald tiny man didn't ask questions. Frankly, Gecko didn't want to know what had happened, or why Hawke was even out of prison to begin with. He was a man of few words, opting to just assess the wound and take care of it.

Smart man.

He patched up the cuts along Hawke's arm and then began stitching the gaping wound shut. All the while, Tyler watched, not at all disturbed by the gruesome scene.

God, she looked different. Two years had transformed her. Curves had sprouted. Soft ones, but ones nonetheless. She wasn't a little girl anymore.

"He didn't have to shoot you," she whispered to him just then.

Hawke didn't respond, but he stared at her hard, and she felt it deep in her bones. That stare was razor sharp. There was no way to shrug it off because when Hawke looked at you, he *really* looked at you.

She fidgeted a little before meeting his gaze and they looked at each other. He saw her chest move faster, watched the way her lips parted. She still looked at him the same, he realized. Like he was some kind of god. He never understood her fascination with him, but he liked it, and he missed it, and he hoped to fucking god she didn't look at anybody else in the club the same way.

Tyler. Again, there was always…always something about her. Hawke couldn't place it. Couldn't put it into words, either.

When Gecko finished, he dosed Hawke up with painkillers strong enough to put a horse down. Then he packed away his things and the first thing he asked was, "How do I get paid?"

"Hector is in the room next door," Tyler responded, avoiding Hawke's eyes. "He's expecting you."

"What's he doing?" Hawke cut in.

Tyler was uneasy. "He's…with a girl."

"You're shitting me right now."

She shook her head slowly. "He stopped off at some titty bar on our way here and found some girls. He thought you'd be into the idea too."

"Jesus Christ." Hawke clenched his teeth.

Here he was in a dump of a place, hiding out from the law, and his brother was already getting his dick wet. This was why he doubted Hector taking over when everything had gone down. He couldn't think past his own dick.

Gecko, sensing the tension, managed a stiff nod and strode out of the room as fast as possible, shutting the door quietly behind him. Tyler looked at the door for a few moments and then back at Hawke. He was already drowsy; his head swam and his body felt contentedly numb from the pain.

The room was still and the silence felt heavy. Hawke began to feel groggy, like his limbs weren't working. With heavy blinks, he watched Tyler shove the covers off the bed. Then she rested on the mattress, pressing her body against the length of his. Her head sat on his chest, her cheek pressed against dried blood and she was completely unbothered by it.

"What are you doin', Tyler?" he asked, his voice slow and sluggish.

"You got busted out of prison," she replied quietly. "I won't see you again for a long time. All those months piled on top of one another, and it was a giant blur. I don't know if I can handle that happening again, Hawke."

"You'll be fine."

"Your bedside manners suck."

"You say that like you're the one that's bleedin'."

She let out a shaky breath. "I am bleeding."

He sighed and tried to lift his arm up. He groaned. His body felt far away. He hadn't felt this vulnerable in a while and it didn't sit well with him.

"What are you doing?" Tyler asked.

"Trying to lift my fuckin' arm up. What's it look like?" he grunted.

"Do you need help?"

"No."

It took him several awkward moments, and then his arm went up and dropped around her frame, good hand cupping her small shoulder. Her body relaxed at the gesture and she breathed deeply, wrapping her arm around his hard torso.

"Everything is gonna be alright," he told her. "You don't worry about me, Tyler. You worry about yourself. I see you when I see you."

"How long?"

"I don't know."

"That's not good enough." Her voice broke. "The club's not the same without you, Hawke. You have to find a way back."

"You were just talkin' about how incredible Hector's been doing –"

"Yeah, *in front* of Hector. It's not like I'm going to trash him when he's three feet away from me. I mean, don't get me wrong, he's trying really hard and I don't want to downplay his efforts, but it's not the same and he struggles. You're the real president and we need you."

Barely hanging on to consciousness, Hawke closed his eyes. "It's not up to me anymore, darlin'. I can't go back. I'll never be able to, and that's something you have to accept."

"It's not fair."

"Yeah, well, Ty, you're fifteen, and you're gonna find out soon enough how unfair life is. And instead of whining about it, you gotta suck it up and learn to evolve. That means accepting I'm not gonna be around the club for a very long time."

"Take me with you."

"I don't know where I'm headed."

"I don't care. Take me."

"No."

He felt her anger. She tried squirming back out of his arms, but he tightened his grip so she wouldn't move. "Stop fightin' me," he told her sternly.

"Then take me with you," she pleaded. "I want to be with you."

"Ty –"

"I love you!" She went limp again and sniffed, hiding her face against his chest. She couldn't face him after that admission. Instead, she kept her lips sealed and coated his skin with her tears.

Hawke stilled, taken completely off guard. "Ty," he said, "what in the fuck do you know about love?"

"I know love is home, and I feel it most when you're with me."

He sighed and shook his head to himself. This girl was so fucking naïve. And ridiculously sweet. What the hell had he done to just claim her from the other guys? He didn't want her, but the thought of her growing and fucking around with someone from the club grated on his nerves. They would just lock her away in a nice little house on the other side of town while they fucked other women. It would be living her mother's life, and he couldn't risk that possibility.

But…love?

She's a teenager. She probably loves a different boy every week.

"It's not love you're feeling," he said to her. "It's fantasy. You're young. You don't know what you're talking about."

"What if I do?"

"You'll find someone," he vaguely said. "Get a cute little pimply dude from your high school. Have fun with him in the back of his thirty-year-old truck. Experience shit, Tyler. Don't be deluded enough to just wait around for me because I sure as shit am not gonna be waitin' around for you to grow up. You gotta stop whatever you think you're feeling because it's not real."

"What if you want me one day?" she asked. "And what if it's too late when you do?"

"Tyler, actin' cryptic isn't in in your nature –"

"What if you want me? Just *answer.*"

"Tyler, one day every fuckin' man will want you. And by then, even if I looked at you and wanted between those legs, you'll have your eyes open to the world, and you'll be having too much fucking fun to stop and want some dead fugitive."

She didn't agree with his words, but she didn't argue. She was stiff in his arms, and though he was barely hanging on to consciousness, he tried to comfort her. He rubbed circles over her shoulder and kept her glued to his side. She felt good like this. He knew it was because he hadn't felt the warmth of someone in a very long time, but he liked this.

He liked it a damn lot.

"Your letters helped," he murmured, unable to put a lid on his thoughts. Mostly, he wanted to make her feel better. "They helped a lot, Tyler. No one else wrote to me. Only you did and…"

Every time he'd read them, they'd made him feel like he was part of her life still, and he hadn't known how important that part was until he was gone. It meant something deep to him that she hadn't forgotten about him; she'd clung on hard, and it'd deterred him from some very dark thoughts.

"It helped writing them," she whispered back.

His eyes closed and his body slowly gave out. His grip around Tyler slackened. He felt her body shuffle, felt her face move higher. Her cool hands touched his face, her fingers traced down his forehead, along the curve of his nose and over the bump of his lips.

"You're wrong," she whispered, "about everything."

She whispered something else to him, but he was too out of it to know what. Then he felt something… soft brush his mouth, and he knew – he knew before he faded into blackness – that she had kissed him.

*

His dreams were unsettling, as always.

And the same.

They were *always* the fucking same.

He was back there, in solitary again, sitting under a fluorescent light, staring at ancient pictures previous prisoners had drawn on the walls with their blood. He could hear the howls and painful cries from the others surrounding the tiny box he had grown stagnant in.

They were caged, just like him.

They were monsters, just like him.

Starved, abandoned, watching their sanity bleed dry as the hours blurred and time no longer existed.

He felt tightening in his chest, and he struggled breathing. It was maddening. Like being buried alive, but worse because it went on and on and…on.

He'd kill himself easily just to escape, and he wanted to. Dear god, he wanted to because what was the fucking point?

In his dreams, he dug his nails into his throat and tore his lungs out and died in a pool of his own blood. But in real life he had just stared at the drawings and punched his head to feel pain.

Because pain…pain was better than this pit of nothingness.

five

Hawke

Hawke woke up hours later to Tyler curled to his side, sleeping peacefully. He looked at her for a very long time, stunned by the softness of her body. He hadn't seen softness like this in what felt like an eternity. He also hadn't felt warmth in that period of time, either.

Tyler was soft.

She was painfully beautiful.

She was warm.

Or maybe isolation had made the world and her more brilliant to look at.

He slid out of bed, careful not to disturb her, and went to the bathroom to shower the filth off him. Even that required strenuous effort. The entire place, shitty as it was, was paradise compared to where he had come from. The hot water was bliss, and he had to shut his eyes to savor the heat flowing through him.

After he finished, he proceeded to stare at himself in the mirror, studying his reflection while he rubbed at his bare cheeks. He needed to disguise himself, grow a beard maybe. He had a very distinguishable face; the cheekbones and sculpted jaw of a fucking model. He would be seen and recognized immediately if he wasn't careful.

He exhaled and dropped his head. He was still weak everywhere, but that wasn't what was bothering him. It was the soft body sleeping in that bed feet from him that was fucking with his head and the words she'd said last night.

Love is home, and I feel it most when you're with me.

He opened the bathroom door and looked at her, feeling regret he had marked her for himself when he spoke to Hector last night. He had just ruined any chance of her being with another member in the club.

Part of you likes that. Look how stunning she is two years later. Imagine another three?

He frowned at himself for that train of thought, but he didn't take the words back like he might have long ago. He was needy. Really fucking needy and vulnerable at the moment. Truth was prison was a nasty place that forced one to think of their own desperation. And he'd been desperate and… lonely. *So* fucking lonely. The kind of lonely that made a man like him ache for something real.

Those letters were real.

Tyler struck a chord in him. He didn't expect it, but she had. She would consume him, he knew it. She was the kind of innocent that was still rough around the edges. The kind that was worth waiting for.

But then he felt the throb in his hand and realized he couldn't have anything real anytime soon. Maybe never.

He sighed and threw his dirty sweatpants back on. Then he stepped out of the motel room and into the morning sun. Just the sight of it gave him pause. He looked up at the sky, taking in deep breaths.

Freedom.

So why didn't he *feel* free?

He tore his gaze away and moved to the door next to him. He opened it without knocking, not surprised that it was unlocked. He found Hector in bed wrapped around the arms of a naked girl. Another girl was up and in the middle of sliding her jeans on. She didn't look bothered at the sight of him. Her eyes were still unfocused, and he figured it had something to do with the countless empty bottles of alcohol strewn on the floor.

The nameless girl smiled at him from behind her black locks. Hawke skimmed her over fleetingly, at her large breasts and wide hips decorated in flower tattoos. A solid ten out of ten. He should have felt that familiar adrenaline shoot through him. This was a naked girl. He hadn't seen one in the flesh for far too long. This was every prisoner's fantasy come to life.

But he didn't feel his cock stir in the slightest. It was bizarre and unexpected how dead he was. The girl's movements slowed and she turned to him face on, looking at him expectantly, waiting for him to say something. He recognized this behavior. She was used to bikers. Used to being told what to do. And that was surprisingly a turn off.

Hawke looked away and shut the door. He was about to return to his room when the sound of a motorcycle caught his attention. He watched a black Harley turning into the parking lot of the motel, and he immediately recognized who it was.

Gus.

Vice President of the Warlords since Hawke was a kid, and a father figure to him since his old man bit the dust.

Again, he should have felt something, but he didn't. The wall he had built in prison would take a long time to crumble.

Gus tore his helmet off and came bounding his way, a look of relief and excitement on his face. "I can't fuckin' believe that psychotic man pulled it off!" he hollered. They hugged it out for a few seconds and then Gus took Hawke's face into his hands and gave his cheek a light slap before dropping them. "Look at you," he said, his voice hoarse. "Like a fucking ghost come to life or somethin'. Didn't Gecko give you anything? You look like you're on your death bed."

"I'll be fine, old man," Hawke replied.

"Fine would be seeing you come back, not seeing you run away."

Hawke sighed. "He had no choice, apparently."

Gus nodded solemnly. "You know the amount of dough that was sittin' on your precious head the entire time you were there? You could have made someone rich."

"It was a fight every day."

Gus looked over Hawke's bare chest, at the new scars Hawke had earned during his imprisonment. "I'm sure it was.

Let's never see you go back. I got enough money to float you a long time, got a black spot on this motel so you won't find any cockroaches coming around. You can stay here and take time out to heal before you decide where you wanna go –"

"I want to leave as soon as possible," Hawke interrupted firmly.

Gus looked at him peculiarly. "Why?"

"The longer I'm here, the staler I'll become."

"Where will you go?"

"I haven't figured that out yet."

Gus watched him for several moments, trying to figure out the blank look on Hawke's face. Then he asked, "Where's your brother?"

Hawke gestured to the room next to his. "He'll be out for a couple more hours, I'm sure."

"He's still asleep?"

"He had a rowdy night, our boy," Hawke explained bitterly. "Decided to fuck a few girls, but he offered me one, so I guess he was thinkin' of me too while I was bleeding, huh?"

"You're kidding me."

Right on cue, the door opened, and the nameless girl stepped out. She stumbled past them, looking at Hawke again with another smile.

"What the fuck you lookin' at?" Gus roared at her, his face reddening immediately. "Look away if you know what's best for you!"

The girl's smile disappeared and she did just that.

"Gonna have to take care of that one," Gus told Hawke after she had stumbled her way out of the parking lot. "Can't afford anyone sayin' they spotted you anywhere."

"Don't worry about her. The girl's still so drunk, she won't remember what I'll look like," Hawke replied.

"What the fuck was Hector thinking?"

"When does Hector ever think?"

Gus cursed under his breath. "He spent most of the time you were in prison fucking women and drinking himself to sleep. Nothing will change after you leave. You understand that, don't you?"

Hawke didn't respond. This wasn't something he had control over anymore. He had to think of himself now and figuring out his next step.

"He never dug deep enough to find out who sold us out with that video, by the way," Gus added, darkly. "The boys talked about it and it got us wondering…" His words trailed off, but Hawke didn't need more to understand where he was going with this.

"We may have our differences, but my brother would never sell me out," Hawke told him, feeling certain.

"Not even to take over?"

"No."

The thought had entered Hawke's mind over the months, but quickly disappeared when he remembered the rare moments of loyalty they'd shared together. Hector would never have sold his brother out because he never cared to be president.

Gus didn't look convinced, but he stiffened a nod anyway. "If you want to leave as soon as possible, Hawke, you can take my bike."

"I'll need your shirt too. Can't be riding with the club's emblem on my back."

Gus agreed, though his eyes dimmed. He wasn't happy about this. It was too soon, and Hawke needed more rest.

"Take whatever you need," Gus told him, patting him on the shoulder. "I'll go grab us some breakfast, huh?"

He left and Hawke returned to his room. This time Tyler was awake and sitting up, staring at him with a fallen face as he came through the door. He stopped and looked back at her, raising his brow questioningly.

"You're leaving," she whispered, tipping her head to the window. "I heard everything."

"Always hearing things," Hawke replied lightly. "Always eavesdropping."

She didn't smile. "Please stay."

He exhaled slowly and collapsed back on the bed, dropping his head down. His blinks were still slow. He was shattered. "I can't," he told her. "I can't have everyone risk their neck to keep me hidden. The sooner I'm gone, the better."

A flash of anger showed in her eyes, and she petulantly kicked the covers off and crossed her arms, staring back out the window. "Dad said you'd always be there for me," she quietly remarked.

"I don't think your father knew I'd be busted out of prison."

"Can't you buy the cockroaches off?"

"With what money? Hector drained the club's pockets just to order my escape."

Tyler frowned, blinking sudden tears. "This is so unfair. I get you for one minute and you're gone again. All I got now is Hector and Jesse –"

"Who the fuck is Jesse?"

"He's a prospect, about to turn member."

Hawke's eyes dimmed. "Been spending a lot of time with him?"

She nodded absently. "He likes to work with cars too. He's got this garage in his father's name they just passed to him. He said he'd make that an asset for the club, which is why his prospecting's been cut short."

"Is he someone the club can trust?"

"Yeah, he's done his fair bit. Helped burn down the Lone Horseman's new shop."

Hawke tensed, working his jaw before he asked, "Another MC moving into Norwich, Ty?"

She shook her head slowly. "Not after that, but…they're small time anyway. No big threat. Jonny's been on top of it, riding out all the time nowadays and making sure nobody will do business with them."

Hawke relaxed.

He fucking hated how invested he was in this club, but already he was thinking of ways he could burn this new MC to the ground. Because that was what you had to do with a threat: you had to cut its head off the second it opened its mouth.

Hector won't do that. He's too soft.

"I'll be around," Hawke then promised, looking at her gravely. "To help Hector out, I'll be around every now and again when the heat cools."

Tyler just nodded, looking at him so fiercely, like she was committing his face to memory.

It made the void inside him ache. He wanted to make more promises he didn't know he could keep so she could feel better, but he didn't.

Ty was old enough not to fall for them anyway.

When Gus returned, Hawke didn't have it in him to eat. He just looked at the old man standing by the door, breakfast in hand, and Gus knew – knew with just one look – that he wasn't preparing to stay, not for another minute. Tyler saw it too, and tears fell from her eyes.

Hawke would leave Tyler like that, broken hearted and empty, unable to look away from him as he stepped out the door, dressed and ready for the open road. He'd grab the money Gus left him and jump on his bike and eventually unite with the man that broke him out. He'd work for him and disguise himself from the world, learning to exist instead of live, until everyone forgot all about the man that escaped prison.

Yeah, that's what he would do.

Only…life had a thing for throwing curveballs because…

None of it ended up working out that way.

six

Tyler

Five years later

"Fuck, you are a hot little minx, Tyler," Hector said from behind me.

His hand touched at my exposed back and he pushed me down slowly. I closed my eyes and breathed as the tattoo gun came alive and its needle pierced into the flesh of my back. I bit my lip and concentrated on the music blasting through the tattoo parlor, but the pain was almost too much. I squirmed and clenched my teeth. It was like a fiery scratch being dragged across my skin.

Ouch!

"You feelin' okay, hot stuff?" Hector asked me, noticing my discomfort.

"No," I whimpered, tensing. "I feel like shit."

"Suck it up, princess."

I raised my hand and shakily flipped him off. I heard his faint laughter as he continued to lay havoc to my skin.

"I know why they call you the butcher now!" I hollered.

"Welcome to the butcher shop!" he hooted.

Fuck, he was rough. I'd heard the horror stories back in the day of people who were in the tattooed hands of Hector Navarro. But he was the best in town, and though he'd stopped working at Warlord Ink since he assumed the role of president of the Warlords MC, he still did favors from time to time. When he found out what I wanted on my skin, he was more than willing to do me this favor. This was my fourth and final session, thank fuck, and I was eager to see the result and get the hell out.

I kept my eyes glued shut. The only sound in the empty parlor was that of the gun and the loud music blaring from the stereo. Every so often, he'd pause what he was doing and give me a reassuring pat on the shoulder. It didn't do shit to calm me down.

At some point, I pulled out my phone and tried to distract myself by scrolling through my current messages.

Mother: *I met a man, and I'm pretty certain he's the one.*

I rolled my eyes. *Sure he is, Mother.*

One message in and that was too much text reading for the day.

I put the phone back down and counted my breaths.

When Hector finally finished, I wanted to cry with relief. He turned the music off and left me on the chair while he grabbed a few things in the backroom. He returned moments later and rubbed some kind of ointment on my back. His movements were gentle, nothing at all like his every day nature. "I'll keep treating your skin for you," he told me softly. "Come for me in the morning."

"That's what she said," I muttered, unable to resist.

He grabbed my ponytail and gave it a sharp tug. "Don't be a smartass. You gotta take care of your tats. It's serious."

I handed him my phone. "Yeah, yeah, now take a picture for me. I wanna see the hell I went through without craning my head in front of a mirror."

"Believe me, it looks sexy as fuck on you. You'll be impressed."

He took a picture and handed me back the phone. I stared at the picture of my back, at the tattoo all filled out, every detail added in from the last couple hours. My skin was red and sensitive, and I knew it would take a while to heal, but Hector was right: I loved it.

I looked over my shoulder and smiled brightly as he began to apply my bandage. "Thanks," I told him sincerely. "It looks great. Better than I could have imagined."

His lips quirked up, happy at my compliment. For a second I'd wished nothing had changed. That he still worked here where he was happiest and didn't have to worry about the obligations he absolutely sucked at (ex: the club). He nodded once and started cleaning up the station. "No problem. Now, while it's healing, I will advise you be topless for as long as humanly possible. This baby needs to breathe."

I burst out laughing and stood up, hiding my breasts with my arm as I grabbed my shirt and bra off a nearby chair. "So you want me to walk around the clubhouse with my boobs hanging out?" I asked, turning my head to look at him.

"Why not?" he replied with a wink. "Your tits are nice."

"You haven't seen my tits!"

"I've seen you in tight tops, Ty. I know they're probably a fucking glorious sight. Put your arm down and let me see."

"That's not gonna happen."

"Since when have you cared about your modesty? You're living with us, and chicks walk around in their birthday suits all the fuckin' time."

"Maybe it's good to have a bit of mystery to my body," I replied cheekily.

He paused from his movements and glimpsed me up and down. "That's true. I think you're the only girl I've been around for so long and haven't seen naked."

"And that's the way it's stayin'," I whispered to myself.

Hector probably fucked more women than Genghis Khan ever did in his reign. I wasn't interested in being another notch on his bed post, although I couldn't lie that it never crossed my mind once or twice in my lifetime. I was only a girl and loneliness was a bitch. Plus, Hector was gorgeous. Had that dark hair, tatted tanned skin and deep brown eyes a gal could easily lose herself in. He would be perfect if he spoke less and kept his dick in his pants, but neither of those two things were going to happen any time soon.

Plus, he wasn't Hawke.

And Hawke? He was better, in every way.

I turned my back to him and started to put my hand through the strap of my bra. I heard him curse under his breath before he yanked the bra from out of my hand.

"The bra strap is going to press against your tattoo, Ty," he told me. "Throw on your shirt. That's all you need right now. Seriously, you have to take it easy."

"Alright, don't bite my head off, I just forgot." I grabbed my white loose off-shoulder top and threw it on. My breasts were on the small side, so not wearing a bra wasn't all that noticeable. I doubted it mattered anyway. Like Hector said, the bar would be sprawling with loose women wearing much less than I was.

"We got company at the place tonight," Hector told me.

"Who?"

"Yuri and his crew. They'll be dropping in some cash and stayin' over to party for the night."

I cringed. "God, Hector, Yuri's really touchy and demanding."

"So are the guys."

"But they keep their hands off me. Yuri is intense."

Hector shrugged. "What am I supposed to do about it? He's Abram's cousin. I can't necessarily tell him to fuck off. Abram's fond of the little shit."

"I'd have to keep an eye out then."

"So you gonna stay back for drinks?" he asked me.

"I don't know," I said. "Depends how obnoxious everyone is."

"They'll be obnoxious."

"Including you?"

He chuckled and grabbed his bike key. "Especially me. I got a date with Jack Daniels and a hot bit of ass."

What was new?

I shrugged again. "Well, we'll see how that ass-hat acts. You have no idea the grief he gave me last time."

Yuri and his crew were part of the Russian counterpart the club did deals with on the side. They weren't regular buyers of the club's product, but whenever they did buy, it was apparently a lot. Enough to keep them over to bleed the bar dry. And Yuri was a dipshit. A real nasty guy with a bad temper and demanding hands. The last few times he had been around he'd tried touching me like I was some club slut ready to put out for him. I had done my best to be patient. Had excused myself every time he got near, but then he grabbed me by the ass the very last time and I had had enough. The drunk dick earned himself a knee to the balls, and he was too drunk to remember.

I pulled a wad of cash out of my wallet and turned to Hector. "By the way, this is for the last two sessions."

He glowered at the bills. "Put the money away, Tyler. You're not making shit at the garage."

I shook my head. "I'm doing really good, actually, and I saved for this so you need to take it. I'm not one of your sluts you get to shower with gifts and send on their merry way. I would have paid for this with anyone else, and this is the last half you quoted me."

He scratched at his scruffy jaw and stared at the money for a few moments. Then he sighed and snatched it out of my hands. Walking past the reception desk, he threw the money there and unlocked the entrance door.

"Come on," he told me, motioning me out the door.

Feeling good, I smiled at him as I stepped out into the warm stuffy air. It had just started drizzling and my hair would undoubtedly pay the price in under five minutes. Hector stood under the awning and had a quick cigarette while I looked up at the stars.

Nights like these reminded me of Hawke, of our time together that night as he drank himself away while he stared at the sky like he'd taken it for granted his whole life.

When Hector finished, we walked to his Harley and I climbed on behind him, wrapping an arm around his waist. In direct view of his patched vest, I momentarily ran my finger over the insignia on the back: of two battle axes crossing, a sword running down the middle and a fiery skull dead center. On top of that was the word PRESIDENT in white bold letters. This was the very same vest Hawke used to wear. My smile wavered just a little, and a feeling of melancholy washed over me.

I missed him.

Hector started the engine, distracting me from my thoughts of his older brother, and we took off into the quiet streets, back to the clubhouse.

Back to home.

seven

Tyler

From the front, the non-descript clubhouse was a plain red-bricked building with the Warlord banner on the front. It had been renovated over a decade ago when the club bought the entire building. It was originally a bar and a couple apartments on top, and the actual bar had changed very little; the other two floors had their walls between apartments knocked out of them and rooms were placed to accommodate every member of the club. It wasn't anything fancy. There were no ten foot walls bordering the place like people often imagined when they thought of a motorcycle gang's stronghold. There were no illegal activities done here either, nor were there weapons of mass destruction like many townsfolk gossiped about. No, all that was done way out of town in a warehouse somewhere secluded. I only knew about it because Hector secretly told me everything.

Instead, our clubhouse was reserved specifically for day to day life. It was where I grew up and ran amuck, and nobody could do a single thing about it. My dad used to be the Vice President of Warlords, and that earned me a first class ticket in their circle. I was everyone's little princess. The guys adored me, even when I was annoying the shit out of them.

My childhood was great and filled with wonderful memories, and then… I thought of the day Dad died; the victim of a random attack by some coward without a face. That cockroach of a cop had been right about it being brutal because I'd heard the club talking about it amongst themselves one time. They said he bled out slowly. As he lay dying with Hawke by his side, he'd made him promise to look after his family.

He left behind Mom and me, and at the time, Mom was a stay at home wife and I was only twelve years old and Hawke was in charge. He'd been president almost four years and was the youngest leader the club had ever seen, but he excelled unlike any other. He promised us the club would look after us no matter what, and that he would personally see to it I would never go without.

But that also came with certain conditions. He wanted me to distance myself from the club and live a normal life. Even today, almost nine years after my father's death, he was still stressing the same damn thing.

I defied him, of course. I was a club brat, after all. You can't just introduce a girl to this lifestyle and march her out the door when she's been living and breathing black leather and bikes all her life. That was just insensitive. The Warlords were my family and this clubhouse was my home, and no former President biker with a beard to his chest was going to tell me otherwise.

The bar was roaring with activity. Deafening laughter and screams could be heard just outside the black entrance door. Upon entering, I had a quick glance around. It had turned into a rowdy bar where laughter and music was all you heard. The pool table was crowded for once, but not from playing the game, but from the guys licking alcohol off the belly button of a giggling topless girl lying on her back. Other topless girls roamed from member to member, and drinks were passed around.

It was chaos, but hell, this club only functioned on chaos.

Hector was already scoping out the selection of females. He settled on Holly, our newest waitress they'd hired last month. She was currently bending over a table and passing a beer over to one of the guys. Just as Hector stepped in her direction, I grabbed his arm tightly.

"Don't screw the staff, Hector," I sharply told him.

He smirked at me. "What if I fire her and hire her back tomorrow?"

I scowled at him. "I'm being serious. Every time you do this, Gus gets pissed and has to hire someone else. You don't seem to realize you're sending mixed signals when you're taking a girl to bed and treating her the way you do."

Hector wasn't a selfish lover, or at least that's what I'd heard. Countless freaking times. I also meant that in the literal sense – I'd *heard* him with women, way back when I was a kid even, and knew he was some kind of fucking guru in the sack.

He took his time with a girl, nurtured her, spoke spine-tingling words in her ears, and as a result, the poor woman on the other end felt wanted and cared for. It was fucked up. Hector was fucked up. The man harbored some serious issues, and he didn't seem to realize that he wouldn't find answers thrusting into meaningless girls.

But I wasn't Dr Phil, so what the hell did I know?

His smirk intensified. "She won't regret it."

"Holly has a kid," I retorted. "She is a struggling mother. This was the only job she could find. Do not fuck that up, Hector."

That smirk immediately fell and he glanced at Holly curiously before muttering, "Fine. I'll do her some other time."

He led us to the bar where Gus was downing a beer. Gus was the VP. He'd been close to my father, and when he died he sort of assumed that father role in my life along with my father's role. He barely glanced in our direction when we sidled up next to him. His eyes were glued to the other side of the bar where a group of faces sat. I recognized them after a few moments.

Yuri's crew, minus Yuri himself.

Hector gave Gus a hard slap on the back. "What's going on, man?"

"Not sure," Gus responded, frowning. "The deal never happened. Yuri says he has extra conditions this time around that he wants to pay a little extra for."

Hector followed his gaze to the group of four men rowdily fondling a few girls as they stopped by. His eyes narrowed in thought. "I don't get it. This isn't a fucking candy shop. We have one goddamn product at the moment that's getting shipped in. What could he possibly want?"

Gus shook his head. "Don't be pissed, but after Jesse spoke to him, he said he wanted to talk to the *real* president of the club."

I watched as Hector's face darkened, and immediately I went on guard. Hector took immediate offence when his leadership skills were called into question.

"What the fuck is that supposed to mean?" he demanded, his voice turning harsher.

Gus simply motioned to a nearby table where Jesse sat with Marshall, playing cards. "You should ask him."

Hector immediately moved in his direction, and I went to follow when Gus grabbed me suddenly by the arm and shook his white head. "Don't, Tyler," he said tiredly. "You should go upstairs to Hawke's room."

"My room," I corrected for the millionth time, my eyes on Hector. "Hasn't been Hawke's since he left, Gus."

"You know what I mean. It's best to keep you out of sight."

"What's going on?"

"Nothing you need to know."

But I did need to know. I didn't like the vibe in the air, like something was wrong. I watched Hector grab a chair and sit himself down next to Jesse. Jesse, as usual, was in a black suit. He was an oddity, this man. The only member in the club who didn't wear his vest and chose Armani instead. Which was a freaking contradiction to him, given his white crisp sleeves were rolled up and his arms were covered in tattoos, or that his blond hair almost reached his shoulders and was messy as hell, or that he had piercings in his ear and lip. You wouldn't normally put a man like that in a suit, but I'll admit he pulled it off impeccably. Plus, I had nothing bad to say about the guy. He was my closest friend in the club aside from Gus and Hector.

Marshall quickly excused himself when he got a call, slinking past the girls undetected. He did stop to ruffle my hair though as he passed and I smacked it away. He was in his mid-thirties and he was the only guy here that escaped the women instead of embracing them. Ever since he had his kid Colin two years ago with his off-and-on again girlfriend Brenda, he wasn't interested in fucking girls. I really liked that about him. It was refreshing to see a faithful dude in a culture that didn't really advocate that one-woman philosophy.

I sat down on the stool, my body turned in their direction. "Yuri wants to talk to Hawke, doesn't he?" I asked quietly, ignoring the way my chest tightened. *Hawke. Hawke. Hawke.* I loved whispering that name in my head.

Gus let out a long sigh. "I don't know more than you do right now, Ty."

I glanced at him and my eyes roamed his crinkled face. "Is he coming?"

I'd seen Hawke from time to time, and they were very short visits and spent behind closed doors talking business with the club members. He always made the time to speak to me directly, but everything about him was different. He was more serious and quiet. He observed more than he spoke, and it used to make me feel like a bullseye when his eyes settled on me. I never knew what ran through his mind when he stared at me, scrutinized me head to toe, and then never said a word about what he saw after he'd taken me in. Those gazes troubled me.

And then the interrogation would follow. The same question fired first.

"Whose bed are you in?" he'd demand.

"No one's," I'd answer.

"Well, you're here, *aren't you?"*

"Yes."

"Then whose bed are you in?"

"Yours."

Then silence.

The man I'd regarded as my best friend was gone and replaced with a hard stone wall that barely showed emotion. Plus, his hair had grown. *A lot.* The sexy face I used to admire was hiding beneath inches of facial hair. It was a tragedy, and it was also a curse. Because the less I saw of Hawke, the more I craved him.

Gus ignored my question and responded instead with, "The problem with Hector is he's too open. He doesn't know how to put up a front. Doesn't know how to keep his emotions under check. He's transparent, and that can be dangerous for the club. Can be dangerous for business."

I knew what he was getting at. Hawke was the most indecipherable man I had ever met. He was also scary. Whereas Hector was fluid and predictable with his emotions, and the edge wasn't as strong in him as it was in his older brother.

In a nutshell, Hector wasn't leader material, and everyone knew it. Fortunately, Hector was damn good with business and had a gift with numbers. He'd managed to float the businesses around town impeccably, and on top of that, had the gift of the gab and made a lot of connections on his own (though he wasn't all that great at keeping them). Plus, he had his ruthless moments. In what way I was never told, but he used his hands well, or so I heard.

"Would Hawke come if he was asked to?" I asked, unable to resist. I needed to know. God, I was desperate to see him.

"He was already asked," Gus answered, frowning.

My breath thinned. "And?" I pressed, anxiously.

"He never made it clear if he would. He's working for Borden, and that comes with a lot of responsibility."

Borden. I cringed at the name. Marcus Borden was a very bad man who had the entire city of New Raven under his thumb. He'd risen to notoriety after he'd disappeared and come back years later mysteriously rich and untouchable. Then he'd taken over the streets, ridding gangs and placing himself at the top of the food chain.

And Hawke was his second in command; a role I didn't think he deserved given his life here. But those two men were close, and I didn't see Hawke pulling back from that job anytime soon.

Gus tapped the bar twice before he slid off the stool, eyes still on Yuri's men. "I'm going to have a walk around, honey. If you need anything, just come right to me. Oh, and stay away from the Russians."

I narrowed my eyes at him. "I don't intend on being near them, Gus. That would be an extremely dumb move and a total violation of my nature."

He raised his brow, giving me a peculiar look. "I understand."

"But you're saying it like I'd be stupid enough to want to."

"I don't mean it like that."

"It's all in your tone, Gus."

"I know, it's just" – he grimaced – "we don't need trouble, and I want you safe."

"I'm here. I'll be okay."

He nodded once and left. I sat alone for a few minutes, watching Hector and Jesse deep in conversation. Shay, the clubhouse bartender, slid a beer in my direction. I took it and picked at the sticker, opting not to drink when it wasn't just the club around.

Plus, I didn't want to be tipsy if Hawke came around.

God, I hadn't felt this perked up in ages.

"Did you get your tattoo done?" Shay asked, distracting me from thoughts of Hawke.

I smiled at her. "Yeah, but it hurt like a mofo."

"Mofo?"

"You know, motherfucker."

"Yeah I know what mofo stands for, I just haven't heard someone say it in a while."

I swallowed my sigh. "Okay."

"Was it nice to have Hector touching you?"

"He did… a good job."

She stared at me for a while, not blinking, barely moving. Then she casually turned away, like she hadn't just stood there for twenty seconds, staring like a creep.

"What do you think of Holly?" she then asked, her voice piqued with interest.

"What about her?" I returned, confused. Holly seemed to be the flavor of the day.

Shay looked across the room and at Holly. Her green eyes followed her as she smoothly transitioned through the room, respectfully keeping a distance from bikers and at the same time smiling with friendliness at them as she served their drinks.

"She's not fitting in," Shay said. "I just don't get why the guys like her so much. Do you?"

I shrugged, prodding harder at the sticker on my beer. "I don't know, Shay. Don't even care to be honest."

"But do you like her?"

"I don't know her that well."

"Hector keeps looking at her and I don't like it."

Ah, Hector again, and there it was, the real problem exposed. "Hector looks at every girl with a working vagina."

"But he's staring at her *too* much. Have they fucked? Do you know anything? Like do you know if they've fucked?"

"You asked that twice in one go."

"I know, but it's obvious, isn't it? Because I feel like the way he's staring at her is personal, like he's seen what she looks like naked. She's a fucking slut, though, right?"

"I don't –"

"Look at her, making her way around the bar, playing hard to get. I see straight through that bullshit. What do you think?"

What in the fuck?

I blinked in surprise at her, wondering what she put in her water recently to make her so…unhinged.

"Like I said, Shay, I know nothing about her, but I know she hasn't caused one bit of drama like you are right now."

Shay's eyes went to mine and her brows shot up. It looked all wrong, to be honest. Her brows were so black, obviously the color of her real hair, yet she dyed her real hair so white it gave me an eye ache just staring at it. On top of that, her face was orange and caked with make-up, and it didn't blend in well with her pale neck. I didn't get why girls did this.

"I'm not creating drama," she said defensively. "I was just asking you a question, Tyler. If you're on the rag you should let me know ahead of time so I don't burden you with my *drama*."

"Then consider me on the rag every day of the year," I countered back, narrowing my eyes at her.

"That's not possible, Tyler, you'd bleed to death."

"It was a figure of speech."

She looked at me queerly. "Why can't you just be a normal girl?!"

"Define normal."

"Just someone to talk shit with!"

I shrugged, weakly. "I don't know why, Shay. I clearly have a problem."

"I see that now."

"If you're looking for a pal, consider joining the whores walking around. I'm sure they'll indulge your love for Hector since you've all shared the same bodily fluids with him and you'll have plenty in common to talk shit about."

"While I appreciate your suggestion which is so clearly laced with mockery, I won't do that, Tyler. I'm nothing like those whores. They don't care for Hector the way I do."

I resisted cringing. Instead, I just stiffened a nod and she moved down the bar, continuing her perpetual glare at Holly before smiling at the nearest guy.

Shay was in her late twenties. Aside from the brow issue and carrot colored skin, she was a very beautiful woman, but she was also absolutely fucking obsessed with Hector. And with his eyes constantly following Holly all week, I knew it was getting to her on a nuclear level.

I distanced myself from drama. The second I sniffed it, I was out of there. Girls weren't easy to get along with for me. They could be your best friend one minute, taking an interest in your life and talking to you twenty-four seven, and then the next minute they used up what they wanted out of you and moved on to other things, leaving you feeling like a piece of used up tissue. I got burned enough to want to escape that mind-fuckery every time I caught a glimpse of it.

Which was why I was currently working at a car garage as an apprentice motorcycle mechanic. There were no girls there. No bitchy office politics to be had. I was surrounded by guys who told filthy jokes and stared at Playboy magazines during their breaks. It was just what I wanted.

From the corner of my eye, I saw Holly suddenly rushing to me, her face panicked. My eyes instantly fell to her white top; it was drenched across her chest. *Ugh, fuck, here we go again.*

"Serious?" I said, scowling at her chest. "What dickhead spilled that on you?"

She stopped by my side and just shook her head. "It's okay, really, but –"

"You need another shirt, I know," I cut in.

This wasn't the first time. In fact, it happened every time she left Kirk's table. I glanced at him over my shoulder seated in the far back corner, glaring into his mug. I'd always hated Kirk. Ever since I was a kid he was such an asshole. He once removed the front wheel of my Barbie tricycle so I couldn't ride around them and then hid it in his toolbox. Dad was so pissed, he ended up kicking him in the balls and forcing him to put my bike back together. And when he did put it back together, the fucking Barbie faces were scratched to shit. Dickhead.

I never understood why they kept him around. At some point, a person needed to just die already, and he was probably pushing a hundred and was just a miserable old cunt. And he picked on Holly. A lot. For absolutely no reason at all.

Like before, she followed me down the hall and up the staircase to the second floor. I heard the sound of moaning the second I reached the top and switched my gaze to the living room. It was large enough to accommodate most of us, and it backed on to a kitchen that I spent too much time making tea in.

On the couch was family man Jonny openly getting a blowjob by some topless chick who wasn't his wife.

"Fucking seriously, Jonny?" I growled in disgust. "I watched Harry Potter on that couch just yesterday."

Jonny grabbed the couch pillow and hid his dick from view. "Just keep walking, Tyler," he told me, distractedly.

I could still see the chick bobbing her head, unconcerned in the slightest I'd just snapped at him. He wasn't allowed to do this, goddammit. I'd been specific about the living room. *Anywhere but that couch, Hector,* I'd pushed, and Hector had obliged and made it a rule. None of the other guys disagreed either. That's why I loved it here; they were willing to compromise, except fucking Jonny.

I made a disgusted sound and moved down the hallway, ignoring the way Holly's body stiffened, her eyes stuck to the ground now as she paced beside me.

"I don't know how you get used to that," she whispered to me, grimacing.

"Honestly, it's nothing," I replied.

It really was nothing. Jeez, I'd seen things as a kid that could make a Pornstar blush. It was just another one of those things that faded to white noise. I quickly grew desensitized to it, not one bone in me perturbed in the slightest. People like Holly, obviously brought up in modest households where you turned away when a couple so much as kissed on television, always found it the hardest to adjust here. I didn't think she had much time left in her, but her desperation for a job had kept her around longer than I had predicted. Which was impressive.

"But you're not like that," she noted. "You've never been with any of the guys...that I know of, anyway."

I nodded as we stopped at my room at the very end of the hallway. "Yeah, I don't fuck where I sleep, Holly. In a place like this, that shit gets complicated."

I never wanted the guys here to look at me as an object. So far I'd done well with that. The only biker that was ever into me was Jesse, and he'd tried his moves on me for a long time after I turned eighteen almost three years back, but I had shot him down constantly (was *still* shooting him down constantly). I didn't want to be some club wife that got shunned by all the others and put away in some nice little house on the other side of town, only allowed here when there was some familial function going on. That would be like living Mom's life, and I hated Mom's life. All she cared about was her hair and nails and keeping a competitive streak with some Pam bitch down the street who always donned Miu Miu heels and pink diamond earrings some poor cunt had mined in some shitty outback somewhere.

I opened the door and walked in, moving directly to my dresser. Holly stepped into my bathroom and threw her top off, dabbing the dry part of it on her chest. I pulled out a black top and threw it at her. She caught it mid-air and immediately dressed, covering up her massive boobs. She was an enviably curvy girl with a tiny waist and wide hips, whereas I was more of a beanpole. My hips were soft and small, my breasts a handful at most. What I didn't make up for in the chest department, I more than compensated in the ass, so it wasn't all that bad.

"Thanks, Tyler," she told me kindly, smiling at me. "You know, you're one of the few here who has actually been nice to me."

I smiled back. "Well, you haven't given me a reason not to be."

Instead of leaving, she just awkwardly stood there, staring at me. I was about to ask her if she needed anything else when she said, "Um…you're close to Hector, right?"

I nodded carefully. "Yeah."

"He's been looking at me a lot."

"Is that right?" I muttered, glancing over my shoulder and at the door. I really wanted to go. I didn't want to talk about shit like this. I was awkward, man. And I could sniff drama.

"I don't know what to do about it. I feel like if I rebuff him, I might lose my job, and I really need this job, you know?"

I looked back at her and sighed. "Or you can give in and just fuck him. He'll leave you alone straight away, I promise."

"I don't want to sleep with him."

Wow, I was impressed by how adamant she was by that. This girl was definitely unlike others that came through the door.

"You can rebuff him, Holly," I told her. "Honestly, it would be a first, but it would probably be a good chip to his ego."

She laughed lightly and nodded. "Yeah, but…he's the president."

"So?"

"So…I mean, I've heard things, right?"

My face tightened. "If you've heard things, you keep that to yourself, Holly."

She nodded quickly. "No, I know that, of course. But what I mean is I don't think he's the kind of guy that takes rejection well."

"You're right, he doesn't."

"And that's what I'm scared of."

"Holly, he's not Stalin. Well, I mean, he's kind of an asshole, and he's not very kind to people sometimes, but he won't cut off your head or anything, I promise." I paused, thinking. "Well, unless you cross him. Really badly. But I don't see how you could. Unless he takes *serious* offence to you rejecting him…"

She went white with shock. *Fuck, you suck at this, Tyler.*

"Chin up, you're fine," I told her firmly, and then I hurried to the door, needing to escape. "Seriously, Holly, you have nothing to fear, alright? Now let's go."

She left the room with me, her pace slow and indecisive. She wanted reassurance. She wanted me to make her feel better, and I was sure I made her feel worse. I wasn't good at making people feel better. I found it hard enough to make myself feel better at times.

We returned to the bar, and she went back to her shift, staring at Hector with a frightened look. Hector wasn't paying attention to her anymore, or any girl for that matter. He was still talking to Jesse, and at this point, I really couldn't hold back any longer. I needed to know what was going on.

I tip-toed to them and casually looked around the room, playing it cool. I stopped a couple feet behind Hector and leaned my head in his direction.

"Abram's just doing this because he had a good business relationship with Hawke, man," Jesse whispered. "Don't sweat it."

"It's insulting, Jesse," Hector replied. "How am I going to gain the respect of the club if Hawke's going to keep coming around here taking care of my responsibilities? He taught me the ropes for the first couple years, but I don't need his shit anymore."

"Look…all I know… is Tyler is a terrible fucking spy, man, and I'm embarrassed for her right now."

I tensed as they both turned their heads to me. Jesse grinned and Hector shook his head.

"You know, Ty," Jesse said, "if you wanted to be all incognito, you could have just sat in my lap and twirled my hair."

"Fuck you, Jesse," I retorted.

He cackled. "I love a filthy mouth, Tyler."

"I'll send Regina your way then. I'm sure her mouth's on the sixth dick tonight."

Hector laughed. "Tyler, you shouldn't curse so much. It looks fucking hilarious coming from you."

"Yeah, she's like a baby unicorn, huh?" Jesse added, biting his lip as he looked me over. "Look at how angry she's getting, all ferocious and red. I want to squeeze her cheeks."

I narrowed my eyes at him. "I'll squeeze your balls if you don't shut up."

"Oooh, baby, please do," he growled, standing up and moving to me. I was still as a statue, unwilling to move because that was what he wanted. He wanted me to be uncomfortable and pushing him away. He pressed himself against me, surrounding me with the scent of his expensive cologne, and I rolled my eyes as he brushed my hair past my ears. "Fuck, Ty, am I still a no-go for you?" he asked, amusement alive in his voice. "Give me a chance to change your mind, baby. I promise you won't regret it."

I looked into his light blue eyes and bit out, "Yeah, Jesse, give me a chance to bite your dick off and feed it to your asshole. That would make my night."

"Kinky girl." He pulled away, laughing with Hector as he rejoined him. "Tyler's the best thing about this club, man. Every time I second guess my patch, I think of Ty's little mouth and how much of a rainbow kitten she is."

"Yeah, she's like one of those fuckin' ponies Marshall's daughter plays with talking about harmony and shit. What're their names?"

"Fucking Rainbow Draft or some shit."

"Dash," I corrected sharply. "Not Draft, idiot."

Jesse winked at me. "You want a dash of my white stuff, sweetheart?"

I flipped him off and that just made them happier. Ugh. Such assholes. I left them to laugh at me and sat back down on my stool. I grabbed the beer bottle again and continued tearing off the sticker, thinking about the tidbit of information they unknowingly fed me.

Hawke was coming. He had to be. I felt delicious tingles at the mere thought.

I may not have messed with the guys here, but Hawke was technically not a part of the club anymore. And that meant he was a territory I could tread upon. God knows I'd always wanted to.

Yeah, and once upon a time, you made it clear to him you wanted to.

I cringed when I thought of myself declaring love to him like the fucking teenage idiot I was. Who did things like that?! What was I thinking? Answer was simple: I wasn't. I'd just been so freaking happy to see him, and so unbelievably terrified of losing him, the words just exploded out of my mouth, and I still regretted that moment deep in my bones.

Like…what was I expecting from him? To declare love back to a fifteen-year-old moron?

Maybe you thought you had a chance with him.

While Hector was a playboy all throughout the years, Hawke was more reserved. I only ever saw one girl leave his room years and years ago, and she was this pretty blonde thing with legs that went on for miles. I remembered her legs more than her face because I'd watched her put these sexy platform heels on right before she did her walk of shame. She didn't mind the walk, though. She'd been smiling with this dazzled look in her eye.

I wanted that dazzled look in my eye.

I'd never had it. My sex life was abominable in that non-existent kind of way, and I needed a man, goddammit. There were only so many batteries a woman could buy.

And with Hawke…maybe he felt attainable to me. Like there was a chance he'd notice me because of the few women he had taken to bed during the time he'd been here. That could have been different now, of course. Maybe he was slumming it like his brother was.

The thought depressed me.

I was about to turn back around to look at Hector and Jesse again when suddenly a chest pressed against my back. I winced at the pain on my just-inked skin just as a mouth touched my ear. "You're comin' home with me tonight, Tyler."

I glowered, recognizing the voice. *Yuri.* Fuck, he found me fast, didn't he?

"And all your little secrets will be mine."

He pulled away and I watched, disgusted, as he sat down next to me, his body turned in my direction. His grey eyes were bloodshot, like he'd sniffed a bit too much coke, and he sniffed like crazy, which confirmed he probably had a while ago. His hair was oily, his face (which would have looked semi-decent if cleaned up) had red splotches along his chin and jawline. Everything about Yuri was slimy, but it was his smile that sickened me the most. It was that self-entitled kind of smile, the kind that said, "I get what I want and there's nothing you can do about it".

I looked away from him and at Hector and Jesse. Giving Yuri notice would only encourage him to continue. My fingers dug at the sticker harder, peeling away clumps until I was grinding my pink nail against the glass.

"You wanna know the best part?" he continued, yanking the beer from out of my hands and downing a large gulp. Droplets ran down his chin and to the lines of his greasy neck. He slammed the bottle back down and grinned at me. "The best part is you're gonna have no choice."

God, he seemed extra unusual tonight, looking wired and antsy like he needed another hit.

"What do you say about that?" he asked me, grinning like the creep that he was.

I didn't respond for a few reasons.

One, I would have probably cursed at him and that would have made him angry, and you never wanted to make a semi-sober man from the Russian mob angry.

Two, I was admittedly unsettled. Nerves ran rampant throughout my body because of how certain he sounded, and he wouldn't sound so goddamn certain without a reason.

And three, I didn't respond to Yuri because the entrance door opened and Hawke walked in.

eight

Tyler

I felt disarmed when I saw him.

He came.

He… actually came.

I wasn't prepared for this. Nothing *ever* prepared me for the sight of Hawke.

Standing by the entrance of the bar, Hawke's eyes searched the room slowly, roaming over every inch of the place with a look of determination. When he found my face, his eyes stopped moving. He stared at me for a long moment; at my face, at what I was wearing, at the awkward sitting position I was in, before turning his attention to Yuri. Some dark thought showed in his expression before he masterfully concealed it.

Then he moved.

The guys noticed him immediately and the room quieted down. Hector and Jesse were already on their feet. Meanwhile, Yuri smiled in Hawke's direction, looking calm and relaxed. The slimy bastard was uncomfortably smug, and something about it made me feel on edge.

Hawke was wet everywhere and his boots squished along the floorboards. I knew right then he'd ridden his bike from the city; a forty-minute hike that must not have been comfortable in the rain. He was wearing a black leather jacket and faded jeans. His beard was still unnecessarily long, and his hair was loose down his back. Still, I could see the prominent facial features hair couldn't hide. Like his long straight nose, and his high cheekbones poking out behind the scruff. His eyes were dark – darker than Hector's – and almond shaped. His skin was bronze, and I could see the top part of his chest tattoos peeking out from the collar of the black shirt he wore beneath the jacket.

He was exquisite, to be honest. Not handsome in the classical way. He was scarred, he was tatted, and he had the eyes of a caged animal looking to break loose. He carried himself well, concealed every emotion expertly, and the product was a brooding biker any girl would happily lust after from a distance. Maybe, after everything, I sought to find beauty in him; a beauty that was rough around the edges, and you only ever saw it in the right light when his face softened, or when he smiled.

God, when he smiled…

It had the same effect on me since I was thirteen.

My heart thundered in my chest, and every part of me felt more alive than moments ago. I straightened my spine, suddenly conscious of what I was wearing. The shirt sucked, goddammit. It'd been over eleven months since he last saw me, and he had to find me looking like a hobo in tiny pink shorts, a baggy shirt, and my tits probably visible through the white fabric.

"You showed up fast," Yuri remarked on a smile as he neared.

Hawke didn't look at me once as he slid into the stool next to Yuri and faced him. "It took a lot for me to come out like this," he replied coolly. "This better be serious, Yuri."

"It is."

Hector and Jesse stopped alongside Hawke, and Jesse whispered something in his ear. Hawke's face remained clear of emotion as he told him quietly, "Clear the room, Jesse."

Jesse immediately moved and began clearing out the room; all the while Hawke stared at Yuri, his lips pressed tight in a line. It took about five minutes for Jesse to kick the women out. The workers disappeared in the back and half the members of the club, drunk and useless, meandered to the second floor of the clubhouse, leaving behind a few others, including Gus who was now on the other side of the bar facing us. He watched Yuri warily, an unimpressed look in his eye. Hector and Jesse moved swiftly to the entrance doors, feet behind Yuri's men still seated at the end of the bar, and I knew that was a deliberate move.

Feeling dramatically out of place, I began to slide off my stool when Yuri snapped, "You're staying, baby. This concerns you too."

I froze and looked confusedly at the side of his disgusting face before I glanced at Hawke. He didn't look back at me. His eyes remained on Yuri, unperturbed in the slightest that I was being ordered to stay like a piece of property.

The bar, moments ago alive and buzzing with noise, was dead quiet now. As the silence continued to build, Hawke idly licked his top lip and said, "Let's get to the point. You refused the deal and asked for me to be here. What's going on, Yuri?"

"Abram wants a change in our supply and he wants the discussion to be made with you," Yuri explained, bopping his knee up and down anxiously or…because he needed another hit. "He wants to triple our demand. Shipment made every month now instead of every two. Problem is he wants a better price."

"It's going to mean getting paid upfront before the shipments are organized."

"How about half before and the rest after?"

"No deal. For a shipment that size I need to make sure I've got the money. I can't be making deals without covering my ass. You've dropped this on us at the very last minute."

"*Abram* did," Yuri corrected sharply. "Not me."

Hawke just stared at him for a beat. "Alright, Abram did. It doesn't make a difference. We'll need the payment beforehand."

Yuri let out a long irritated sigh. "Fuckin' fine! We'll get you the payment beforehand, but that shit's on my shoulders. I can't afford a bad batch."

"Has there ever been a bad batch?"

"Well, no."

"So there won't be a bad batch, and it's settled. Anything else?"

"From now on, the exchange is to be made in random locations. We can't afford the heat from the law if we're picking up your shit at the warehouse, or having it dropped off at our place."

"Fair enough. I can see the logic in that if we're going to be making more frequent transactions."

"Abram also wants to discuss limiting your supply dealings with rivals of his that are encroaching on our territory."

Hawke looked thoughtful about that. "That's tricky for us. This is one of our main sources of income, and we're supplying for a number of key players. Axing somebody out means dealing with some kind of retaliation."

"Better it come from them than us."

"This is something I'd have to discuss with Abram in person."

Yuri shrugged. "Well, fine, that's up to you, but Abram has a bad side, remember? You don't want to oppose him too much, you understand what I mean?"

Hawke didn't look like he gave a shit. "Sure. Anything else?"

Yuri nodded and gestured to me with his head. "And I wanna take this one back with me tonight."

Whoa, whoa, whoa.

My heart spiked in my chest. Where in the hell had that come from? I balled my fists and opened my mouth to speak when I saw Gus at the corner of my eye furiously shaking his head at me. Was he seriously ordering me to keep my mouth shut?

Hawke still didn't pay me attention, or at least he didn't seem to care that my eyes had widened into saucers and I was pissed beyond belief. In fact, he looked bored as he watched Yuri carefully and replied, "Who? Tyler?"

Yuri sniffed and nodded again. "Yeah, I want her."

This time Hawke pointed in my direction, still keeping his gaze locked on Yuri. "Just to be clear, *her?*"

Another sniff. "Yeah."

"Then you've misunderstood."

"Misunderstood what?"

"Tyler doesn't come around here whorin' herself."

Yuri just shrugged. "So what? I want her."

"We have others."

"Look, I've done this before. I've had others, and I don't want others. If I did, I would have said that, but I didn't say that, right? I want *her* and that's all there is to it."

This time Hawke's eyes flickered to me. It was half a second, but it was enough to make my blood turn warm and ease my anger. There was no way in hell Hawke would pass me up like some prostitute. No way in hell.

As the feeling of tension arose, I noticed Jesse and Hector had briefly exchanged glances. They moved even closer to the entrance, like they were planning on blocking anyone from leaving. It was such a coordinated move, like they'd done it a million times before.

"Look," Hawke calmly replied, "I'm not going to have this back and forth banter with you, Yuri. Truth is, she's part of the club, not some hangaround that's looking for a next fix."

"I know that," Yuri retorted confidently.

Hawke gave him a strange look. "Then you know she's not for sale. She's free to come and go, and she gets to decide who she wants to spend her nights with. You can't just come around here and lay claim like this, right? It's not normal."

Yuri shook his head repeatedly. "No, no, you don't seem to be understanding me, Hawke. These-these are my fucking *conditions*, alright?"

"Alright, and I'm listening –"

"No, no, you're *hearing*, not listening. There's a big difference."

"Either way, we can't be talkin' about throwing people into the mix of our deals. I mean, this is a drug operation, if we're going to be honest. This isn't human trafficking. I can't go, 'oh yeah, sure, have the girl and do what you want with her' like she's a fucking cigarette you're bummin' off me. I can't turn a cheek to that. That's rape, right? There's a lot I do but rape? Rape's not one of them."

"It's not rape. She wants it."

"She wants it?"

"Yeah."

Hawke made a face. "Really?"

Yuri twitched. "Yeah, really."

"Then turn around and ask her if she wants it. If she says she does then all is good and we didn't even need to bring this shit up in the first place. So go on, then. Ask her, Yuri, don't just stare at me –"

"Look, don't tell me what to do, alright?" Yuri snapped, baring his teeth. "Nobody tells me what to do! I'm not a fuckin' follower, man! I'm just as high as you, Hawke. Just as high. I'm fuckin' Abram's cousin, remember? You think he'd take kindly to you telling me what to do?"

Hawke nodded steadily, his patience impeccably intact. "Okay, I won't tell you what to do, but I want to hear her say it. I want to know she wants to go home with you."

Yuri sniffed again and looked around the bar for several moments. He glimpsed at Gus, smirking at him, which made Gus even more pissed. I kept waiting for him to turn to me and ask me, but he didn't. Because he knew damn straight what the answer would be. Instead, he cracked his knuckles one by one. Then he grabbed the bottle of beer and downed another big gulp. Hawke kept his gaze fixed on him, like all the others. I couldn't believe they were even entertaining this hotheaded bastard.

He slammed the beer back down and belched loudly. "Hawke," he started, clearing his throat, "how much money do you want? Because we've got lots of it, man!"

Hawke furrowed his brow. "What are you talking about?"

"Name a price."

"Why?"

"So I can give it to you and be on our way."

"I don't want your money, Yuri."

"Well, *we* want the girl."

"We? I thought it was just you."

Yuri stiffened and ran a hand through his hair impatiently. "This is fucking ridiculous. You are being very stubborn, Hawke, and it's really pissing me off, man."

"You're pissed because you're not getting your way."

"No, no, no, that's not why."

"Yuri –"

"You know, I didn't want it to come to this, but if you don't fucking do this, we'll find someone else to buy our fucking shit from."

Hawke looked completely unconcerned. He tapped the index finger of his wounded hand on the top of the bar and shrugged. "Then go find another supplier."

"You'll lose a lot of business."

"We'll lose *some*, but not a lot."

"Just gimme the girl, Hawke. She's just a fuckin' girl, man." It startled me how desperate Yuri sounded. I didn't understand it. In fact, it made me terrified. Had this creep been watching me and I didn't know it? I was beyond unsettled now and fighting to keep my body from trembling.

Hawke still spoke calmly and slowly when he replied, "Don't insult me by coming to my place and not taking no for an answer. This thing with the girl, it sounds really desperate and pathetic, and frankly, it's starting to wear me down, Yuri. Now we can agree to up our supply for Abram at a discount and you can go on your way… *or* you'll start seein' a different side of me, and you'll regret bringing out that side of me."

"Don't fucking threaten me," Yuri barked, completely dissolving now as he pointed in Hawke's face. "You're just a fuckin' wash out. Not even part of the fuckin' club anymore, either! You think I won't go back to Abram and tell him you didn't give me what I wanted? You think I'm that fucking beta? You don't intimidate me, Hawke. Nothing about a fuck-up ex-biker intimidates me."

Hawke didn't respond. He just watched Yuri detonate with empty eyes. I'd quickly learned this was Hawke at his most dangerous.

"Now this is how it's gonna go," Yuri continued, talking speedily. "You're going to accept the discount and the shipments every month, and you're also gonna let me walk out with this bitch on my arm."

Hawke tapped his fingers on the bar some more. He stared intensely at Yuri long and hard before softly responding with, "But that's not going to happen, Yuri."

"No? No it's not going to happen?"

"No."

Suddenly digging a hand into the waistband of his jeans, he produced a gun and aimed it in my direction. My heart lurched in my chest and I jerked away, about to jump off the stool when his other hand grabbed at my hair. I sucked in a breath as he smashed my head against the bar, my vision going blurry. My entire body seized at the lightning bolt of pain shooting through my nose and skull. Tears sprang to my eyes and I let out a small cry, my face pinned to the bar so hard I couldn't move it.

"Is it going to happen now?!" Yuri shrieked, the tip of his gun tapping at my head. "You *listening* to me now, Hawke?"

"Oh, you fuck," Hawke whispered, "you really shouldn't have done that."

"Or what –"

I didn't see it happening. All I felt was the harsh tug on my hair as Yuri was tackled off his stool, a bullet ringing out of his gun and narrowly missing me. He took me down with him, and I fell in a heap to the floor, air knocked out of my lungs. I heard a struggle and turned my head to the commotion. They weren't more than a foot from me, on the ground. Hawke was on top of Yuri, straddling him. With one arm across the asshole's throat, Hawke effortlessly ripped the gun out of his hand and threw it haphazardly away from them.

Then he turned his dark gaze back to Yuri and smashed his fist into the man's face. Yuri's head snapped back against the floor, a sickening crack sounding out.

"It could have been easy," Hawke calmly murmured as he dug his free hand into his pocket, pulling out a switchblade. "You could have been on your way and none of this would be happening."

My heart thundered inside of me, desperate for oxygen, but I couldn't suck in a breath. Everything went still around me. To my horror, my body refused to move. My gaze locked on them. This was my curse: my inability to look away.

With wide eyes, I watched the gruesome scene. Watched as Hawke murmured more words and dug the tip of the blade into Yuri's eyes. He carved them out of his face one by one, quickly and steadily. Yuri screeched at the top of his lungs, his entire body exploding in tremors beneath Hawke's mountainous frame.

"I'm not unreasonable," Hawke continued, breathing quietly as he worked the blade into the man's throat. Blood splattered everywhere. Over his jacket. On my face. All over the space between us. "I'm just surrounded by unreasonable fucks that take advantage of my hospitality."

Then he stood up, drenched in Yuri's blood and stared down as the man gurgled and fought for life.

With a shake of his head, Hawke spat out with disgust, "Now look at the mess you made."

nine

Tyler

Oh, my God.

Oh, my God.

Oh, my God.

I was…immobilized. Just a part of the scenery as I stared on with wild eyes.

Yuri had stopped gurgling and convulsing for a full minute when Hawke turned to Hector and Jesse across the room. His face cracked with anger. I could feel it radiating out of him, and I didn't know how detached he was, or whether he was going to mutilate somebody else.

"Isn't it just great how we allow people who aren't part of the club to just come blowin' through the door armed with guns?" he growled.

Hector stared at the bloody scene and frowned. "I wasn't here."

"The sign of a good president is taking responsibility over the actions of your members," Hawke retorted. "No matter what!"

Hector looked away from his brother's stare and stiffened a nod. Hawke turned to Yuri's men, drunk and crimson red with horror, and spread his arms out, asking them, "Does anyone else have any fuckin' problems?"

Four of them shook their heads.

"Are you sure? We can keep discussing this girl if you want."

They shook their heads again.

"Fine. You pussies can go back to Abram and tell him I'm fine with the arrangement. But first, you can get off your drunken asses and clean this mess up. I want the floors sparkling like a sea of fucking diamonds before the sun comes up. We're not responsible for the body either, so you take that maggot on your way out."

All four heads nodded.

He then proceeded to turn in my direction. He casually stepped over the unmoving body and bent down to my level. He didn't pay attention to my startled face and terrified eyes. He just slid his arms around me and picked me up.

"Come on, darlin'," he murmured gently, moving us in the direction of the staircase in the back of the bar. "Let's get you cleaned up."

*

Hawke carried me upstairs to our room. Upon entering, he vaguely looked around it, at all my stuff covering every surface of what was technically his before he opened the bathroom and gingerly set me down on the counter. Then he took his jacket off and threw it on the bed. Turning back to me, he bent down and opened the cabinet under me, moving aside my dangling legs for a moment with his bloodied hands to grab a pink hand towel. Standing back up, he turned on the faucet behind me and soaked it with warm water.

"You got a nasty cut," he remarked, pressing the dripping cloth against the top of my forehead.

I jumped, surprised by the pain I felt. I didn't realize there was a cut. I'd been too concerned with Hawke removing Yuri's eyeballs to notice.

Hawke just killed a man and didn't blink once.

I knew he was scary. Hell, I saw him smash a helmet against the head of that cockroach. He needed to be scary because being scary meant being powerful too, and god, he was such a figure of power around these parts.

But witnessing the violence out of his own two hands was something I couldn't prepare myself for. It really hit me – and it felt like ice cubes crawling down my spine – that I had been infatuated with a killer since I was thirteen years old. He fucking beat cockroach and proceeded to have him executed, but my eyes had been shut. I'd been in denial and was comforted by that denial.

This, though? This was madly confronting because I'd seen…*everything*.

And now he was cleaning me up with the gentlest eyes narrowed on my wound as though it was a gunshot to the heart instead.

There was suddenly nothing exciting about this at all.

"It hurts, huh?" he asked softly.

I just blinked. I could hardly form words in my head let alone out of my mouth.

"That fuckin' punk," he murmured with a frown. "I can't stand people like that, darlin'. They are the scum of the earth, you know that? They don't deserve to breathe."

I blinked again. Dear God, he just killed someone, *right in front of me.*

The men here were fucking crazy, but not like this. Not like *him*.

"I had to," he finally whispered gravely, catching my haunted expression. "You listen to me carefully, Tyler, and you remember what I say. You *never* let men like Yuri go. You make that mistake once and they'll keep comin' back with this entitled attitude and overinflated ego. They'll *never* go away, darlin'. They're there to stay until they fuck shit up so bad you can't fix it. And, besides" – he let out a long breath as he stared at my cut some more – "he hurt you."

As he pressed the towel against my forehead, his other hand rested on my bare thigh. His fingers soothingly rubbed at the skin. I was still a little too numb to feel it, though I hated to admit I wanted to.

"And what I did say about anybody disrespecting you?" he added, thoughtfully. "Your face is a temple, and he marred it. My fault for not reacting sooner. I give people too many chances. I let them talk. I should have known better. Should have seen the way he was shaking, obviously the maggot was in withdrawal."

He moved a little closer to me, until I could feel the warmth of his body.

"Now he's gone," he told me sternly, and I was drowning in his dark eyes. "And you understand he needed to be gone, right?"

I stiffened a nod, too out of it still to speak. Hawke dabbed at my forehead and then rinsed the towel with more warm water. He seemed concentrated on his task, like it was surgery work that needed his absolute attention. He'd never tended to me like this. I felt like a china doll handled with care. It was strange being on the receiving end like this.

"You gonna be giving me those doe eyes all night, or you gonna talk?" he then asked, running his teeth over his plump bottom lip as he studied me.

How could I talk?

I was speechless.

Petrified.

And, worse yet, I was intensely attracted to this man regardless of all the fuckery.

What did that say about me?

I stared at him, drawn in by his rugged face and the tattoos visible above the collar of his shirt. God, he *screamed* trouble. And I foolishly listened.

He rested his hand on my thigh again – a little higher than before – and rubbed more circles over it, until slowly my body began to thaw and relax beneath his touch. My heart rate slowed down and goose bumps broke along the flesh he was touching, sending light little tingles through me.

"Why did he do it?" I finally asked, my voice quiet but surprisingly steady.

"Why did he do what, Ty?"

"Why *me*? It doesn't make sense to single me out like that."

Hawke's eyes roamed my face. Again a look I couldn't understand. He moved even closer to me, until his chest practically touched mine. Then he leaned down, and I felt his breaths on my cheek before his mouth touched my ear. My eyes fluttered shut as his scent enveloped me. I felt warmth travel all the way to the spot between my legs.

The tip of his nose ran along the curve of my ear, and then he parted his mouth and answered, "Maybe he singled you out after he saw the outline of your tits in your transparent top. And maybe, as he got closer, he saw that your painted on shorts accentuated the folds of your pussy. And then maybe, for a sick little fuck like him, he couldn't resist the teasing show you put on any longer. What do you think of that theory, Ty?"

Blood drained from my face. Hawke pulled back, his eyes inches away from mine. I saw the amusement in them, and my warmth was replaced with sudden anger.

"So it's my fault then?" I hissed. "Girls walk around with their tits hanging out but it's *my* fault I got singled out like that because I decided to wear more than they did?"

"You're an idiot, Tyler."

"Why am I an idiot?"

He abruptly grabbed me by the chin and forced my face in the direction of the mirror behind me. My body broke out in tremors as I saw the drops of blood still coating my face. Yuri's blood.

"Look at you, darlin'," Hawke then said, his voice laced with fury as he looked at me in the mirror. "Look at how fucking beautiful you are. None of those girls with their tits hanging out have anything on you. You are simply fucking breathtaking."

Turning my body away from the mirror, I shook my head and pushed his hand away. "That's not why he singled me out and you know it."

"You know what I know?" he snapped, the warmth from before evaporating. "I know that I told you a thousand times to stay away from this club. I know that if you just listened, none of this would have happened. If we're lucky, Abram will let this go, but Abram won't because to him it's probably a sign of weakness that he sent his moronic cousin in here to renegotiate a deal and wound up dead."

"You didn't have to kill him!"

"He made you bleed." He stopped there. Like that was all the excuse he needed to cut a man's eyes out and gut him like a pig.

"You're crazy," I let out in a rush, my head swimming in shock. "You're fucking crazy."

He threw the towel down and looked away, a conflicted look crossing his face. "I know that already," he whispered harshly.

He turned around, hiding his face as he opened the shower stall door and turned the water on. The room filled up with steam very quickly. He kept his face averted, determined not to let me see it, but his body was half turned in my direction when he ordered me to, "Get in, Ty. You need to wash yourself."

"I'll do that when you're gone," I replied evenly. I wasn't going to strip in front of him and breeze past him.

He suddenly looked at me. "You can't. You're shaking and need my help."

"I'm not shaking."

"Then get off."

"I'm not shaking," I repeated confidently.

Trying to prove myself, I slid easily off the sink. The second my feet touched the tile floor, my legs suddenly buckled and I nearly collapsed to the ground, hands struggling to grasp the edge of the counter. Every part of me quaked, and I couldn't understand it. I felt fine two seconds ago.

Hawke was instantly at my side and wrapping an arm around me. "I got you, Ty."

"Let go of me," I demanded.

"So you can fall back down?"

I glared at him, embarrassment flooding me. "I don't want you to touch me."

"You do want me to touch you," he replied in a hard voice, searching my eyes. "Isn't that what you begged for in that motel room?"

"I was a *kid*."

He let out a chuckle and it didn't reach his eyes. He leaned back into me, his nose barely touching mine. "So why are you still looking at me like that?"

My chest tightened and I shook my head. "I'm not looking at you like anything, Hawke."

"No, but you are."

"I'm not. You're crazy. You just killed a man."

"He had a gun to your head."

"You killed him."

"And it's not changing the way you look at me." The corner of his mouth went up in a soft smile. "Not one bit. You always manage to surprise me, Tyler."

I didn't respond. I hated that he was right. I couldn't stop looking at him with that stupid fucking revering look. For as long as I could remember, the sight of Hawke did something to me. He made my insides go soft. He made my heart pump harder. He…seemed to *touch* some part of me that nobody else ever could.

Like a coward, I turned my face away from him. I didn't want him to see that look from me. Not now.

He didn't press the matter. No, that wasn't something Hawke did. He didn't like to talk. He liked to just *stare* nowadays.

"Lift your arms," he then said, grabbing at the hem of my shirt.

"Hawke –"

"I don't want to keep staring at you covered in a dead man's blood, Ty."

I shuddered, appalled and freaked out. I lifted my arms immediately, feeling sick to my stomach. Blood and gurgling sounds invaded me. Yuri's face burned in my brain. I had half the urge to smash my head against the wall in an attempt to rid it from my mind.

"Put your arms down, Ty."

I didn't realize he'd already taken my top off. I dropped them immediately and covered my breasts with my arm. My head felt light and I sucked in air. I was ruined, wasn't I? I'd asked for this, didn't I? I was a spoiled little club bitch that felt like I belonged here, and one death later and I was already disintegrating into a giant baby. This is what they did, and I knew that already, but I dug a hole and put my head in it, loving the ignorance like the fucking idiot that I was.

You're freaking out. Just calm down.

"What the fuck's on your back?" he suddenly asked me.

I didn't respond. I was still thinking of Yuri's eye-less face. I'd never seen a face without eyes. I always thought it would just be two black holes, not…fleshy, or pink, or bloodied. How did Hawke manage to remove those eyes in less than five seconds? That took serious skill, didn't it? And experience.

It would have taken *a lot* of experience.

Hawke was behind me, hands at my back while I lost myself in dark thoughts. He peeled the bandage off and went still. I glimpsed at the mirror, needing to see his reaction. His face was pale, his eyes wide with horror. Oh, so *this* bothered him? Not Yuri, though, no. But…this. My tattoo. My tattoo was what broke through Hawke's wall. How fucking brilliant.

"The club insignia, Tyler," he said in disbelief. "Why?"

"Because I belong here," I simply replied, though my voice sounded hollow.

He exhaled and ran a hand over his face. "Fuckin' hell."

I waited for him to explode. I knew this was a step too far in his books, and it wouldn't sit well with him, but I stood by the tattoo, even now.

"When did you get this done?" he asked.

"It was finished tonight," I answered.

He frowned and his fingers shot up. I felt him touching at my skin, tracing over the tattoo. "You got ointment for this? It's going to need another coating soon."

I shook my head. "Hector said he'd treat me in the morning."

Hawke's jaw clenched. "Of course he did. He did this then, didn't he?"

I nodded. "Yeah. I wanted him to, Hawke."

His fingers stopped moving, and solemnly he asked, "Has he touched you, Tyler?"

I knew what he was asking me, but I was shocked that he would even think it. Hector was playful and flirty, but he *never* put the moves on me.

"No," I told him firmly, not masking my surprise. "Not like that. Never."

"Good."

Why *good*? If I wasn't such a pussy, I would have asked. But Hawke was intimidating, and breathing alone was a hard enough task to handle.

Hawke circled me until he was standing in front of me. As I looked up at his dark eyes, I felt his hands on my shorts. Felt him unbutton them before he slid them down a few inches. They fell on their own the rest of the way. I was naked. In front of him. Yet he was staring at my face instead of my body, and it made the situation surprisingly worse.

"Put your arms down," he told me.

I hesitated. I couldn't remember the last time a guy saw me naked. Probably never. I had fucked in the dark a few times with my high school boyfriend. Something about the light made it too intimate, and I didn't want to have intimacy with just anyone. Not living this lifestyle, anyway.

But Hawke…

Hawke could make me do anything, I realized.

I dropped my arms and I was still too busy trying to breathe to feel entirely conscious of the way I looked. His gaze immediately shot to my breasts. He scanned my body slowly, going over every inch. I knew that he liked what he saw because his eyes looked heated and his body went tight. Any other day I would have loved the tiny little victory I felt about that, but right now I mostly felt exposed, and not in the obvious way, but in a way that made me feel like he'd peeled a layer off of me with just one look.

"When did you get so beautiful?" he muttered, his brown eyes meeting mine.

I didn't reply, but something heavy stirred in me. It was enough to block out the bad images for a few moments. My stomach tightened at the way his eyes continued to run the length of me, like some meal he wanted to devour.

I wondered if he was going to touch me.

I knew I wouldn't stop it from happening.

It was the kind of thing I felt I somehow…*needed* right now. Because I wasn't thinking of Yuri and blood and eyeballs on the hardwood floor.

I was solely thinking of Hawke's masculine face, his soft plump lips and delicious bronze skin. Adrenaline fired through my bloodstream; it felt like a kick in the deepest part of me. I wanted to move forward. Wanted to inch my way so that I could feel my nipples press against the hard plains of his chest.

Hawke seemed to understand the look on my face. His jaw tensed and then… he let out a small sigh and stepped back. His eyes instantly cleared as he ordered me to, "Get in the shower and clean yourself, Ty. Don't get your back wet. I want every drop of blood gone."

I went so still, surprised by his reaction.

He was leaving me? Just like that? What did I expect though? For him to *console* me all night? For him to touch me and give me a way to expel the goddamn energy that was buzzing through my body right now at a dizzying pace?

Disappointment gnawed at me. Leave it to me to want to be touched by a man that'd just killed a human being and had us coated in his blood. The reminder made my bones stiffen, sending reality crashing down and the images to come bursting through.

Blood. All that blood. Everywhere. On me still. His choking, dying sounds. Gurgling on blood.

Swallowing back a sudden sob in my throat, I turned and moved to the shower stall hastily. I was going to throw up. I needed the hot water. I needed to wash it all off – that red blood that was sprinkled all over me. But as I opened the door, my knees buckled and I nearly collapsed again.

"Shit," Hawke cursed as his arms caught me again.

"I'm fine," I panted, even though I felt like the walls were closing in on me.

I didn't know what was happening, why my vision spotted, why my legs couldn't stand upright. I broke out in tremors in his arms, swamped by overwhelming fear.

"You're having a panic attack," he whispered. "Calm down, Ty."

I sucked in air and my head swam. I went to close my eyes, but more images of blood ran through me, until I felt like I was covered in it. In all that blood.

He settled me on the floor, and I couldn't focus. I grabbed at his arm, panicked to find he was moving away from me, detaching his body from mine.

"Don't leave me," I whispered.

"I ain't leaving you," he assured me.

He stood and I looked up as he threw his clothes off, stripping every article of clothing until he was naked. Then he bent back down and collected me in his thick arms and stepped into the shower. My arm wrapped around his neck as he sat us down on the tile ground. He held me tight as I shook uncontrollably, the water pounding over us.

"It'll pass," he promised me, his voice gentle. "You'll be alright because you're tough, Tyler. You've always been that way."

I didn't respond. I rested my face against his hard chest and closed my eyes again. This time I didn't see bloody images, not when I was surrounded by Hawke's touch.

He moved around, grabbing my loofah and running it down my legs and arms. He made sure my back wasn't against the water, but he piled my hair over my front and ran it under the spray. Eventually, my grasp around his neck loosened and I turned my face up to look at him. He was concentrating on his task of soaking up the loofah and squeezing the hot water over parts of my body. It was relaxing, and slowly I felt the scattered pieces of my mind come together again.

"You…" I paused, sniffing as my eyes wandered his thick neck along the curve of his pronounced jaw.

He looked down at me as I spoke, staring into my eyes, waiting.

I was shaking so bad, my muscles ached. But I opened my trembling lips and forced out, "You…you always…take care of me."

Hawke's face relaxed and he barely blinked as he searched my eyes. Droplets scattered all over his face, falling from his eyelashes and over the soft curve of his cheeks.

This moment.

This moment meant everything to me.

"Breathe, Tyler," he then told me, his voice like silk and filled with warmth. "Breathe with me."

He brought me closer to him, resting my head against his chest. With his heart beating in my ear, I breathed along with him, and let the air out at the same time. I repeated the action, my eyes running along his biceps as I went, idly taking in his tattoos and thick scars that ran along so many parts of his body.

I was seeking safety in the arms of a beast. He'd murdered ruthlessly, yet doted on me with a level of compassion you wouldn't expect from that kind of evil.

There were two men in Hawke, and despite the terror I felt, my heart still swelled because I wanted both of them.

I'd *always* want both of them.

After I'd calmed down, my eyelids had gone heavy. Hawke had lulled me into half-consciousness. He carried me out of the shower, drying us both with a towel. Then he laid me down on the bed and dressed me.

I was barely awake by the time he finished.

I felt his hands over my face, gently caressing my cheek while he said, "Sleep, baby. You need it."

ten

Hawke

No matter how hard he tried, Hawke was always being forced back to the club. There was no escape. He was doomed to be the ghost president, taking care of Hector's messes and somehow keeping out of club affairs. Fucking hell, this whole night could have been prevented. How could you not do a body search of outsiders coming through the clubhouse? If they fucking had, Yuri's gun would have been found and that entire situation would not have escalated.

Though Hawke couldn't deny he was glad the seedy shit was out of the picture. Killing that entitled punk ass was easy. Yuri always had been a loose cannon. The fucker had been impulsive for years, but Hawke would have preferred quietly taking care of him in some part of the bush somewhere. Not in front of the club and Tyler.

Fucking Tyler.

After he dressed and left her on the bed, Hawke paced the hallway outside her room. No, *his* room. That little wench had hijacked it. Turned it into her temple. Once upon a time the walls had been pink. Fucking pink. Like…*really* rosy pink. And there'd been half-naked posters of beta guys on his wall with their airbrushed abs on display. He couldn't believe she'd brought her teenage shit to the clubhouse, among murderers and drug dealers. And not one of the bastards downstairs had discouraged her from doing it either. They just welcomed Tyler in with open arms, like, "hey, Tyler, yeah, baby girl, come on in and sidestep the bodies and bags of cash on your way inside the clubhouse of horrors" – the fucking idiots.

But the walls weren't pink anymore, thank every holy fuck in the world. They were grey. The curtains didn't have polka dots on them; they were plain and boring. She didn't have any more CDs of wailing male singers – you know, the ones with the cheap looking tattoos, pussy-black eyeliner and gelled up conditioned hair – singing about how depressed their pampered lives were. Her dresser was now covered in make-up, brushes in all shapes and sizes, and – to his horror – a supply of birth control pills.

Tyler had evolved and it was a miracle. She still dressed girly as fuck in her pink shit, and don't even get him started on those sexy as fuck pampered nails, but she was…sharper looking and more aware. She was surer about herself than she had been a year ago. He saw it in the way she carried herself. She knew she was beautiful, but she never used it like a weapon. He really liked that. It was refreshing. Too many fake bitches roamed these rooms, bleeding every poor fucker dry – and not just of cum, but money too.

Hawke had wanted her to be independent. He'd hoped for it. Hell, he imagined her growing out of the clubhouse, finding some white collar douche to shack up with, and then settling down in the suburbs with two point five kids and a tiny little dog. But…no, that wasn't the case. Instead, she was working at Jesse's auto shop as an apprentice – who in the fuck saw that coming? – and she was getting closer to the guys every day.

He thought this crazy obsession to be part of the club would fade. He thought she'd stop staring at him in that cat-in-heat kind of way.

But Tyler *still* looked at Hawke with that longing so deep he could feel it in his bones. He saw it every time he came around, and he saw it when he stepped into the bar and his eyes caught hers. She'd immediately straightened herself, suddenly conscious of the way she looked. It mattered to her that he liked what he saw, and he wasn't going to lie to himself – he fucking *loved* what he saw.

He'd wrapped his arms around her naked. Felt the curves of her body as she shook in his grip. She was so fucking gentle. So beautiful and sweet. He couldn't erase the grating feeling of want in his bones, or the way she nestled into him, needing him the way nobody else ever had.

His hopes for her were dashed. That fucking girl was here to stay, and she was proving it to him day by day, entrenching herself deep in club affairs. She was laughing at him, wasn't she? Every fucking inch of her called out to him. Her tits, her legs, the dark little hairs between her silky thighs, her slender back – and that fucking tattoo – it all started to call out to him.

I've grown up. She shouted at him with her eyes. *I've grown up and you promised me more.*

*

It was midnight when the Russian fucks sobered up and picked up Yuri from the floor and carried him out of the bar. He was in a body bag, because the Russians conveniently had a spare one of them lying around.

"Can you believe this shit?" Jesse had muttered when he first saw them unrolling the damn thing. "They've got a body bag, man."

"You can't seriously be surprised," Hector replied back.

"Just a little bit, Hector, because we don't have that shit in our back pocket, and I'm starting to wonder if we should. I mean, where do you casually buy a body bag from? Is there a wholesaler around? This shit needs looking into."

The Russians backed their car to the entrance of the bar. It was pitch black when they stepped out and quickly threw the body in the opened trunk. When they returned to clean up the mess, Hawke was already there, standing inches away from the puddle of blood, tapping the face of his watch to hurry them the fuck up.

"Could have been done an hour ago," he snapped at them. "Get a move on."

They did. Because the Russian fucks also had a case full of cleaning supplies.

"What in the fuck is this?" Jesse hissed at Hector. "They're packing bleach too, man."

"We always travel prepared," one of them explained after he overheard him. "Too much blood. Too many bodies. Once we cleaned with toilet paper because it was all we had."

The others chuckled, like it was a fond memory between them. Yeah, ha-ha, we butchered a man and cleaned the crime scene with toilet paper, ha-ha. *Fucking imbeciles.* Hawke took a deep breath so he wouldn't fucking lose it at them.

Gus stood by the entrance door, carrying a shotgun in one hand as he watched them carefully. They cleaned quickly and efficiently. The fuckers never dared make eye contact with Hawke once as they scrubbed and polished the floor. The gravity of the situation weighed on them hard, and they were going to return to an inevitable shit storm with Abram – the last thing they needed was Hawke to explode.

When they finished, Hawke looked to Gus, and Gus inspected the scene before he okayed it. The second he had approved, the Russians rushed out of the bar and into their car and sped out of there, practically doing a burnout as they turned the corner of the parking lot and disappeared.

Jesse walked over the space Yuri died in, looking down at his feet at every step he took. Looking chuffed, he shook his head. "Drunks did a good job, Hawke. I think this is the cleanest spot in the bar."

Hawke just stared at him, not saying a word. The shit that came out of this guy's mouth sometimes…Fucking hell.

Hector was already lighting up a cigarette and joining Jesse on the walk-on-the-spot-the-sick-fuck-died-in. Then, acting like nothing happened and they hadn't fucked up so bad, they spoke about pussy, and wanting pussy, and nothing else but pussy.

"You want pussy, Hawke?" Jesse asked him with a grin, stopping. "Still some bitches around, hey? We can salvage the night. Let's smash 'em."

Hawke exhaled deeply and rubbed at his face. His fingers tingled with the urge to beat the fucking idiots for bringing this shit to the club, but Hawke knew how important it was to keep his cool. Working for a kingpin like Marcus Borden taught him that.

"Hawke?" Jesse pressed, still staring at him.

Hawke glowered at him. "You think this is funny, Jesse?"

Jesse's smile faded. "No –"

"I killed a man under our roof," Hawke interrupted, his calm voice laced with an edge. "I shed blood in the clubhouse. Think about that before you think about your precious pussy."

Jesse just stared at him with this blank expression. Holy fuck, this club had lost a lot of IQ since he left. He'd never seen the men so fucking wayward. There was no structure within the walls. None of them were walking the line, and he knew it was only a matter of time before the police (the clean kind) came knocking. And if it wasn't the police, it was an enemy.

Just one enemy would be enough to remove the Warlords from the face of the earth forever.

Jesse turned away from Hawke. "Hawke's right. I uh…I better call it a night, brothers. I'll see you guys in the morning."

When he disappeared, Hector took a seat at the bar and Hawke gestured Gus over with a wave of his hand. Gus moved to him immediately, settling his shotgun down on the top of the bar as he went.

"We need to bury this," Hawke told him sternly. "No one is ever to talk about this night again, unless we're in a club meeting."

Gus nodded adamantly. "I agree."

"No slipups, either. I want the workers and the girls questioned. We have no room for mistakes."

"You got it."

Hawke gritted his teeth as he continued to hold back his anger. "And there needs to be something done about this club letting anyone in without getting searched, Gus. This ain't a joke. This was a major fuck up. We used to have conditions. We never let just anyone come walkin' in."

Gus frowned. "Everyone's been relaxed. We've been at peace for some years now."

"Yeah, and everybody's forgotten what it's like to be at war, and that's the problem. Nobody here is prepared."

Gus looked over his shoulder and at Hector whose back was turned to them. He was lazily drinking a beer, keeping a distance from Hawke. Gus let out a long sigh, and Hawke could hear well and clear what the old man wasn't saying.

The guys loved him, and he was useful when he knew what to do, but Hector fucking sucked at being president.

"I'll talk to him," Gus promised, turning back to Hawke. "We'll figure something out, don't you worry. I'm not wearing this patch just to look good. You know I can handle it if he's on board with what I have to offer."

Hawke exhaled slowly as he scanned the bar, thinking of how packed it had been only hours ago. At least he'd cleared it before he dealt with Yuri. He thought of the sick bastard's demands, thought of Gus telling him without words that Hector was failing hard at being president, and then he thought of Tyler and…

He rubbed at his face again, exasperated by it all. "What's going on with Tyler?" he then asked, looking back at Gus intently. "I'm not getting it. Is she sticking around for a reason?"

Gus couldn't hold back the small smile on his lips. "She's…part of this, Hawke."

"Part of *what*?"

"The club. We've had her for years, you've known that. We love her. She reminds us of her old man, and I fucking miss that dick's face."

Hawke clenched his jaw. "Gus, don't get all emotional on me, alright? Tyler is a problem."

Gus widened his eyes. "A problem? No fucking way, Hawke. She has not created one bit of drama. The goddamn barmaid causes more drama, believe me. Tyler lives and breathes our life. She is loyal and she is strong. Christ, she is hacking this life better than most wives in here."

"And what about after tonight?"

"Well, I don't fucking know. You took her up, what was she like?"

"Shaken."

"Shaken like broken?"

Hawke hesitated, thinking of how she acted around him. By the end she'd appeared…lustful. "No, not broken."

Gus shrugged. "Then she'll be fine, and I know for certain she won't open her mouth…"

Gus rambled on about Tyler like he was part of her fucking fan club. Hawke drowned him out and glanced at Hector, at the way he circled the bottle in his hand and stared glumly at the counter. He was beating himself up about his failure, which meant he was going to find someone to slide his dick into to forget.

Some things never change.

"And anyway, Jesse will keep an eye on her when she gets to work and we'll know if she's alright," Gus finished.

Hawke stiffened and stared at Gus seriously, the image of those birth control pills flashing before his eyes. "Has she been with Jesse?"

"What?"

Hawke pointed at the entrance door. "I walked into the bar, and when I looked around the place Jesse was staring at her, and not staring at her decently, you feeling me?"

Gus chuckled, making light of the situation. "They're good friends."

"How good exactly?"

"Well, he wouldn't say no to her, if we're going to be honest."

"What about her?" Hawke pressed, hating how demanding he sounded, but he needed to know, especially as her naked body swirled in his mind. "Has *she* said no?"

Gus gave him a strange look. "She's rejected Jesse already. Many times, actually. She doesn't want him and…you already know that."

"So it's just been that one guy?"

He nodded slowly. "Yeah, the high school pencil-dick jock. Don't get me started about him."

"Why?"

"The slimy little fuck bragged about bagging her after prom night. Said it was going to buy him a first class ticket into the Warlords."

"I already know about that. I had you guys take care of that."

"Yeah, but he still goes on about it."

Hawke's face darkened. "I thought you beat his ass until it was black and blue."

"I did. Some people don't learn, you know that."

"He still work at that gas station?"

"Yep."

Hawke sighed. "This town is fucked up. This club is fucked up. This situation with Yuri and the fucking gang demanding more shipments is fucked up."

"You know Abram better than me. Is he going to get pissed?"

"Yuri was his moronic cousin that he felt responsible for. Abram is going to be livid."

Because Abram was worse than Yuri. He wasn't an obvious lunatic like Yuri, but fuck, that man was sadistic in ways even Hawke shuddered to think. He exacted revenge with patience and struck when you least expected it. If you were on his shit list, chances were you were going to end up stuffed in a barrel and thrown in some ditch.

Gus was concerned as he looked away and rubbed the back of his neck. "Is he crazy enough to go to war?"

"Yeah," Hawke said steadfastly. "He is, which is why this needs mending as soon as fucking possible."

"Fuck." Gus went quiet, mulling it over. "We didn't have a goddamn choice, though. He was gonna shoot Tyler."

"That's what we tell him."

Gus sighed. "Look, Hawke, I don't want you worrying about this shit. You got enough on your plate as it is working for Borden and all that. I mean, that guy is fucking crazy enough as it is. Just…go back to the city and forget all this. Hector and I will take care of Abram. We'll explain Yuri's erratic behavior. It wouldn't come as a surprise to him."

"This was my doing," Hawke replied solemnly. "I killed Yuri. I'll fix it."

Gus took a step closer to Hawke and muttered, "*We'll* fix it together. I'm not going to risk you getting found out here with you ridin' around on your own, Hawke. Most people in town won't open their mouths because of what we do around here to help out, but…it takes just one to fuck us over."

It wasn't just fear that kept the residents quiet. It was what the club did in town. They helped out whenever they could. Sometimes families came around asking for help with medical bills, rent, anything they were short on. The club wasn't all bad. In fact, once upon a time they were clean, until Hawke's old man Red became greedy, wanting the taste of the better life. He dabbled in side incomes, and then he got even more hungry, tackling on distribution where the money really was. Red had decided it was better to have dirty money than be in squalor and watch another gang come strolling in town to fuck things up. At least the town had the Warlords, who were a lot more decent than the others.

Better the devil you know, or so the saying went.

The only member that didn't morally agree with it had been Tyler's old man Dennis, but at the time there had been nothing he could do about it. Plus, he grew to love the attention. Dennis used to love the girls and couldn't keep it in his pants. Power did things to men. It made them overlook the moral bullshit just so they could enjoy the high of the present. And the high involved a bag of coke and a blowjob from some big lipped beauty that would never have dared blink an eye at Dennis if it weren't for that patch.

Women were powerful in their own right when they knew how to work an easy man. And Dennis had been a very easy man.

With a pat on the back, Gus said, "We'll discuss it in the morning."

He left Hawke standing there and returned to his room. Hector was still drinking his sorrows away feet from him, and Hawke sensed the aggression in him without having to look at his face to confirm it.

"You can't be here," Hector told him moments later, glancing at him over his shoulder, eyes glazed and, like he expected, filled with fury. "You gotta go back to your other brother, right? The one you'd rather take a bullet for, even though he orders you around like a fucking puppy."

Hawke didn't respond to that. In fact, he barely blinked in his direction. Hector would always be bitter with his older brother. A lifetime of jealousy did that to someone. Arguing was pointless.

They stared at each other for some time, the tension always lingering between them. Shit was never easy. *Never.*

"And don't you dare get wrapped up about Ty," Hector spat angrily. "The girl stays. We function well with her around. She soothes everybody."

"You're playing with fire," Hawke replied quietly. "You know she needs to be safe."

Hector suddenly slammed his hand down on the bar hard. "Where else is she safer than here?! Huh? Answer me that fucking question, Hawke. You got a bunker somewhere you can hide her in? You want to keep her a prisoner 'til she's twenty-one? Well, fuck, she's gonna be twenty-one in a matter of weeks, asshole! If nothing happened to her the last eight years, then ain't nothing gonna happen to her before then!"

Hawke smirked. "Then why did Yuri come around asking for her, brother?"

Hector shook his head. "Like I said, there's no way for him to have known about it. He just wanted her. That was it."

"And what if you're wrong?"

His younger brother clenched his teeth. "Fucking hell! I'm not, alright? You need to go. Fuck knows I'm tired of you coming here and putting me in second place. You said you'd leave it to me. You said you didn't want to take the patch back, but you're a distraction every time you're around. This chapter isn't your fucking concern anymore. Now let me take care of things."

If he'd been taking care of things, Hawke never would have received the call to take care of *this*. He could have mentioned that, but again, it was pointless with Hector. You couldn't say a damn thing without his fucking ego taking a nosedive.

"Get a shut eye, Hector," Hawke finally said. "And I'll go when I decide to go."

With that, he turned around and walked out, heading back to his room. He didn't know what he needed to do about the mess with Yuri, but he knew he needed sleep. He'd figure shit out when his mind wasn't filled with rage over the cunt that'd put a gun to Tyler's head and thought he could demand shit from him.

He opened his bedroom door and found Tyler still asleep in his bed. He stopped mid-step and stared at her. She was wearing purple boy-shorts and a white singlet, the only two articles of clothing he could find in his haste to dress her sweet body. The covers were between her soft legs, her dark hair partially over her face. But that wasn't what made him lose his breath.

It was his jacket she was using as her pillow, her face pressed against the leather, breathing in his scent.

She'd cuddled his fucking jacket to her like a goddamn teddy bear. He didn't expect to like the sight of it so much, and it irritated the fuck out of him that he did.

"What happened to you?" he whispered aloud. How in the hell had she grown so much in such a short amount of time? It was doing his head in. She was so fucking beautiful, it made his balls ache and his chest go tight. And his chest never went fucking tight, nor did his balls ache for pussy before. Women had been the same for him all his life. He'd grown so desensitized to the act of fucking, he hadn't touched a woman for months…and months. It was like his will for sex had died. Which wasn't a joke. He'd fucked like a rabbit since he was fourteen years old living the club life, and it was only when he became president that he started to feel like a numb shell for it. Yet one gaze at Tyler's naked body made him feel ravenous to fuck.

Maybe she was reminding him what he was missing out on.

Or maybe that was just the excuse he was using so he wouldn't admit he wanted *her*.

Sometimes a person could be standing in front of you your whole life without you knowing it. Then one day you walk into a bar and see that person not as a child from your memory, but a grown ass woman with curves in all the right places and a face so fucking beautiful it hurt your eyes.

Hawke sighed and shook his head at himself. Sleeping in this bedroom with her within arm's reach would be a bad idea.

"What're you doing?" she suddenly said in a groggy voice.

He tensed, surprised to find her awake.

"Nothing," he replied tightly. "Get some sleep."

Instead of doing as she was told, she stretched and rested on her back. Her tank shot up and part of her hip and stomach were visible. Her legs – disproportionately long compared to the rest of her small frame – looked like satin heaven.

Fuck, he thought of her breasts, small and perky, easy to cup. He thought of her hips, soft and rounded in all the right places. He couldn't get the image of her wet, naked body out of his head.

She blinked at him slowly. "You can sleep here. It's your bed."

He shook his head. "Doubt you'd want me near you after tonight."

"I don't know what to think about tonight," she whispered back, staring at him gravely. "I…I can't get his face out of my head, Hawke."

Her voice broke near the end, and it gutted him. Fuck, she wasn't going to handle this shit well at all. He moved to her quickly and took a seat on the edge of the bed. He swept the hair from her face and cupped her cheek, turning it so that she was staring at him.

"Do you hate me for what I did?" he asked her, needing to know.

She shook her head. "No."

"How do you feel about me then?"

A tear fell from her eye. "I…I'm scared of you."

She was *scared* of him. He'd rather she hated him instead.

"You wanna know somethin'?" he replied quietly, his chest heavy. "I'm scared of me too sometimes."

Her hand went over his, and he thought she'd remove it from her face. Instead, she held it tightly and cried. He brushed away her tears, but they kept coming. Her other hand grabbed at his arm, and she hauled herself to him, crawling into his lap. She buried her face into his chest and shook.

He should have felt angry at himself for putting her through that sight, but he couldn't feel anger toward himself. He did what he felt he had to do at the time, and with how unstable Yuri was holding that gun to her head, she might have been blown away impulsively if Hawke hadn't reacted so quickly.

Hawke wrapped his arms around her and rocked her against him. He was filthy – clothing still covered in dried blood – but he couldn't leave her. Not like this.

"How do I get it out of my head?" she begged, her voice tight.

"You don't," he replied calmly. "Fighting it makes it worse. You force yourself to think it."

"There was so much blood."

"Yeah."

"I feel so dirty."

Fuck, his chest hurt for her. "Yeah."

"How do you handle it, Hawke?"

He paused. "I turn off."

Otherwise he'd have gone mad years ago.

She nodded and stopped talking after that.

He ran his hand down her spine, never telling her it was going to be okay, never saying anything actually. His fucked up hand slid down her leg and back up, rounding her ass with all that junk and back up her spine again. After a while, she calmed right down and breathed quietly, liking the feel of him. He sensed it soothed her. Mostly he wanted to show her that the hands he'd killed someone with were also the very same hands capable of making her feel better.

The last thing he expected was her breaths to thin, or her body to tighten beneath his touch. She was *responding* to his touch, and not in the relaxing way he'd hoped.

Suddenly the room felt too small, and her body felt too good. Her shampoo – some kind of feminine shit that smelled like fucking heaven – wafted into his nose, making him lean in closer to her head for more of it.

He closed his eyes as his hand continued to move, but it didn't feel like it was moving in the same way it had been before. It was far from clinical. No, he *really* felt her skin this time, memorizing every curve on his way to her hip.

The second she squirmed for more, he stopped suddenly and opened his eyes.

Fuck.

He pulled away abruptly and started to set her back down in his bed when she grabbed his hand and forced it between her inner thighs.

Right on her pussy.

He tensed and looked down at her, at her glistening needy eyes and parted lips.

"Hawke," she whispered, breaking the silence.

She stared at his mouth.

He stared at hers.

Fuck again.

"You ain't thinkin' straight," he told her, frowning.

"I want you to touch me."

"You want me to distract you, babe."

"I want both."

He didn't know why he kept his hand there.

Well, he did fucking know.

He liked the feel of her pussy through the sad excuse of fabric. More importantly, he liked the feel of *her*. And his dick hardened as a result. He was a man, after all; it was fucking chemical.

His fingers barely moved, but they moved nonetheless. Enough for him to feel her folds.

Enough to make her breaths stop.

Enough to make *time* stop.

Fuck, she was sexy.

She sucked in a breath, closing her eyes for a moment to the feel of him. The look wound him right up. Warmth spread from his head down to his fucking toes. He wanted her.

Wanted.

When was the last time he wanted someone so bad?

Never.

Not like this.

Fuck again and again.

"You wanna know why you're horny?" he asked her, running his teeth over his bottom lip as he looked her sexy body over and, fuck, she had an ass. "It's because you're still firing with adrenaline. You're wound up tight and you're sensitive all over. You're on a hair trigger, and your sweet pussy's throbbing for a release. And you wanna know what happens after you orgasm, darlin'?"

She didn't respond. She just stared at him, waiting.

"You feel dirty," he said. "And you regret it. Because then you don't know if the fucked up situation hours ago excited you, or made you lose your mind."

"Hawke –"

"Maybe when you're thinkin' straight you'll be sure."

"Hawke –"

"But right now, you ain't sure."

He removed his hand from between her legs and set her down on the mattress, her face pressed against his jacket again. She immediately turned her body away from him. She was embarrassed. Or disappointed. He didn't know what. All he knew was he wasn't going to fuck a girl after he'd murdered some tool in front of her.

Hawke was fucked up, sure.

But not *that* fucked up.

"You get some sleep now, Tyler," he forced out.

It took a surprising amount of willpower for him to turn around and leave.

eleven

Hawke

He paced the hallway outside his room eighty-seven times. That wasn't a guess either – he'd fucking counted.

Eighty. Seven. Times.

He was wound up. His dick hadn't softened, his mind still raced with images of her vulnerable eyes, and his hand tingled from the touch of her pussy.

And it had been his *injured* hand too.

Nobody – especially a woman – had ever touched his injured hand without cringing.

Ty hadn't even flinched… and it did his head in.

This was Tyler.

TYLER, YOU DIPSHIT!

Not some random bit of fluff that he wouldn't think twice about fucking and discarding. That's what they'd all wanted, wasn't it? To be used without commitment, without question, without expectation for more.

Tyler wouldn't be like that, though. She'd latch – he saw it in that fucking stare – and that's why he needed out of here right now.

It was like this every time he saw her, and every time he was taken aback by how stunning she was. It was maddening, and he'd find himself going through the mental steps trying to convince himself to walk away and not let her sweet wanting eyes make him weak enough to take her.

But tonight was especially difficult.

Because tonight she'd made the move.

Out of desperation and vulnerability, sure, but she'd done it nonetheless, revealing her want in a bold manner that triggered every primitive urge in him.

He tried to make it work in his head. What would it mean to taste Tyler? How far would he be willing to go? But every time he thought it, he'd hit that motherfucking roadblock. Wanting her meant staying, and staying was out of the question.

Finally, after an agonizing hour, he left. Sleep wasn't going to come, not after Yuri and Tyler. Too much adrenaline coursed through his veins. He needed to get back to New Raven – to Borden and the guys. Maybe they'd figure something out with Abram. Borden always had the best plans.

But as he cruised down main street, memories flooded him. He past shops he was familiar with: the barber shop his old man frequented with him by his side; a club owned strip club that Gus organized Hawke's first lap dance at with some strawberry blonde babe by the name of Cherry (and Cherry died of a drug overdose a year later); a salon that had once been a diner they'd ended up shooting up when the owner skimmed off their slice of the pie (that was the first time he'd confronted violence and he had been fourteen years old and armed with a pistol his father had given him upon instructing him to "learn to be man").

Hawke felt nostalgic. Sticking around had never been the plan. He'd usually showed up to the clubhouse and then left right away, and while he knew the shit with Abram needed to be sorted out, something about Tyler struck a chord in him. He felt reluctant about leaving her, and he couldn't understand the emotion coursing through him. Curiosity about her? Temptation to be near her after he'd seen her naked and touched her pussy in bed? Or maybe it was just Yuri's request fucking his head up.

He didn't know for sure, but he thought about it as he roamed the quiet streets, down neighborhoods and parks. Norwich was a pretty little town now. Not so much a dump anymore, though he noticed the south end was still packed with homeless people sleeping in tents on the side of the road.

He didn't know what possessed him to stop his bike in front of the motel room where life took a strange turn. It was a night he had tried very hard to forget, though it niggled at the back of his mind every single time he thought of Tyler.

Leaning back on his bike, he took a deep breath, staring at the room Dennis had died in. It had been the night he'd begged Hawke to care for Tyler right before he choked on his blood and died.

Take care.

Take care of her.

I took it.

I took.

Don't trust.

Don't trust.

Don't...

There was never a day that had gone by that Hawke never thought of those words.

Tyler had been thrust into his life forcefully and without question, but now he was beginning to realize just how ingrained she was in his world.

Because he didn't want to see her out of it anytime soon.

twelve

Tyler

I woke up in the stillness, feeling like last night was a thousand miles away. I was pretty sure my mind had built a wall, eager and desperate to bury the blood and fear I'd experienced. The last time it'd done this was when my father died, and now I felt like I was putting another event inside that box I never wanted to reopen. Regardless, whatever my brain was doing, it was working, and I didn't want to leave the quiet peace I was in.

My head was a lot clearer. The adrenaline and tension had washed from my limbs, and I felt malleable and limp. For a while, I floated in semi-consciousness, my face still pressed against Hawke's jacket.

Hawke.

Hawke rejected you.

That was the first clear thought that entered my mind when I finally opened my eyes. The second thought was,

God, what was I thinking making him touch me like that?

I was suddenly embarrassed at myself. I didn't know why I did that, or why the urge to be touched was stronger than ever. I threw the covers over me and groaned into my pillow. How would I face him? That's not something you could easily brush off.

I lay like that for a while under the covers; it was my version of a black hole I could crawl into. Then I heard the door creak open, and footsteps approached. My eyes immediately shot open, and I tensed, wondering if it was Hawke.

"Sweets, are you up?"

The tension dissipated. It was Jesse.

"Hmm," I groaned back.

The bed sank and his arm dug beneath the covers, finding my frame. "You alright?" he asked me, running his hand down my bare arm.

"Mhm," I returned, not in the mood to speak.

"You gonna stay in today?"

"What?"

"It's back to work for you," he explained softly. "But you can take the day off. I would understand. I just wanted to know because I'm down there getting ready –"

"I'm coming," I cut in, my voice stronger.

I felt him pause before he peeled the covers off of me. His blue eyes met mine, and goodness, they were particularly bluer than usual. His hair was a mess, like he'd just gotten out of bed and came stumbling to my room like I was his first priority. He was wearing just his black briefs, his built tattooed chest and pierced nipples in plain view, inches from my face. It was a wanted distraction, but not one that stirred any warm feelings in the pit of me the way Hawke did.

Jesse looked at me closely, studying me with this perplexed look on his face. "You sure?" he asked, biting at the piercing on his bottom lip.

I nodded. "I'll be down there in thirty."

He nodded back. "I'll get ready then and wait for you outside."

He got up and moved slowly out of the room, tossing back a glance over his shoulders at me. "If you need anything before then, let me know," he added right before he disappeared.

Typical of Jesse to want to be there for me, and I should have asked him to stay so I could explain the heavy feeling in my chest I was carrying from last night, but I didn't want to burden him with it. He'd just order me to stay and the clubhouse was the last place I currently wanted to be.

I needed work.

I needed to put my head down and forget.

I was thinking of all that when my phone rang off its tits. I groaned again, grabbing it off the night stand and opened my eyes to read the name on the screen.

Mother.

I frowned and ended the phone call. Five seconds later it erupted again. Christ, she was persistent. I'd been dodging our monthly call for days now, and really, the best thing to do was get it out of the way.

Glaring at the phone, I finally answered it. "Hello?"

"Tyler, this is Mom," she said, her voice already slurred and it was…what, eight in the morning?

"Yeah, I know that, Mom. I don't know why you always tell me that."

"In case you forget my voice."

"Believe me, nobody forgets your voice."

She ignored my bitter tone. "You've been avoiding my calls."

"I've been busy."

"Well, I just wondered when you could come around and meet Paul."

"Who?"

"My other half. I met him at the church and he is the one, Tyler."

"You go to church?"

"They had this free baking event on, and I love that religious bitch's cupcakes from down the block. It's great how they let anyone in, isn't it? I just have to make the sign of the cross and they're forgiving me and shit."

"That's not morally right, you know that?"

"Fuck morals. You know better than anyone else that's not how we lived."

"Dad would never have crashed a church and made the sign of the cross to get free baked shit."

"Honey, Gandhi would have cut a bitch for those cupcakes. On that note, your fuckin' father really messed up my reputation."

"You were a stripper when you met him, Mother."

"And then I moved to High Gate to start over and live an elegant life."

"On his dime working for the club."

"Look I'm not complaining. It's not all bad. When people look the other way, it just makes it easier to steal, am I right?"

She cackled on the other end and I just…didn't say a word. Like…what could be said?

People harped on and on about a low life father being a sperm donor, but I had yet to hear an equivalent term for the mothers who didn't give a fuck.

"Womb donor?" I whispered under my breath, wondering if that worked. Or… "Egg donor? Fallopian tube donor?"

"What?" she asked, confused. "Are you drunk?"

"Uh, no, because that would mean I'm an alcoholic if I'm drunk by eight in the morning, wouldn't it, Mother?" I said pointedly. "I'm just trying to figure out an all-encompassing word to define your parenting. I'm reflecting on your qualities, things like being an absentee mom who only cares about her tequila and calls me up to tout her good news but never asking me what is going on in my life. That sort of thing. Do you have any suggestions, Mother?"

"Fuck you, Tyler Wilson, you're just like your father."

I nodded. "Your compliments are so sweet, per usual."

"That's not a compliment. He was an unfaithful jackass."

"You fucked my karate instructor."

"How the hell do you know about that?"

"Because you forced me to watch fucking Maury of all shows in my karate suit while you took him into the next room!"

"Why are you talking to me like that?" She suddenly played the victim card the second I cornered her about something she couldn't get out of. "I was a struggling mother. I had no shoulder to lean on! How dare you? Turning into an animal like the rest of those chimps at that club."

"Great, well, wow, this was a great conversation. I look forward to having it again next month with Christopher being the one instead of Patrick."

"Paul!" she screamed.

"Have a good day, Mother dearest."

I hung up and angrily threw the phone back on the night stand. It slid off and landed on the floor. Ugh.

It took everything in me to finally throw the covers off and slide out of bed. I took a quick shower, scrubbing myself everywhere and feeling horrified to find I was still sensitive and throbbing between my legs. I was half-tempted to take care of myself, but just as I brushed my fingers along my clit, pleasure formed along with nausea. I couldn't do it. Couldn't masturbate when my body still shook from the aftermath. I let out a few tears, trying to shake off that immobilizing fear, and made the water hotter so my muscles didn't tense so much. When I finished, I dug up my grey work overalls and threw it on. I avoided looking at the pink rag on the counter, opting to stare at myself in the mirror instead. I cringed at my raccoon eyes. Now I not only felt forlorn, I looked every bit of it too.

It was pitiful.

This was all Yuri's fault. If he hadn't pulled out that gun, he wouldn't have died and I wouldn't be feeling traumatized. Selfish bastard. Something about him niggled at the back of my head, though. His demand to have me just didn't make sense, and I knew Hawke was aware of it.

Again, the rejection ran through my mind, and I swallowed a groan. Humiliating. So, so humiliating.

Move on, Ty. So what if he rejected you? He's a fugitive and his beard is ridiculous.

That pep talk worked, and I began to feel a little better.

I tried applying a medium coverage of foundation on my face, but gave up two seconds in. I couldn't pretend to give a shit what I looked like. So I skipped that step and lazily removed my pink nail polish and trimmed my nails short until there was barely anything left of them. This was always the sucky part: finishing another theory block in the classroom and then returning to the grime of the auto repair shop. I was always gone just long enough that my hands were back to feeling smooth as silk.

I did my make-up, tied my hair up, and then sat on the toilet seat for a very long time, trying to breathe through the distress that made my heart squeeze and my breaths short and fast.

Yuri's dead and you're alive. It happened. It's over. Move on.

I walked out of the bedroom. The clubhouse was still. This was the only time of day it wasn't noisy as hell. All the bedroom doors I passed were shut. I stopped at Hector's room and knocked. When I didn't get an answer, I opened the door and glimpsed in.

I rolled my eyes at the sight: Hector butt naked on his stomach with Shay's naked body sprawled over his back, cradling him like he was her lifeline. He must have been desperate for a lay because he knew how clingy she was and he'd claimed on more than one occasion that she did little to push his buttons. Regardless I knew the drill: he'd toss her out the room the second he opened his eyes, but she'd carry on wanting his babies and striking when he was desperate to get his dick wet again.

This place was a broken record sometimes.

"Hector," I whispered to him, still standing in the doorway.

He didn't budge. I moved into the room, tiptoeing quietly. I stepped over articles of their clothing they'd aimlessly tossed around them. I tried not to snoop too hard, but really, it was hard when his used condoms were haphazardly strewn in plain sight and I didn't want to fucking step on one.

I should have worn a hazmat suit for this shit.

"Hector," I whispered again, shaking him by the shoulder. "You told me to come to you for the ointment."

I shook him a few more times, but he still didn't wake up, much less move. Jesus, how much had he had to drink?

On a sigh, I went to his bathroom (it was a goddamn bombsite) and searched his cupboards instead. I found a container of ointment under the sink and I tucked it in my pocket, wondering how I was going to apply it myself. Jesse would have to do it. I hurried out seconds later and strode down the hallway.

Jonny wasn't in the living room anymore, hallelujah, but I did notice the head of Mercy, a black mutt the club had adopted years ago. He was a vicious motherfucker, and his name had little to do with his personality. When Mercy was around strangers and he felt threatened, the last thing he showed was mercy, but I guess that was the joke. I patted his head once on my way to the kitchen and he lazily wagged his tail in response. Our merciless beast had a soft spot for me, probably because I smuggled him treats more than what was allowed.

"Where you goin'?" a voice sounded.

I jumped and spun around. It took me a moment in the dark to find where Hawke's voice had come from. He was seated on the couch recliner in the corner, arms crossed. He looked tired as hell, like he too hadn't slept a wink last night.

"I didn't see you in here," I said quietly, my cheeks warming up quickly thinking of last night. "Could have taken the couch."

He jerked his head in Mercy's direction. "That dog wanted to tear my face off."

"He doesn't know you very well."

"Yeah, well, he's a fucking asshole."

I smiled and it felt genuine. God, just the sight of him made all the fears disappear. "Then he's doing his job well."

The corner of Hawke's mouth quirked up. I stood awkwardly for a few moments, unsure if that was the end of the conversation or if I was meant to end it in a different way. Truth was, I was elated to see him here. Part of me thought I'd step out and find his bike gone along with him.

However, another part of me would have totally been okay if he was gone. I mean, having to face him after I made him touch my vagina last night when I was needy – and I was still currently needy – horrified me.

I wondered if we were thinking the same thing. About last night. About his hand there and me panting like a fucking porn star and telling him I wanted him. But he was acting normal, so…I felt normal…*ish*.

Suddenly remembering the original question he asked me, I pointed to my overalls and said, "Oh, and I'm heading out for work. I'm back at the shop after my block of classes."

He nodded once. "Right. Have fun at work."

Now *that* was a conversation ender. I nodded back, a little disappointed at his blasé mood. Yeah, he was totally turned off by me. And it was *definitely* because of the vagina grope. Or more accurately, the *coerced* vagina grope of motherfucking doom.

I cringed the mother of all cringes and entered the kitchen. I stood there for a while, trembling at the awkwardness before I grabbed a breakfast bar from the kitchen cabinet. I almost cursed that my box of twelve was down to two. Bastards never replaced what they ate, *ever*.

I stared down at the bar for a few moments, wondering how I could face him. I reasoned that if I didn't act normal, it would make the situation that much worse. I needed to just…relax.

I took a deep breath and nodded. Yeah, relax and just…act normal.

I walked back out and just the sight of his sexy fucking face and I was thinking about the fucking coerced vagina grope of doom.

Goddammit, what's wrong with me?!

I stopped in my tracks and turned to him for a second. He was still staring at me, intently I might add, and I couldn't handle it. I made to turn away when I stopped again and turned back to him. Fuck I looked like a human revolving door. I was making things worse and –

"You need anything, Ty?" he asked me.

My heart sped in my chest as I tossed his question in my head. I should just say no and walk away, but then…what if he was gone when I came back and I could have used this opportunity to talk to him and…

Feeling uncertain, I pulled out the ointment from my pocket and raised it to him.

"Hector won't wake up," I explained, avoiding his eye. "Do you think you can help me out?"

"You want me to rub it on you?" he asked, his voice lower than before.

You know, I was around filthy people every single day, but fuck, when it came to Hawke, my face couldn't resist burning up. And I didn't even think he was trying to be filthy.

"Yeah, Hawke," I answered, fighting my blush, "that's what you do with ointment."

"I'm just asking you to clarify, Tyler."

I just looked at him because my head was empty and I would have said a bunch of stuttering "*ums*." So I just raised my hand and gave him a thumb up.

A fucking thumb up.

What the fuck?

He stood up and stretched his arms out on a loud yawn. The act caused his chest to expand, and by god, he was broad and hard and that black tight shirt rocked his body to a tee. He came to me and took the ointment from my hand. I was a bit shaky when I turned around and unbuttoned my overalls, sliding it down to my hips.

At least you're not looking him in the eyes.

"The tank top too," he told me, his voice still unusually low.

"What?" I asked.

"Your top. Take it off."

Right.

I peeled it off, holding the fabric against my chest. I felt exposed all over again, and strangely enough, not looking at him made me instantly relax.

"Is telling me to undress your thing now, Hawke?" I cheekily asked, trying to make light of the situation.

I felt his fingers on my back, rubbing the cool ointment over my tattoo. "Only when you're covered in blood or need your tattoo lubricated, Tyler," he answered.

"Is that all?" I pressed, more out of curiosity than anything. "Because I saw the way you looked at my body last night, and it didn't feel clinical."

"I like to admire a beautiful woman when I see one."

"Oh, I'm a *woman* now."

"You sure as shit look like one."

I bit my lower lip and, thinking of last night, asked, "But not one worth touching?"

His fingers slowed and he let out a soft chuckle. "Fuckin' hell, you've grown some balls here, haven't you?"

"I'm surrounded by dudes. It comes with the territory."

"Yeah," he murmured. "Don't know if that's a good thing."

There was a few seconds of silence, and I knew I needed to acknowledge the obvious elephant in the room, or else I would never escape this awkwardness.

"Um, Hawke" – *here we go* – "about last night when I took your hand and put it between –"

"Don't know what you're talking about," he cut in, ending my would-be apology before it even began.

I smiled to myself, thankful that he was burying it.

"Now what the hell is up with your occupation? Motorcycle mechanic? Where the fuck did that come from?"

I laughed. "Jesse. He wasn't being serious, I don't think. Probably taking the piss. I was struggling after high school because I didn't know what I wanted and he jokingly invited me to the car shop. I took him up on it just to take that shit-eating grin off his face."

"And then what?"

"And then I decided I'd give it a go because I was bored and had nothing to lose."

"Girls don't usually do that."

"Do what?"

"Work on cars."

"Yeah, I think we know by now I'm not like most other girls."

Thoughtfully, he muttered, "No, you aren't."

After a few silent moments, he dropped his hand and screwed back the container. I quickly threw my tank back on and turned to him, trying to gauge his mood.

"Do you disapprove of me working there?" I asked him curiously.

He looked me over again, this time lingering on my fingers buttoning up my overalls. "I liked the pink nails."

My fingers slowed and I glanced down at my short nails, feeling a little regretful for removing the nail polish. "Yeah, I did –"

"I like the greasy look too," he cut in, his lips shooting up in a heart stopping half-smile. "Women who get their hands dirty rile me up, darlin'. You're capable, and that's sexy."

Heat rushed to my face. "You find me sexy?"

"Why do you look all constipated? It's what I said, isn't it?"

I bunched my lips to one corner to keep from smiling. Using his words, I replied, "I'm just asking you to clarify."

He smirked at me, and my heart picked up at the sight. He knew what he was doing to me. He knew how beautiful I thought he was, even with all that damn facial hair.

He took a step closer to me and I felt his hand at my hip. The touch was so unexpected, I went still. I looked at him all wide-eyed as he neared me, eyes on mine and never straying. He closed the gap between us, and I was starting to wonder what he was going to do when something hard hit my side. He slowly slipped the container back into my pocket, the sneaky bastard. Leaning his mouth to my ear, he said huskily, "Yeah, you're sexy as fuck, Tyler. You're also a club brat that needs to move out of my bedroom."

He gave me a final look – and I swear there was something there in his eyes that was far from neutral – and then he brushed past me, his arm touching mine. I stared after him as he walked out of the room and down the hallway.

I felt this urge to follow after him, to try the coerced hand-on-vagina thing again, but I resisted, knowing Jesse would be outside waiting to give me a lift to work and…knowing I couldn't survive another humiliating rejection.

I walked out of the room and stopped in the hallway, noticing my bedroom was partly open. I tip-toed to the room and, stopping just outside it, I peeked in and saw Hawke standing with his back to me, phone to his ear.

"I need to get ahold of Abram. Have him call me as soon as he gets this."

Then he turned the phone off and peeled his dirty shirt off, discarding it on the ground as he walked in the direction of the bathroom. Christ, he was built, and it was a sexy kind of built, not the nasty kind when guys popped steroids and their muscles looked like inflated balloons.

Fuck, I felt like a horny teenager all over again. The excitement, the maddening tingles just the sexy sight of him brought on, was all too much.

"Unless you're about to join me in the shower, I don't see what else you could want, Tyler,"
Hawke called out.

Shit!

My heart jumped, and I couldn't move away fast enough as I turned and hurried out of there.

Jesse was there when I stepped outside. When he saw me, he started up his Harley and waited for me to climb on. My movements were slow and forced as I moved to him, putting more distance between me and Hawke. He handed me my helmet and I carefully put it on. I buckled the straps and stared at Hawke's bike sitting in the parking lot in his very own spot.

Now *there* was a bike I wanted to be on, wrapped around a man that wasn't Jesse.

"You okay?" Jesse asked me, looking back at me with concerned eyes.

I nodded and reluctantly wrapped my arms around him. Shutting my eyes, I pretended for just a few seconds that it was Hawke instead.

thirteen

Tyler

The morning was spent doing gopher work. Shit that slaves should be doing; like fetching coffee and breakfast for the boys before being sent on another errand to pick up parts from a couple equipment manufacturers. I consoled myself that at least I wasn't getting filthy in the heat like all the others.

By the time I got back early afternoon, the boys told me Jesse wanted to see me in his office. I found him leaning back in his chair, eyes closed, with his latest "assistant" assisting his dick.

"Fuck sake!" I cursed loudly, turning away in disgust at her head bobbing up and down. First Jonny, now him?! He'd never done this before.

I heard Jesse's chair squeak. "Time to go," he ordered her.

"I can finish you," she insisted.

"I said go," Jesse repeated, angrily.

She quickly jumped up to her feet and buttoned up her blouse. She strode out of the office, a smirk on her flushed face. I slammed the door shut loudly the second she was gone and glowered at him. "You could have locked the door, Jesse."

"You could have knocked," he retorted, straightening the sleeves of his suit shirt.

"I've never knocked. Every time I have come to see you, I have opened this goddamn door and there's never been a problem with it."

He rolled his eyes and tucked himself back into his pants. I didn't know if it was just my imagination, but I thought I saw a tattoo on his freaking dick. "Alright, calm the fuck down, Tyler," he muttered. "I didn't think you'd be this fucking prudish about this."

"Prudish?" I crossed my arms, irritated beyond belief at the shit I had to put up with. "That's the last thing I am and you know it. It's not wrong that I don't want my eyes to see that shit during work. It's about being professional, Jesse."

"I'm the boss," he cut back sharply. "I owned this fucking place long before I fucking joined the club. I can kind of do what I want and *who* I want. You don't get to talk to me like I'm not your boss, you got it?"

I took a few breaths to keep myself from losing it and just stared at him pointedly. He looked exhausted and annoyed. It wasn't a combination I was used to seeing. Jesse was always smiling and joking. I wondered what was pissing him off.

After a full minute, the anger creases on his face disappeared and he looked at me with remorse. "Sorry, sweetie, I didn't mean to bite your head off. I'm just...wound up, you know? I needed a release."

"Didn't get it last night?"

"No." His face darkened again for a fleeting moment. "Sorry you had to see that. I don't know what the fuck is getting at me. My head's cloudy, and I didn't get enough sleep, I guess."

I nodded in understanding. "We all have our bad days. Now what do you need, Jesse? The boys said you asked for me."

At my lack of hostility, his shoulders relaxed and his face glowed again. "If it were up to me, I'd have you the same way Miranda was just moments ago."

Ah, yes, the funny banter was back.

I resisted smiling. "If it were up to me, I'd cut your dick off so bitches like *Miranda* weren't around in the first place."

His eyes lit up. "You jealous?"

"Not in the slightest."

"Well, I need her."

"You need her servicing you."

"Nah, she's my personal assistant."

"Personal cum-bucket, you mean."

He just smiled. "I'm usually doing the pleasing, Tyler. I like it that way more, but she doesn't really do it for me. I thought her lips were plump enough she could help me out instead. But her suction was off, and she bared her teeth like Jaws."

"Too much info, buddy."

"You know what would do it for me? Servicing *you.*"

This guy. "I kind of have more self-respect than to be with a dude who was just getting sucked off."

"I'm limp as a noddle, Ty. She wasn't accomplishing shit. But you…god, we'd rock each other's worlds. I'm still waiting for you to give in."

I rolled my eyes. "How about I'll consider it if we're both single at ninety? Make one of those pact kind of things."

"Ninety?"

"I'll be experienced then. Think of how good my suction will be without teeth."

"Fuck, that actually sounds like we're going somewhere. Do you want a taste of me right now so you have something to look forward to?"

"I'm sure your dick tastes like raspberry saliva after what I just saw, so no."

"You make it sound like a death sentence, and it's hard to understand. Girls want me and you don't."

I sighed at the note of somberness in his words. "Okay, I'm not getting into this. Tell me what you want, Jesse, so I can go back to work."

He leaned back in his chair and that smile began to slip as he closely eyed my face. "Look, to be all fucking serious, Ty, I wanted to see how you were feeling."

"What do you mean?"

His brows shot up. "I mean you witnessed Hawke kill a dude a foot from you and instead of still losing your shit about it you end up coming to work the next morning."

"Oh, you want to talk about *feelings.* I didn't think you had a therapist in you."

"Tyler, seriously."

I looked away from his intrusive eyes and at a spot on the wall. It took a lot for me to hold it together. "To be fair, Jesse, Yuri had a gun to my head."

"Yeah, I know, but…fuck, sweets, that was heavy shit. I know you've seen the guys brawling. You're used to some blood here and there, but nothing like last night. I'm worried for your sanity. That's not something you can easily come back from."

"I'm fine," I lied, trying not to relive Yuri's eye-less face another second. "You don't need to worry."

"'Course I do," he heatedly replied. "You're one of us! Part of the family. That means we need to look out for each other. One thing we never brought to the clubhouse was that sort of violence. We would never in a million years want you to have seen that shit. I don't know what the fuck Hawke was thinking. He should have stopped the second he got the gun off him."

"Hawke was protecting me," I replied steadfastly, thinking of his words last night. "Men like Yuri don't change. They just keep coming back and pushing their boundaries. Hawke needed to do it, and I understand that."

Jesse looked at me perplexedly. "It was fucking savage!"

"It was necessary."

Now he paused for a moment. "Do you…you got a thing for him or something?"

I looked at the wall again. "No."

"Then why are you so chill about this?"

"I'm not. I'm just…more capable at handling this shit than other people."

Lie. I was totally not capable of handling this shit, hence why Hawke had to rock me back and forth like a fucking baby. But shit, he cared enough to, right? Before I fucked it up by putting his hand between my legs, anyway. He'd touched me all over even. Maybe it was my imagination, but I could have sworn he'd lingered on my ass longer than everywhere else.

Wow.

He definitely had.

That made the rejection heaps more bearable.

Jesse didn't appear totally convinced. In fact, he looked horrified. "No one is capable of handling that shit!"

"Jesse –"

"I think about you a lot, did you know that?" he cut in, his voice softer now. "I think about how to make life better for you here and better for you at the club, all so that you don't run for the hills at the shit that goes on. I'm terrified you'll leave."

"I know that, and I appreciate it. You've been a good friend."

"Friend?" he scoffed, the smile on his face fake. "I'm not doing this shit to be your *friend*, Tyler. I'm doing it so you open your fucking eyes and realize I can keep you safe if you were on my side and sharing *my* bed instead of sleeping in Hawke's every single night."

I clasped my hands together, feeling more uncomfortable by the second. I really just wanted to go back to work and think of Hawke's hands on my ass instead of dealing with Jesse's crap.

"What the hell do you want me to say to that, Jesse? I'm totally struggling here. I've got a lot on my plate right now, adding your invite in your bed is something I don't need."

He leaned over his desk and stared at me sternly. "You know I'd have killed Yuri for you too, right?"

I frowned and looked back at him. "This isn't a competition –"

"Everybody knows about your schoolgirl crush on Hawke. I saw the way you were blushing up a storm the second he entered the clubhouse last night. Even now you're fighting it."

"Congratulations for really making shit awkward now."

"I'm being straightforward, and I'm not going to tickle your ear about Hawke. He murdered a fuck of a lot more people than any of us ever did in the *history* of our club, Tyler. Did you know that? He is merciless. He's Borden's fucking hitman for crying out loud. You've grown him in your mind to be something he isn't and forgetting what's already in front of you."

I hated Jesse for putting me on the spot like this. Was he seriously trying to compare himself to Hawke right now? Because that was like comparing oranges to apples, and I wanted my broody apple instead of an orange that fucked stupid girls in offices and compared their blowjob teeth to Jaws.

I narrowed my eyes at him. "What's in front of me, Jesse, is a man that got sucked off minutes ago. A man that is constantly around bare-breasted sluts and constantly getting his dick wet by them too with his good pal Hector. So excuse me for not buying your sincerity and sliding into bed with you like some hussy with half a brain."

"I was just telling you how it is."

"I don't want to hear it! Hawke doesn't even want me, and I learned that the hard way, alright? And it was embarrassing and I'm still humiliated, but that's *my* business and not yours. And even if he did want me in some other parallel universe, I can decide for myself what *I* want."

He sulked. "I know that, alright? But you also know my past enough to believe I wouldn't have a thing to do with other girls if you wanted my side of the bed, so don't be throwing that shit in my face either."

"We have a *friendship*, Jesse. I don't look at you like that. The idea of fucking you is like incest to me."

He shrugged. "That's not unsexy if we acted out on it in a fantasy kind of way."

"You'd only act on it if you're into that kind of shit, and I am not at all remotely interested. It's just fucked up and I'd never look at you the same."

"You're an only child, so it's not like you'd be thinking of a particular sibling, Tyler."

What the fuck? "Why are we even talking about this? It's sick."

"I don't fucking know. There was a point and I've just forgotten it. Gimme a second to remember."

He brainstormed for a few seconds, and I couldn't believe I was actually giving him a chance to.

I finally sighed, giving up. "Jesse, stop, you're being silly."

"I'm trying to make you understand Hawke is nothing like me, and that's a good thing. I'm there for you. I would be mindful killing someone around you, you know? I'd have you look away at least."

"That's very sweet of you," I said dryly.

"I'm better."

"Why can't you both be good in your own ways?"

"He's got a fuckin' mannequin face, Ty. You don't even know if he can feel half the time you're around him. Plus his beard is getting fucking ridiculous now. He's fulfilling the stereotype of a biker, and making pretty boys like Hector and me look soft."

"Jesse –"

"Look, I'm real and I'm *here*," he interrupted me, tapping his desk to emphasize how *here* he was. "Don't get close to him. He's a fugitive and he's leaving soon. Hawke's a dead end, sweetheart."

And just like that, I was knocked speechless over two lines of brutal truth. *That* was how you slapped someone in the face with reality.

I felt like fucking Ralph in the Simpsons getting his heart broken on Valentine's Day by Lisa. Thought of his face cracking in pain when she didn't *choo-choose* him.

Fucking Lisa.

Fucking Jesse.

Bunch of heartbreakers, the lot of them.

Jesse studied me, grimacing at whatever devastation I was so obviously displaying. "Tyler," he said quietly, his voice like silk, "I'm sorry if I'm being a dick. I just don't want you wasting your time wanting someone you can't be with."

I looked away from him and cleared my throat. "Yeah, sure," I returned, trying to come off as casual but failing.

"You're struggling," he stated, sadly. "Maybe you should go home –"

"I'm fine."

"Where the fuck did you get this armor from? I've never seen a girl like you."

My armor felt brittle and cheap like plastic. I just pretended it was hard so people like Jesse would leave me alone.

"I gotta go back to work, Jesse," I told him, the life in my voice gone. "I'll see you later."

I didn't give him a chance to stop me. I fled from the office and sat at my work bench for a long time, wondering why the hell I felt like I lost Hawke when he wasn't even mine to begin with.

fourteen

Hawke

It was noon and Hector still hadn't come down.

The guys had conglomerated in the meeting room behind the bar to discuss Abram, and were currently *not* discussing Abram because they were waiting on princess Hector to emerge from the room of Sleeping Beauty. Hawke leaned back in his chair, arms crossed, staring at the head of the table where his brother should have currently been sitting in.

No, where *he* should be sitting in.

He couldn't help that thought from slipping in.

Hawke gritted his teeth and turned to Jonny. "What is this?"

Jonny shook his head, glancing at the watch on his wrist. "Yeah, he usually gets up right about now. Maybe he had more to drink than what he usually, uh, drinks…"

Gus sat across from Hawke, staring at him expectantly. Fuck, he was giving him *that* look, the one that said: *See, Hawke? Your brother fucking sucks at this shit and it should be you at the head of the table.*

"Marshall," Hawke spoke, "go wake him up. We can't wait anymore for this shit."

Marshall nodded and took off.

They waited ten more fucking minutes, and it was a shit ten fucking minutes because Hawke spent every second of them trying to fend off thoughts of Tyler. She had latched onto his mind the second he stepped into this place, and he couldn't stop thinking of her.

That tight little body.

Those lips.

Those soul-sucking eyes.

That. Mother. Fucking. Stare.

Then this morning. He almost groaned. Christ, she looked fucking delicious in those ugly overalls. He was half-tempted to just get the fuck out of there and see her kneeling before a bike, getting her hands filthy. If it was his bike, he'd have stripped her naked, back against him, ass out, tattoo on display as she worked it with those sexy little hands. He'd have kept her nail polish on, though, because pink nails wrapped around his cock would be sexy as fuck.

Shit, he was actually *fantasizing* this shit, enough to make his dick hard.

Fuck. Fuck. Fuck.

Hawke rubbed his face, exasperated by his inability to operate without her clouding his head like a pussy-whipped fool.

You can't be pussy-whipped without havin' that pussy first, idiot.

He wanted to have it. He wanted to have Tyler bent in all kinds of ways. That much was obvious, but she looked so fragile standing in front of him pretending to be strong. He saw right through her façade and it concerned him that she was gone. That he had let her go in the first place.

The door finally opened, thank fuck. He watched Hector stumble into the room, his hair a mess, his face sullen, his eyes black from exhaustion. He wasn't even wearing his patch. No, his stupid fucking brother was shirtless and holding tight a freshly opened bottle of beer.

Well, this was just fucking great, wasn't it?

A drunk, alcoholic president strolled through, looking like he currently didn't give a rat's ass about being here.

He smirked at Hawke as he rounded the table and took his sweet old time sitting down at the head of it. Hawke didn't react to that arrogant expression, though he would have given anything to have smashed that Brad Pitt smile off his face with his fist.

"Where's Leon?" Hector asked, looking around the room. "We're missing our Road Captain, and I can't have this meeting without him."

Gus let out a long sigh. "Leon has been on the road since last Friday, and we ain't expecting him back for another month, Hector."

"Prez," Hector corrected. "That's what you call me officially when we're in a meeting, Gus. You know that."

Gus didn't reply. He just looked at Hawke. Again, he said that thing with his face.

Hawke dragged his teeth along his bottom lip and turned to his brother. "Alright, Prez, we gotta talk about –"

"I haven't addressed you," Hector interrupted, taking a long swig of his beer. "You don't talk unless I address you, Hawke, and to be fucking honest, I'm not sure why you're even in here. You're not even part of the club anymore."

Gus clenched his hands into fists. "You are still drunk, Hector," he said, trying his hardest to keep the anger out of his voice. "Because need we remind you that Hawke can take your place any fucking second he chooses."

Hector didn't seem ruffled in the slightest, putting on that Pitt smile again. "But Hawke doesn't want it. Right, bro? You can answer that because I'm addressing you now."

Hawke didn't rise up to the bait. Instead, he calmly said, "We were about to try and get ahold of Abram again to smooth this through when you came through the door."

Hector took another gulp of his beer. "I don't see why we bother. We should just shoot the fucker and sell the shipments to somebody else. We got lots of buyers on the market."

"You haven't spoken to them in over a year," Gus snapped. "What makes you think they'll even want our business? There's a gap now that we're not keeping contact with 'em, and it's being closed by other small time fucks who'll only get bigger if we don't do something about it."

Hector shot Gus a dark look. "Yeah, you fuckin' said that already, Gus."

"And you're not demanding anything be done about it. We're losin' money! The fucking cockroaches keep comin' back for more money, and soon, we're gonna have nothing to give 'em if we don't start sellin' more."

Hawke tapped his fingers against the table, keeping his eyes pinned to Hector as he said, "Abram is not an enemy we want to have. He is ruthless and he is untouchable."

"Yeah, and so was Borden before he got fucking tortured. Remember that?" Hector retorted.

Shit, this was an impossible task. Hawke couldn't believe how fucking STUPID his brother was.

"Let's just settle this," he told him as he pulled out his phone, opting not to indulge his alcoholic *president* any longer, and called Abram again. He put the call on speaker and settled it on the table.

It rang four times before someone picked up.

"You wanna fuck with me, Hawke?" Abram angrily shouted on the other end.

Everyone in the room stilled in surprise, but Hawke expected this.

"I don't want to fuck with you, Abram," he replied. "It happened for a reason."

"It happened for a reason?!" Abram repeated, angrier by the second.

"Let me explain –"

"I want to see your fuckin' ass on my fuckin' doorstep, you hear me? I want to hear every fuckin' thing that you did to my cousin to my *face*, and not over a fuckin' phone call like a pussy. You got it?"

"Yeah," Hawke replied. "I got it."

"And if you fuckin' run, I'm gonna come after that filthy club of yours. I'm gonna tear them to pieces, you hearing me? I'll pay your cockroaches double so they'll throw your asses in prison, and I'll put a price on every single head in there! Then I'm gonna make that whore of a girl that lives there eat a bullet as I fuck her from behind."

Tyler.

Hawke fisted his hands, trying his hardest not to explode.

"I know *everything* that goes on in there. If you don't have a decent excuse this will get fuckin' ugly, Hawke. I got ties, you stupid fucking idiots. You wanna know who you're fuckin' with? You don't wanna fuckin' know."

Hawke kept his voice steady as he responded, "No, we don't want to fucking know."

"I'm gonna be back in two days and you better be at my place, and don't you fucking dare drag your sorry excuse of a president there either. I'll just end up shooting that useless pussy fuck."

The line went dead, and the room fell silent.

Hawke stared at his brother, gauging his reaction. Hector looked paler, his lips sealed as he kept his eyes away from him. He didn't have anything to say, which shouldn't have surprised Hawke, but fuck, he was disappointed in the little shit.

He was over it.

Fucking OVER his bullshit.

Standing up, Hawke grabbed Hector's bottle and tipped it upside down, emptying it on the floor beside Hector's chair. "And this," Hawke gritted out, watching his brother's scowling face, "is why we don't fuck with Abram. Sober the fuck up, *Prez*."

Then he tossed the beer on the table and turned to everyone else.

"I know all about Abram. He doesn't want a war. He's just really fuckin' pissed about his stupid fuckin' cousin bitin' the dust. We'll deal with him but not in a gun's blazing kind of way. We gotta be careful. We are in no fucking shape to tackle on a war because this fucking club is a goddamn mess. In the meantime, take care of security, stock up on our weapons, and do a fucking search of anyone comin' through that door. Can you handle that obvious goddamn instruction?"

They all nodded.

"Good, and keep a fuckin' eye on Tyler, will you? This fuck just threatened he'd rape her, and believe me, that's not something he's against doing. Got it?"

They all nodded again.

He walked out of the bar, needing air. He paced out front, wanting nothing more than hard liquor to ease the coil of stress in his chest.

The fuck had threatened not just the club, but Tyler, like…like he fucking knew all about her. He probably did. Probably had eyes on the outside, and hell, at the rate Hector was letting people in, maybe there was someone in the inside too.

This shit had suddenly escalated. Hawke wouldn't be able to just return to the city. Now he had to prevent a big fucking war from happening because his stupid fucking brothers didn't do a simple body inspection.

"Fuckin' hell, Hector," he muttered under his breath, shaking his head.

His brother wasn't fit to lead, and nobody wanted the position. Everyone knew how big the role was. It was an inevitable death sentence if you didn't know what you were doing. Besides, they wanted Hawke back and he…he went through too much shit to get where he was.

He wasn't sure if he had it in him anymore.

fifteen

Tyler

The day got easier toward the end. Working distracted me nicely, and with some good music and small chats with the guys, I was feeling pretty normal again.

I didn't expect Hawke to be around when we got back to the clubhouse. I was so surprised – and so fucking elated – to find his motorcycle sitting in the parking lot. Just like that, I perked up more than before, and my body came back to life. I jumped off the bike and nearly sprinted to the entrance. I stepped in and paused, analyzing the scene before I found a seat.

The brothers had sat on opposite sides of the room; Hector was at the front of the bar, and Hawke in the back. It seemed very purposeful, especially as I caught Hector currently glaring at Hawke. Hawke, as usual, was ignoring it entirely.

I felt the tension between them as I studied them both. I knew that Hawke taking care of Yuri and the deal about the shipments appeared like he was undermining Hector's power in the club, but I was thankful he'd done it. I wasn't sure what would have transpired if Yuri had been negotiating with Hector instead, and that's not to say that Hector would have allowed the creep to take me home with him because I knew he wouldn't have agreed to that. No, it was that I was unsure how quick he would have reacted to the gun being pointed at my head.

Would that have been enough reason to piss Hector off? Or had something else happened while I was gone?

I stood back for a while and watched Jesse join Hector and Marshall. Then I observed Hawke, who had Gus, Jonny and Kirk by his side. The rest of the members were in the middle, not wanting to confront the obvious split between both brothers.

It was so *obviously* awkward.

After a few moments Hawke and Hector simultaneously looked up at me. Talk about psychic sibling connection or something. I couldn't read Hawke's expression, but Hector's had an expectant look on his. He was waiting for me to join him, and I felt caught in the middle like my loyalty was being questioned.

I hesitated and started moving in Hector's direction. This was the right thing to do. My loyalty was to the *current* president, not to the man I'd tried to force between my legs.

Right?

Only… halfway there, my body turned so abruptly, I found myself moving to Hawke instead. I didn't once stop to question it, though I knew I should have. Because it wasn't just them staring at me, it was everybody else too. But I just couldn't seem to stop myself.

Hawke watched me intently as I moved to him, taking in every inch of my body like he was committing it to memory. I stopped in front of his table and waited for him to invite me to sit down.

He took a swig of his beer bottle, his eyes never straying from mine. Then he set it down on the table and slowly said, "Go back, Tyler."

"What do you mean?" I asked, blankly.

"You don't know what you're doin' by comin' to me," he answered, his voice a warning. "You're pickin' my company instead of his, and you know all about Hector's ego. So think very carefully about what you're doin' before you decide where you want to sit."

I paused and glanced over my shoulder. Sure enough, Hector and Jesse were staring at me, and they didn't look too happy. Logic told me to go to them because I didn't want to rock the boat, and Hawke was only here temporarily anyway. Better not to get on their bad side, right?

But then I looked back at Hawke, and god, my heart burst at the thought of being near him. I couldn't help myself. I grabbed the chair facing him and sat down.

Hawke smiled behind his bottle the second my ass hit the chair.

"Hector will get over it," I said, returning the smile that didn't reach my eyes.

Fuck, what had I done?

Jonny cackled. "This is the only female that can survive the bullshit of club life, Hawke."

Hawke nodded, licking his bottom lip thoughtfully. "I'm starting to realize that. How about you get her a beer, Gus?"

"That I can do," Gus replied, leaving the table.

Okay, that was an encouraging start. As long I didn't look behind me, I could pretend the atmosphere was happy.

When Gus returned, he gave me a beer and I sipped on it and chilled with them. It wasn't very exciting because the guys didn't talk and Hawke spent the whole time watching me. When the women started flooding through the door, everyone in the bar perked up and started to really have some fun. Even miserable Kirk was drawn in by the tits being flashed around the place and excused himself from the table.

For a while, Hawke and I didn't talk, but he wouldn't stop looking at me. He startled me with his attention. I felt warmed by the depth of it and panicked at the same time. Growing up, long before my father died, it took a lot for me to catch his attention because he'd ran the place non-stop, and as a result, he'd been swamped with business and girls dangling around him like starved kittens. And while girls were currently nearing him for a piece of his attention, he wasn't giving it to them.

No, he was giving it to *me*.

Even after last night's brutal, horrifying, feel-the-shudder-in-your-bones kind of rejection.

Mind. Blown.

"You don't know what you just did, do you?" he suddenly asked, looking thoughtful now. "You just made a statement to everybody, Ty. That shit has consequences."

I hid my hesitation with a shrug. "It's done with. I can't just get up now and turn back."

He didn't seem impressed by my response. "Just watch yourself," he told me grimly. "And choose your prez next time."

"That's what I did," I muttered before I could stop myself.

He went still, and then he tensed his jaw. "Fuckin' hell, Tyler, don't you be saying shit like that around here, alright?"

"I'm not. I'm saying them to *you.*" I leaned forward, smiling softly. "And you secretly like it, don't you?"

He dragged his teeth over his bottom lip. "You're transparent, Tyler. I know what you're trying to do. Trying to stir me up."

"I'm trying to make you miss it."

"Why? So that I can reclaim my title?"

"It's still yours technically. When you went to prison Hector was substituting for you. Nobody made it official, and the club's been in purgatory since."

He chuckled. "You think you know everything, huh?"

"I've got years of seeing things, Hawke, and when no one knows you're around, they show themselves to you. So, yeah, I'm pretty confident I know everything."

Hawke shot me a sideways glance. "Hiding under tables."

"In closets too."

"See a lot of dirty things?"

"Only the dirtiest."

His face brightened, and my heart swelled at the sight. How a man could go from a shade so black last night to a heavenly white tonight was a mystery.

"So tell me 'bout Hector then," he then said, looking past me and at him. "How's he handling his role? Be honest."

I shook my head slowly. "He isn't handling it, Hawke. He's either violent or doesn't know what to do. He doesn't show it, but his hands tremble when they ask him how to handle something."

"How often does he tremble?"

I frowned. "Often enough."

"Hmm." Hawke was inquisitive now as he thought of what I said. "I learned today they're losin' money."

"Yeah. A lot. It's the cockroaches. Their ringleader Duggard comes around negotiating all the time. They keep asking for more money."

"Bloodsuckers."

"Oh, yeah. It stresses Hector out, and Gus just throws more money at them, which is the wrong way to handle it."

"You're right."

"What would you do?"

He didn't skip a beat replying, "Bleed one of 'em dry to send the rest a message."

"That goes against your rules."

"*Old* rules," he corrected me. "After working for Borden I realized fear is the biggest weapon. Worse than guns, and violence. Fear is a tool that can silence an entire crowd. Much like the town now. They're afraid, but if Hector's doesn't do anything soon, gangs will rise up and start tryin' to take over the streets and the cockroaches will keep taking advantage."

"Maybe we need you more than ever right now."

"Maybe that ship sailed five years ago."

I smiled wistfully, looking at him closely as I asked, "But do you miss it, Hawke?"

"Being president?"

"The life, being president, all of it."

He looked at me peculiarly. "Why? You thinkin' of leavin' and seein' what else is out there?"

"God no, I can't see myself out of this place. I wouldn't even know where to begin. There'd…be no purpose."

His smile flattened, and when I realized what I said, I shut my eyes momentarily, wincing out, "Shit, sorry, Hawke. I'm not saying you have no purpose –"

"You can say what you want, or whatever you feel," he cut in, softly. "Don't censor yourself around me, alright?"

I nodded, not meeting his eye.

Then he said quietly, "I do miss it, Tyler. Yeah, I ain't gonna lie. I miss it a fucking lot some days."

His voice sounded pained.

I looked back up at him, surprised by his admission. It was all he was willing to say; I knew that already when he gulped back his drink and slammed the beer down harder than he should have.

I didn't know how to make him feel better with words. I wasn't sure how sincere they would sound anyway.

Without thinking, I leaned over the table and rested my hand over his injured one. As I looked at him, I gently rubbed at the callouses, over the scars and thickened flesh. His eyes shot to mine, his face no longer pained but…curious. Then he watched my movements, the way my fingers roamed his hand. There was such a stark difference between them. He was such a man, his hands so big and vicious looking, while mine were soft and little.

Hawke visibly relaxed and warmth flooded his face as he took me in, looking over every inch of me he could. The more he did it, the more my skin ignited.

We drank. Maybe I had one too many beers, but it was just enough for my head to feel that pleasant cloudiness.

"Can I ask you somethin'?" he suddenly said, running his tongue along his lip thoughtfully.

"What?" My voice was quiet as I trained my gaze to his mouth.

"Would you have regretted it if I touched you?"

My lips parted and my heart raced. He was talking about the ultimate rejection, and I felt my face go red just thinking of my brazenness last night.

"Yeah," I admitted steadfastly. Because he'd been right. I hadn't been in the right frame of mind.

"What about now?" he asked, his voice huskier, lower.

I let out a light breath. "No."

His gaze dropped to my mouth and he looked at me for a while, intrigued and wanting. I was in my fucking overalls, there were girls wearing nothing, and he was staring at *me.*

That spot in the pit of my stomach fluttered and tugged. I wanted him badly. I'd happily take him if he offered. I had no time to play games like the bitches around me did. The longer I was deprived, the more pained I felt.

And Hawke?

He deprived me of something big, and I was scrambling to understand it.

"You're starin' at me in that way again," he growled, gritting his teeth like he was trying to rein in an emotion. "You're killin' me, Ty."

"Good."

There was a ghost of a smile on his wet lips, and I felt that part of me throb a little more just wondering how good he would taste if I kissed him.

As the alcohol flowed in, the awkward divide in the room lessened, and everybody began to merge with one another. The guys migrated to where we were and Hawke's attention was abruptly forced from me when they crowded around us.

I moved my hand away quickly, hiding it under the table, watching him interact. Figures they'd flock to him like moths to a flame. Hawke was revered. He barely opened his mouth and he sought me out every few moments, but our moment was over. I could feel him pulling away, growing reserved again.

Goddammit.

Hawke was an uphill battle, wasn't he? Like a butterfly, you caught one and cupped that baby in your hands, and the second you opened your palms, even just a little bit, it flew away.

Looking for an excuse to leave the table, I finished my beer and got up, bringing the empty bottle back to the bar. I slid it to Shay, who was barely paying attention to me and was gawking at Hector. He had moved to a table at the bar, arms wrapped around a regular sitting on his lap and stroking his groin.

Hector was a different kind of butterfly; one that bit before he flew.

"Sorry, Shay," I said, sympathetically.

Her eyes flickered to mine and she narrowed them. "What the fuck for?"

"For Hector's behavior –"

"I don't care," she interrupted, shrugging. "Don't look at me like that. I'm fine with it. That's what it takes to be an old lady."

"You're okay with him fucking you last night and then fucking someone else tonight?"

"That's who he is and I'm not going to change him. In his heart I know he wants me. He just hasn't realized it yet."

I frowned but decided not to press it. Shay was going to spiral out of control one of these days and the sight wasn't going to be pretty.

I moved down the bar to where Jesse was knocking back a fat glass of whiskey. He didn't look at me as I approached, but I could tell he was still not his normal self.

"He'll keep using her," he said quiet enough for me to hear. "Hector's not looking to slow down, either."

"To be honest, she didn't seem concerned by that," I replied.

He eyed Shay. "She's lying. That girl is hooked on him like crack."

"I know," I agreed. "But there's nothing to be done by it. She'll have to get burned to learn. Even then…I don't think she'll ever get it."

He took a gulp from his glass and then wrapped an arm around my waist, bringing me to his side. He turned his face to me, and I could smell the whiskey on his breath as he whispered, "You should have picked us over him, Tyler."

I swallowed, knowing damn well that he was right.

"Everyone was watching, sweets."

"I didn't mean anything by it."

He tugged at the piercing in his lip, studying me. "You were wrong, you know. He didn't look at you like he didn't want you. He's actually still looking at you. Do you feel the burn from his stare? Because I do. I feel like a big fat fucking X is on my back for touching you right now."

I wanted to turn my head and see it for myself, but then it would be obvious to Hawke that we were talking about him.

"If Hawke wants you," Jesse continued, swallowing hard, "then I can't fight that. But once a girl is with a brother, that's it for the rest of us. We lay off for life. You gotta think of that before you decide to give yourself up to one of us assholes."

"I'm not here to be on the back of someone's bike."

He chuckled scathingly. "Until it happens."

He called for Shay to give us another drink. She slid two beers at us and I sat down next to Jesse, his arm secured around my stool, an obvious possessive display that had me rolling my eyes.

As I worked on my drink, I tried to make my glance around the bar look casual. It failed miserably when I saw Hawke and stopped.

He was staring right at me.

He didn't look threatened, didn't look angry, didn't look upset at all at Jesse touching me. He kept his eyes pinned to mine, like everything else around us didn't matter. Like he was so sure he could have me and nothing was going to stop him.

It was absolutely territorial.

Holly suddenly stood in my line of view, looking distressed as she held out the collar of her shirt and said, "Tyler, I need another shirt."

Jesse chuckled, staring at the puddle over her breasts. "Fuck, not again, Holly."

"It's ridiculous, isn't it?" she cried, exasperated.

"You should get Gus to stop you from going near Kirk."

I fumed. "Kirk is so fucking senile, nobody wants to go near him. They think he'll just drop dead if they upset him."

"He's outlived everybody. He's kind of a fucking ornament now."

"Well, the ornament is harassing Holly on the daily."

Jesse laughed harder. "Maybe Holly needs to fight her own battles."

Holly scowled at Jesse, and it surprised me when she retorted, "Funny when that's coming from *you*."

My eyebrows rose as I looked between them. She had on this cutting glare, and it was the first time I'd seen the angelic woman angry. Jesse's laughter faded and he turned his attention to his glass, taking another massive gulp this time. She'd silenced him.

O-kay then.

I slid off the stool and as Holly and I began walking, I stopped by Kirk's table and snapped, "You can't keep pulling this shit off, Kirk! You cut it out or else I'll ask Hector to ban your ass from sitting here."

Kirk just smiled into his nearly empty mug. "She likes it."

"I don't," Holly hissed.

"Oh, you fucking do and you know it," he belched out, smiling slyly as he licked the rim of his mug, staring at her like a fucking creep. Honestly, he was whacko and something needed to be done about this.

We went back to my room and I pulled out another shirt to throw at her. “I owe you for this,” she told me as she changed. I waved it off, telling her it wasn’t a big deal before she left again, determined to keep away from the old bastard.

Now that I was in my room, I didn’t know if I wanted to go back down. Hawke just seemed like a giant tease dangling in front of me. I genuinely didn’t trust that I wouldn’t throw myself at him again, and I cringed at the thought of having to endure rejection number two.

I unbuttoned my overalls and slid them down to my waist. Then I kicked off my boots and grabbed a towel, figuring it would be best to have a quick shower so I wasn’t smelling like grease and oil.

I didn’t see Hawke standing there in the doorway until I turned to close the door. I froze, looking at him with wide eyes. How long had he been standing there?

His demeanor seemed different. He looked at me so intently, so hungrily, the knots he’d caused from before only worsened at the pit of my belly. His eyes ran the length of me again, lingering over my tank top and crawling up my neck.

When he reached my eyes, his voice was thick when he said, “You’re temptin’ me, Tyler.”

Those were words I heard in my dreams, but they weren’t executed with the same passion. He looked tormented, like he was fighting himself just being here.

“I paced the hallway almost a hundred times last night after I touched you,” he continued, quietly, blowing me wide open with his admission. “You seem to have an effect on me that I’m not used to, and I felt it the second I walked in here. You’re vexing me and I don’t like it. Worse yet, I can’t even tell you to stop because you don’t even know you’re doin’ it.”

I couldn’t breathe. The air was stuck in my lungs as I listened to him talk. My heart was all kinds of fucked up, beating so hard one second and then clenching and unclenching the next. I was sure it wasn’t healthy.

"I wouldn't want to stop even if I was doing it," I pushed out, feeling triumphant after the last word fell from my mouth.

His lips flinched upwards. "Yeah, I figured that too. You're desperate for me. I can see it in your eyes."

I felt taken aback. Desperate?

Whoa, whoa, whoa.

Desperate screamed *pathetic*. Pathetic screamed *pity*, and I didn't want his pity.

I felt insulted.

I blinked hard, feeling a slither of annoyance at that word. "Desperate? You think…you think I'm desperate for you?"

"I do."

"No," I fired back. "The only thing I am toward you is scared, and I told you that already."

He shook his head slowly and stepped into the room, closing the gap between us. "No, see, you're scared of *yourself* because you still want me, even after I beat a cop and killed a man in front of you. Which also makes you confused and disgusted with yourself, and now you're wondering if there's something wrong with you. If there's *always* been something wrong with you. I've never seen a girl go through life like this desperately wantin' an ugly biker so much. Hell" – he scoffed – "I'm not even a biker anymore."

"I'm not desperate, Hawke," I icily said, trying to keep my feet rooted in place as he neared. "I've been living life just fine without you here. I party, I work, and hell, I've *fucked* too."

His hand suddenly shot out, gripping the back of my neck and pulling me to him. My chest hit his and I stared up at him, stunned speechless at his reaction.

I felt his breaths on my face and mouth. Felt his eyes dig deep beneath my own and into me as he retorted, "Baby, you've been with *one* boy and that was almost two years ago.

You stop everythin' when you know I'm coming around, and you just chose me over your president and I've barely been here two days. Even now, you keep starin' at me in that way again. The way you've been starin' at me for *years*. It ain't fear I'm looking into. It's want. You want me wrapped around your tight little body. You can't help yourself."

I gaped at him, not responding.

"Am I wrong?" he pressed. "Tell me if I am, and try to be convincing about it this time."

I studied his face, and then the tattoos crawling down his bulging arms. He was thick and strong. He called himself ugly, but he reminded me of a Viking, all hard and savage. Hell no, he wasn't ugly. If he was, the girls wouldn't be looking at him so much, and I wouldn't be…what, panting for him? Yeah, I totally was because my breaths were short and fast, my heart was squeezing and my mouth was dry as dirt.

I shut my eyes and muttered, "You're not wrong."

He stopped moving, and when I opened my eyes, I found him staring back at me seeming utterly perplexed by my response.

Had he expected me to lie?

"Say something," I pleaded, not understanding the silence.

His lips twisted and his brows came together in confusion as he muttered, "I'm weighing my options right now, Tyler."

"About what?"

"About whether I should fuck you or walk away."

Please, fuck me.

I felt doused with desire. My head was swimming, both from lust and the alcohol I'd knocked back. He was conflicted, caught in the middle as though there was something forcing him not to move.

I wondered what it was.

At the same time, I didn't care.

Feeling brave, I tipped my head higher up and leaned into him, my lips intent on touching his. Before I could, his grip moved to my hair and he pulled it back sharply. I winced, feeling my scalp ache as he kept me an inch apart from his mouth.

"I'm not your knight," he told me, his voice vibrating all the way down to my toes. "There are things I've done that you would never forgive me for. I'm a killer and I'm dead. I don't have a purpose, darlin'. I exist, nothing more. Don't make me want you. You won't like me if I want you, Tyler."

He was warning me in a *really* fucking tragic way, but I still didn't care. Not when my pussy was clenching with white hot need for him to touch me. How long had I wanted this?

Forever. A part of me whispered.

He stopped pulling back my hair and watched me carefully, waiting on my next move. I didn't even think. I'd wanted Hawke for too long to care about his stupid fucking warning.

I'd rather be burnt than stand by the fire, wondering how nice the heat would feel on my skin.

I looked back at his mouth and leaned straight in.

sixteen

Tyler

I brushed my lips against his. His eyes were open, watching me as I gently tasted them. God, they were soft, softer than I could have ever imagined.

I studied him for a quick moment, wondering if this was okay. He didn't look indifferent. In fact, he ran his tongue along his bottom lip just then, as if tasting me back.

Fuck, that did things to me. It made my knees weak and my breaths lighter than before. I moved in again without thought. The second kiss was longer. I pressed a little harder, flicking my tongue at the seam of his lips as I drew away. This time he leaned forward, keeping his lips on mine. His hand tightened in my hair again, but instead of pulling me away, he brought me closer, his mouth coming alive the second our lips collided.

I couldn't control the way my body felt. I couldn't hold back, and not a single thought entered my mind as all my energy focused on what he was doing to my mouth and the delicious pleasure it gave me.

In seconds, the gentle kiss turned more urgent, more… heated. None of it was mechanical. It was sloppy and needy and…god, it was amazing. His large hands were everywhere, running along the length of my body. Then suddenly he was picking me up, his hands digging into my outer thighs. My legs wrapped around him as he moved us to the nearest wall in direct view of the hallway. Our tongues clashed and I groaned into his mouth. The second his tongue met mine, my entire body shook and I wrapped my arms around his neck, groaning into him.

Wow, wow, wow.

It was just a kiss. It wasn't sex. Yet…it was so fucking hot, and already I was wound up, my core clenching with the need to be touched.

His mouth left mine, kissing and sucking feverishly at my neck. My legs were spread wide, and his front rubbed against my pussy. I felt how hard he was through his jeans and my eyes rolled to the back of my head, needing the friction, but more so, needing him inside me.

"Hawke," I moaned, my body burning now.

His mouth covered my breast through the fabric of my shirt and he sucked at my nipple, until it was taut and hard. God, even that felt good. Everything felt good. Like I was sensitive in every place.

"Fuck, you are so sexy, Tyler," he groaned. "It's doing my fucking head in."

I grabbed at his face and forced his mouth back to mine. His kiss was so consuming, so urgent and wanting, I barely pulled away. I was deprived of oxygen until my lungs ached, but I didn't stop kissing him. I didn't care. I needed this.

I needed *him*.

He rocked into me, and that ache turned into a full throb.

He cut off the kiss, groaning as he moved against me, tugging at the bottom of my lip with his teeth. This wasn't enough, though. I needed more.

"I want you to touch me, Hawke," I panted, unable to stop myself. "Please, touch me. I'm going to explode."

His eyes were drunk on lust as he looked at me. I wondered what he saw.

I wasn't fearless.

I wasn't smooth in my movements.

I felt like a needy woman stripped of her senses and wanting.

God, he'd been right; I was *desperate* for him.

"Yeah, you're gonna explode around me," he promised edgily, licking at the corner of my mouth. "God, look at those lips. Fuck, what I'd give to have them wrapped my cock, Tyler. Would you like that?"

I nodded, whimpering – and I'd never whimpered in my life.

His hand slid beneath my tank and he cupped my breast, knocking his forehead against mine. "Fuck, and your perfect tits. I'd come across them if you let me. Would you like that too?"

I nodded again, unbelievably turned on.

"What about your ass, Tyler?" he asked, that hand sliding to cup a chunk of it. "You got a big ass. Would you want me to fuck you gripping that ass?"

"Yes," I whispered.

His hand roamed back to my front and pulled my overalls down further, guiding his hand inside. I gasped as he ran his finger along my sex, slipping his hand beneath my underwear.

"Fuck, you're wet," he said incredulously, shaking his head against me. "You really want this."

It startled me how surprised he was by that. Like he couldn't believe he had this kind of effect on me.

He grazed across my opening and I moaned. Slowly he caressed me, up and down my slit, watching my reaction while he sucked at my lips.

The second his finger moved inside me, my hand tugged at his hair sharply.

He grinned against my mouth. "Shit, Tyler. You are so tight."

He pumped his finger into me slowly, and I could feel my walls clenching him, desperate for the way he filled me.

"Jesus," he whispered. "You feel good. How the fuck could you want this from me, baby? You are so fucking beautiful, so fucking sweet…"

He pushed another finger in and I gasped, barely able to kiss him now that there were sparks shooting through me.

God, it felt good. More than good. It was dirty, and I liked dirty.

He pushed his fingers as far in as he could go, rubbing against a spot that made me shake against him. He kept me pinned in place as I shook, unable to control myself. He watched me intently, like he needed to see me unfold around him.

"That good?" he asked, his voice so low I barely heard him.

"Yes, yes, yes," I chanted. "More, Hawke."

He chuckled deep in his chest. "Yeah."

He rubbed his thumb along my clit as he moved in and out of me. I bucked my hips, losing myself as the pleasure built bit by bit. He stole kisses from me, heated short bursts of his tongue caressing mine. At one point, I kept my mouth open and he swallowed my moans. He sensed how close I was to coming because he moved faster, working me perfectly.

God, yes.

It felt incredible.

I closed my eyes and moaned, nearing the edge. "I'm going to come, Hawke."

He groaned. "Yeah, you're tightening. I can feel you throbbing. Fuck."

More thrusts, more whimpering. Then words started to flee my mouth in a rush. "I want you."

"You want *this*. You want what I'm doin' to your perfect little pussy."

I shook my head, not thinking as the pleasure began to double in intensity. "I want you. Just…Just you."

Just as I said that, I came around him, my walls clenching his fingers tightly as I rode it out. I trembled as my head fell back. The feeling was so unusually good coming from his hand. The entire experience was brand new and I absolutely fucking loved it.

By the time I opened my eyes, Hawke's movements had stopped suddenly. I didn't understand the look on his face until I realized what I'd stupidly said as I came, and then I remembered his warning.

I'd pissed him off, and while he didn't necessarily look that way, the lust in his eyes had cleared. His fingers moved out of me and slowly he set me back down. My feet touched the ground, and I felt unsteady.

What the fuck just happened?

A second ago he was inside me and I'd come around his fingers, and now he had taken a step back, looking darkly at me.

I licked my lips and uttered, "Hawke –"

"Don't," he interrupted, running a frustrated hand through his hair.

"I didn't mean it like that."

"You did."

"No."

"Baby," he paused, looking at me sharply. "You did."

"You made me come and I said something in the heat of the moment. That shit doesn't mean I really want you."

"You're a terrible liar."

I swallowed, feeling suddenly sweaty with my hair plastered to the side of my face. I brushed it away and looked back at him. "So what if I did mean it?" I asked, my voice hard.

He chuckled, dryly. "You've naïve, Ty."

"I'm twenty years old, Hawke. I'm not fifteen anymore. It doesn't have to be serious. No commitments, nothing. I'm a big girl, I can handle being touched and not clinging."

As if to prove my point, I moved to close the gap between us but he shook his head. "Don't you fucking move right now," he ordered. "I'm really wound up right now, Tyler. You came and I fucking felt it and it was sexy as fuck with you moaning and dropping your head back like that. I don't think I've ever been this hard."

I hesitated, itching to come closer. "Hawke –"

"Stop."

I stopped moving and stared at him, waiting. He seemed troubled, looking at me differently now. I could tell a thousand thoughts were running through his mind, making him appear conflicted. He looked me over, taking in my flushed state, my chest rising and falling fast. I had "just came hard" all over my face and body, I was positive.

"Fuck!" he hissed, rubbing at the heavy scruff on his face, shooting me an accusatory expression. "Fuck, Ty."

Before I could even wrap my head around his anger, he dropped his hand and was about to say something else when ringing erupted from his pocket. He cursed and pulled it out with a frown. "I gotta take this, Tyler."

After I stiffened a nod, he swiped the screen and put the phone to his ear.

"What do you want, Linda?" he clipped, impatiently.

I could hear a female voice on the other end, but I couldn't hear a word she was saying. Hawke rubbed at his face, the tension lines forming around his eyes as he listened.

"Don't yell at me like a crazy bitch," he told her. "I swear to Christ, Linda, I'll hang you to fuckin' dry if you don't ask me nicely."

Pause.

"Nicer than that. You got it in you."

Another pause.

"That's fuckin' better. Keep an eye on him and don't lose sight of him. I'm on my way."

On his way? He was leaving just like that? I felt panicked. I needed more of him. I wanted him to stay.

He hung up and pocketed the phone, looking at me thoughtfully now.

"You wanna go on a ride with me?" he asked.

"A ride where?" I replied, surprised by his invitation.

“To the city. I got something to take care of there and…between you and me, we’re not done yet with whatever this is.”

I should have pretended to at least think about it because, let’s be honest, that whole desperate speech thing really hit a nerve.

But…

I couldn’t stop myself. He made me come and I was all loose and shit. It was inevitable that I would answer straight away. This was Hawke, after all.

“Okay,” I said quietly, hating myself just a little bit.

seventeen

Tyler

I thought a ride meant finally being on the back of Hawke's bike, but I was wrong.

It meant taking Kirk's old red truck.

Before we left Hawke removed the license plate on the back of it, and I should have been wary about that, but nothing about the guys in the club surprised me anymore. They were outlaws, and whatever Hawke was intending on doing was going to be illegal. That part was obvious.

I hopped inside the truck just as he got behind the wheel. The clunker turned on and he peeled out of the parking lot, stopping just before the road to lean over.

I tensed the second his hand brushed past my lap and grabbed at the seatbelt. God, a tiny touch and I was still sensitive all over.

He tugged on it with a knowing smirk and said, "Put this on, Ty."

"It doesn't click in," I replied, showing him. "You think I haven't driven his piece of shit before? We should take someone else's car. Like Jonny. He's got a sweet race car."

"We need to look unassuming."

"What are you planning on doing?"

He turned the corner and accelerated. The truck sounded like it was churning metal under my feet. Ugh, not a good sign.

"There's this guy that's just started showing up at the club every Friday," Hawke explained, frowning. "He's been spikin' drinks and takin' girls home and then dumpin' them in alleyways."

My heart jumped. "Killing them?"

"Nah, they're alive, but they're bruised and hurt and…obviously violated. Anyways, a couple girls kept comin' around the last couple weeks and tellin' Borden about it."

"He wouldn't care."

Hawke shot me a severe look. "Of course he fuckin' cares. Borden doesn't tolerate rape, Tyler. He may be a brutal motherfucker, but he's still got a conscience."

Well, shit, I didn't think Hawke would get so passionate about defending the bastard who took him away from the club and me.

"So why haven't you guys been on him sooner?" I asked, moving away from the topic of Borden.

"Nobody knows what he looks like. He doesn't chat the girls up. Doesn't go near 'em actually. He just slips shit in when he passes by and stalks them 'til they're blacking out someplace."

"Creep."

"Yeah, well, Linda was on top of it tonight."

"Linda?"

"The club manager. She said they spotted a man puttin' some powdery shit in a woman's drink. He's hanging back and waiting."

"Why don't they stop him?"

"I left so quickly, I didn't leave anyone in charge. I take care of security, and I'm gone two nights and this shit's exploded in my face. Plus, I wanna take care of the fucker myself."

"What are you going to do to him, Hawke?"

Hawke's grip on the steering wheel tightened and his teeth clenched. "I'm gonna teach him a lesson, Ty."

Hawke had a soft spot for taking care of women. I was sure it had something to do with his mother. He'd been so close to her. I still went to see her from time to time with Hector, and god, she was a stubborn and strong woman, closer in nature to Hawke than Hector. She'd always ask Hector what Hawke was up to, looking immensely agitated when she waited for him to respond. Hector would always assure her Hawke was alright, but she'd fidget anyway and mutter prayers under her breath.

From what I heard, she had a very trying life married to Red, the former president who'd died years before my old man had over a deal gone bad. Red had been a very cruel man, never once showing the club any kind of soft spot because, in my opinion, I never believed he had one. But from the little Hector had told me, his mother Adella had grown up on the streets, even alluding to the possibility she'd been whoring herself before Red came along and took her for himself.

Though I'd never gotten a straight story, it made sense why Hawke never disrespected women. Back when he was president, there was a lot of prostitution in town and the women were often found brutally beaten, and not just by their customers, but by their pimps too who had taken most of their earnings for themselves. There wasn't a corner in town that wasn't talking about it, and when it got back to Hawke he was livid.

I remembered my father's face when they got ready to ride out and "take care of it". I'd never seen him so dark in my life.

"These women need protection," he'd told Hawke. "They're not all druggies; they're mothers or homeless, barely scraping by. We can help them."

It was the first time the club had gotten themselves involved in a violent circle they weren't trying to profit from.

It was what made Hawke unlike all the other presidents before him and solidified the respect the club showed him…and the town too.

They eradicated the pimps and put the women in a motel they owned. They made the women keep a log of dangerous costumers and they sorted them out every time there was a complaint. There was a whole system put in place to ensure they didn't get hurt, and the system worked.

Until Hawke left.

It fell apart under Hector's control, and the pimps returned, hiding in shadows as they whored women out like strips of meat. The problem was more fixed in place now, and the women no longer turned to the club, because the club had failed them (and Hector didn't concern himself about it).

The thought made me a little bitter. I looked at him, brows knitted together and said, "You realize we have women in need of saving here too."

He caught my expression and sighed. "Tyler, did it ever occur to you that maybe I'm just not interested in going back to that life? The rules have changed, and the club's gone soft. The men are sloppy. Hector's recruited at least a dozen assholes who only carry the patch because they think it's fucking cool, but the second they have bullets flyin' past their heads they're gonna cower back."

"You can fix that."

"You just can't let this go, can you?"

"No."

He shot me a strange look. "Why do you believe in me, Tyler?"

I stared out the window, getting lost in the streets as they blazed on by. Why did I believe in him? I gripped the seatbelt and shrugged. "Because you're the best man I ever met, and…and among other things, you make me feel safe."

I could feel the heat of his eyes on me, but I couldn't meet them. No way. He would see that I cared for him deeply. Had always cared for him. I didn't want to be so utterly vulnerable. It was terrifying.

"I don't think you realize, Ty, what I would become if I went back to that," he finally said, his voice indiscernible. "You wouldn't like me as president this time around."

"Why?"

"I'd have to be unforgiving and do things – violent things so others wouldn't cross us."

"I understand."

"No…you don't."

I mulled that over, frowning. I'd seen the club do bad things.

How bad could Hawke be?

"This piece of shit needs fuel," he grumbled minutes later, already turning us into an empty gas station. "Be right back, babe."

He got out and strolled in there. I watched him carefully, checking out that hard back and nice ass. Even when he used his hand to open the door, I kept thinking how nice his fingers felt inside me and my face burned just thinking it.

I thought having a taste of him would have quenched my want at least a little bit, but instead it made it stronger and more urgent.

Seeking a distraction so I wouldn't babysit the entrance door, I opened the glovebox compartment as I waited and rummaged through papers and wrappers and…women's underwear? What the fuck?

"Ew, Kirk," I whispered in disgust, shutting the compartment immediately.

That old dude had underwear in his car.

Used underwear judging by the crumpled look of them.

Underwear!

With roses on one and…and hearts on another.

Ew. Ew. Ew.

This was the kind of disturbing shit I wouldn't miss about club life.

I wiped my fingers on my overalls, shuddering in my seat when I heard a sudden smash. My breath escaped my lips in a *whoosh* as I looked back at the convenience store.

The entrance door was obliterated. There was a man on the ground, hurt. Hawke stepped over him and walked casually back to the car with two cans of energy drinks in his hands.

"What the hell, Hawke?" I shouted after he slid into his seat. "What happened?"

"I had to take care of him," he replied, barely looking at me with that stoic face of his as he set our drinks in the cup holders. "Couldn't miss the opportunity."

"What are you talking about? Why did you have to take care of some guy?"

"Because that asshole's been bragging about bagging you, babe, and that shit's no longer acceptable."

My whole body stopped moving. I stared at him, horrified and confused, before I turned my sights back to the man on the ground slowly getting up. When I saw his face, I let out a groan and smacked my forehead against the window.

It was my douchebag ex-boyfriend from high school.

I didn't even know he was talking about me. How the hell did Hawke – someone who didn't even live in this town anymore – know something that personal?

Why are you even surprised, Tyler?

Hawke started the car again.

"Thought you had to fill up," I said blankly, already knowing the answer.

"Didn't need to, babe," he replied, putting us back on the road.

*

"What'd you see in that spider lookin' boy anyway?" he asked me ten minutes later.

He'd gotten some of that energy fueled drink in him and looked a lot more alert and less dark and broody. I was still trying to process what happened when he asked it. I looked away from the night sky and at him. "Maybe I thought he was interesting."

Hawke chuckled wryly. "Fuckin' hell, you gotta try harder than that to help me understand. You lost your virginity to that sack of shit, Ty." His lips pressed down hard and his nose flared. "That fuck didn't deserve it."

I dug my fingers into the dashboard paint and peeled away at it. "What do you expect me to say?"

"Did he force himself on you? Because you're too sweet for that kind of boy."

"That kind of boy?"

"Horny type that probably lasts a minute in the back of his car."

I rolled my eyes. "No, he didn't force himself on me. As if. I'd have ripped his balls off if he had. He was nice."

"Nice?" Hawke repeated, skeptically. "He used you to try and get into the club. Does that sound like *nice*?"

"No, Hawke, obviously not."

"Were you desperate for attention? I just don't get it."

"There's that word again," I snapped, angrily. "*Desperate*. You think I was desperate for that guy?"

"Yeah –"

"Fuck you, Hawke. I was not desperate. I was *curious*. I wanted to know if I could feel a certain way to a guy that wasn't…"

He glanced at me curiously. "That wasn't what?"

I hesitated and shook my head. "Doesn't matter."

"That wasn't me?" he prodded, keenly. "Is that what you were going to say?"

I didn't answer.

"It sounds like you were going to say it. It was me, right?"

"Don't get all egotistical."

He laughed lightly. "Fuck, I'm not egotistical, but the way you look at me, Tyler, it makes me feel like I'm Tom fuckin' Hardy."

I hid my smile and muttered, "You have no idea."

"So why him then?"

I didn't answer.

"Tyler," he pressed, "I'm just tryin' to understand, babe. I really want to know this. It's been sittin' in my head for two years now. I know you had this crush thing on me for a while, and then outta nowhere they're telling me you're with some high school jock. I always thought that was odd and unlike you. I just wanted to hear it from you instead of the guys."

I dropped my hands from the dashboard and sighed, resignedly. "It's not a fascinating story. I was curious about boys, okay? I was a teenager and…you don't know what it's like being a girl, Hawke. You get laughed at if you're fat, called anorexic if you're skinny, told you're ugly if you're wearing too much make-up, and ugly again if you aren't. You never win with that crowd. I was ostracized, and I wanted a connection outside of the club. When I hung out with Rohan, it felt nice, and I'd started to really explore myself around that time."

"Explore yourself," he repeated, inquisitively.

"I…touched myself… and the more I did it, the more I wanted to be kissed and touched by someone else. I wanted a boyfriend. I wanted to know what it felt like to have someone inside me, and…Rohan seemed sweet enough."

He nodded in surprise. "That was a simple answer."

"Because my needs were simple."

"Was he good? Did he make you moan the way I made you moan in that bedroom, Tyler?"

I swallowed and looked at him. He was already staring back, waiting.

"No," I whispered bitterly. "I threw it away, alright? I cheapened myself for him because I should have known he wasn't all that into *me*. It was just the club he was after."

It was the first time I had officially felt used. In hindsight, I should have been wary of his intentions. He ruined guys for me, and now I wasn't interested in guys outside of the clubhouse, or inside of it too.

It was a remarkable shit-fuckery.

"Fuckin' pencil dick," Hawke muttered under his breath, fuming.

"He *did* have a pencil dick."

"Yeah?"

"I didn't even feel it inside me."

He surprised me with a hard laugh. "Really?"

"Yeah, I kept asking him, 'Is it in?'"

His chest shook as he lost it. "I fuckin' knew it."

I couldn't help but laugh too. "Maybe I'm still a virgin."

He looked at me, amused. "Didn't even make you come?"

I shook my head. "Not once."

"Shit, that is rough, babe," he told me. "Not a way to treat a woman."

I smiled. "All bullshit aside, Hawke, the way you touched me was glorious. I never felt that way before."

He smiled back. "That's called experience, Ty. Believe me, my first time was a fucking disaster."

"You're a liar! Don't tickle my ears."

"No way, I'm not lying!"

"Fuck off."

"Fuck off nothing. Gus set me up with a stripper, and I was a horny fourteen-year-old, too fuckin' young to question that moral fuckery. I was too busy being all bright-eyed thinking I was on top of the fucking world."

"What happened?"

"You really wanna know?"

"Yeah." I nodded, surprised that I did.

He chuckled and rubbed at his beard. "She was really young and sexy, not as sexy as you, but fuckin' sexy, I'll give her that. She did this lap dance for me and stripped. Then she danced her way over to me, and suddenly my jeans were off and wrapped around my ankles and I was touchin' her everywhere. I'm talkin' there wasn't a place she didn't want me to touch."

"And then?"

"And then she sat in my lap and the show was over in under a minute."

"Under a minute?"

"At the time, it was the best minute of my life. As I got older, I realized a minute wasn't all that impressive."

I wrapped my arms around my stomach as I laughed. That wasn't what I expected. No, in my head, he was a pro right from the get-go.

He smiled wistfully. "Anyway, I guess my point, babe, is that it doesn't matter all that much about your first time. There's no point regretting what you can't change."

I rested my head against the seat, watching him. "I like you, Hawke," I said, unable to keep it to myself. "I like you a lot."

"Yeah," he responded carefully, "I'm starting to realize that, Tyler."

eighteen

Tyler

The club was bigger than any in our town, and the room was dim and flashing with lights and dancing bodies. There were people *everywhere*.

Hawke took my hand and we waded through the room. He took me to the bar area and searched it, stopping his sights on a tall redhead in a tight red dress. When we started to move to her, I shot him a confused look.

Surely this model wasn't Linda.

Club managers were not *this* hot, right?

She caught Hawke's gaze and her red lips pursed. It wasn't a fond look she was giving him; it was rage.

"Where the fuck were you?" She demanded before she jabbed her long red fingernail against his chest. "Forty-five fucking minutes, Hawke? What the fuck?"

Hawke just looked at her. "Tell me where the guy is, Linda."

"Well I don't fucking know anymore, Hawke. We are short-staffed for this shit, and there are double the bodies permitted in this place. I no longer know where the fuck this douchebag is because we didn't think we would have to babysit the fuck for forty-five fucking minutes! And who the FUCK is the hillbilly standing behind you looking at me like I'm the FUCKING Mona Lisa?!"

Hawke motioned to me. "This is Tyler."

She shot me a look of disgust. "A man?"

"Obviously she's a woman."

"With a man's fucking name! And why is she wearing fucking overalls?"

"These are my work clothes," I snapped.

"There are dressing standards in this club, so the next time you show your face here, try putting on something that doesn't make you look like a yodeling bumpkin."

"What the hell is your problem?"

Her face reddened as she snarled, "My fucking problem, little girl, is I have a fucking rapist on the loose in my fucking club and if Borden finds out I couldn't have my useless fucking asshole workers keep an eye on him while King fucking Hawke got here, I might lose my fucking head!"

"Linda," Hawke cut in, "you need to keep your voice down –"

"Easy for you to say! I've been pacing for almost an hour now, Hawke."

Hawke took a step closer to her and set his hand on her bony shoulder. "Hey," he said gently. It was like watching an ant try and tame a lion. "Calm down, alright? I'm sure he's still kickin' around waiting to make his move. You need to breathe because acting like a crazy woman isn't going to help matters."

She blinked rapidly, looking back at him with a hardly put together face. "The stress is getting to me, Hawke. I can't handle this shit anymore. If I have another woman coming through the doors telling me she got touched by a man under my goddamn nose, I'm going to lose it. It's my fault as it is –"

"It ain't your fault," Hawke cut in sharply. "You cut that bullshit out. You ain't weak. Quit actin' weak, Linda. Have the men keep searching for the cunt. I'm not going anywhere until he's taken care of, alright?"

She nodded, taking a deep breath just to calm herself down before she hardened her face again. "Okay, alright. I'm going to pass the word you're here. Maybe one of these chimps found him."

He nodded and she took off, meanwhile I just stood there, staring at him with a gaping mouth. He didn't pay me attention as he sat down on the stool and grabbed me by the arm. He hauled me to him so that my body was pressed against his side.

He kissed my forehead and said, "Stay close. I like you next to me." I wasn't sure he realized the effect his casual words had on me.

I leaned into him. "That woman is crazy."

"Linda is a piece of work," Hawke confirmed on a nod, his lips spreading into a soft smile. "But she's good at what she does."

"She called me a hillbilly and a man."

"She was actually being soft on you."

"She acted like I committed murder for dressing the way I am."

"Because this shit is personal to her. The club may belong to Borden, but it's her baby too. She lives and breathes it."

Wow, he was defending the red-haired bitch a lot.

I studied him suspiciously for a moment. "You sleep with her?"

He looked back at me in surprise. "What?"

"Don't make me repeat my question."

"I'm giving you the opportunity to withdraw it."

"But I want to know."

He smirked. "Are you jealous, Tyler?"

"No," I lied, suppressing my irritation. "Just answer."

"I don't fuck where I work, babe, and I have standards."

I turned away from him and faced the bar, closing my eyes briefly. God, what was wrong with me? One beautiful woman talking to him familiarly and I automatically assume he bedded her?

Idiot. Idiot. Idiot.

His hand grabbed at my chin, turning my face to him. He looked amused as he leaned into my side and whispered, "Whose tongue was I sucking just recently?"

"Yours," I whispered back.

"And who made you come so hard you had your head banging against the wall?"

My face heated as my gaze dropped to his mouth. "You did, but…you pushed me away after."

"You think I wanted to?"

"Yeah. Maybe."

He narrowed his eyes at me. "Baby, you are the hottest thing I have ever touched in my entire existence on this green fucking ball of waste. You are so hot, so fucking sweet, I'm already fantasizing about bending you over this bar and fucking you in front of everyone. Now that would be a really good reason to go back to the club life, huh? Make you mine in front of everyone and have you marked with my cum and watch you enjoy it."

His words…

Holy fuck.

He couldn't say things like that without…

I grabbed his shirt and smashed my lips against his mouth. He kissed me back, crashing his tongue against mine until every single inch of me burned and tingled. How could a kiss turn me on so much? I pressed against him, wanting his warmth against that hungry spot between my legs.

He pulled away, looking serious now as he said, "And I have never seen a girl want me so bad. It's kinda fuckin' me up, Tyler."

I took his lower lip between my teeth and tugged. He growled in my mouth and nipped me back.

"You could have taken me by now," I said, anguished. "I'm aching, Hawke."

He ran his hand over my hair, contemplating. "Maybe," he muttered, more to himself than me. "Maybe there is something."

Maybe?

"It's not maybe when I'm this wet for you," I told him.

Fuck, I was brazen. But he brought that bit out in me because the only way things would ever progress with Hawke was by being completely honest.

"Christ," he murmured to himself, looking at me. His thumb lightly traced my lips. Again, I could see him holding back, fighting to reserve himself, but he couldn't. I'd wound him up too much.

Linda returned suddenly, looking flushed as she took his large arm in her hand. "We found him," she said. "Come on."

nineteen

Tyler

Hawke told me to wait at the bar while he disappeared to handle the situation. I sat on the stool, watching as plush looking girls and dudes with polo shirts or expensive silk button-up shirts ordered fancy, colorful drinks. The clubhouse drank beer and hard liquor, not this rainbow colored shit.

Still, this place looked amazing and sleek. I understood why it was the most popular club in the city. I looked around and then up at the second level where it was closed off by a red rope barrier. There were a few bodyguards standing out front of it, conversing. Obviously that was the VIP area.

I was about to look away when I met the eyes of a man standing there, feet from the guards, arms on the balcony overlooking the club. I stopped moving, entranced for a moment at the clean shaven face of the solid man I had seen on the front of countless newspapers.

Marcus Borden.

He had a hard face. Ridiculously gorgeous, but also frightening at the same time. He was staring fixedly at me – staring like he knew who I was – and never looking away. Christ, I imagined Hawke standing by him and knew they'd make a scary duo. No wonder everyone feared them. They just had that look – that scathing you-can't-hide-from-me kind of look.

I eventually glanced away from him and turned my body so that it was facing the bar again. I didn't want to see him watching me. That man had buried enough bodies they'd probably be discovering mass graves for hundreds of years to come, and I didn't want one of the discoveries to be of a twenty-year-old moron that died trying to have a staring contest with a kingpin. Melodramatic maybe, but you had to think this kind of shit through.

Minutes passed by when Linda reappeared at my side and said, "Hillbilly, I've come to fetch you." She didn't look as stressed as before, but the bitch-face was still strong in her.

I glowered at her. "It's *Tyler*."

"I don't care, just get your ass up and follow me."

"I'm supposed to wait on Hawke."

"Well, who the fuck do you think I'm taking you to?"

"Why can't he just get me?"

"Because he's cleaning himself up."

I stared at her for a moment, trying to understand what she meant by that. But her bitch-face was intact as ever.

"You gonna move, or do I have to fucking drag you out?"

I reluctantly slid off the stool and stood up straighter. I shot Linda a scathing look before retorting, "Stop being a cunt to me, alright? Your attitude is fucking ridiculous. I'm surprised nobody's beaten it out of you yet."

"You forget who I work for."

"Yeah, well, I'm part of the Warlords and I don't take kindly to insults. So unless you want a face full of acid, try to be kinder to me."

She paused, her eyes betraying her bitch-face as she looked at me with surprise. Then she slowly smiled at me. "Oh, I get it now," she said, reflecting. "You're that girl he used to talk about. Now it makes sense."

He talked about me?

I was curious. If she wasn't such a wench, I'd have asked her what he said, but I had a feeling that unless you were threatening to remove her vocal cords, she wouldn't tell you anyway.

She turned and started walking, and I reluctantly followed.

"Your club crashed here once for business," I heard her say without looking back at me. "They fucked up the place bad."

"The latest members in the club aren't the most respectful," I lamely explained.

"They fought each other for the sake of it."

"They do that sometimes."

"One of them was dragging around a drugged up weeping bitch."

"You're referring to Ellen, and she cries a lot when she's high."

"And don't get me started about your president. That guy thought he could spread me wide open."

I suppressed a smile. "Hector does a good job of it from what I hear. Maybe you missed out."

Linda shot me a strange look. "You really are part of them, aren't you, knowing all this."

I nodded. "I know everything."

"Club brat."

"Yeah."

So low I could hardly hear her, she replied, "Yeah, I know what that's like."

As we waded through the room, it occurred to me *he* might still be watching me. Feeling tense, my eyes shot back up to the balcony just then, and I sighed in relief.

Borden was long gone.

*

Linda took me back outside and to the red truck parked in the handicapped spot because Hawke was a douche like that. She stopped to give it a disgusted look. "Why is he driving this trash can?"

"Apparently to look unassuming," I replied.

She scoffed. "What, is he hiding from someone?"

The law. "Yep."

She pursed her lips and, despite looking wary, said, "Right, I forgot about that."

I leaned my back against the front of the truck and crossed my arms. "To be honest, it was probably an excuse so I wouldn't be riding on the back of his bike."

Linda looked at me funny. "It's just a fucking bike. I don't get why you bitches have so much symbolism behind that shit. It's fucking pathetic."

"Because it's a form of rejection."

"It's mental and naïve."

"It means a lot to us."

"What are you, twelve?"

"No, I'm not twelve!"

She waved at the club. "He took you here, didn't he? Which is a fucking first. Hawke doesn't bring girls *in*, he usually takes them *out*."

I narrowed my eyes at her. "Wow, thanks, that makes me feel *great*."

"Well, it should, you oblivious idiot," she retorted, impatiently. "Can't stand when morons like you spill your life story to me like I give a fuck. I don't, so keep your woes about not being on the back of his stupid fucking bike to yourself."

Oh, my God, she was right. I was being dramatic.

You're turning into Shay.

"I swear to God," she went on, "Borden ended up with a fucking tarantula of a bitch, and if you're like her in the slightest and I have to deal with two melodramatic bitches, I'm going to cut someone's throat."

"I like Borden's girl," I muttered under my breath, reflecting for a second on the time I met her almost two years ago. She'd been an emotional mess, but still managed to notice me in the strife of it all. I'd been an emo teen at that stage of my life. "She was epic."

Linda clenched her teeth. "I fucking hate you already."

I heard footsteps just then and turned to find Hawke approaching us. He didn't blink an eye at Linda, but he did say, "I took care of it."

Her demeanor changed remarkably. Her face softened and she nodded at him. "Thanks, Hawke," she said sweetly.

I blinked at her in surprise. Was this chick bipolar or something? She glanced at me briefly with this strange look of pity. "Take care, Tyler," she told me. Then she turned away and walked back to the club, leaving me utterly perplexed.

"Is everything okay?" I asked Hawke after she disappeared.

He was already opening his driver's side door when he morosely replied, "Fuck, Ty, just get in the car."

I did, all the while watching him and wondering why his face was all screwed up looking.

He drove in silence, but his hand on the steering wheel was tight. He drove a little too fast on the road, cutting people off and then cursing under his breath like they were in the wrong. I clutched the seat on each side, feeling annoyed at his sharp turns and said, "Remember my seat belt doesn't work, Hawke, so take it easy."

He didn't.

"Hawke," I hissed, my shoulder hitting the window. "Slow down!"

He abruptly veered the car off the road and slammed on the breaks, causing me to jerk in my seat. Holy fuck, what was his problem?

Looking dark, he punched at the steering wheel, and the horn sounded out. Then he got out of the car, slamming the door so hard the whole car shook. Bewildered, I watched him walk over the short strip of dirt that bordered a cluster of closed businesses. His fists were closed at his side as he paced, his chest heaving up and down, his hair covering part of his face. Tall and built, he looked absolutely intimidating in the dark of night.

Was this why Linda gave me that pitying look? Because she knew Hawke was in a mood?

I sighed and opened the door. I climbed out and walked over to him, stopping feet from where he now stood, blankly staring ahead.

"You got some serious road rage," I whispered to him, my voice light. "If you're shitty because of that young dude cutting you off, to be fair it was kind of karma."

His eyes moved to mine, and his lips didn't flinch because I wasn't funny. "I'm not feeling too good right now, Ty."

"I can tell."

He exhaled long and slow. "I've got that adrenaline firin' through me. I've still got blood on my hands."

I studied him for a minute, concerned at the way he was shaking. He couldn't keep still.

It reminded me how I felt when he took Yuri's life. All that adrenaline coursing through my body, and I had only *witnessed* it. I couldn't imagine what it would have been like on his end having to do something like that to keep me from getting hurt.

"Is this about the man at the club?" I asked.

His eyes fell and his nostrils flared as he gritted out, "He deserved it."

I nodded, understanding. This was about what Hawke did which, up until this point, I had no idea affected him so much.

He was about to lose it again. The dark look on his face intensified. I quickly moved closer to him and took his hand into my own. I brought it to my mouth and gently laid a kiss on his calloused skin. He went stiff, surprised by my move, and looked at me.

We said nothing for a while, but I could tell I hadn't done much uncoiling the tension in him. Eventually, he let my hand go and returned to the car. I followed and we both slid in, not a word spoken between us.

He didn't start the car, just tapped his finger on the steering wheel.

"It's a vicious cycle," he murmured. "I have to hurt a bad man, and then I feel riled up, and all I wanna do to forget is hurt again and…again. My head is heavy with images of the shit I've done. I've got bad blood runnin' through me. I've taken from people – good people even – and I've played god too long. Sometimes I think I should've stayed in that prison, rotting away."

Just as he'd said that, he looked out the window and his body started to quake again. I quickly left my seat and moved over to him, settling myself over his lap before he could think of leaving again. He went stiff, surprised by my move, before he looked at me. Knees on either side of him, I relaxed my body so that we were face to face. This position made me feel small next to him, but small in a way that I liked.

His eyes dropped to my mouth. "What're you doing, Tyler?"

"Distracting you," I said.

His face cleared a little, his anger was replaced with need. He pulled me to him, my chest hitting his. He stroked my face lightly and brushed the strands of hair behind my ears, curiously looking at me. "What did I tell you about distractions?" he asked, his voice low.

"That you regret them after." I paused just then, staring at him intently. "Will you regret it if I made you feel better right now?"

His finger brushed along my bottom lip and he licked his own just then, like he was imagining the taste of me. I could see the darkness still lurking in the depths of his eyes, and I knew he needed this.

"Honestly," he muttered, "something sweet about you tells me I wouldn't regret a single moment tasting you."

I smiled when he gripped a fistful of my hair and crashed his mouth to mine. He kissed me hard. His other hand dropped down to my overalls, and like before he unbuttoned them and slipped them down to my waist. Then he slid his hand under my shirt and found my breasts. He cupped one in his large palm and squeezed before moving to the next. I arched my back, telling him with my body that I loved what he was doing. It wasn't like before, because this time I could feel him hardening beneath me, and he wasn't slowing down. He wasn't waiting for me to make the next move. He was *taking* me.

His entire body shook, and he groaned as he tore his mouth from mine and buried his face in my breasts. He dragged his hands down my spine, the pressure deep as he wrapped his lips around my nipple and ravenously sucked. I moaned and grabbed a fistful of his hair, grinding myself against his hard dick.

I wanted it out.

Wanted it in my hand.

I reached for his jeans when I heard the sound of a siren suddenly chirping close by. I stopped and looked up, my eyes barely registering the sight before me.

Flashing lights.

Red, then blue.

I froze in his grip as he pulled away, glaring up at the rearview mirror.

"There's a cop car behind us," I dumbly said, stating the obvious.

"Yeah, I can see that," he replied.

"Should we make a run for it?"

"In our race car?"

I frowned. "I told you to take Jonny's car."

"Mm, indeed you did."

Just then a cop approached the car, flashing his annoying fucking flashlight inside. I squinted my eyes and looked away. I made to move, but Hawke's hand tightened around my hip, keeping me in place. The cop used his flashlight to knock on the window, and Hawke unwound it slowly, staring the cop down.

"License and registration," the cop ordered just then.

"What for?" Hawke retorted.

The cop looked between Hawke and me. "You're not allowed to park here."

Hawke smirked, unconcerned. "There ain't a sign up sayin' that."

"There's one in front of you." The cop pointed to a no parking sign in plain view.

Hawke chuckled. "Fuckin' hell."

The cop slid his gaze to me. "You alright there?"

I avoided looking back at him because my tits were sort of visible. Hawke's hand was currently cupping one. In fact, he was still hard and the slightest movement made my core pulse.

"I'm fine," I told him.

"Can you get off so this man can fetch his license and registration?"

"I don't have either," Hawke returned, casually.

"Then I'm going to have to ask you to step out of the vehicle –"

"I'm not stepping out, and if you knew what was best for you, you'd turn the fuck around and go to back to your car and play cops and robbers to somebody else."

Cop looked mad. "Sir," he heatedly said, "I'm going to have to ask you once again to step out of the vehicle –"

"Name is Hawke," he cut in sharply, narrowing his eyes at him. "And as far as I'm concerned, we're paying you to turn the other cheek and walk back to your fuckin' car. Word gets back to Borden that I've been cuffed and you're going to disappear come morning."

The cop's face fell as recognition flashed in his eyes. "Shit," he muttered, stepping back. "Shit, I didn't recognize you, Hawke. You can leave. I'll tell the other boys you're riding a red truck. I apologize."

He kept apologizing seven or eight more times before Hawke cut him off by turning the car on. The cop moved away and by then Hawke's grip around my hip went loose. I moved back to my seat, with his hand copping a feel on my ass. I laughed and flicked it off as he put us back on the road with a giant smile on his face.

"You got everyone here in Borden's pocket?" I asked after a minute.

"They're in my pocket too," Hawke replied. "I'm technically still the president, after all."

*

Everything was set in stone. Hawke was going to fuck me when we got back, I was sure of it. The tension between us was thick. Every time we looked at each other, I saw the heat in his eyes. He was going to do it.

I felt jittery, wondering how it was going to play out. Would he throw me on the bed and strip me naked? Would he go down on me and –

My knees instinctively shut. Fuck, I needed a shower. Would he give me the time? Or would that disrupt things if I bathed? I was flushed everywhere, excitement bubbling within.

I leaned my head against the window, trying to calm myself down. The last thing I expected was to be lulled by the bumps in the road, or for the ride to feel longer than it was.

My eyes closed, and I fought – with everything inside of me – to keep them open, but it was a losing battle.

Hawke wasn't going to fuck me.

Because I fell asleep.

My stupid fucking body let me down.

twenty

Tyler

He carried me inside, and I was wrapped in the woodsy scent of him. I heard him say something to Gus and then he was carrying me up the stairs and to the bedroom. He set me down in bed, and by then I'd opened my eyes just barely, my hand reaching out to his.

"Don't go," I murmured, tiredly. "I don't want to think of him."

"Think of who, baby?" he asked me.

"Yuri."

He paused, and then pulled away. I heard his movements and moments later I felt the bed dip. He undressed me, pulling off my overalls and socks and discarding them somewhere close. Then he brought me into his bare chest and wrapped an arm around my waist, spooning me.

I wasn't completely asleep, but I was halfway there. I felt his kisses on my shoulder; the way he grazed my skin with his teeth sent goosebumps down my arms. I was so relaxed, sinking into him as he continued his wet kisses.

Right before I fell into blackness, he whispered, "Whose bed are you in?"

I licked my lips and breathed out, "Yours."

"Yeah," he groaned, his hand cupping my breast. "Fuck, I like you, Ty. That's a real problem for me."

I was literally too tired to respond.

I was long gone by the time I even thought to ask why.

*

I had a fitful sleep. More blood, more images of Yuri, more unsettling feelings ran through me. I was weak and unable still to find a permanent way to erase that goddamn event from my mind. As a result, I thrashed in my sleep, whimpering as his lifeless face tormented me.

"Hey," I heard Hawke say, "I'm here, Ty. Relax."

Hearing his voice quieted the fears inside me. My body relaxed immediately. He tucked me back into him as he rained more kisses on me.

There were no more nightmares after that.

It was barely morning when I cracked my eyes open and stared at the figure standing beside the bed. I didn't know how long he'd been standing there, but the second I opened my eyes, Hawke said, "I gotta go, darlin'. Have to take care of Abram."

I blinked back my sadness as I gazed at his reserved face, barely visible in the darkness. "You won't be coming around anytime soon?"

"Not for a while."

I reluctantly nodded.

He made to get closer and stopped before he did. He stared at me hard for a long moment, a fleeting conflicted look on his face before he masked it and turned.

"Hawke," I let out in a rush before I could stop myself.

He turned around and looked back at me.

My throat was too clogged up to speak, but I wanted to ask him about last night, about what we did. Understanding donned in his eyes and he moved to me and sat down on the bed. He brushed my face tenderly with his hand, stroking my cheek before running his thumb over my mouth.

"When did you get so beautiful?" he whispered under his breath, the same question he'd asked aloud before.

I kissed his thumb, my breath thinning as I watched his reaction. He closed his eyes for a few seconds, his chest rising and falling faster. When I kissed his thumb again, I slipped my tongue out and lightly brushed it against his skin.

He opened his eyes and they looked feral as he growled, "Don't tempt me, Ty. You don't want to see that side of me. I am not soft, you understand? I take, and I take *hard*."

Chills ran down my spine, and I felt a deep tightening in my core. I kept waiting for him to back away, but he didn't remove his hand. He kept it there, watching me with sick fascination for what I might do next.

I considered his warning, but frankly, I didn't give a fuck about it. I opened my mouth and wrapped it around his thumb, sucking it gently. His breathing stopped, and he ripped his hand from my hold and before I knew what was happening, his mouth descended over mine. He kissed me roughly, tasting my tongue and lips in a mad, abrupt rush. His arms came around me, squeezing me to his chest as he deepened the kiss, consuming me. I felt his erection against my thigh, felt the need in his mouth.

I moaned and the sound spurred him on. His hands shoved my legs apart and he rubbed my pussy through my panties, causing me to jolt beneath him. I didn't know until later that I was begging him to fuck me, to put me out of my misery, or that I was particularly vocal about it.

I could feel how pent up he was. His self-control was weaning, his hand gripped my hair and he pulled at it sharply, angling my head so that my mouth remained on his as he settled himself between my legs. Every inch of me was on fire. My hand grabbed at the collar of his shirt, keeping him near me in case he pulled away.

I was beyond turned on.

Wanting to come came second to breathing.

It was vital.

Completely necessary.

Animalistic, really.

Hawke felt the same way. He was wound up tight, needing inside me with a fury.

He pulled away just enough to slide my underwear off. I was completely spread open to him, and if it'd been lighter in the room, he'd see how wet and glistening I was for him.

My hands immediately flew to the buttons of his jeans, and they were shaky and unsmooth. I didn't know what the hell I was doing. This was Hawke, not some high school moron I didn't care about impressing. My heart was in my throat the entire time I unbuttoned him, and the second it was undone, he tore them off.

This was seriously happening.

Or I was dead and in hell.

Because heaven couldn't be this cool.

He kissed me again, languidly this time as I felt something hard prod my sensitive flesh. I moaned against his mouth, my hands clenched tight around his shoulders as he ran the tip of his cock along my slit, lightly brushing against the bundle of nerves that had me seizing in bed.

"You're gushing," he said, his voice in awe. "Fuck, Ty, I love that you want me this bad."

I shut my eyes, anxiously waiting for him to slip inside me, but he rubbed his cock along me for a while, watching my reaction closely.

"Take your top off," he demanded.

I slid it over my head and threw it aimlessly on the floor.

"Cup your tits."

I did, and he leaned down and sucked at one nipple before moving to the other. All the while, he continued his torment, until my throat was dry from breathing so hard. It was alright, though, because along the way I discarded his shirt too and ran my hands down his ridiculously impressive torso.

"You're so hot," I told him, unable to keep my mouth shut. "I fucking want you, Hawke."

This time the words didn't make him angry. Impossibly, his dick hardened against me. He dropped back down and kissed me again, possessing my mouth with the harsh and rhythmic strokes of his tongue. Then he gripped my thighs, digging his nails as he spread me wider.

"Hold me tight, Tyler," he told me tightly.

I gripped him as hard as possible and closed my eyes.

"No, look at me, baby."

I opened them and peered into his eyes. I wished the lights were on so I could see the need in them.

He rocked into me, the head of his length pushing into me slowly. I felt myself stretching around him, and it took a couple minutes just to get him wet enough to slide in. The anticipation was brutal. Neither of us were breathing right.

I felt like a virgin all over again, and I may as well have been because, *fuuuck*, he was thick. How bloody big was he? I tried to raise my head to get a better look because he was still moving in. The sensation was almost unbearable and so ridiculously foreign.

I knew he was deliberately being slow, savoring the sensation with drunken eyes. Inch after inch, he filled me, and I was so sensitive for waiting, the feeling was absolutely explosive. Grabbing at my breast with his other hand, he continued to guide himself back and forth, filling me one minute, emptying me the next.

My eyes rolled to the back of my head as he continued. My walls clenched him tightly, sparks shot through me.

As my body molded to his cock, he started to move faster, driving his cock deeper and harder inside of me. They were controlled movements at first, like he was testing the waters, watching how I would react. I thrashed beneath him, moaning louder, the pleasure growing.

He wasn't wrong about warning me.

He took hard.

His hand caught in my hair, forcing my face in place as he thrust inside me. His other hand wrapped around my ass, gripping it. He grunted, cursing under his breath, telling me how good I felt.

The headboard slammed against the wall.

Repeatedly.

I was sure the plaster was coming off.

My hands slid down his back, past his tattoo I wish I could see, and I gripped his ass as he drove inside me, rubbing against my clit along the way.

I exploded so suddenly, my body not expecting the unrestrained pleasure soaring through me. I cried out, and he swallowed my cries with his mouth, groaning back as he continued to move roughly inside me.

"I felt that, Ty," he gritted out as he moved.

He didn't fucking stop.

And it was so good, I couldn't bear it.

He kept pounding into me, spreading my legs impossibly wide and pulling his chest away from mine so he could watch himself disappear inside me.

"Oh, my god, Hawke, don't stop!" I begged. "Please, like that. More, Hawke."

His dick was slick with my come. I watched his lips press down hard as his pleasure began to climb. His thumb moved between us, rubbing at my clit, forcing more sparks to build.

It was almost too much.

I cried out again as he forced another orgasm through me.

"Fuck, Tyler," he growled, thrusting in one last time.

I felt him pulse within me and his body shook through his release as he filled me with his come. He collapsed over me, his chest rising and falling fast. He stayed inside me a while, his forehead against mine, as he muttered in agony, "Fuckin' hell, Tyler."

My heart was beating fast and hard. My mouth was still open, sucking in air. Every inch of me ached to be touched by him again.

He eventually pulled away, moving out of me one last time. He looked stunned as he gathered his jeans and shirt and slipped them back on. Then he ran a frustrated hand through his hair. I hadn't moved once, but I continued to watch him as he fought to contain himself.

"You and those fucking eyes," he growled, standing up. "Tired of that look, Ty. It fucking strips me."

I continued not saying a word. He wouldn't be listening to whatever I had to say anyway. He was too wrapped up in the clusterfuck of what had just happened between us.

He stopped pacing, and his eyes went back to me and over my body. My legs were still spread open, and his jaw locked. "Fuck," he groaned. "Goddammit, Tyler. I have to go and I'm going to look like a fucking cockhead fucking you and leaving you!"

A few more minutes of indecisiveness passed by.

The guilt was eating at him. He looked at the door and then at me, uncertain of what his moves should be.

I just stared.

"Do you hate me?" he suddenly asked, his voice raw.

I shook my head.

"Do you…regret what we just did?"

Christ, he seemed so broken, like he was terrified of my response.

I shook my head again.

His shoulders relaxed and he swallowed thickly. "I don't regret it either, Tyler, it's just…fuck, it's bad timing."

I continued waiting, knowing he had to leave and take care of the shit-storm with Abram. He just seemed too reluctant to move, like he knew he had to but his body was unwilling.

"I'll see you when I see you," he finally said, determined not to look at me, as if one stare might cause him to come back to me. On a deep breath, he forced himself to move and then he hurried out of the room without a glance back.

My heart was still hammering long after he was gone.

I should have been upset he'd just walked out. I had the ability to work him up; he was clearly unhappy about it. I seemed to strip him of his control, and it was such a sight to behold! Seeing Hawke undone like that.

Only…I wasn't upset, nor did I feel used. Instead, this stupid weird smile flitted across my face as the taste of his tongue overwhelmed me. I felt tender between my legs and deliciously sore, and god I wanted to slip my fingers inside myself and come again to his grunts in my ear and his dick pounding into me.

What he did crashed into me over and over again, making me hot to the touch.

It happened.

He fucked me!

It was better than I had imagined, than I had hoped it would be! Even on those nights I went beyond my expectations, thinking of how wild he could make he feel.

He was better because his face in the end said everything I needed to know.

He tasted me and he had wanted more. And instead of taking it, he was running away, determined to beat what he felt for me. Silly man didn't realize it wouldn't work, so I smiled brightly in the darkness of my room.

Hawke would come back. I was sure of it.

twenty-one

Hawke

He ran.

There was no sugar coating it.

Yeah, he fucking ran.

For reasons that didn't concern Tyler, by the way. Just…he ran because he had obligations. He needed to go back to the city. Back to Borden. Staying at the clubhouse blurred the lines.

Not with *Tyler*.

With the *club*.

Yeah, that was it. Hector felt threatened whenever he was around, and he wasn't wrong to feel that way. The guys really looked up to Hawke. They longed for his leadership and it made the tension he already had with his brother ten times worse.

So that's why he ran.

Yep.

Plus… there was *kind of* an issue with the whole touching Tyler's pussy thing. Not massive, or anything, just enough to give Hawke instant blue balls and a headache and…constant visions of her on the end of his dick.

Fuck.

Yeah, okay, so it had a *little* more to do with Tyler and how fucking sexy she was naked, and how needy she was the other night when she placed his hand between her legs and silently begged him to fuck her.

And there was last night.

Feeling her tits.

Sucking on her tongue as she moaned.

The walls of her pussy clenching around his fingers as she came hard around them. Fuck, she'd been wet because of him. *Him!* He felt like a fucking god.

And then there was this morning.

That was unexpected. He'd been prepared to leave, not stare at her like a fucking creep for a long period of time. He just…couldn't seem to get his legs moving, and when she opened her eyes and looked at him? No way could he go. He was a goner. He *had* to touch her a little bit at the *least*. The last thing he expected was her to suck on his fucking thumb, for fuck sake. Even more than that, he hadn't anticipated the blood to rush to his cock that fast.

He had felt…primitive.

Possessive.

Absolutely fucking animalistic.

She was so goddamn carnal.

Couldn't forget the walls of her pussy gripping him so tight, he almost blew inside her straight away.

Couldn't forget her heavy breaths, and her pleas as he moved in and out of her.

"Fuck me, Hawke," she panted, gripping him tight as she writhed beneath him. "Please, like that. More, Hawke, please. Please."

She was so wet for him. *Him!*

He couldn't fathom it. He hadn't been looked at in that way for years. Not with his fucking beard and constant habit of staying in the shadows. And yet Tyler had seen straight through that, unconcerned in the slightest his hand was fucking mangled and disgusting to look at, or that all he needed to look like a homeless dude was a fucking trench coat and a can to shake for coin.

She looked at him the way Emma looked at Borden: lustful, wanting, *needing*.

The only thing he wished he'd done was savor her more. He never got to taste her pussy, never got to slam her from behind or stick his dick inside her mouth – and fuck, imagine the sight of that, her little lips wrapped around him, swallowing his load.

She had practically given herself to him on a silver fucking platter. She wanted him and any sane man would have taken that offer – because what kind of fucking idiot would say no to Tyler with those bouncy tits and that pleading mouth asking for more?

Hawke.

Hawke was the fucking idiot.

Because he couldn't have her, and he didn't know why he gave in like that.

Well he did actually.

He'd felt so pent up as she'd sat before him, staring at him with those deep brown eyes while she'd rubbed his fucking butchered hand. Even just the memory caused his hand to tingle.

He'd tried to remember this was the angelic daughter of Dennis. The one that rode her annoying pink fucking tricycle around the clubhouse, and he wouldn't admit it – not to her or to anyone ever – but he had instructed Kirk to get rid of that stupid fucking tricycle because it was annoying and didn't belong among bags of guns and bottles of alcohol and needy naked bitches. Mostly, though, it had squeaked like a rusty hinge and drove everyone up the fucking wall.

And then there was that thing with her stare.

Fuck, she stared at him in such a way. It was borderline creepy. He almost wanted to just put a bag over her head so he wouldn't see it so much.

It was constant – **that stare** – of want and need, a dangerous combination that fucked with his head. She needed to stop with that stare of fucking doom because it kept chipping away at the ice block in his chest. He was a hardened criminal; a murderer; a fugitive. What the hell was he feeling all gooey like a chick over a fucking *stare?*

So, yeah, in a nutshell, that was why he was leaving.

Because of the stare.

And other things.

twenty-two

Hawke

"Let me get this brilliant story straight, shall we? You killed my cousin, a man I had come to trust over ten years of loyal servitude, because he… wanted to *fuck* a girl?"

Abram looked at Hawke from across his gargantuan dining table currently covered in food. There was some soulless looking girl – soulless because there was absolutely no life in her eyes – sitting beside him, staring down at an empty plate.

One of Abram's many slaves.

He had too many of them lurking around his mansion. All dressed in colorful gowns. All unimaginably beautiful.

All dead in the eyes too.

Hawke didn't know how Abram found these women, or how he got away with having them. Frankly, he wasn't that curious to ask.

Gus fidgeted by his side, looking at Hawke and Abram, not knowing what to do. Abram had silenced him upon arriving, said he wanted to talk to Hawke and not Gus or Jesse (who was currently staring at the soulless girl with a confused expression on his face).

Hawke had spent the early morning (before creepily staring at Tyler) sitting on the armchair with that horrible dog growling at him for no apparent reason other than breathing too close. It wasn't six in the morning when Abram called Hawke and ordered to see him right away.

They'd had to sneak out of the clubhouse thereafter, which wasn't hard because Hector was plastered in bed with some fucking no-name generic bird he'd taken to his room last night.

And now the three of them were in Abram's space, completely unarmed. Hawke didn't want to start trouble, so he knew they had to be vulnerable to appease Abram. He needed to give the bastard the feeling he was in charge, and Hawke wasn't going to lie, he felt powerless at the moment.

"Yuri was in withdrawal," Hawke explained to him calmly. "He was very aggressive in his demands, and I tried to be cordial."

"Cordial? You fucking *KILLED* him!" Abram roared, pounding his fist on the table. The soulless girl next to him barely blinked.

"He was acting like a lunatic," Hawke retorted.

"For a girl? You know how fucking insane that is? He can have any fuckin' girl he wants under my roof, and they're better than your clubhouse rats. Why the fuck would he go through all that effort for one of yours, Hawke?"

Hawke studied the Russian for a moment. The man was deceptively good looking; he was the kind of guy who didn't need to demonstrate his power to lure beautiful girls in.

He was also impossible to read.

Even his anger was a charade that he used to throw people off.

Hawke kept his face neutral, looking almost bored as he explained, "Like I just said, he was in withdrawal and aggressive. He would have fought me over any girl. It just so happened the girl he wanted was already spoken for last night by another member."

"His actions were very excessive."

"It didn't help he said you gave him the okay."

"I said to enjoy himself. I never mentioned a particular girl, much less kidnap one."

"He seemed pretty goddamn keen."

Abram leaned back in his chair, his anger lines fading. "This doesn't make any sense. The girl he wanted, what's her name?"

Hawke felt Gus and Jesse's stare boring into him, and despite their barely concealed concern, Hawke didn't pause in his lie as he answered, "Shay."

"Beautiful?" Abram proceeded to ask.

"That's relative."

"Well, she'd have to be fucking beautiful, wouldn't she, Hawke?"

"Suppose so."

Abram shook his head, scoffing. "Now what the fuck am I supposed to do about this? You think you can just kill family and I would let it go? I look weak if I sit back and let your club get away with this."

"This wasn't the club, it was me. I take full responsibility."

"And see, that's why you're still leader material. Unlike your unfortunate brother who has more of a reputation inside the bedroom than out. You really do need to take back that cut. I'd be a lot more cordial to those animals if I knew you were in charge."

"I'm a fugitive."

"I can make that disappear."

Hawke's face hardened. "Nobody can make that disappear."

Abram smiled. "Money can make *anything* disappear, Hawke. Your good friend Borden would agree."

Hawke didn't reply. That wasn't a topic he wanted to invite into this shit-storm. He'd already made peace with his current reality, no point looking back.

"What would you have me do to settle this?" Hawke asked.

"Eye for an eye," Abram answered.

"And that means what?"

"I want someone in your filthy tribe to bite the fucking dust."

Jesse growled and Gus went still, cursing. "What the fuck?"

Abram pointed at him. "You shut the fuck up, old man."

Hawke raised his hand to Gus and Jesse, silently telling them to calm down before he turned to Abram. "That ain't happenin'."

"Then we'll burn your clubhouse to the ground with everybody in it."

Was this dick serious? Or just talking shit?

Hawke chuckled sardonically and narrowed his eyes at Abram. "You really wanna make more enemies? Especially with one that has connections to Marcus Borden, a man who owns an entire city and its thugs under him? You want to sabotage sales from your business by cutting off supply now in search for another one? And what happens if that other one is shit and your buyers fuck off, or worse, die from whatever shit is found in it too late? Then think of what dead bodies will bring to you: a whole shit load of cockroaches sniffin' up your alleyway lookin' for someone to blame."

"Is that right?"

"Yeah, that's fucking right, and I've been around the block one too many times to tell you with fucking certainty how right that is. So don't play games with me, Abram. Just be straight and own up to the fact you had a man with a drug addiction that was also a poor excuse for a human being."

Abram went quiet for a few moments, contemplating. Hawke took the opportunity to look at the two meat heads standing between them and their way out. If things went to shit, they might have to take them on, but if they were armed…well, it'd get ugly.

He really didn't want it to come to that, but Abram was too unpredictable and he'd killed for less.

"I'm not afraid of war," Abram started, thoughtfully. "My demand for a bigger supply isn't crucial. I do it to build a network, like you and Borden. Your threat is hollow to me, Hawke, because I wouldn't lose anything vital for business if your club turned its back on me, but…I'm not a believer of making enemies. Like you, I'm not impulsive."

Was this dick ever going to get to the point?

"Yuri's loyalty was never questioned," he continued. "But" – he sighed irritably – "he was a liability too with his drug addiction. And my men did back up your story about his aggression, so…maybe this was necessary."

Shit-storm averted.

"But that doesn't change how I deal with the club. I want the deals to be made with you."

"Abram, you gotta handle it with Hector."

"Hector is fucking clueless, Hawke! Your boys here know it too judging by the look on their faces. You would be insulting me right now to think I would want to even look at that man. He is disorganized and answers problems with unnecessary violence or nothing at all. He doesn't know what he's doing. He has a network of people in his pocket, and that would have taken you and your old man years to build, and he doesn't know how to use them."

Hawke glared at him gravely. "Have you been spying on us?"

"Occasionally people whisper in my ear. And what I've gathered is pretty black and white. Nobody respects Hector. They respect *you*."

Fucking hell. "You're putting me in a situation that forces me back to the club frequently."

Abram shrugged. "And you plucked the eyeballs out of my cousin's face before you cut his throat clean. I'd say my fucking conditions are pretty pleasant compared to what they could have been."

Well, shit, when he said it like that…

Hawke reluctantly nodded. "Good point."

"But there's still this problem about the girl."

"There is no problem about any girl. Yuri was high, drunk and horny. *That* was the problem."

Abram didn't respond for several moments. He cut his eyes to Gus and Jesse, studying them intently. "So there's nothing else you need to tell me, Hawke?"

"Like what?"

Abram shrugged again, looking over Hawke meticulously. "Just…*anything*."

The fucker was on to him. Hawke could sense it. "Just that I'm glad we have an *honest* relationship," he replied carefully.

"Yeah." Abram smirked. "Honesty is relative too, isn't it, Hawke? I'll see you at the next drop. In the meantime, pay my respects to Borden."

Borden wouldn't give a fuck.

With that, Abram nodded at his meatheads and they cleared the way.

Without another word, Hawke, Gus and Jesse turned around and walked out. It took them five minutes just to get from one side of the mansion to the other. Cameras and men and soulless girls crossed their path the whole way.

"Fucking rich people," Jesse uttered under his breath.

"He's a fucking asshole," Gus hissed just as they exited the mansion. "I don't understand him."

Hawke understood him.

Men like Abram thought they could buy their loyalty without having to work for it, and then wondered why they couldn't buy bikers so easily. When you were a community – a family, more like – loyalty was earned, not bought. Abram was fascinated by that, which was why he didn't end up putting bullets through their heads.

Gus slowed down just as they reached their bikes sitting outside the black iron gates. "You sure you don't want to come back with us?" he asked Hawke.

Hawke shook his head. "Nah, I gotta go back."

"Abram was right, though, about Hector."

Even Jesse stiffened a nod, reluctantly agreeing to that. He still hadn't looked Hawke in the eye once since the morning. Hawke knew it had something to do with Tyler, what with him trying to mark his territory over her last night and failing miserably. Hawke hadn't felt threatened once, though. A Navarro got what he wanted. And if he wanted Tyler, he'd have her.

"You boys need to go back," he told them. "I'm not going to have this talk about throwing Hector under the bus. The cut is his."

Gus shrugged. "Whatever you say, Hawke, but I know this isn't the last of Abram. He *will* retaliate."

It wasn't in Abram's nature to go back on his word, but Hawke had been wrong about many things in the past.

"Keep security high," he told them solemnly. "No mistakes this time, Gus."

Gus assured him there would be no more mistakes. Hawke watched them jump on their bikes, nodding their heads at him one last time before they took off down the long rounded driveway. When the dust settled and the sound of engines were replaced with utter silence, Hawke found himself standing by his bike, staring emptily at the sky, wondering what his next move was.

Back to the grind, motherfucker.

Already he felt the weariness in his chest. Dread was heavy, like a cinderblock stuffed inside his ribcage. He rubbed at his beard and pulled at it. Fuck it itched something awful. He should just shave it off already and stop hiding behind it like a pussy. But it was a kind of armor for him. A symbolic way to separate him from his old self because, let's be real here, the old Hawke was dead.

And that was the problem: he suddenly wanted to revive him and go back to…her.

Now he was officially pussy-whipped.

He jumped on his bike and let the engine roar to life. Then he went for a very long ride, and for a while he pretended it was like before: riding with his brothers, following his lead.

The heavy wind against his face.

Empty road ahead.

The smell of leather in his nose.

He felt alive when he rode.

He felt *whole*.

Better than that, he felt at peace.

It was only when he stopped and life came rushing in that he remembered where he was and he… *hated* it.

The loneliness within him was like slow decay, and with time it would rot its way into his soul.

twenty-three

Hawke

Hawke parked his motorcycle out front of a tiny white house. From the outside, it looked like any house on the quiet, old street. The yard needed trimming and the fence's white paint had mostly peeled off.

Hawke frowned as he stepped off his bike and looked around. The condition was nowhere near what it had been years ago. Everything looked all wrong. The white concrete bordering the front of the house had yellowed, and the tree that sat next to the house was overgrown, its fallen leaves from who knows how long ago clogging up the gutters.

He walked to the gate, and its hinges creaked as he opened it and moved down the path to the porch. When he got to the front, he pressed the doorbell, but nothing sounded. He hit it again, this time harder. When there was still nothing, he grunted in irritation and opened the screen door, pounding on the front door.

He was pissed.

This place wasn't meant to look like this.

Fucking Hector.

The door creaked open, enough for the head of a shotgun to poke out.

"Get off my land," growled a voice. "I ain't sellin'!"

Despite being pissed, Hawke's mouth quirked up. "It's me, and I ain't buyin' this house knowin' the assholes that ran amuck in there, drawin' on walls and stompin' holes into the floor."

There was a moment of stillness. Seconds passed before the gun dropped and the door slowly creaked open. A dark and white headed woman poked her head out and stared at him with huge brown eyes. Her mouth fell open, and all at once her eyes watered.

"Hawke," she pressed out, sniffing, looking him up and down. "Is that really my little boy lookin' like a drugged up hobo on my front porch?"

Same old humor.

Hawke chuckled deep in his throat. "I wouldn't say I'm little, and I ain't on drugs either."

Immediately she grabbed him by the arm and hauled him to her. Her frame was only tiny, but she was stronger than she looked. She buried her face in his chest and wrapped her arms around him, stroking his hair and face like he wasn't some grown ass man but a little boy.

Hawke let out a long breath, hugging her back. The smell of her took him back to a time before his world was black and filled with blood.

When he got lonely, and he felt like there was a sick, twisted monster moving around inside him, he came here.

And he hadn't been here in three years.

Adella shut the door the second he was in. She used the sleeve of her night gown to wipe at her tears before she ushered him along, through the tiny living room and into the equally tiny kitchen.

"Sit down, my boy," she ordered him, already rummaging through the cupboards.

He collapsed in the kitchen chair and watched her move. The kitchen was a bombsite. The floor and counters were covered in crap. His mother had always been a hoarder, and just plain messy. She'd always claimed it was organized chaos, but that organized chaos was up to her ankles in crap.

"Let me make you something," she said, already flushed in the face. "Are you hungry? What would you like? I can make you Gringas, or you can have leftover stew from last night –"

"I want you to sit down," he interrupted, motioning to the chair next to him. "I can't be here for long, Ma."

She was trembling when she got to the chair and sat down. Her small hand shot out to his, and she squeezed it tightly, gazing at him in astonishment.

"I missed you, I missed you," she repeated sadly, looking him over as she clutched the cross around her necklace with her other hand. "I pray for you. I tell Jesus to look after my son, and I always feel warmth in my heart, like he's telling me you're okay. Now you're here, in one piece, like my prayers have been answered. How have you been, my boy?"

"Everything is fine," he replied steadfastly. "You takin' care of yourself?"

"I'm makin' it by just fine."

"The house doesn't look too great."

"I'm pushin' sixty and my limbs ache when I move. I ain't no spring chicken, Hawke. Looking after the place is harder these days."

"Where's Hector in this, Ma? I thought he was supposed to help you out."

She nodded. "He is, he is. He gives me money, he takes me to the doctor for my diabetes and he's got some lady comin' around to do my laundry and buy me groceries. I got clean clothes, food, and my medicine, and that's all that matters."

"But the house –"

"Houses get old, Hawke," she interrupted, waving the argument off with her hand. "They don't last forever. You can take care of one every minute of every day, but it's no way to live life, and you never end up on top of it. Things fall apart left and right. It's a never ending battle, and I'm only here for a short amount of time. It's a stress that makes no sense at the end of it all."

Hawke sighed, not bothering to respond.

Adella was stubborn like him, and she never complained. Even when his father put her through hell with his unfaithfulness and violent temper, she stood up for herself and never backed down. It was why he had barely come home most nights; he didn't want to deal with a raging wife.

Hawke suddenly wondered how he let his old man make him abandon his mother to join the club life. What in the fuck did he see in him to make him want to leave it all behind at fourteen?

Adella stood back up shortly after, determined to make him eat something.

Pulling out the leftovers from the fridge, she warmed him up some stew and gave him a wet kiss on the face.

"You need to get rid of this fur," she told him, running her hand through his beard. "It's looking like a nest. How are you going to get married and give me grandbabies? No girl is going to look at you seriously with this."

Hawke smirked. "You'd be surprised. Women love it."

"Yeah because they're little whores. I want a nice girl. You should see how grown up Dennis' daughter is now."

Hawke's chest went tight and he looked at her strangely. "How do you know about Tyler these days?"

She smiled thoughtfully. "She always comes around with Hector, gives me these beautiful lilies and mint chocolates I like but can't find around here. You want a girl who can handle herself? She's got it all, and she's still a goddamn lady about it. No belly tops or ass hanging outta her shorts like she's beggin' for attention. You should take note what a woman is really like. Modest and tame, but also feisty and sexy when she wants to be. Don't be takin' home anymore strippers from that club you work at."

Hawke didn't want to talk about Tyler, but fuck, she plagued his head, and it didn't help his mother was talking about her. His mother was a hard ass and she actually liked a girl? And not just *a* girl, but *the* girl that had been haunting Hawke since the second he left her wet with his come in bed.

What the fuck?

But maybe that was just the power with Tyler. She had such a way with people. Nobody loathed her. She wasn't catty, she didn't backstab, she minded her own business and was loyal to a fault.

Fuck, he already missed the taste of her lips.

"I don't take home strippers," Hawke vaguely said, steering the conversation away from Tyler. "Borden's got lap dancers, and they swing from a pole, sure, but they don't get fully naked unless you're getting a private showing."

"Do I wanna know, you shit head?"

Hawke smirked. "You raised me to be a man, Ma, not a priest."

She shoved the bowl closer to him, motioning him this time to eat before she replied, "I can't be responsible for you being a man, Hawke. That was your father's doing, and I should have fought harder to keep you away –"

"You couldn't do anything," he cut in, solemnly. "Some things were outta your control, but you taught me things nonetheless."

Things that made his conscience heavy with regret.

She looked away from him, not meeting his eye. "I wish I felt that way."

His mother had tried to give him and Hector a straight life. For a while, she'd done a good job sending them to a private school on her own dime so his father didn't know about it. They'd done well too. It turned out Hector had a gift with numbers and Hawke could build anything with his hands.

Unfortunately, shit didn't work out the way his mother wanted it to.

His old man found out and pulled them out of school. Convinced they were soft, he brought them into the club, and while Hawke was fourteen, he was aware of what went on inside closed doors.

But Hector?

He'd been twelve and impressionable, and the second he stepped foot inside the clubhouse Red had thrown a girl his way, telling him to be a man. Ever since, Hector couldn't give up the pussy and Hawke could kill anything that had a pulse with just his bare hands.

It was one of the reasons he didn't deserve Tyler.

The other reason would destroy her.

"She wants me, you know," he said before he could stop himself.

Adella stilled and looked at him confusedly. "A stripper wants you?"

He chuckled dryly. "No, Ma, Tyler."

"You're pulling my leg."

"No, she…she wants me badly. She looks at me in this way and…" He paused and rubbed at the back of his neck. He'd never talked girls to his mother, or to anyone for that matter. This shit was weird.

She took a few moments processing his words and then she smiled warmly at him. "Why are you so surprised that someone wants you?"

"Not just someone, this is Tyler we're talking about here. She's ridiculously sweet, and it fucks with my head. I can't think straight around her, and it makes it harder."

"What's so hard? You both want each other and you should pursue that."

"No," he firmly said, shaking his head as he looked at her seriously. "Not after the lies. She would never forgive me if she knew..."

"You lied because you had to."

"That's not good enough."

His mother frowned. "You're a Navarro," she replied. "Navarro boys don't care about forgiveness. They take what they believe is theirs."

"That's really bad advice."

"They don't let the woman they want walk away, Hawke."

"Is that what Dad did? Took you until you hated him so much. See, I don't want that."

Adella shook her head slowly. "Power and corruption found its way into your father's soul, and that's what changed everything. It's what's going to happen to Hector if you don't put a stop to it. I'm not proud of that boy. He needs a woman."

"He's not the type."

"Every man has a woman out there ready to drop him to his knees."

Hawke laughed lightly. "Maybe."

Maybe meaning *no*.

Hector would never, ever settle. He was a loose cannon, a giant question mark that Hawke didn't know how to fix.

"Are you going back?" his mother asked just then.

"Yeah, Borden is waiting –"

"I was talking about Tyler."

Hawke went quiet.

"Are you going back?" she pressed, staring at him carefully. "You wouldn't break that girl's heart, would you?"

"Ma, as far as I'm concerned, Tyler's heart was made to be broken. I can't stop it from happening."

"She will hate you, but you must be strong for her. You must stand by her and let her hate you. It'll make her feel better."

"Maybe."

Maybe meaning…*maybe*.

*

He stayed back until night, and he tucked his mother into bed and kissed her on the forehead.

"How did we get here, Hawke," Adella asked sadly, staring at his damaged hand just before she fell asleep. "What could we have done differently?"

He frowned, thinking of her question.

He'd never been given the choice.

"Nothing," he finally said, looking blankly back at her. "There was nothing we could have done, Ma."

She let out a tear and nodded, staring at him still like he was her little boy.

It was devastating.

The other night he'd murdered a man, removed his eyeballs and almost severed his head with a blunt as fuck knife he'd used to cut rope at the port Borden owned.

And tonight he was soft and tucking his fucking mother into bed like a gentleman would.

It never ceased to amaze him the different lives he led.

He was a loving son to a strong willed woman.

First in command henchman to the city's most ruthless man.

And the ghost president of a notorious MC that was falling apart at the seams.

He knew one day he would have to simplify his life to make it work.

He just couldn't figure out what the fuck he wanted.

twenty-four

Hawke

Borden was in the office of his club when Hawke walked in the next morning. His other half Emma was sitting at her desk next to his, eating a ham and cheese sandwich. She looked particularly flushed, the top two buttons of her blouse undone, her dark hair unkempt when it was usually pristine in the mornings.

Hawke had to pause to stare at them after he closed the door behind him. The picture before him was always set in stone.

Emma ignoring Borden.

Borden watching her meticulously as he fiddled with his folders.

Emma catching his glances and smiling slyly.

Borden on the verge of making a demand that would wind up with them fucking like rabbits in the office.

Shit never changed, and it wasn't a bad thing. Petite fiery Emma with all her faults and annoyances had levelled Borden out so he wasn't growling at everyone every five seconds. It made for a more pleasant work environment, although Borden was still a hostile motherfucker when he wanted to be.

Once upon a time, Hawke had been wary of her. She'd been a distraction, a temptation to Borden (and even him because she was so fucking beautiful) that had him focusing elsewhere instead of his priorities. A man like Borden made enemies; ones that made Yuri look like a tiny kitten.

"Look who's graced us with his presence," Borden muttered, popping a pistachio (what he ate when he was pissed) in his mouth as he scowled in Hawke's direction. "Glad you could take a break from shit when it suits you, princess."

"I had club business," Hawke replied.

"Club business," he repeated slowly. "You working for me or for those bikers, Hawke? Because now I'm confused."

Hawke frowned. "You got a port, Borden, and we get our supply shipped in to sell shit to them. I had to up a supply for a customer. The guys needed me."

"He's technically still their president," Emma told Borden quietly.

"Doll, if he was their president he wouldn't be here, now would he?" Borden replied, looking back at her.

She rolled her eyes and turned back to her computer. "It's complicated for Hawke. He's a fugitive. He can't go back."

"Yes, he can. It's been five years since his supposed death, and from what I've sniffed, he's not on anyone's radar. He can find himself an identity, a legit one, not some fake one some idiot makes in his garage somewhere dirty. It would cost him about a couple hundred grand, but it's within his means."

"They'll recognize him," she complained.

"He can continue looking like an alpaca, or he can shave that shit off and look exactly like his old self, it wouldn't make a difference. All you have to do is bribe the authorities, and not the fucking cockroaches on the bottom. I'm talking he'd have to take it to the top, which means he'd need a network, one his club already has, because we all know the fucking authorities aren't so fucking innocent, either, huh?"

"It wouldn't work," she argued. "You're talking about a shocking amount of money here."

"If you had it, it would work."

"Sounds like something out of a movie."

"Except I've done it."

Emma paused and her jaw dropped. "Fuck off."

"Fuck off nothing. I've done it. Of course I charge an arm and a leg. Couple hundred grand? I make that in interest."

"You fucker."

"I am a fucker, and you love that shit."

She grinned. "I do."

Fuckin' hell, these two.

Borden smirked. "So, my point is, doll, if Hawke wanted to go back and lead his feral club, he could. But he doesn't, which is why he's here."

She looked over at Hawke with a curious look. "Why don't you want to, Hawke?"

Hawke tensed his jaw. "Because it's none of your fucking business."

"Aggressive, are we? What's happened to you to make you flip a switch at that question?"

"With all due respect, Emma, this isn't an episode of Days of our fucking Lives, alright? I don't have to unload my feelings and make you understand shit. It's my business."

"I ask because I'm concerned."

"You ask because you're nosey."

"That's part of it, I won't lie. It's just…I don't like your brother. He's a pussy worshipping jerk."

"You don't have to like the people you deal business with, like the fucker I had to deal with. It was Yuri."

Borden cringed. "I hate that fucker. He's a creep."

"What's wrong with him?" Emma asked, curiously.

"He's got sick fetishes."

"Why do you even know that? You always find out this shit."

"You wanna find out about the people you deal business with? You find out what their sexual triggers are to get a picture of what they're like. The seedy fuckers like violence, and that loony liked waterboarding shit. Apparently it made him cum like a hose."

"That's feral, Borden. God, I'm eating!"

"You asked the question, Emma. He's a sick fuck."

Hawke clenched his jaw. "I killed him."

Emma froze and Borden's bites slowed as he peered at Hawke curiously now. "You leave for a few days and come back with a death wish?"

"I've sorted it out with Abram."

Borden chuckled dryly. "You are a fucking idiot if you think you got it sorted out with Abram. He's a liar. He'll shake your hand and stab you in the throat at the same fucking time."

"He sends his regards."

"Couldn't give a fuck if I tried." Borden leaned back in his chair, staring hard at Hawke. "You just made yourself an enemy, Hawke. Yuri meant something to that piece of shit."

"Yuri was unstable and on to me about something."

"Like what?"

"Tyler."

Borden's eyes lit up with understanding. "You're kidding me."

Emma looked confusedly between the two of them. "What's going on?"

Borden didn't answer. Hawke and him stared at one another for several drawn out moments, silently communicating, and all he saw in Borden's expression was, *You're fucked.*

"Emma, can you give Hawke and me a couple minutes?" he asked softly.

She nodded and stood. She was about to leave when he said, "You're forgetting something, doll."

She rolled her eyes, trying to appear annoyed but Hawke noticed the blush in her cheeks as she turned around, bent to his level, and kissed him softly on the cheek. Then she walked out.

"Let's run this over," Borden started, thoughtfully. "How would Yuri know about Tyler?"

"He shouldn't."

"Well, he did obviously."

Hawke frowned. "It would have to have come from Hector, me, you, or my mother. Those are the only people that know about it."

"Who in that list is the most probable?"

He hesitated. "Hector."

Borden nodded. "It's the only thing that would make sense."

Hawke rubbed at his face and began to pace the office, feeling his chest tighten as he ran the possibility through. "It doesn't make sense," he argued. "It's not in Hector to betray me like that."

"Maybe he's been betraying you all along. Think about it. You excel at being president and he's stuck in the shadow of your success. Your men revere you and then all of a sudden you're pinned on a murder with evidence up to the roof –"

"You're suggesting Hector handed the authorities the video."

"It's just a suggestion."

"It's not one I believe. Why would he get me out?"

"Because he knew you'd be a fugitive and you'd never be able to return."

Hawke continued to shake his head, growing more and more frustrated as he went. "I can't believe that, Borden. It doesn't work."

"You can't believe that, or you don't *want* to believe that?"

Hawke stopped, glaring at Borden, wanting nothing more than to argue that point but knowing damn straight that he was right.

Still.

He couldn't get himself to consider it.

"Look," Borden said calmly, "I'm not going to accuse that manwhore for this. He's proved his worth time and time again, but…this requires digging."

"We've been digging," Hawke stressed, exasperated.

"I've got more resources to tap into, Hawke. We're going to find out everything, and I know the answer is sitting in that information. So hold tight and don't fuck back to that town just yet."

*

He walked out of the office, stopping in the hallway to smack his forehead against the wall. He took in deep breaths, attempting to keep the suspicions of his brother in the middle of this shit-fest at bay.

Hector wouldn't.

He just…wouldn't.

He felt a hand on his back, and smelled Emma's perfume as she moved next to him, rubbing his back.

"I've seen a change in you," she whispered. "You've never come back from that town this shaken up before. Something's happened, hasn't it?"

Hawke stiffened a nod. *Tyler happened.*

"You're going to go back, I know it."

"How do you know?"

"Because you can't keep running away forever. There's only so much road left until you hit the end."

Emma would know. She'd had a hard life.

He turned his head and looked at her. "How did you know Borden was it?" he asked her, curiously.

She smiled thoughtfully. "Because as much as I wanted to push him away, he wormed himself inside me. It didn't happen overnight. It took time, and then…one day it just hit me. His absence made me confront what he meant to me."

He didn't respond to that. His head was too clouded with thoughts of Tyler and how she'd grown before his eyes over the years. He'd taken her presence for granted, determined not to focus on her because he knew how beautiful she was inside and out.

Emma was right. Now that Tyler was absent from him, the ache was quickly wearing him down.

If he hadn't touched her then maybe he would not be so fixated. But…after just one taste, Hawke was hooked.

Tyler was intoxicating.

twenty-five

Tyler

It'd been five days since Hawke left and Hector wasn't the same. Everybody sensed it. He was harsher than he was before, and his temper flew at a flip of a switch.

It didn't help the cockroaches paid him another visit. Their negotiator Duggard, who was a middle aged man, rugged and suited to take the bikers on, had disrespected Hector in front of everyone by starting the conversation with, "I've got a list of orders that you're going to follow."

Orders to the president of the Warlords? Was this fuckhead serious?

But Hector, angry as he was, didn't punish the asshole for disrespecting him. Instead, he appeared conflicted, like he was uncertain of how he was meant to show authority when his answer to everything was violence. So he'd just stiffened a nod and taken Duggard into the meeting room where Gus cursed up a storm outside it, talking about how weak Hector was behind his back.

Duggard had come out of there a half hour later looking smug, his eyes cheerful, his demeanor laid back and relaxed. He was not in the least intimidated by anyone. In fact, he looked like he owned the place, and it had Marshall boiling in his blood and Jesse itching to tear the cockroach's face off.

Everyone was fuming and Hector resorted to breaking a chair in the meeting room apart after he'd gone.

Since then, Hector spiraled out of control. He was drinking more and following Holly with his eyes like a predator. The poor girl ignored it as much as possible and left work the second her shift was over. Sometimes she'd leave minutes earlier and Hector would ask about her whereabouts and grumble curses when he found out she was gone.

So he fucked Shay a lot, and Shay was starting to realize she was just warming his bed instead of owning half of it.

I was enjoying my solitude when she stopped by me to unload.

"That bitch is stringing him along," she said darkly. "You need to tell Hector that Holly is a cunt, Ty. Not for me, but for *him*."

"I thought we had this speech about drama," I replied, genuinely confused as I looked at her sullen face; it was extra orange today. "Like…you were there when I told you that you were creating drama, weren't you?"

"This is serious."

"You are stirring the pot, dear Shay, and you need to back away before the pot tips and burns you."

She gave me a look. "That doesn't make any fucking sense, Tyler."

"Neither does your logic about Holly. She's done nothing wrong."

"I fucking loathe her. I'll fucking kill her if I have to, I swear."

"Now you're being plain stupid."

"But I will."

"Stop channeling the inner trailer trash in you."

Shay leaned over the bar, staring evenly at me as she retorted slowly, "But she. Is. A. Whore!"

Eyes descended on us, and I wanted to sucker punch her because – *ughhhhhh* – I'd really started to have enough of this fucking Hector obsession and Holly bashing. I was just trying to enjoy my fucking drink!

I glanced around the bar and then leaned forward at her, growling out, "Bitch, *you* are the one whoring yourself to Hector, not Holly. And you need to be real fucking careful with that mouth because if you start talking this way about killing some waitress to anyone else, your ass is going to be used for a whipping post, and those two holes downstairs? They're going to be big enough to slide ten sausages through, you feeling me? So keep your fucking. Mouth. Shut!"

She froze, her eyes bulged, and she stared at me like I'd stabbed her in the heart. "I thought you didn't care about me," she whispered.

What in the fuck? "I don't."

"But you care about my wellbeing like I'm…I'm part of the club too."

"Are you taking drugs?"

Her eyes glistened with tears but she started to laugh, and now I was seriously confused. "You are the golden girl, and the golden girl actually considers me part of the club."

"Oh, my god, you are insane."

"I love you, Tyler."

I groaned, disgusted. "No, Shay, you don't."

She giggled again and slid another beer in front of me. "This one's on the house, honey."

"They're *all* on the house."

She moved down the bar to serve more drinks, but not before winking at me.

Oh, lord, my nose tingled something awful. I could smell the pungent reek in the air.

The smell of *drama* on the horizon.

"Hey, you alright?" Jesse asked, sidling up next to me. He grabbed the beer Shay had set in front of me and took a long swig.

"Yeah," I replied simply.

Ever since that conversation in the office about warming his bed, I'd taken a big step back from Jesse. He was my friend – my hot as fuck tailored suit biker friend sure – and I didn't want to blur the lines. He never brought the topic up again; my guess was because Hawke wasn't around and he didn't feel threatened. He acted like everything was normal and still took me to and from work, but…yeah, I was very reserved.

"Why is Shay hollering at you?"

"She's not."

He bumped his shoulder against mine. "Hey, what's wrong?"

"Nothing, I'm about to go find Hector –"

"He's already in his room."

I searched the bar suddenly, and my heart paused when I couldn't find her. "Holly?"

"What?"

I cut my gaze at him. "Is he with *Holly*?"

He shook his head, giving me a strange look. "Nah, not Holly. She left already. I didn't see him with anyone either."

Oh, thank God. My shoulders slumped. "Okay, good."

"Why good?"

Because I felt overprotective of Holly lately, and helped smuggle her out of the bar sometimes to avoid Hector.

Yeah, it'd gotten that bad.

The more she pushed him away, the more he wanted her.

Instead of saying any of that, I just shook my head. "No reason."

He leaned into me. "So I'm going to the club in a bit and thought you'd wanna tag along."

"Not tonight."

"If you're deterred because you think it'll be just me, let me assure you that most of the others are comin' along too."

My brow rose. "Thought the clubhouse was supposed to be high on security."

"We're doing fine."

"Well, I'm staying. Think I'll order Chinese and flick through some Netflix."

He winked. "Netflix and chill?"

God, no matter how hard I wanted to keep my distance, he couldn't *not* put a smile on my face. "No," I said, fighting back a laugh. "There will be Netflix without the chill."

He chuckled, his blue eyes sparkling. "Alright, I'll crash the couch with you."

"Jesse –"

"There is no hidden agenda, Ty-phoon. I come in peace."

I let out a soft sigh and looked at him seriously. "Jesse, I want to be alone."

There was a short pause. The kind of pause when someone was processing something. Hurt flashed in his eyes before he covered it up and nodded at me. "Yeah, sure," he said, trying to sound upbeat. "That's cool. You can be alone."

"You're not pissed?"

"Why would I be pissed? I'll just end up getting wasted and fucking another airhead. Isn't that what you think I'll do? What's new?"

"Jesse…"

He began to move and I grabbed at his suit shirt and forced him back to me.

"Hey," I said, sharply. "I didn't mean it like that, alright? I know I came off cold."

"You've been coming off cold since I told you I wanted you in my bed, Tyler," he retorted, frowning. "I get that you don't, alright? I'm not trying to fuck you every time I'm near you, though."

My brow rose. "Seriously?"

He rolled his eyes. "Look, of course I wouldn't say no if you wanted it, but I respect that you don't is what I mean. I'm tired of you pushing me away. I want my fucking friend back, not this switched off bitch who looks at me with dread."

Now it was my turn to feel wounded. "You…think I'm a bitch?"

He looked at my expression and sighed hard. "Fuck, goddamn it, Tyler, no. You're not a bitch. I meant… ugh, fuck, you know what I meant."

I didn't respond.

He groaned and moved closer to me. "I'm sorry, sweetheart."

"I'm sorrier."

"No, that's fucking stupid, you shouldn't feel sorry. I'm sorrier."

"No, I really am sorrier, Jesse –"

"Oh, would you guys shut the fuck up with the sorry bullshit!" Marshall hollered. "Fuckin' migraine just hearing your playground bullshit."

I cracked a smile, keeping my eyes on Jesse. "You can crash the couch with me."

He smiled back. "Yeah, but I really am horny, though, and I kinda thought I really could lure you in –"

I smacked him on the shoulder. "I knew it!"

He laughed. "I'll see you later, alright?"

I nodded. "Yeah, yeah."

He left sometime later, taking half the guys with him. I spent the evening eating ten pounds' worth of Beef Chow Mein on the couch. When Jonny came up with a girl, I snarled at him. "Go the fuck away, Jonny. You think it's easy to disinfect a couch after you?"

"Calm your fucking tits, Tyler," he retorted, going back down.

It was nice being the only girl in the club to have a room to herself.

Until Hector came out of his room an hour later. He had only his jeans on, and his upper body was exposed. He was the only one to have space between tattoos, and his chest was completely bare. He had a nice body. Lean and muscular, bronze like Hawke, and tall like him too, but not with the same mass as his older brother.

He looked miserable when he collapsed on the couch next to me, lazily tugging on my ponytail. "Why is it so quiet?" he asked, his voice tired and blank.

"The guys went out," I answered.

Hector frowned. "They went out without even letting me know? Who the fuck is taking care of security?"

"Jesse said it should be fine."

"Is Jesse here?"

"No."

Hector's eye twitched, his anger palpable now. "They don't take me seriously, do they? We make meetings, they agree to upping the security around this dump, and they just forget the second they want to party. God!" He groaned, rubbing at his temple. "How the fuck did Hawke do it? They faced two wars, Ty, and he knew what to do every time!"

"To be fair, we haven't had to face any crisis."

"Abram could have been one," he said, shaking his head back and forth. "And that was only fixed because of Hawke. I'm drowning, Ty, I'm…"

I looked back. "What?"

"Nothing."

He didn't look at me like it was nothing. The pressure was eating away at him, I realized. That was why he'd been acting out like a rage case.

Forcing his eyes from me, he let out a long breath and straightened his emotions out.

"What're we watching?" he then asked, focusing on the television.

I studied him, trying to figure him out. "Um, Orange is the New Black."

His lips went up in a half smile, and just like that, the mood lifted in the room. "Girl on girl?"

"Yep."

"Is, uh, Holly around or anything? Maybe she'd like to watch too."

I pretended to act casual, though I was surprised that he was asking. Chilling with a girl besides me? That was a first.

"Uh, no," I answered. "If you've forgotten, Holly's a mom, so…"

He nodded inquisitively. "Son?"

"Daughter."

"How old?"

"Four."

"Huh. You know where she lives?"

I frowned. "Hector –"

"I'm not asking because I wanna fuck her, Ty. I'm just curious."

I was skeptical about that. "I don't know where she lives," I lied.

He caught it and scoffed. "Fucking liar. You drop her off at her place some nights."

"That is a little bit true."

"I'm not trying to fuck her," he repeated firmly.

"How about inviting Shay instead? She's kicking around, I'm absolutely *positive* of that –"

"Not Shay," he interrupted, adamantly, looking around the place like she might pop up out of the walls or something. "I can't stand her, Tyler. She won't go the fuck away."

"Then stop taking her to bed."

"She lets herself in and crawls into my fucking bed naked. She's unhinged, Tyler. What the fuck do I do to get rid of her?"

I wanted to tell him to be a leader and kick her the fuck out, but…it wasn't my place.

Changing the subject, I threw half my blanket over him. "Get comfortable. I got some food too, if you want."

He nodded and took my fork from out of my hand. "Yeah, I need this."

"Just don't eat all of it, okay? There's two people here."

"I won't. Fucking hell, so bossy."

"Gotta be bossy with you boys."

"Anything to drink?"

"Sprite."

"That's weak."

I rolled my eyes and sarcastically mumbled, "Sorry for disappointing you, my lordship."

We watched half a season, ate all the food, and somehow alcohol appeared out of the blue. Keeping conversation short, Hector drank himself to sleep on the couch, and I went back to my room at quarter to midnight, sober.

The heat was unbearable, so I threw my clothes off and slid into bed naked, snatching Hawke's t-shirt off the floor along the way. He'd taken it off the morning after he'd murdered Yuri. I should have been repulsed that it was the same shirt he'd killed Yuri in, and covered in his blood too. But I'd completely lost my sanity after what happened, and was Hawke deprived and depressingly lonely.

So I made it into a ball and used it as a pillow, and with Hawke's scent in my nose, I fell asleep easily, no nightmares chasing me.

twenty-six

Tyler

I woke up not two hours later to the sound of water sloshing nearby. My eyes burned from fatigue and the sting of light coming from the half-opened bathroom. I sat up and glanced tiredly around the room, catching sight of black boots set neatly by the door. Next to them was a pair of jeans and…a black leather jacket. The scent of Hawke wasn't in just my nose anymore, but all around me.

My heart tightened in my chest.

He was here.

Showering.

I quickly ran my hand over my hair, neatening it. Then all at once I dropped back on the mattress and shut my eyes. Maybe I needed to pretend to be asleep.

My eyes opened twenty seconds later and I sat back up. I was jittery. He'd see me flinching if he stepped out, and if he figured out I was faking sleep, there'd be that awkward feeling in the air, and I didn't want *another* awkward encounter with him.

It felt like a lifetime passed by before the water shut off and a body stepped out. He was naked. *Obviously.* And standing side on, glancing at himself in the mirror. He seemed focused on a part of his chest, meanwhile I was focused on the way his ass jutted out.

Wow.

I was actually seeing him naked this time. I wasn't immobilized in terror and rocking in his arms under the water. Nor were we in the dark with him pressed against my chest.

He was completely visible and, holy fuck, he had a very muscular ass, and thick corded thighs that –

He turned face on and stepped out, and holy fuck…

Holy fuuuuck.

My mouth dried entirely. He looked incredible. No, better than incredible; he made the posters of guys I used to hang up around the bedroom look like broomstick sissies.

I could see the line and shape of every muscle on his body: his traps, biceps, abs, and a V that put all other V's to shame.

But that wasn't where I was currently looking.

No, it was his giant fucking package blaring at me shamelessly or, rather, swinging.

It looked nothing like Gavin's dick. Actually, his dick looked like a stale Cheeto compared to Hawke's. Hawke was beautiful. Yeah, I called his dick *beautiful*.

This sexy, huge dicked beast had fucked me, and I'd practically taken it for granted by not turning on one simple light switch.

He stopped moving when he saw me. "Did I wake you up?" he asked, his baritone voice causing flutters in my stomach.

I shook my head, forcing my eyes away from his beautiful D. "No, I've been stirring all night."

"You got a towel that isn't pink, babe?"

"No."

He nodded, and that made the drops in his hair fall all around him. He went back into the bathroom and pulled my fluffy pink towel off the hook and ran it through his hair and chest. He stepped back out and moved to the edge of the bed, collapsing into it on a heavy exhale.

Then he sat there for a while, his back to me, not moving.

My brow furrowed. I was about to ask him if he was alright when I saw the bruises – giant ones the size of large fists – running along his back. My eyes widened and I crawled to him quietly. If he heard me, he didn't care. I stopped behind him and softly rested my palm along one; his muscles flexed beneath my touch and his breath left his lungs in a whoosh.

I gasped. “Hawke?”
“Hmm?” he grumbled.
“Your back…”
“Yeah.”
Both hands slid along his back. His flesh was hot and moist, and I could tell by the way he shuddered that he was in a lot of pain. “What happened?”
“Work, darlin’.”
“Club?”
“No.”
“Borden?”
“Mm. Had to roughen up some men.”
“They hurt you.”
He chuckled scornfully. “You should see them.”
He turned around suddenly and I shifted back, covering my breasts with my arm as he looked at me. He hadn’t turned the bathroom light off, so there was plenty of it flooding into the room. He had a cut lip and a deep black bruise over his eyebrow. I didn’t like seeing the marks. It reminded me he wasn’t indestructible.
I felt sad. “You look like shit.”
His tongue lapped at the cut. “I always look like shit, babe.”
I lightly touched his beard and then quickly dropped my hand. “Maybe you should lose the beard then.”
“Not your thing?”
I shrugged, not meeting his eye. “I like it. It’s just… I miss your face.”
“You know I got called Chewbacca once?”
My lips twisted up and I fought smiling. “Oh?”
“You think I’m a Wookiee?”
“Wookiee, no. Gandalf, though? You’re halfway there.”
He grinned. “Great.”
My heart burst at his smile. It bared teeth, perfectly white ones, and it opened his face right up. God, I wanted him again.

"Why are you back so soon?" I then asked him, trying to play it cool so I didn't look like a salivating egotistical idiot that wanted to be told I was the reason.

"You know why," he answered, eyes all over me.

My breath thinned. It was me. It was totally me.

"Took care of shit on my way here, and I was filthy. Used your shit smelling body wash."

"I know."

"I smell like a chick."

"Well, I like it."

He smirked, eyes now on mine. Fuck, he was staring hard, and I was getting red all over. "You usually sleep naked, Tyler?"

"No."

Those eyes flickered *everywhere* again. "You should."

I chewed at my lower lip, not responding.

"Get back in bed, Ty."

He stood back up and made his way to the bathroom. He flipped the light off and darkness fell. I shuffled further back and rested my head on the pillow. I could just barely see him moving around. He walked around the bed and fell into it. Right next to me. Still a couple feet away, and we may as well have been miles apart.

Still.

He was in my bed. Well, *his* bed.

I turned my face to him, eyes adjusting to the dark. He turned his head, meeting my gaze. Neither of us said a word. I was hoping he'd just jump me and cut the tension, but he wasn't moving an inch. I swallowed thickly and grabbed the covers, throwing them over me. Then I turned my back to him and closed my eyes.

I needed to sleep. Please, God, I needed to sleep and pretend I didn't have a six foot two naked beast next to me, but all I kept thinking about was his smile. I squirmed, feeling my lower belly flutter and throb.

"Hey Ty?" he said a minute later.

"Yeah?" I barely sounded out.

"Why is my filthy shirt in bed with you?"

My eyes whipped open and I froze. *Fuck.*

Very slowly, I turned my body to him. He was holding up his shirt, still wrapped in a perfect ball. I stared at it for a horrifying moment…and then I grabbed it abruptly, leaned over the mattress and threw it under the bed. He was still staring at me when I laid back down.

"I didn't know it was there," I lied, my voice tight.

His silence killed me.

He was judging me.

So much for avoiding an awkward situation. I'd just wandered straight into that shit-ville.

"Were you sleepin' with it?" he suddenly asked.

I cringed deep in my bones.

Somebody kill me.

"No," I answered.

"You weren't smellin' it?"

My pulse pounded in my ears now. "No," I repeated.

"You're a terrible liar, babe."

An axe to the head. Hell, throw me in a fire, I don't care. ANYTHING but THIS.

What the fuck was wrong with me?

I had so many opportunities to get rid of it, or…at least *wash* it. Now I was worse than those creeps that stole panties from clothing lines and sniffed them at home with their grubby hands down their pants.

The bed shifted and he got closer. I tried to resist looking at him. I was too humiliated to even move. Then…

I felt his fingers at my mouth, tracing the shape of them. My breathing stilled and I turned my face to him before I could even think. He watched me, his eyes heavy on my mouth as he continued, forcing me to part my lips. When I did, he slipped his finger inside and grazed his fingertip against my tongue before moving back out and wetting my lips. His breaths were longer and deeper.

"Whose bed are you in?" he asked, gruffly.

I sucked in a breath, barely moving. "Yours."

Silence.

Then, "Yeah."

His jaw clenched as he trailed his fingers down my neck and along my shoulder. Then back up again, to my mouth, to my tongue, wetting my lips and sliding the wetness down my neck. I was burning everywhere. This was worse than the heat of summer; it was inside me, running through my veins, burning its way into my heart.

What was happening?

I waited for…*something*, and the anticipation killed because he was doing…*nothing*.

I raised my hand, and I brushed my fingertips along the cut on his lip. He had soft lips; the kissable kind that you probably melted into like butter. I wanted to kiss him, badly. I wanted to run my hand over his beard and down his chest and abdomen. I imagined grabbing at his cock and feeling it swell in the palm of my hand.

What would that be like with Hawke?

He parted his lips for me too, and when he licked at my fingertip, my entire body tingled. I swallowed thickly and traced his lips and down his throat, over that adam's apple, and back up again. By the third round, I felt bolder, and my fingers trailed lower than his neck and down his chest. He was so built and rock hard, my hand went lower, over the speedbumps of his abs and to the trail of hair.

I had just barely brushed the beginning of his cock – smooth like silk and far from limp. My eyes shot to his, and his expression went dark. Lust-filled and charged with need, I moved to him and captured his mouth. It was a quick kiss, just enough for me to taste his lips and feel how soft they were. God, I'd missed them. When I pulled back, his eyes were still open, staring deeply into mine.

I didn't know what he was thinking.

I made to move away from him when his hand suddenly grabbed at my neck. It was a firm grip; he didn't squeeze and it didn't hurt, but his grip forced me back to him. Back to his eyes. I gasped, my face inches from his, as he looked me over.

"Fuckin' hell," he whispered. "You're trouble for me, Tyler. I can't stop thinking about you. Can't stop thinking about being inside your sweet little cunt. Can't get enough of your lips, your taste. Can't get enough of you period."

I opened my mouth to speak when he pulled me to him, smashing his lips to mine. I closed my eyes immediately and opened my mouth to him. He kissed hard, with an urgency that knocked me breathless. He quickly moved over me, moving his hand from my neck to my hair and fisting it so hard my scalp ached.

"Open your mouth wider for me, Ty," he demanded, his voice hoarse.

I did, and I felt his tongue swiftly clashing with mine. I groaned, my body already seizing and coiling with need. He sucked at my bottom lip and I felt his hand grabbing at my breast, kneading it and squeezing hard at my nipple. A lightning bolt of pleasure shot straight down to my core, and I groaned again, squirming beneath his huge frame covering every inch of me.

Without thinking, I ran my hand back down his chest and to his cock. The second I wrapped my hand around him, he hissed in my mouth and dropped his forehead to mine.

"Fuck, Tyler, yeah," he panted. "Squeeze harder, babe."

I squeezed around his thick length, shocked that it grew even thicker, until not even my fingers met the whole way around. I pumped him and he continued to tell me to go faster. His hand left my hair and gripped the bedframe. He breathed heavily, eyes closed, as I pleasured him, exploring his length and feeling a bead of moisture at the tip of him.

I wanted to lick it off him.

Oh, my God, his noises only added fuel to my desire, growing feverishly bigger within me. So this was what it was like to pleasure him. It was hot and sweaty, even his breaths against my face did strange things to me.

He kissed me again, this time not as hard. It was a soft kiss, languid and sweet. He lightly bit at my bottom lip and then sucked it. Still stroking him, my other hand gripped the back of his neck, keeping him to me. My hips moved on their own; it wasn't enough I was kissing him, my body did its own thinking and sought pleasure.

Seeming to understand, I felt his hand slide down to the sensitive skin between my legs. My head fell back as he trailed his finger along my slit, teasing around my opening.

"Fuck, you are drenched," he murmured, kissing down my neck and moving lower.

My entire body responded to his touch and kiss. There wasn't an inch of me that wasn't going crazy. Jolts of pleasure ripped through me as he slid his finger up and down. I was forced to let go of him as he journeyed the way down, settling himself between my legs. And like instinct, my legs quickly made to close and my hands pushed at his head, trying to move him away.

"Relax, Tyler," he told me, forcing my legs apart. "You'll like it."

His finger continued to tease my opening when the heat of his mouth centered around my clit. I went still, trying to relax, and when I felt it, that hot slide of his tongue, I let out a harsh breath. More jolts of pleasure tore through me. It was indescribable. My fingers found their way back into his hair and this time I squeezed to keep him there.

He was soft and slow, getting me used to the feeling and pace. I shook hard, and he had to grip my hip to keep me still. My whole body shivered and I moaned shamelessly, grinding myself against his mouth. My pleasure climbed, and my whole body bowed to him, centered solely on his mouth and tongue.

"Please."

There I went with the begging again. It tumbled out of my mouth, forgotten the second it hit the air, making me repeat it time and time again.

"Please, please."

Hawke went faster, sucking feverishly at my sensitive bundle of nerves towards the end, and I froze, holding my breath as the orgasm ripped through me. Like a chant, I repeated his name in a breathless whisper over and over again as I rode through the feeling.

I felt him chuckle, and it vibrated through my sensitive skin, causing more swells of pleasure.

He moved back over me and took my mouth against his. I cringed at the taste of myself so thick on his lips, and he chuckled again, his chest pressed against my sweaty body.

"That was good," he muttered. "You *taste* good."

I was all for vulgarity, but this was so personal, I burned from embarrassment. Avoiding a response, I grabbed at his length again and squeezed, and he situated himself on his elbows. He looked down at my hand. "Spread your legs for me, Tyler," he demanded tightly. "Real wide."

I spread myself wide for him.

"Rub me against your pussy, babe," he instructed. "Soak me with your come."

I rubbed the glistening head of him against me, and I shivered again, closing my eyes at the pleasure. He kissed my eyelids and laughed. "Good, huh?"

I nodded. Oh, yeah.

"Wait until I'm inside you, Tyler, fucking you again." His voice turned edgy. "You'll feel me everywhere, all the way down to your toes. Fuck, I want inside you. It's all I think about. I want to own every hole. I want to take you on your knees, make you suck me while I fuck your little pussy with my fingers."

My god, his words were like another form of sex.

"Guide me inside you now."

I opened my eyes and looked between us. I pressed the head of him at my entrance and tried to draw him in. Like before, I felt extremely small, like I was nudging a gulf ball through a hole the width of a pin. He nudged his hips forward to help, and I had just begun to feel my body stretching to accommodate him when he pulled away abruptly.

I looked back up at him questionably, but he wasn't looking back. His face was on the door, concentrated.

"Hawke?" I asked.

"Shh, baby," he replied in a whisper.

I held my breath, already catching on that he was listening to something. I tried to listen to, but I caught nothing but the sound of my heartbeats.

He frowned and suddenly slid off the bed. I leaned up on my elbows, watching him move to the door. He opened it a crack and pressed his ear against the opening.

Then…

I heard it.

Mercy's barks and something crashing, over and over again from somewhere nearby.

twenty-seven

Tyler

"What is that?" I asked.

Just as I asked, voices erupted from the hallway and doors opened and slammed loudly. Hawke quickly grabbed his jeans and slid them on, not bothering to do it up as he opened the door all the way and yelled, "Where's it coming from?"

"Outside!" I heard Jonny yell back.

Hawke barely looked at me as he demanded, "You stay here, Tyler."

Then he disappeared out of the room, and my head was still spinning when another body came rushing in seconds later.

"Tyler?!" Hector shouted, panic in his voice.

I froze and then scrambled to cover my body with the covers. "I'm here! Get out!"

Hector briefly looked me over, his face gentling. "Thank fuck."

"What's going on?"

But I didn't get an answer. He'd already hurried out.

I slid out of bed and threw my shirt and shorts on and wandered out. I caught Shay standing in Hector's doorway, covering her body with a bedsheet.

"You're not allowed down there," she said.

I ignored her and made my way down the staircase. She called after me again, but I was already on the first floor, listening to the shouts and curses from the guys. The commotion was coming from outside, and as I slowly entered the bar area I stepped on something sharp and pain shot up my foot. Jumping, I looked down at a trail of glass, scattered throughout the room, and as I continued to look, I noticed the glass had come from all four windows, smashed to hell.

Fuck.

Gunshots suddenly fired, flying through the broken windows. I dropped to the ground and threw my arms over my head. Glasses nearby smashed, sending more shards soaring through the air around me. I wanted to move, wanted to get the hell out of there, but I was plastered to the ground, too afraid of getting hit to budge an inch.

It ended seconds later, and my heart was battering in my chest when I finally looked up, hearing angry voices.

Was it over?

Shuddering, I moved to my hands and knees and crawled over broken glass to the entrance door.

Most of the guys were outside when I cracked it open and looked out. They were seething, screaming curses and threats in the direction of a truck speeding down the street, laughter and hoots disappearing with it.

"Fucking dicks," Gus growled, looking darker than I had ever seen him in a very long time.

"What were they screaming?" Kirk barked angrily. "Do we got a new threat?"

"These were Abram's men! He fucking sent them, I know it. They even looked fuckin' Russian."

"We got intel on them?"

Gus made a face at Kirk. "Do you even know who the fuck Abram is, you old shit?"

Kirk appeared confused, and Gus scoffed before looking around, inspecting. "Anyone hurt? Fuckers fired a lot of bullets."

They all looked at one another, searching for visible wounds.

"Hector, you okay, man?" Marshall suddenly asked, rushing to his side.

Hector was quaking, his gun still pointing in the direction where the truck had taken off. His other arm was bright red and dripping in blood. Even from where I stood it was a gory sight.

“They shot me and threw bottles at me,” he gritted out, breathing heavily. “It’s just my arm. I’ll be fine.”

“Fuck,” Jesse hissed, walking back from the edge of the parking lot to Hector. “They’re going southbound, man. We can catch up to them.”

When Hector didn’t respond, everyone turned to another figure, waiting for his instruction. I followed their gaze to Hawke standing in the front. His back was to me, the club’s insignia visible on his skin. I couldn’t see his face.

“Hawke,” Jesse pressed, “what do you want us to do, man?”

As if sensing me, he looked over his shoulder and caught my eye. I stiffened, waiting for him to scold me for coming when he’d told me to stay. Only…he didn’t bark at me all. Just stared for a few moments, his eyes no longer heated and wanting. No, now they were just cold, like staring into ice.

Finally, he said, “Check your bikes, see if they’re not littered with bullet holes. We’ll head out right now. Get armed. You got sixty seconds or we’re leaving without you.”

Immediately everybody scattered, hurrying to get ready. They passed me in a flurry, knocking me back a step before I straightened again and looked for him.

He’d moved to Hector and had a hand locked around the back of his neck. He leaned into him and whispered something in his face, and Hector nodded, staring at his brother with emotion flooding from his eyes. Hawke patted him on the back in a consoling move before gesturing him back to the bar. Hector moved and didn’t look at me as he walked by.

“Get back inside, Tyler,” Hawke told me, completely void of the need he’d had not even minutes ago.

I stared at him, wanting to say something, but…nothing made its way out.

So I just nodded instead and disappeared inside.

*

Gecko showed up an hour later carrying his medical bag with him. He found Hector sitting at a table in the back, his shirt off, his grizzly arm out and ready. He went to him and took a seat beside him, already grabbing at his arm to examine the damage.

The cuts were deep and messy. Hector had spent the last hour drinking heavy liquor and pulling out bits and shards of glass.

"This is going to require stitches," Gecko explained, frowning. "I need to remove the bullet and I need to clean up the site, and that'll take a while."

I took a seat beside Hector and patted his good arm. He was sweating from pain, but he hadn't complained once. Gecko used a headlight to peer at the wounds and remove the remaining glass with this tweezer looking tool. He placed every shard in a kidney dish and continued on, instructing me to get rags as he disinfected the sight.

The bullet was the toughest bit. Gecko had to prod deep, causing Hector to hiss and groan in agony.

After that, he visibly relaxed.

"I froze," he muttered sometime later, looking far off. "I fucking froze when they stood on the back of their trucks firing shots, throwing bottles. And then when it was all over, everyone wanted me to tell them what to do, and I had nothing. My head was empty."

"It's okay," I replied dumbly. What the hell else was I supposed to say?

He looked at me, and his jaw tensed. "It's not and you know it."

"Hector –"

"I fucked up."

I turned my focus on Gecko cleaning up the wound so Hector wouldn't see my expression. He was right, and I hated to admit that. But…yeah, he was fucking right.

"Every time this happens, I fuck up," he continued, clenching his teeth. "You want a debt repaid? I can handle that. You want me to balance the books? I can do that. You want me to ink your fucking skin? I'm excellent at that. But ask me to make an order, and I fucking freeze."

I held his hand and squeezed. "Stop beating yourself up, Hector."

"Don't you get it?" he snapped, looking at me hard. "I'm not good at this shit, and you want to know why? Because you can't just fucking learn it. You gotta be wired to be a leader. You gotta be tough and call the shots right there on the spot. Not get whacked by a bunch of bottles and have men terrorize the one place your club should feel the safest in."

"Nobody knew about these guys."

"You don't get it, Tyler. There will always be these kinds of guys coming around, and I should have been ready for that to happen. I've been naïve and brazen. I let everyone believe we were untouchable, and then trouble comes knocking right at our doorstep and everything goes to shit."

"Hector –"

"I let the surveillance cameras age. I don't have men keeping guard. I've got a whole fucking network of paid guys walking the streets and I never bother to use them because I don't even fucking know what to order them to do. It's not in me, so I let myself down, and then I *fuck* meaningless pussy because the release calms me!" He angrily grabbed an empty bottle and smashed on the ground, causing Gecko to pause what he was doing.

Hector closed his eyes for several moments, breathing through his nose, whispering at one point, "The Navarro family were meant to carry this club through future generations, and I'm going to be the one that fails."

It seemed to help him saying that, like it soothed him. His face cleared and the anger in him ebbed away. His breaths were long and calm, and I could do nothing but hold his hand and worry over the others.

Where were they?

Was Hawke safe?

Why had everything suddenly gone to shit? I was under the impression everything had been fine with Abram.

"Were you in bed with him?" Hector quietly asked me, out of the blue. "Is that why you were naked on the mattress and he had just his jeans on?"

I tensed, not expecting that question after his tormented words. I couldn't even look at him.

"It's alright if you were, Tyler, I'm just asking."

"No disrespect, Hector, but…I don't ask about your conquests," I replied evenly.

"I know, but Tyler, this is my brother we're talking about here."

"I know –"

"He's supposed to be dead."

"I know, Hector!"

"I'm not against it, but you're like a sister to me. Just be careful."

I stiffened a nod, grateful that was all he had to say on the matter.

"What did he say to you?" I wondered aloud, risking a glance in his direction.

Hector pursed his lips, reflecting. "He said he'd get even with the fuckers for hurting me. They could have done more damage if they'd aimed higher."

"They could have killed someone."

"Yeah."

"They drag us through the mud like we're monsters, but we don't act unless we're provoked."

"We've just been provoked, and water finds its level. Believe me, Hawke keeps his word and he delivers."

I hoped he was right.

When Gecko finished wrapping Hector's arm up, he got his money and left. Not ten minutes after that, the roar of engines sounded, stopping out front. The guys were back. Relief ran over me as they came flooding through the door, none of them looking particularly happy. The last to come through was Hawke, whose fists were painted red with blood. He didn't stop to look at anyone as he disappeared out of the room.

I looked at Jesse and mouthed, "What happened?"

Jesse shook his head and mouthed back, "You don't wanna know."

Judging by the pale look on some faces, it was best I didn't push it, but the next day I'd hear all about it on the news.

About the shooting just outside town, and five bodies burnt to a crisp inside a burning truck.

twenty-eight

Hawke

He watched the blood drip from his hands and into the sink. He stared at his raw knuckles, at the top layer of flesh gone from them.

"Nine," he murmured to himself, hollowly.

He'd just killed nine men in the span of four hours.

That was a personal record.

First, the four fuckers in the city that robbed three of Borden's businesses. They'd been big men and, worse, the sober kind. He had to tear down the door to the small apartment they'd hid out in with all of Borden's cash sitting in a neat pile on the couch.

Hawke had never been more grateful to be the size he was.

He kicked one man's head flat. Number two ended up with a knife to his heart; quick and effortless. Number three was tough, the biggest of them all, and Hawke had to go back to his roots, using every ounce of his strength to gain the upper hand in a fight that earned him a dozen strikes across the body.

Number four was the most pathetic. When he realized it was a losing battle, he'd tried to abandon the men by gathering all the cash in his arms. Hawke ended up tackling him to the ground on his way to the door and buried his head in the hundred dollar notes, thinking it appropriate the man died suffocating on the paper he had risked his life to steal.

When all was said and done, Hawke had gotten up and collapsed on the fuckers' couch. Then he sat there, with his elbows on his knees, and the strangest thing happened.

He felt fear.

Fear because if he'd failed, he wouldn't see her again.

Tyler had been on his mind every minute of every day, but never so aggressively as on that couch. Hawke was utterly disturbed by it.

And fascinated.

He tried to be rational about his growing fixation on the girl. It was just her beauty, wasn't it? He attempted to convince himself she was a gorgeous piece of eye candy, and no man goes through life without crossing a kind of beauty he'd drop everything for. Physically, she was everything he'd ever dreamed of in a woman, with just the right of meat to grip as he pounded into her.

Yeah, it was just physical.

But…fuck, it wasn't just physical, because he'd loved the sound of her voice. Loved the faces she made. Loved what she'd had to say. When she'd handed him that ointment and he'd rubbed it on that fucking tattoo, he remembered thinking, "I could hear this woman's voice all day."

It was dangerous liking a girl this hard.

He'd always known she'd be different, but never in a way that made him *want* her.

And wanting her made him paranoid.

What was she doing?

Was Jesse around her, trying to get between her legs again?

Was Hector keeping a close eye on her?

The thoughts dragged him down, until he was growling into the silence and so fucking annoyed that he was where he was, he ended up pacing the apartment and kicking one of the dead fucks just to get it out of his system.

He wanted her.

Yeah, it was good to at least be honest with himself about it, but…what did it mean to want her? Enough to *have* her?

Suddenly her words flooded through him, biting him in the ass:

What if you want me one day? And what if it's too late when you do?

The fucking girl was fifteen when she'd asked him that question, and now that he thought about it, it sounded more like a fucking threat. A threat that was causing him serious anger issues.

It was never too late. Even if she was with someone – with airhead Jesse – he'd force her to him, and the thought didn't even bother him. Nothing that was morally questionable bothered him. It was the only way he'd made it this far in life. Borden, in all his fucked-upness wasn't as far gone as Hawke was, and it was Hawke that had to carry out the tough calls when Borden lost sight of the real goal.

Hawke ended up calling Borden right there and then.

"What?" Borden barked on the other end.

"You free?"

"It's fuckin' midnight, Hawke," he retorted. "Don't you have fuckin' things to do than to call me up at fuckin' midnight?"

"I found the fucks who did the robberies."

Borden sighed. "Fuckin' hell, Hawke, we'll take care of them in the morning, alright?"

"I already took care of it."

"When?"

"Twenty minutes ago."

"Alone?"

"Yeah."

Borden muttered another curse. "You need a fuckin' life, Hawke. You keep tryin' to clean the streets like some night crawling vigilante. You tryin' to be a superhero?"

"Do superheroes murder the criminals?"

Hawke heard Emma's soft voice in the background asking Borden what was going on. "Nothing, kitten, go back to sleep," he murmured to her. Then, "Hawke, call the kills in and we'll have the guys take care of it. Anything else, you fucking psycho?"

"Yeah, I'm headin' out," Hawke said. "Going back to Norwich to handle the shipment."

"Thought that wasn't due for another three weeks."

"Yeah," was his reply.

Borden went quiet on the other end. Hawke heard him shuffling around and the sound of a door closing. Wind whipped through the phone, enough for Hawke to know Borden had gone outside.

"Is everythin' alright, brother?" he asked him, a note of concern in his tone.

"I gotta make sure she's alright," Hawke answered.

"Going soft over a girl?"

"My bottom half is sayin' hard."

Borden chuckled. "You fucking pussy."

Hawke cracked a smile.

"I saw her at the club," Borden said thoughtfully. "Very pretty girl, Hawke, but she was fucking scared shitless looking at me."

"Is that right?"

"Oh, yeah. I was pretty sure she thought I would add her to one of my mass gravesites or some shit."

"That's something Tyler would think."

"Go and see her, Hawke, but don't leave me for long, alright?"

"I didn't think we were an item, Borden."

"Fuck you," Borden retorted. "I'm being serious. You can't leave me, man. I need you in my life. We've been through hell together, huh?"

"Yeah, you fuckin' risked your neck to bust me out of prison."

"I did that for money. I didn't even fucking care if you made it at the time. I ain't talking about that. I'm talking about everything else we've been through. I owe you."

"Yeah."

"So go then and…teach your brother some fuckin' manners."

"Alright, man." Hawke rubbed his beard, thinking. "You got any new information from your sources, by the way?"

Borden paused. "It's not easy. This is a very fucking difficult world to crack into. I ain't seen something so buried in the underworld this much."

"Can you unbury it?"

"Fuck, man, you unburied my girl once upon a time, I can unbury this."

Hawke nodded, grateful. "Thanks, Borden."

"See you on the other side."

With that, Hawke had hung up and jumped on his bike and took off to Norwich. The last thing he had expected was more trouble – more *bodies*.

Were they really Abram's men? He just couldn't understand it. It wasn't Abram's style to do something so fucking stupid, but if he had…

This would mean war.

War because his stupid fucking cousin died because he was a crackhead loser.

Hawke cursed under his breath and scrubbed at the blood. He grabbed Tyler's pink soap, its fruity smell already hitting his nose, and he barked out a laugh.

A crazy fucking laugh.

He'd just killed nine men and here he was, standing in a bathroom with pink shit everywhere, washing blood away so his hands could smell like *fruit*.

And then, just like that, his laughter died and he bent over, breathing deeply with his eyes shut to keep the sick bile down his throat.

Think about it before you block it out, motherfucker.

He sucked in air, and it sat in his lungs until his chest burned. He let the air out slowly and repeated the process.

He forced himself to relive every kill, every drop of blood, every look of life bleeding out of every pair of eyes he'd taken tonight.

Adrenaline shot through him. He sucked the air in and out, until his body started to unwind and his mind had had enough, and those images drifted off to join all the others in nothingness.

Fingers ran down his back, and he opened his eyes, wondering how long he'd been bent over the sink, breathing it all out of his system. He looked up at the mirror and found Tyler standing behind him, trying to comfort him.

She met his eyes in their reflection. "Hey," she whispered, "you okay?"

No, he wanted to say.

"I'm alright, babe," he mumbled instead, feeling exhausted.

"Turn to me."

He did, very slowly. She ran her hand over his face and down his bare torso, wiping away the dried drops of blood with her fingers. It burned wherever she touched, and he watched her intently as she continued.

"Gotta wash this all off," she whispered to him.

She turned from him and started the shower. Then she turned back and began unbuckling his jeans. This was like a role reversal of the first night, *her* tending to *him*. The beautiful thing didn't realize he didn't need tending to.

This was just another day in Hawke's fucked up life.

After she pulled down the zipper, she tugged his jeans down and then froze.

Her eyes shot up at him. "Why…" she started, not finishing.

"Why what?" he pressed. "Why am I *hard*?"

She just looked at him, her cheeks reddening. "You did things tonight."

"You didn't see any of it."

"You're looking for a distraction."

He moved closer to her, dropping his head down to hers. "Maybe."

She looked at his mouth and then his eyes, breathing more heavily as she replied, "You're not thinking straight, Hawke. I don't want you to regret anything."

She was throwing his words back at him like she'd been analyzing them for days. She probably had too.

Instead of answering, he grabbed her hand and forced it to his dick. She wrapped her hand around it but didn't stroke him.

"Hawke –"

"You wanna help me right now?" he cut in, his voice hard. "Then squeeze me. Fuckin' do it, Tyler, because I'm going to lose my mind if you don't."

She must have sensed his need because she squeezed his cock and he hissed sharply, knocking his forehead to hers. "Good, fucking good, Tyler. Start movin' your hand now."

She did.

Up.

Down.

Squeezing around the head.

Repeating.

He groaned, moving his hips back and forth to control the pace.

She was fucking him with her soft little hand, and he grew harder, thicker, just staring at her watching herself pump him. Her other hand crawled up his hard abdomen, feeling his chest, running her fingers over his nipple with this drunk look in her gaze.

The girl wanted him, but he couldn't make it decent with this fog in his head.

Hawke didn't feel entirely like himself because she was right, he was seeking a distraction. He didn't want to remember burning bodies, or a face pressed against a bunch of money. He wanted Tyler, and he wanted her mouth wrapped around his dick, sucking him 'til he came on her tongue.

Spurred on with pleasure, he grabbed the back of her neck and forced her face to his. Then he kissed that sweet mouth, already parting her lips with his tongue to taste her. She moaned lightly, gripping his cock harder. He groaned back, his other hand grabbing at her tit, squeezing it through her top. She was so fucking sexy, it was killing him with need to be inside her, feeling her walls wrapped around his cock.

"Fuck, Tyler, you are perfect. Can't get you outta my head…"

He saw how fast she was breathing, saw the way she licked her lips when she stared at his cock. He would have easily come, but…fuck, he was too weak to deny her.

It would be wrong to fuck her.

He knew that.

She would hate him later.

He was certain of that.

But… he wanted her something fierce. When he grabbed at her top and tore it off, everything – all the bullshit of tonight, the guilt of the past – ebbed away into the background.

He wanted her.

She wanted him.

That was all that mattered.

The rest was a train wreck for another day.

The second her top was off, he closed his mouth around her nipple and sucked hard. She squirmed beneath him, sucking air sharply at the sensation. She was so sensitive, he could blow on them and she'd come.

"Take your shorts off," he told her, panting.

She stripped immediately, obedient and eager. He pulled his jeans down and stepped out of them. She was naked and he couldn't stop his eyes from taking all of her in. He moved back to her, and when he kissed her, it was rougher, more carnal than before. His hand moved between her legs, touching at her clit, slowly rubbing circles until she could hardly kiss him back from the pleasure.

Hawke tried his hardest to maintain the slowness, to not be rough in the way he wanted, and for a few short moments he concentrated on her pleasure, on the way she arched her back as he sucked at her perfect tits.

And then…

He saw lifeless eyes, and blood…

So much fucking blood.

Nine. Human Beings.

Monster.

Monster.

Mon...

His heart came up to his throat, and he swallowed the heavy lump. It sank straight to that motherfucking cinderblock in his ribcage.

"Turn around," he said hoarsely, unable to keep the ache from his voice.

He helped turn her around before she could see the look on his face.

Vulnerability was for the weak.

It was an emotion that didn't suit him.

He just wanted to fuck, not feel like a man trying to run away from his past.

He should have stopped for real. He should not have put his arm around her, or let his hand slide back to that beautiful bare pussy of hers. He should not have pressed down harder, causing her to buck her ass out to rub against his cock.

But he did.

He centered his cock at her entrance and he wanted to enter her. His entire body broke in tremors, primed for it, but…

He'd be using her.

Hawke didn't want to use her. He'd never forgive himself.

He spun her back around, her wide eyes meeting his.

"Your hand," he gritted out, deprived of her tight pussy. "Just your hand, Tyler."

Without waiting, her hand wrapped around his cock again, and she pumped him like before, this time her eyes on his, studying him. He wondered if she saw it: his raw desperation to escape, to forget, to *feel*. Her other hand went to his face and stroked him gently.

He kissed her again, but it wasn't out of anger. The adrenaline was strong, but it was contained too. Tyler made it bearable.

Her tongue sucked at his bottom lip as he tugged hard at her puckered nipple, rolling it between his fingers. He felt hot everywhere and tight…so fucking tight, he could barely move his muscles. He stopped breathing and…

He came.

Hard.

All over her hand, and she still squeezed and thrust his length as he shuddered through the pleasure.

Only…it wasn't all pleasure.

It was disgust too.

With himself, and what his hands were capable of.

Even his groan sounded tormented, and she was looking at him like she knew. He couldn't look back. He moved his face to the side and sucked in air. His chest hadn't felt this light in a while, and his head…oh, thank fuck, his head was clearing.

It was a temporary respite, he knew that. But it was better than feeling like a snake had coiled itself around his heart and squeezed.

"I'm sticky," he heard her say.

He looked at her, and she was flaring her nostrils at her hand coated in his come. It was fucking hot, he had to admit.

"If you were mine, I'd tell you to lick that up," he said, half-serious, half-amused.

Ty smiled and rubbed her hand against his torso. "Here, take it all back. When you decide I'm yours, I'll take it down my throat."

You're already mine.

He took her hand and gave it a soft kiss, looking at her solemnly as he spoke. "Thank you."

"For what?"

"For taking care of me. Distracting me."

She looked down at the floor. "Sure."

He ran his hand up her neck. "What's wrong?"

She pursed her lips. "If it was anyone else standing here, would you have told them to do the same thing? Like Shay, or Holly, or the whores that come walking—"

He cut her off with another kiss. "Shut up, Ty. I told *you* to do it. Not anyone else."

She stiffened a nod, saying nothing else. He led her inside the shower, and it was a fucking miserable one because it'd been on for-fucking-ever and the hot water was nearly depleted. But he got to clean her, and it made him oddly satisfied.

Any man would give his left testicle just to touch her, much less rub his come off her flushed skin.

He knew she was still wanting. He saw her thighs tremble every time he neared, so he brought her to his chest as the spray soaked through them, and he rubbed her to orgasm. She cried and her knees buckled, and he caught her against him, sucking at that beautiful little spot between her neck and shoulder.

Afterwards, he carried her to bed sopping wet and she curled against him. With half her face pressed against his chest, she fell asleep within minutes.

Hawke wasn't so fortunate.

twenty-nine

Tyler

Hawke was still in bed with me when I woke up the next morning. I felt his fingers running down my bare spine. I could hear his strong heartbeats through his chest, and it relaxed me.

"Are you leaving me?" I pushed out, my throat feeling closed at the thought of him going again.

"No," he replied softly.

I relaxed and ran my hand across his vast chest, unable to resist touching him. His skin was smooth, his abs hard. I took his other hand into mine and kissed along it. I felt him stilling beneath me and his other hand stopped moving.

"What's wrong?" I asked.

"It's my bad hand, babe," he answered indiscernibly.

"Then your bad hand deserves more kisses." I kissed it again, this time over the fleshy scars, his abs tensing as he lifted his head to watch me.

After a few more kisses, he bunched my hair into his hand and pulled me up to him, capturing my mouth against his. He kissed me for a long time, languidly exploring my mouth, coaxing my tongue against his. He worked me so well, and he knew it.

"Is it like this for long?" I asked him after he pulled away and my face was level with his.

"Like what?"

"Is it this good? Or does it dull with time?"

He looked at me for a few moments, his tender eyes moving over me. "I don't think it could ever get dull taking you. You're stunning, Tyler, and your personality shines."

I stifled a laugh. "My personality?"

"I love it."

"Mr Hawke the biker liking me for my personality? No one will buy this."

He smirked. "It's not just your personality."

"No?"

"You've got a big ass, that has something to do with it, and your tits are so fucking beautiful, I imagine coming on them at least a dozen times a day."

"Charming."

"I can be."

"They're small, though."

"They're perfect."

My face flushed. "Stop it, you're making me blush."

"I know, and it makes you look deceptively innocent."

My brows shot up. "Deceptively?"

"Mm," he groaned, that smirk still strong. "You've got that girl next door face, but you've seen everything under the sun. Learned about sex when you were a preteen, I'm guessing?"

I giggled, and the sound was so foreign coming out of me. "Try ten."

"No."

"Yeah."

He groaned, this time in dismay. "How?"

"You don't want to know that one."

"Give me a hint."

"Something to do with hiding in closets."

He laughed deep in his chest, the rich sound escaping his lips. "Fuckin' hell, Tyler, why the fuck have we kept you around so long? I don't get it. So many guys have kids, and they've never stepped foot in here."

"I'm different."

"Yeah?"

"Yeah."

He searched my eyes, that content smile reaching them as he agreed on a breath. "Yeah."

Feeling warmer than ever, I nuzzled into him, kissing him slowly. My hand roamed his chest, never getting tired of the bruises and marks along his skin. I could feel his heart beating furiously beneath the palm of my hand as I dipped my tongue against his.

"You think this will get old with you?" he suddenly whispered, his voice masked as he studied me.

My fingertips grazed his happy trail and softly brushed along his length, which was already halfway erect. Looking back at him seriously, my eyes bright, my smile real, I replied, "No way."

Hawke appeared startlingly vulnerable right then and there, swallowing thickly in his throat as he nodded at my response. Then he grabbed my legs and situated me over top of him, breasts against his chest, legs on either side of him. Both hands travelled down my back, gripping at my bare ass and grinding me against him. He was hard already, the ridge of his cock brushing against my clit. I moaned in his mouth, wet and needy.

"You are ridiculously responsive," he murmured.

"Only because of you."

He pulled away, breathing heatedly into my mouth. "You want me, Tyler?"

I nodded.

"Sit right up."

I did. He grabbed his cock with one hand and gripped my hip, situating me over him. His eyes moved up and down my naked body, tongue sliding along his bottom lip as he brought me down on top of him.

"Holy shit," he groaned, watching himself enter me. "Now that's a fucking beautiful sight, Ty."

I stretched around him, and this time his invasion was beyond familiar. He kept me pinned on top of him like that, filling me and not moving. I liked that he did this again, getting me used to his size instead of just bulldozing his way inside of me.

He teased my nipples, staring up at me with this lazy grin. "Not wonderin' if I'm inside you?"

I smiled back. "Fuck no, I feel you everywhere, Hawke. I'll know where you've been hours from now."

"Sore from my cock hours from now? I'm really liking the sound of that."

His cock pulsed inside of me, proving just how much he liked the sound of that.

He rubbed at my clit as I began to move, causing me to moan at the flutter of pleasure he brought on. His calloused hands glided up my body, feeling every inch of me with this stark look of awe in his eyes.

He made me feel so beautiful.

He let me work him, in and out slowly. It was remarkable how full I felt, like he was touching every nerve inside of me, rubbing it so tingles built. I wanted it harder as I went. I slammed down on him, seeking that explosive jolt of pleasure he'd later tell me was my g-spot. I threw my head back and he sat up, taking my nipple in to his mouth and thrusting inside me in such a perfect angle, rubbing along that spot…

"You're tightening," he whispered, sucking fiercely at my skin. "Fuck me, Tyler."

Wrapping my arms around his neck, I rocked into him, every inch of me burning. I whimpered and came, chanting his name like I chanted it last night. I felt his mouth at my neck, licking, his teeth scraping against my bare flesh, hard enough to leave marks.

"So good," he groaned breathlessly, moving into me one last time before he came, his head buried between my neck and shoulder.

He flopped back down on his back, taking me with him. Still half-erect inside me, he ran his hand up and down my back as we caught our breaths. God, I could do that every day. Every hour of every day.

Hawke made my chest full and yet ache at the same time. I wondered if I was the same for him. Judging by the way he looked at me, I was inclined to think I was.

"What are you going to do about Abram?" I asked sometime later, tracing circles along his pecs.

He sighed. "I don't know yet, babe."

"Did he really send those guys?"

"It looks like it, but…fuck, I never took him for an idiot."

I frowned. "If this is all to avenge his stupid cousin, I'd say there's something else, something you don't know about."

Hawke went quiet, and then he murmured, "Maybe."

Hawke

He lied.

If Abram was behind this, he knew exactly what he wanted.

Tyler.

thirty

Tyler

I had dozed back to sleep, and when I woke up, Hawke was gone. I showered quickly and changed before going downstairs and into the bar area, searching for him. Music was on in the background. Marshall, Shay and Holly were tending to the mess and Jesse was already installing new windows. Hawke, Hector and Gus were nowhere to be seen.

"Where are they?" I'd asked Marshall.

"After last night's shit-fest, they're in the meeting room to sort the mess out," he answered, distractedly.

"Oh. Do you know how long they'll be?"

"No idea."

"Not allowed to go in either?"

"They were all in a shit mood, Ty. I wouldn't step foot anywhere near that room. They're trying to get ahold of Abram, and it's not going so well right now."

Shit. Things were going to get ugly.

All because of Yuri.

Yuri!

How stupid was that?!

I couldn't help but feel responsible. If I'd just gone to my room that night, none of this would have happened. I felt a pang in my chest.

I looked around glumly. "Do you need any help?"

"Yeah, help us with the glass, honey."

Happy not to think, I grabbed another hand broom and dustpan and kneeled down, piling up all the loose pieces of glass. Holly found her way next to me.

"Was it bad?" she asked me quietly.

"It could have been worse," I replied.

"I heard Hector got hurt, but I didn't get to see how bad." Her voice was neutral, but I caught the curiosity in her expression.

I nodded. "He'll be alright, though."

After we cleaned the surface and floor of glass, I was safe to turn on all the fans around the room. It was horribly hot and my hair was sticking to my skin. Jesse wasn't doing too well in the heat either. He stripped down to his boxers, throwing his suit neatly over a chair. Holly nudged me and gestured to him with a huge smile. "He's pretty easy on the eyes, huh?" she said.

I faintly smiled back. "Why don't you keep him company?"

Her eyes widened. "Oh, hell no. Jesse's been a dick to me ever since…" she paused, her face falling.

I waited for her to say more. "Ever since what?"

"Less talk and more cleaning, bitches!" Shay yelled over the music, giving us a pointed look.

Holly rolled her eyes and moved away, and then Shay proceeded to take her spot saying, "Hector's going to need an Advil when he gets back."

"Thanks for letting me know," I sarcastically replied.

"He's in a lot of pain. I might take him up some breakfast. He'll like that too, right?"

I stood straighter, giving her a look. "Didn't you just say less talk and more cleaning?"

She gestured to Holly. "I was talking to that little hooker over there. Look at her, she's giving me evil eyes."

Holly hadn't even glanced at her. "She's not doing anything, Shay."

Shay scoffed and looked me over. "Thought you were on my side, Ty-ger."

I groaned.

She smiled. "See what I did there? Ty-*ger*."

"Yeah, yeah, I see what you did there."

"Smart, huh?"

"Oh yeah, totally ingenious."

She looked real chuffed and I abruptly left her, making an excuse that I needed to give Jesse some water, and I really did just so that my excuse seemed legit. He set his measuring tool down and took the bottle, gulping most of the thing down, and then proceeding to throw the rest of the water of his face. From my peripheral, I saw Holly sigh longingly and I bit back a grin.

"Do you need any help?" I asked him.

He smirked, looking me over. "Oh, yeah."

"What do you want me to do?"

"Sit on my face."

"Cut it out, Jesse," I said, irritated. "I'm not in the mood."

"Oh, shit, you're glum," he replied caringly. "What's wrong, sweets?"

"Nothing."

"Nothing?" He dropped his head to my level. "It doesn't look like nothing. In fact…I think you need a bit of cheering up, sweetness."

"Nah, Jesse, don't even bother. I don't want a pity party, or you telling me how hard and big you are or any of those things you constitute as cheering me up."

"I'm not gonna talk about my cock, Ty. Unless you want me to."

"Jesse, stop."

"What's this about then?"

"I'm upset because this whole fucking drama with Abram is my fault."

Jesse shot me a perplexed look. "How is it your fault?"

"Because Yuri wanted me, and he might not have asked for me if I wasn't around."

"That's stupid, Ty. I thought you were smarter than that. Yuri was a fucking asshole, and none of this is your fault. Now I *know* I have to cheer you up."

"Don't, Jesse."

Ignoring me, he looked up at the girls and said, "Put something more decent on! I gotta cheer up rainbow kitten over here."

"Metallica?" Shay excitedly asked, already leafing through CDs next to the stereo.

"No, not fuckin' Metallica," he retorted in disgust. "I mean, how the fuck is Metallica cheerful?"

"It was a suggestion."

"It was a terrible fucking suggestion, Shay. What's wrong with you?"

Shay's face fell. "Too many people ask me that question," she said brokenly.

"Aw, no. Really?"

"Yeah."

"Well, I don't give a fuck, Shay. I'm trying to cheer *Tyler* up, not you. I don't give a fuck about how you're feeling. Now I want something fun on. Something I can dance to. I got mad skills, ladies. I am a beast in need of some tunes."

Holly was already pressing buttons and looking for a particular song. Then she stopped and gave us a thumbs up and the beats flooded in.

Uptown Funk.

"That's what I'm talking about," Jesse shouted before he ran a finger down my face. "Let's turn that frown upside down, muffin."

At first, it didn't seem like he was doing anything. I looked at him confusedly before I saw it…or rather, *felt* it. My eyes dropped down to his body moving, his pelvic thrusting to the beat of the song. At the same time, he started snapping his fingers.

"Oh, my god," I muttered, already looking away. "Really, Jesse?"

Jesse swiftly moved back into my line of sight and got into his dance mode, busting moves so smooth it looked like he'd rehearsed them. They were also ridiculously sexy.

Especially when he swayed his hips and sang to the song, moving to me with his half-naked glistening body.

Oh, god.

His eyes turned crazy and he pulled a few ridiculous facial expressions and I couldn't resist laughing at the serious look on his face. This guy was crazy. I shoved his chest back as he neared and that only seemed to encourage him. He spun around me, gripping a chunk of my hair at one point to lip sync in my ear.

"I wanna funk *you* up," he growled.

I pushed him away again and this time he turned around and bent over, twerking to perfection, his ass against my stomach. I covered my face in embarrassment and exploded with laughter until my ribs ached.

"Oh, my God, you're insane," I yelled at him.

He stood back up, running his hands down his tattooed body sensually before he took me by the hand and pulled me to him. Still lip syncing. Still with that serious diva look on his face. I was red with laughter, surprised even that my own body was starting to rock with the beat. The fucker was infectious, and he just made me forget *everything*.

"Now that's a smile!" he cheered, gripping me around the hips.

He was right.

He'd cheered me the fuck up.

Unbelievable.

I hugged him, even while he continued to practically hump me, I kept my arms wrapped around his neck, thanking him. He stopped and hugged me back too, kissing me on the neck before he pulled away and migrated his sensuous dance moves to Holly and Shay.

The girls melted right into him.

*

The guys stepped out of the room after an hour. By then, the bar room was almost back to normal, but Jesse was still working on the windows. I was standing next to him, laughing at the way he occasionally bucked his hips to the music in the background, when they came through the door.

Hector looked like shit, Gus was angry, and Hawke was…well, Hawke. He moved into the room, catching sight of me quickly before shifting his gaze to Jesse and how close he was to me, still bucking his hips, still sweating in nothing but his boxers.

"Distance," he said to me sternly on his way to the table in the far back. He collapsed into it and Holly quickly stopped by to give him a beer.

"Hector, baby," Shay cooed loudly, wrapping her arms around Hector as he sat on the stool, "I got you Advil. You want Advil?"

Hector forcefully removed her arms and pushed her back. "Stop."

"But I stopped by at the pharmacy. Wait and I'll grab a couple tablets –"

"Fuck sake, Shay, I need some fucking room to breathe without you breathing down my FUCKING NECK!"

Whoa, whoa, whoa.

Shay dropped her arms to her side, looking startled and bug-eyed. Honestly, I wanted her to slap him for hollering at her because, no matter how ridiculously obsessed she was with him, she was just trying to help.

Instead, she nodded profusely and replied, "No worries, baby. You're sore and need room to breathe."

Girl had no spine for him.

I cringed and Holly shot me a wide-eyed look, concealing her smile as she moved to serve Gus who had just dropped into the chair next to Hawke.

"Anyone making any food?" Gus asked, looking over at me. "Some eggs and bacon, maybe? Think there's something in the fridge you ladies can cook up. Anyone? Tyler?"

I nodded heartily. "Oh, yeah, just change my name to Doormat and I'd be happy to assist."

Jesse and Holly laughed, and Gus glowered. "That fuckin' tongue on you Tyler is too much sometimes."

"Shall I censor myself around you, Gus?"

"I'm being fucking serious. Cut it the fuck out. We're fucking tired. We got a war on the horizon with a fucking lunatic who wants to possibly put the club into the ground, and now it's your fucking attitude. Soon, we'll have those self-entitled fucking cockroaches asking for more money, and it'll be more money out the fucking door! Like we're made of it, huh?!" He slammed the table down with his fist.

Nobody laughed anymore.

"I'll cook up something, Gus," Holly told him sweetly, hurrying to the back of the bar with Shay following. I was pretty certain they'd have agreed to clean the toilets with a toothbrush so long as they were away from him.

With the sudden tension in the air, the anger in Gus, and Hawke's unreadable expression, I found myself moving back to Jesse for comfort.

"What did I say about distance?" Hawke said suddenly.

"Well, you just said the word *distance*…" I faintly replied, blinking at the wall over his head. "That can be interpreted in many ways."

He didn't look impressed, and now I was a little annoyed by this whole set-up. Was it Attack Tyler day?

"I think I'll uh…head out back with the girls."

I made to move when Hawke sounded out, "Tyler, come here."

My face was flushed with anger as I started moving to him, glancing between him and Gus, trying to figure out what the hell was going on.

I stopped in front of him and waited.

"None of this is your fault," he told me softly. "We're just pissed and Gus is spitting shit he doesn't mean."

My shoulders relaxed. "What happened?"

"With Abram not responding to our calls, it appears he's probably responsible for last night. On top of that, we have to prepare in case of another attack, which means spending money we don't really have to improve the security on this place and the warehouse if he's gunning for it next. On top of that, the cockroaches will try and want more money. Enough to bleed us half-dry."

I looked over at Hector, and he had buried his head into his arms, not moving.

"So," I drawled out slowly, "how are you going to sort out the cockroaches?"

Hawke took my arm and brought me closer to him. The gesture shot straight through my heart.

"Things might get ugly, babe."

The bar stool suddenly screeched loudly as Hector slid off it, kicking it hard behind him. It fell over, and he bent down and stood it up, only to kick it hard again and watch it fall back down. Then, still not content with the kicking, he grabbed it again and smashed it repeatedly against the edge of the bar, until it cracked and the seat flew everywhere. By the end, it was a pile of wood, and he stood by it, glaring down at it like it'd somehow insulted him.

"Cool it," Gus told him.

"This is fucking stupid," Hector growled, looking up at them. "Wish you'd just fuckin' say it already! I'm a fuck-up. I fucked THIS up. Just fucking say it."

Nobody said anything.

He clenched his teeth. "Fuck it, huh? I did this. I'm done, man! I'm fucking done with this shit. Just…fuck it."

He stormed out of the room, knocking Marshall's shoulder with his, while I stared at the infinite pieces of stool scattered on the floor.

"Holy shit," Jesse muttered under his breath, drawing my attention. "Some morning then, huh? Hector's fucking unhinged. Looks like he needs a sterilizer to put him down for a while."

Gus exhaled. "He's beating himself up about it. Hector's spiraling and self-destructing. It'd be best we just give him some space. But we gotta figure out what to do. We need to make more money, Hawke. If you know a way…" his words trailed off.

Hawke didn't respond. He looked far off in thought, his face unreadable.

The plotting man was back.

I felt like I was thirteen again, watching the wheels spin in his head. His eyes met mine, and he understood my expression, understood what I wasn't saying out loud.

This was a giant mess, and we needed him.

His jaw tensed and he let out a slow breath. Then he pulled me to him and I collapsed in his lap, his arms wrapped around me. He kissed the back of my head, uncaring that the guys were all looking at us with surprise.

Hawke was marking me.

"Well, shit, Gus was right," Jesse said moments later, his voice low as he looked out the window, scowling. "Cockroaches are here, guys. One car pulling up right now, and that ugly ringleader Duggard is stepping out. What do you wanna do?"

Unconcerned, Hawke's hands ran down my arms, and I felt his mouth at my ear and him whisper one single word that made my breath catch in my throat. "Okay."

Then he slid me off his lap and stood up, marching straight for the door. "Grab your guns, boys," he ordered. "We're holding our ground."

"What are you gonna do?" Jesse repeated, alarmed this time as Gus and Marshall withdrew their guns.

Hawke grabbed a large bottle of rum and a lighter where Hector had sat and growled, "I'm going to take care of this once and for all."

thirty-one

Tyler

Duggard barely made it to the door when Hawke slammed it open and stormed out. The guys followed after him. I stood by the window staring out, unsure of what to expect.

Duggard stopped in his steps when he took Hawke in, looking perplexed at the sight of him, before he started saying, "I'm looking for Hector –"

"No!" Hawke roared, grabbing him by the neck and shoving him back so hard he fell to the ground. "You're looking for more money, and you ain't getting it."

Duggard tried to scramble away unsuccessfully. "You're asking us to cover up five dead bodies!" he shakily hollered. "That's a big job, and it's going to cost more –"

Before Duggard could continue, Hawke pressed his boot on his chest, popped the bottle open and poured it over the officer's uniform. Another cop stepped out of the car, not nearing the site, but raising his arms and shouting, "What are you doing? Leave him alone! We were just here to negotiate –"

"No negotiations!" Hawke shouted, his face turning grave as he added more weight on Duggard's chest and pointed at the other cockroach. "You've been orderin' us around, taking advantage of our fucking hospitality, and you wanna know something, you sick little fucks? We got years of tapes with you assholes tryin' to squeeze more coin out of our pockets. It's a two-way fuckin' street now, you fuckin' maggots. You sell us out, and you'll be sharin' jail cells with us, and we ain't gonna be so nice anymore."

"It's just business!"

"It's robbery!"

The cockroach agreed, shouting that he was right and that they wouldn't ask for more. But Hawke was hearing none of it. He continued pouring the rest of the rum over Duggard's body as he writhed beneath him.

"No," Hawke said, a dark edge to his voice, "you won't agree until there's been some damage involved. That's what you fucks are like. You push and FUCKING PUSH!"

Then he bent down and flipped open the lighter. Duggard's uniform immediately caught on fire and he screamed hysterically as Hawke stepped off him and returned to the clubhouse, throwing the lighter on the bar.

I gaped at him in shock and he looked back at me with an eerie look of determination.

"You said you wanted me back," he started, his voice deep and slow, "this is what it's going to take, babe. Don't say I didn't warn you."

*

Duggard was fine. He'd thrown his clothes off with the help of his partner and then stumbled back to the car. They took off out of there and Warlord territory had been silent and still ever since.

Everyone knew what Hawke had done.

He'd sparked *fear*.

And fear, he taught me, meant power.

It'd rubbed off on me, that fear. I was back to being startled by him and what he was capable of. Not that he would ever do something to hurt me, I knew, but still. The guy was willing to take it as far as possible, something Hector hadn't the balls to do.

"I told you it would come to this," Hawke had told me solemnly. "I've gotta do bad things to get back on top, Tyler. That's just the way it has to be."

"For how long?" I'd asked.

"However long it takes."

Hawke didn't stop there with Duggard. Him and the guys rode out the next day and paid the cockroach and others another visit, this time to renegotiate on their deal. It'd crept up over the years, and they'd made a killing covering for the club, and Hawke was displeased.

I didn't know what he did to them, but the guys came back looking a little green, meanwhile Hawke was stone-faced per usual.

What he was doing worked, and the cockroaches settled on the deal, probably by force than anything.

The news now was that the five "drunken" assholes (all conveniently had a criminal history for being violent losers) had been killed over a car robbery. I did a face palm the second I heard about it. A car robbery that resulted in five deaths and a burning vehicle? Did these corrupt coppers even *try* anymore? But they buried it; total media blackout on the crimes, and after a couple weeks it was forgotten news.

Oh those murders? Yeah, just a bunch of violent SOBs trying to act tough and ended up getting their heads blown apart! No big deal.

Hawke's warning on that car ride whipped through me over and over again, and I'd barely paid attention to it until now.

"I don't think you realize, Ty, what I would become if I went back to that," he'd said. "You wouldn't like me as president this time around."

"Why?"

"I'd have to be unforgiving and do things – violent things so others wouldn't cross us."

"I understand."

"No…you don't."

He was right. I hadn't understood.

Everything swiftly changed after that event.

The club changed.

I changed.

Hawke had taken back his cut, and Norwich had become the wild west again.

thirty-two

Tyler

Hawke wouldn't stop touching me.

I couldn't stop coming.

I whimpered as he sucked at my clit and I exploded around him, tugging sharply at his hair bunched in my fists. My whole body quaked.

His kisses travelled up my belly, over my breasts and back over my raw mouth. They were swollen, and bitten, and now they were numb as he roughly ravaged them.

Hawke situated himself between my legs and took me again, his moves slow, his exhaustion apparent as he thrust in and out of me.

They were lazy thrusts, though his cock was still somehow hard as ever after six hours of off and on again fucking throughout the night. He'd come three times. I'd come…countless.

He grunted things.

Said I was beautiful.

Said I made him feel whole.

I realized he wasn't even aware he was saying them.

It was like he was fucking himself to death, ridding some kind of darkness because he felt good inside me. Maybe I made the bad disappear.

All I knew was that this was a cycle I would come to be familiar with. Every time he did something bad – in this case, setting a man on fire and paying those guys a visit that had half the club looking queasy – he *needed* to be inside of me.

My life would be centered around this truth for months to come as he righted the club and made his presence known in town.

His slick body moved against me, the scent of our sex thick and inescapable. I didn't know how he managed to do it time and time again, but I found myself thrashing beneath him, whimpering uncontrollably as he drew another orgasm out of me. Hawke loved the sounds, loved the way I tightened around him, because he'd growl deep in his throat and fuck me harder, pounding into me, that damn headboard banging so loud against the walls.

Then he came, flooding me with more of his come.

My eyes were heavy, my mouth dry and open, sucking in breaths, my sight blurry as I watched the sun's rays creeping into the room.

*

I wasn't allowed to go to work during the week following the incidents. Hawke was adamant I stay put because whoever was behind the attacks was still out there. I needed to be kept an eye on until it was resolved, and I didn't know how long that would take, but I wasn't going to be dumb enough to go against his orders.

This was what came with the territory being here. I'd accepted that ages ago.

The morning after the cops ran off was wrought with tension. Most of the guys had conglomerated in the meeting room, making calls.

One of them was to Abram, and I'd heard his shouting from outside the room.

"Why the fuck would I have sent men to your place, you stupid fucking dimwits!!" he'd screamed, his anger startling Holly even twenty feet from the room. "If I wanted you all dead, you'd be dead! I wouldn't pussy around and shoot up your fucking rat's nest! This is an insult. You're insulting me with your fucking ignorance! Don't you dare accuse me of this shit anymore, or I'll actually fuckin' do something this time!"

Well then.

Hawke came out looking thoughtful, while Gus was pissed, mouthing Abram off about being a liar.

"He didn't do it," Hawke simply told him, shutting him up.

Clearly disagreeing, Gus's face turned red with anger. "He did do it, Hawke, and the proper thing to do is go over that cunt's place and teach him a fucking lesson."

Jonny and Marshall seemed to agree, nodding their heads, but Hawke didn't respond to that. He sat down in the far back of the room, wheels spinning in his head. Then he shifted his gaze to me, and something about his expression unsettled me.

Something was wrong.

I felt it deep inside of me.

There was something he wasn't telling me.

thirty-three

Hawke

It'd been a week since the five deaths and four days since the cockroaches ran with their tails between their legs when Borden sent Hawke a message.

You're not coming back, are you?

Hawke stared at the message and didn't respond. Everything had happened so suddenly. He'd felt like his life had been split down the middle, and he had to make a choice: Borden, or his club.

He chose neither.

At the end, it came down to Tyler. He wanted her in his bed fiercely. She made him feel, and not just one thing in particular, but a whole range of emotions he hadn't even remembered he could feel.

Plus, he did miss the club life. He could clean this place up, kick the losers out and bring the loyalty back in. He'd ban drugs from entering the place, and there'd be fucking cameras everywhere, followed by structure – dear god, this place needed fucking structure unlike anything he'd ever seen before.

He'd show everyone there was more to this life than partying and drinking and fucking.

The thought gave him purpose.

"I feel like the weight of the world is off my chest," Hector had said after he learned his brother was taking back his cut. He'd approached him in the meeting room. Hawke had been sitting alone at the head of the mahogany table, flipping through the books, looking over the club's income.

He looked up at Hector setting his cut down in front of him; he was returning it to its rightful owner, but Hawke didn't glimpse at it once. His focus was on his little brother.

Hector swallowed roughly and looked back at him. He was sober today, and he looked like fucking shit, but that was a good thing, Hawke supposed. You had to feel like shit before you got better.

"I never wanted the title," Hector quietly told him, staring down at his cut up arm. "I know what they've been saying for years now. The rumors that I sold you out or some shit, and it didn't help I've been an egotistical dick, flaunting it in front of you, but that wasn't because I stole it or anything, it was because I tried to be better than you when I know I'm not. I'll never be.

"But fucking hell, Hawke, I would never have handed over that video. I never wanted you to go away just so I had this stupid strip of leather on my back. I searched for the culprit for years, and never found him. It ain't proof, I know, but…it's my word."

Hawke set the books down on the table. "Why are you telling me this right now, Hector?"

"Because it's been sitting in my head for years now, and I guess part of me wanted you to think I was ruthless enough to do that to you just so you thought I had a spine."

"I never for one second believed it," Hawke replied solemnly. "You got too much love for me, though you won't admit it."

Hector grimaced. "Yeah, well, I've left you in a shitty position right now. Not much love in that."

"The situation ain't so bad."

"We're being bled dry." Hector gestured to the books. "At this rate, we won't have much to sustain us for long."

Hawke shook his head slowly. "That's not true."

"What do you mean?"

"Tyler."

Hector went still and he let out a long breath before he grabbed the chair next to him and sat down. "I thought that wasn't going to happen," he said, confused.

"She'll be twenty-one in a week."

"But she doesn't fucking know and we don't even know how we're going to get ahold of that account."

"Borden's working on it."

Hector shook his head, letting out a long breath. "We can't tell her the truth, Hawke, it'll break her heart."

"What am I supposed to do?"

"Lie. Make it sound less brutal."

"Can't lie anymore, Hector."

"Then she won't look at you the same. She will fucking loathe you, man."

Hawke raked his teeth over his bottom lip, suppressing the panic in his chest. What other choice did he have? He wanted her, but he didn't want secrets.

"Then she'll hate me," he said, his voice deadening. "But she's mine, and I ain't letting her go. A Navarro takes what he wants, and I want Tyler, no matter what happens."

Then he grabbed his phone and responded to Borden.

No, I'm not coming back.

*

They armed the clubhouse and set cameras with men on surveillance 24/7. There hadn't been an attack since, and no word on the streets about who was responsible, though Hawke was bleeding dry every contact he had out there, hoping for some kind of lead because it just didn't make sense for it to be Abram.

It took Hawke a few days to gather up his thoughts and tell Tyler. This was fucking dreadful because the morning was beautiful and she was sleeping peacefully in bed, her ass in direct view of him.

How many times had he fucked her?

Too many times.

His dick wasn't tired of it either.

The world seemed to fade away when he was entwined in her. It was the perfect salve to keeping that monster within him at bay.

But he hadn't touched her since his talk with Hector. He kept his distance, feeling guilty that he'd even touched her in the first place. It felt like the ultimate betrayal.

He didn't know how it happened or what possessed him to do it, but he ended up standing in front of the mirror, chopping off his beard. Fucking hell, what a goddamn mess it was. He didn't shave it off, but he trimmed it so that it was an inch past his cheeks. Then he tied his hair back and returned to the bed, shaking her awake.

"Hey," he whispered, unable to resist stroking that beautiful face.

Tyler slowly opened her eyes, blinking several times and then stilling when she looked at him. There was shock, but mostly confusion, like she didn't know who she was looking at.

"Hawke?" she muttered in disbelief.

He cracked a smile. "You look beautiful all confused and shit."

"And you look like Khal Drogo but without the eyeliner," she replied, her hand already running over his face.

"Is that another one of your literary heroes?"

She choked on a laugh. "Yeah, sure."

"I thought I needed a trim."

"A trim? God, Hawke, I can see so much of you. I just…wow."

He loved the way her chest rose and fell faster as she looked him over. That fucking look; God, it would never get old, would it?

He grabbed her hand and brought it to his mouth, resting a soft kiss in her palm before saying, "Thought we could go on a ride. I want you on the back of my bike, Tyler. Want it bad."

Her cheeks reddened, and she smiled brilliantly at him. "I want that too."

He tried to smile back, but that cinderblock sitting in his ribcage twisted from within, causing him to stiffen and look away.

"I'll be downstairs waiting for you," he told her, setting her hand down at her side.

Then Hawke got up and walked out, unable to shake the feeling of absolute dread.

Tyler was going to fucking shatter in a matter of hours.

thirty-four

Hawke

Fuck, why did she have to look particularly sexy this morning?

He groaned to himself, knocking his head back so he was staring at the sky instead of the girl who'd just come out of the clubhouse in nothing but tiny jean shorts and a tight white tank.

Then there was that smile, so fucking blindingly angelic.

Could he do it?

Maybe there was another way to fix the club up.

Hawke's doubts began to mount within him, especially as she threw the helmet over her head and climbed on the back of his bike, wrapping those slender arms around his front. He held her hand for a few moments, squeezing it tight before he let it go. Then he turned the bike on and edged out of the parking lot, taking off down the road.

Tyler's body felt good around him, her thighs squeezing around his hips, her head against his back as he cut through the streets and went far – very far.

He couldn't have witnesses.

He needed total isolation.

He had to tell her.

There was no other way.

*

They stopped for breakfast at a nice little place. Hawke spent the entire time taking in his surroundings, eyeing everyone that came in and out of the place. He couldn't let his guard down, not for a minute.

"You should get yourself a strawberry milkshake," she told him after they'd eaten. "You used to have those all the time."

He cracked a smile. "I have one every now and again."

"Yeah, and you end up looking like a grizzly bear eating berries."

He didn't end up getting a milkshake, but she did, and she did that stupid fucking thing of taking her camera out and taking pictures of the thing. He didn't get why people did this, but Tyler looked fucking cute, so what did it matter?

Hawke watched her demolish it, and his chest went all tight and shit. Was this what it was like with Borden? He wondered. Did he just...*know* the girl was it for him because of these ridiculous fucking heart clenches?

Or did he just have a fucking heart disease or some shit?

Yeah, more like Tyler's Golden Pussy Disease.

She caught him staring at her, and she smiled at him shyly before saying, "You're giving me that look, Hawke."

Hawke's gaze warmed. "I have a look?"

"Yeah, and it's fucking me up."

She was using his lines and he tried to smile, but nothing happened. His goddamn lips went thin instead, and he just stared at her.

Probably giving her *that look.*

She started to fumble with her milkshake, looking red while pretending his searing look wasn't effecting her.

"I like you, Tyler," he found himself saying, quietly. "I really, *really* fucking like you."

You fucking coward. You don't feel this way because you really, really like her. You **love** *her.*

Tyler licked her lips and nodded back seriously. "I really, really fucking like you, Hawke."

Yeah, she loved him too.

*

They rode for a while after. The weather was just too gorgeous to pass up a nice ride around town.

If Hawke was being honest with himself, he knew he was doing it to delay the inevitable.

Finally, he took her to a small creak near the bush in a quiet untrodden area of town. Killing his engine, they hopped off the bike and walked to the water. She slipped her shoes off and dipped her feet in it while Hawke took a seat on the green grass just ten feet from the edge.

He was covered in the shade, the heavy trees overhead providing him comfort in the heat. Meanwhile, the sun hit Tyler, making her skin glow and her dark hair shine as she cooled herself off.

"We should bring the boys out here," she noted thoughtfully. "Would be a nice place to have a barbecue."

Hawke nodded absently, distracted by her beauty, by the heavy weight in his chest.

Tyler moved to him then, smiling sexily at him as she threw her shirt off and collapsed in his lap, wrapping her arms around his neck. She kissed him before he could think, and his hands instinctively shot to her back, keeping her to him.

Fuck.

This wasn't what was supposed to happen.

She cut the kiss and raised her head, offering her throat to him. He kissed her, knowing she loved being sucked and bitten there. Her breaths came short and fast, her thighs quaked.

"Take my bra off," she demanded, needy.

He pulled it down instead, his mouth already sucking at one of her taut little nipples. She moaned, pressing her hands against his face to keep him there.

"Hawke," she moaned, rocking her hips back and forth. "That feels so good."

He grunted when her hand touched his dick through his jeans. He was fucking hard. What was new? Every sexual encounter with Tyler was better than the last, making him harder quicker.

"Shit, Tyler," he murmured, running his palms down her body, and pulling away to watch the rise and fall of her tits. "Shit."

Hawke wasn't himself.

He was trying to talk his body out of doing what it wanted, but it was a bit too late.

Tyler had the ability to cloud his judgment and make him detest himself less enough that he could convince himself he could have her.

Now she was sitting in his lap, tits out, face pink, and his dick was hard as granite, yet he couldn't get himself to do it. All he was thinking was, *Jesus, what the fuck are you doing? Tell her what happened. She has the fucking right to know.*

He closed his eyes, halting his movements entirely.

"Hawke?" she whispered, uncertainly. "Are you alright?"

He shook his head. "Nah, Tyler, I'm not."

"What's wrong?"

He opened his eyes and slowly pulled her bra back up, fixing the straps as he avoided looking into her eyes.

"I need to tell you something," he finally said, grabbing at her shirt and handing it to her. She took it and held it to her chest, looking at him confusedly.

The silence crept in.

He wasn't going to do it, was he?

"Hawke," she prodded, "is it bad?"

"Yeah," he replied.

"How bad?"

"Very bad."

"What does it have to do with me?"

He raked his teeth over his bottom lip. "Everything, Tyler," he answered. "It has everything to do with you."

Her entire demeanor changed. The lust in her eyes disappeared and he saw the fear in her, saw her fingers tremble around her shirt as she continued to let the seconds pass without a word uttered.

Nothing would be the same after this.

"I lied to you," Hawke finally said, feeling his heart pick up. "About Yuri. I think I know why he wanted you, and it wasn't because of your looks."

Her eyes were wide. She still didn't speak, and it made everything that much fucking harder.

"You've got money," he continued carefully. "A fuck load of money sittin' in a hidden account, ready to be accessed on your twenty first birthday."

Her brows came together in confusion. "What are you talking about? Why wasn't I told?"

"Only Hector knows from the club and…Borden."

"Why?"

This was the difficult part. The part that was going to kill her soul.

"It's the club's money," he let out, his chest constricting. "Millions of dollars stolen and put in your name. Word got back about the account. We know it exists, that you're free to take it back, but we don't know its location or how to contact the person in charge of the bank. It's very underworld business, a banking system reserved for mobs than normal civilians."

Her hands let go of his, and her face fell. "I'm very lost right now, Hawke. Why is there club money sitting in some hidden account for me?"

"Your father stole it. He was going to run with it."

Tyler froze. In a flash, he saw a series of emotions: confusion, disbelief, anger. "That doesn't make sense," she retorted. "Why would Dad steal money from us? He wouldn't. You've got it wrong –"

"He told me," Hawke interrupted solemnly. "When he was dying, he kept saying it he took it, over and over again. Why do you think we're doing so much dodgy shit? We're in debt, babe. The club is struggling, and we need that money so we can pay everything off and clean the club up again."

She looked away from him, her face pale, her lips trembling. She slid off his lap and moved away from him, her hands fisting the grass. "This doesn't make sense," she whispered. "Dad would never have gone. He would never have stolen from the club. It doesn't make sense. You're lying to me." Her voice broke. "Please, tell me you're lying to me."

"I'm not lyin' to you."

Tears fell from her eyes as she looked at him in awe. "Why would he say that to you? Why would he steal, Hawke?"

"I don't know."

"You don't know?!"

"No, babe, I don't."

Her chest rose and fell faster. "Did…did you kill him?"

"No, I found him bleeding out in his motel room. He didn't tell me who killed him. He was dying, and he was barely making sense as it was."

Don't trust. The old man had repeated over and over again. *Don't trust.*

"He'd been acting strange before then," Hawke explained quietly, "and then I discovered the accounts were clean when he disappeared one night without letting us know he'd be gone. I found out where he was because he'd been with one of his favorite girls."

Dennis could never resist a beautiful woman.

"Why didn't you tell me?" Tyler spat at him, anger fueling her words. "Why didn't you fucking tell me, Hawke? You hid this from me, from the club, for *years*!"

Hawke narrowed his eyes at her. "Do you know the shit-storm that would have started if I told the club your old man had robbed us clean? Do you have any idea how angry and impulsive they would have been? Nothing would have stopped Jonny, or fuckin' Kirk, or hell Marshall even, from bursting into your house and killin' your mother and you for his crimes. I kept it from them to *protect* you, because if you haven't noticed, Tyler, we are fuckin' outlaws, and some of us are fucked up more than others."

"So you've been burying it since!"

"What choice did I fucking have?!"

She jumped, startled by his shout. His face fell and he instantly regretted it. "Tyler," he said contritely, "I'm sorry."

She was shaken up, clutching at her chest like she was in physical pain. All those years she'd looked up to her father, and he hadn't the heart to tell her what he had done.

"It doesn't make sense," she repeated, her voice cracking. "Why would he put it in my name? Where the hell is the logic in that, Hawke?"

"He had money in his own account, enough to run for a very long time. We managed to take that back. I think he put it in your name in case he got killed, just to make sure you were looked after."

She shook her head. "No, that can't be it."

"Tyler –"

"That's not it!" she screamed, her face reddening as she glared at him. "All this time I thought you knew him! You didn't know a damn thing about my father, Hawke."

He shook his head, his heart slowing as he replied sadly, "Baby, I don't think *you* did."

She choked back on a sob and stood up, stumbling away from him. She paced aimlessly, her steps prodding the edge of the creak, her hands in her hair, pulling at the strands as she sobbed into the open air. She was losing it, and Hawke couldn't sit there and watch her without wanting to do something, anything to make her feel better.

He stood up and went to her. He approached her slowly from behind and wrapped his arms around her. Tyler immediately flailed, screaming at him to let her go. He dropped his arms, but she turned around and shoved him back, her tears replaced with rage.

"I fucking hate you," she seethed, slapping at his chest. "I fucking hate you for this!"

Hawke just nodded. "I know."

"No, you don't fucking know!"

"I know you're looking for someone to hate."

"Fuck you!" she hollered, continuing to push him back like he was fighting her, though he wasn't. He just stood there, taking her hits and aggression, knowing she needed it out.

"I trusted you!" she continued. "I fucking trusted you!"

He didn't know if she was talking to him, or her father.

"I hate you," she howled. "All this time? All this time you knew and you didn't even tell me!"

"You'll hate me for a little while," he quietly told her as she stepped away, her eyes narrowed and raging. "But you'll come back to me, Tyler, when you realize I'm not the bad guy here, and I'll be waiting."

"Fuck you," she repeated. "I hate you."

"Yeah, sure you do, darlin'."

That just pissed her off some more, and she flew at him again, smacking him across the chest, hollering some more how much she hated him. That he was a monster and a murderer.

"But you knew that already," he replied evenly. "You knew I was all those things and you still wanted me."

She sucked in breaths, growing quiet as his words sank in. He saw the truth in her eyes as he said it. She crumbled, that anger transitioning back to sadness.

She walked away from him and made it five steps before she collapsed to the ground and buried her face in her hands.

thirty-five

Tyler

I'd pined for Hawke for years, wanting more than anything for him to come back.

And now I wanted him gone with a fury.

I barely touched him on the ride back. I was happy to just fall off the bike during those sharp turns if it meant not touching his body.

Though I hated that I still wanted to.

The whole day had been orchestrated so he could tell me the truth. He'd taken me away from the clubhouse so I wouldn't have lost it in there and subsequently inform everyone else of it too. It was the right thing to have done because I knew it would have torn the older members apart knowing my old man – whom they still revered – had done something so atrocious as this. Even now I wanted to protect his name.

How sad was I?

He'd ripped the club apart, would have disastrously put the Warlords name in the ground if they hadn't resorted to doing drug deals, and I still wanted to protect him?

Love didn't make you see right from wrong. It wanted you ignorant so you could shield not just the person you loved, but yourself too.

Like Hawke. I hated him for keeping it from me, but I didn't really want him gone. I was just pissed. Really, really pissed at him, and I held on to that anger for days and days, moving away from his touches, never talking to him except to tell him to get out when he made to sleep next to me.

He never got out. He slid into bed every time and wrapped his arm around me and forced me against his chest. "You don't really want me to go," he whispered to me once, kissing along my bare shoulder. "You want me here."

"No, I don't," I seethed.

"You do, and you wanna know how *I* know?" He sucked at my neck. "Because you still look at me in that way, Tyler."

I swallowed thickly, trying to resist the warmth his touch created inside my arctic chest.

"I know it hurts," he continued, his voice softening. "And you can push me away all you want, but I know you need me just as much as I need you. I've given up everything right now to be here. The law is still out there, and I'm risking my neck just to have you in my bed. But I want you, Tyler. I want you so bad it hurts."

He was right, but I wasn't ready to admit that, so I just listened. I continued to resist his touches, but that only spurred him to try harder.

Secretly, I didn't want him to give up.

I should have seen it from his point of view. How hard it would have been to tell me this. I was just too clouded with anger and looking to take it out on him and blame him when really it was my father who'd betrayed us. I was struggling to come to grips with it, though. My father had been so passionate about this club. He'd been so happy, so involved. I wondered a lot of things about it. Were there signs I'd missed? Had his behavior been off? Was my father angry? I couldn't recall anything out of the ordinary.

At the end, I had to force myself to come to grips with the fact my father wasn't the man I thought he was.

Hawke

It had been seven days of her pushing him away. Just how much longer was she going to keep doing it? She was centering all her frustrations on him and not Hector. How that asshole flew under her radar was a mystery to him.

Hawke got she was pissed and sad about it. Hell, he was too for the longest time after Dennis had died in his arms, but…fuck, he never considered what it meant to care for someone other than him. He never knew the devastation he could feel being cast aside every night.

Why did people want relationships when this was the utter bullshit that came along with it? You could easily save yourself the trouble and play the single game and fuck without caring whether you were in the good graces of whatever hole you were sticking your dick into.

Yeah, that thought lasted about two seconds because…yeah, he fucking wanted her. Didn't care either that she currently held the power between them. The strong euphoria that shot through his veins every time he held her made all that bullshit worth it.

Throughout the day he gave her space. He couldn't risk her going to work, so she kicked around the clubhouse, spending a lot of time with Holly and Shay and avoiding him at all costs.

Meanwhile, he spent his time making the clubhouse into a serious stronghold. He made deals and reconnected with contacts that'd been left cold for eons. Next he was looking to go over every patched member and determine how just essential they were to their role because, shit, there were too many members as it was and they were doing nothing but taking money to support their lifestyle outside the club.

It pissed Hawke off unlike anything else.

In the middle of all this was Hector, who was still sobering up and trying not to touch the drink, though Hawke could tell it was a major struggle. But he was changing, and without the drink he wasn't angry half as much.

"Instead of waiting for her to get over it, maybe you should take her out," he told him as they stood out front of the building, watching Jonny and Jesse drill more bars over the windows.

Hawke scoffed. "Tyler won't let me within a foot of her."

"It's her birthday in a week. Take her to Ma's. She loves it there every time I go around. Maybe she'll warm up to you again afterwards."

"All Ma would talk about to her is how much of a shit I was growing up."

Hector chuckled. "Possibly."

"Fucking women, Hector."

He shook his head. "Yeah, well, that's why I don't fall in love, man. Life's too short to be in pain."

Hawke smirked, nodding before replying, "Actually, the pain's the best part."

Hector sighed, looking at his brother peculiarly. "Fuckin' turning into one of those sad saps now, man? You got woman bits I don't know about?"

"Fuck you."

"No, you want to fuck Tyler."

"Yeah, I do."

"The daughter of Dennis, I have to add."

"She sure is."

"That annoying little turd that used to drive us up the fucking wall with that squeaky fucking tricycle."

"That would be her."

The disbelief was still apparent in Hector's voice as he stressed, "Tyler."

"*My* Tyler."

Just as Hawke said that, he saw Jesse's body tense. The fucker had been listening to them, and there was a wounded look on his face he was doing his absolute best to conceal.

Hector noticed too and he nudged Hawke's shoulder, whispering, "He'll get over it, man. It was just a mad crush."

Jesse's reaction didn't fit that of a mad crush. He obviously cared for her, and maybe it would have pissed Hawke off if it was someone else, but Jesse was loyal and passionate. No matter how devastated he was, he would never cross Hawke or Tyler. It just wasn't in his nature.

Just then the sound of an approaching vehicle interrupted them. Hawke glanced over his shoulder as a black Mercedes turned in, slowly coming to a stop in front of them.

Hawke's eyes narrowed and he let out a long breath. "Fuck."

The passenger door opened and a suited man stepped out, glaring at Hawke with a face as cold as ice.

"Borden," Hawke said, his voice tight.

"We've got to talk," Borden replied. "I've got answers."

"Let's go inside."

But before Hawke could turn, Borden moved to him abruptly and slammed his fist against Hawke's face, causing his head to jerk to the side and ringing to explode in his ears.

"That's for fucking leaving me," Borden growled.

Hawke wasn't going to argue because, yeah, he fucking deserved it.

thirty-six

Hawke

Borden wanted to talk alone with him, so Hawke took him to the meeting room and shut the door behind them. Borden threw a file on the table and turned to him, his mouth set in a hard line, his eyes cold and angry.

"First of all," he started, nose flaring, "you could have fucking told me a long time ago that this was what you wanted."

Hawke crossed his arms and leaned back against the door, retorting, "I didn't know I wanted it."

"You don't just wake up and want to be president again."

"No, you don't."

"So what happened then? You can't possibly be doing all this for pussy."

A sliver of anger tore through Hawke's chest, and he ground his teeth together, trying to keep it together. "Isn't it funny how the tables turn?" he asked, sardonically. "If I recall, I was in your shoes asking you the same fucking question once upon a time."

"This is different. Emma was a struggling waitress that carried a cheap as shit switchblade. Your girl lives with bikers who are pleading for you to come back."

"And I'm back now."

"What about all those talks we had about you being on my side instead of theirs."

"We're on the same fucking side."

"We'll be business partners, and you wanna know how many times shit like that deteriorates between two parties, Hawke? Do you see my reluctance right now?"

"It's justified."

"Damn fucking straight it's justified!" Borden hollered, losing his cool in a way Hawke wasn't familiar with. "You don't seem to fucking realize that outside of you and Emma and my family, I got nothing. I can't have us be at odds with one another."

Hawke moved to the chair and collapsed into it, rubbing his face in exasperation. "Christ, Borden, you think I would ever want to be at odds with you? That shit won't happen."

"Give me your fucking word."

Hawke looked at him, his eyes firm and unwavering as he said, "I give you my fucking word."

Borden didn't look any less tense. He was fuming, his face cracking with anger as he said, "You haven't thought this through. You're blinded by your affections –"

"I'm not giving her up."

"Can you go to war? See your men die all over again? We lost someone too, and how difficult was that to move on from? You don't want the death of people you care about on your conscience."

"No one's dying on my watch."

"Not until you fucking read what I have to show you."

Hawke hesitated, glancing at the file on the table and then at Borden. "What do you mean?"

"I mean you can't knock out threats when you don't even know who they are, and Hawke, you didn't see this one coming."

Hawke stilled, feeling a wave of trepidation run through him as he eyeballed that file again. Horrible thoughts flashed in his head, of all the his doubts, of all the shit he'd heard.

Were the rumors true? Was Hector behind it? That was his nightmare, and the answer was sitting feet from him.

"How bad?" he asked tightly.

Borden frowned, looking bothered for a moment before replying, "Very fucking bad."

*

For a few minutes, Hawke watched Tyler conversing with Jesse. He was making her laugh, which was a welcoming sight. The boys really did treat Tyler like she was part of the family. He'd seen it a lot, the love and respect they had for her.

But Jesse was shirtless again, the asshole. Probably trying to get her to salivate or some shit, only she was barely paying attention to his torso the way Holly was as she distributed beers to the boys sitting in their chairs out front. When she went to hand one to Hector, he shook his head stiffly and she seemed pleased.

Hector looked around and caught sight of Hawke standing by the window, looking out at them. He narrowed his eyes in question, and Hawke looked away, not ready to speak of what he'd learned in that room.

He thought he'd lose his shit after reading that file, but…strangely, a calm wave swept into him. He felt numb, and he supposed that was better than rage.

Maybe, if he'd been around, he'd have figured it out a long time ago.

Maybe…he could have stopped so much heartache.

The monster within twitched, longing for action now instead of later, but…Hawke needed to process first.

Just then Tyler looked up, catching sight of his cold stare. Her smile faded away, and there it was again, that look she was trying hard not to show. Unfortunately, Hawke didn't want to see it. He didn't want this fucking numbness to wear off. He needed it. It was armor. It was the only way he could mentally formulate a plan of attack.

He turned his head and walked away.

*

He ended up sitting alone in his room, his face buried in the palm of his hands. The lights were off, and the silence was deafening. *This is different.* He tried telling himself. *There's a door that opens. The lights are off. You can't hear those...those screams.*

But it wasn't enough, and the monster within stirred as the walls closed in on him.

In an instant, Hawke was back there again.

In solitary confinement.

Bloody pictures on the walls.

A piece of shit fluorescent light over top of him, his only light, the symbol of timelessness as it never changed, never wavered, never even went out.

Screams – fucking hell, he could still hear them echoing inside his skull.

It was a fucking pit. One that made him want to dig his fingers into his throat and rip his lungs out.

He should have done it. Should have died in a puddle of his own blood.

Then he wouldn't be back here.

President.

In love with a woman who currently hated him.

Having to kill all over again.

Having to make the world fear him when all he'd done the last five years was hide, purposeless and void of life.

And now this.

He could see himself, pacing in circles in that pit of misery, then collapsing to the ground, that fucking fluorescent light blinding his eyes as two words chanted all around him.

Don't trust.

Don't trust.

thirty-seven

Tyler

Borden had said something very bad to Hawke, because when he emerged out of the room after Borden had left, he was different.

His eyes were blank, his movements stiff, his gaze guarded.

If I thought Hawke was terrifying before, I was wrong. Very, very wrong.

He distanced himself from everyone, including Hector, and he sat alone in the far back of the room, wheels spinning as he glanced at every single face in the bar with this blatant look of suspicion and distrust.

It was the first time I ever thought of leaving. Not permanently or anything, just until he was back to normal. Because with eyes like those, I knew he was planning something bad.

Over the next few days, he didn't slide into bed with me. In fact, he was riding around a lot with the guys, knocking on doors, forcing businesses to pay their cut they'd avoided for far too long.

At some point, he ended up burning a barber shop down when the owner refused. Of course, the second the guys started breaking shit, he relented and offered Hawke more.

Hawke refused.

Jesse told me what Hawke had said to that man. "You say no once and that's it. No chances."

Hawke was not to be fucked with.

Then, over the following days, he proceeded to kick out three guys who were barely around but carrying the patch, and then he burnt their patches out front for everyone to see.

The guys started pulling in their weight after that.

He never mentioned the attack on the clubhouse. Never made orders to figure out who was behind it. He'd just abandoned it like it mattered to him no more, and then he'd given Jesse the go about me returning to work.

I was surprised, but it was a welcoming release. I needed to be away from Hawke's chaos. I knew this was what needed to be done, but knowing it and seeing it were two very different things.

Hawke was going back to his roots.

He was showing me that to be perceived as bad, he had to do very, very bad things.

*

Everything came to head between us a few days after I'd returned to work. Jesse had driven me back home because apparently Hawke refused to allow him to give me a ride on the back of his bike anymore. Which I understood.

We were stepping out of the car and I was gathering my things from the seat when I noticed Jesse stiffen, his gaze locked on something.

"What?" I asked him.

He didn't respond, but he gestured his head in front of him. I stopped beside him and followed his line of sight to Kirk's red pick-up truck parked at the far end of the parking lot. I stilled immediately when I saw it, and it took a moment for the shock to pass.

Shay was on the ground, her back against the wheel, her arms behind her chained to the chassis. She was in nothing but her bra and panties. I could tell the sun had been beating down on her all day. Her skin looked like a strip of leather, browned and red and cracked all over. I didn't know if she was conscious until she turned her head a tad in our direction.

My jaw dropped. "What. The. Fuck."

"You're tellin' me."

I made to walk in her direction, when Jesse grabbed me by the arm and forced me still. "Don't," he said in a hard voice. "If she's been bound like that, there's a reason for it."

"She looks like she's been baking under the sun all day."

"I know."

"That's fucked up."

"I agree."

I let out a breath. "We can't just leave her like that."

"You know your place here, Tyler," he retorted sharply. "This isn't your business. Leave her alone."

He let go of my arm and moved past me. When he made it to the entrance of the clubhouse, he stopped and turned to me, waiting for me to follow. I could see the warning in his eyes, and I knew he wasn't being a dick about it. He didn't want me involved because he was concerned for the consequences if I was. I didn't listen and go to him. What the hell consequences could Hawke possibly throw at me? Instead, I focused back on Shay, at her matted blonde hair and slicked skin. Then I moved to her quickly.

"Tyler!" Jesse called, already frustrated. "Don't you dare!"

I ignored him. When I approached her, I knelt down to her level and looked her over. Her face was a fucking mess. Mascara ran down her cheeks, her eyes were puffy from crying, her lips chapped and white. Jesus Christ, she was in bad shape. I reached out and touched her shoulder, and she flinched in pain.

"Sorry," I said quietly, my voice thick with remorse. "I didn't mean to hurt you."

She didn't respond, but her lips quivered as she blinked slowly at me. I didn't ask her what happened, or who had done this. Jesse was right when he said it wasn't my place. This sort of shit was what came with the territory living in the club, and I wasn't allowed to question it.

But I wasn't going to lie, it was fucking hard at times. This was cruel, and I hated pretending I had the stomach to handle it. I'd seen some bad punishments in the past – once they'd glassed a prospect in the face for stealing money from the cash register – and every time shit like this happened, I cringed on the inside and distanced myself.

Only this was confronting, and I couldn't entirely look away without wanting to help in whatever way I could.

I looked over at Jesse and he was crossing his arms now, pissed as hell at my disobedience. I mouthed "water" to him and then motioned to the entrance. His face darkened even more, but I stared at him harder, not backing down at all and mouthed it again. He gritted his teeth and disappeared inside. Not a minute passed when he reappeared carrying an ice cold water bottle in his hand. He stopped when he got to me and handed me the bottle, looking in a completely different direction. I took the bottle from his hand, unscrewed the cap, and pressed it against Shay's dried mouth. She went suddenly alive and parted her lips, drinking feverishly as I poured it down her throat. All the while, I examined her; there were no bruises or marks, so I knew she wasn't beaten, but her skin looked thoroughly fucked.

"That's enough now, Tyler," Jesse told me gravely, still not staring at us. "Unless you want me to get my ass kicked by the guys for letting you do this shit."

"Then leave me to it," I hissed back at him. "I'm not asking you to stand here."

"I'm not leaving you."

"Why the hell not?"

"Because you're my fuckin' friend, Tyler, and I'd rather be one blamed than you, even if she might deserve this."

My stomach turned. What the hell could she possibly have done for *this*?

Feeling on pins and needles, I let her finish the bottle and then I stood back up. "Thanks," I muttered to him, my voice softer now. "I really appreciate it, Jesse."

His face gentled and he nodded. "It's alright."

Shay brought her knees to her chest and rested her face against them, looking dead once more. Jesse took me by the arm again and led me away. We walked to the entrance door, and he threw a glance at her over his shoulder. With a smirk, he said, "There's a positive to all this, you know."

I threw him a dubious look as he opened the door for me. "And what's that?"

"At least the rest of her body will finally match the color of her face."

"Too soon, Jesse," I replied, disapproving. "Way too soon."

*

I heard about what Shay did the second I stepped into the bar.

Apparently she'd gone absolutely nuclear this morning after waking up to Hector kicking her out of the room. She lost her shit like never before and went off on him. She told him she wasn't a doormat and that it was time to make her his woman.

Of course Hector said no. Or, more accurately, he'd said, "Bitch, get the fuck out of my face. You don't tell me what to fucking do."

Aaaaand that was when she lost it. Like, off the reservoir and into the fucking hellfire kind of lost it. She'd stormed downstairs and attacked Holly, breaking a part a beer bottle and swinging the sharp ends at her as Holly screamed in terror. Apparently, she'd cut her on the chest, and even Kirk, in his deteriorated state, had roared for her to stop.

Jonny and Marshall were the first to physically intervene. They'd dragged her back upstairs to Hector. Then… it got worse.

She screamed at him, told him she'd start talking about shit she'd been seeing around the club (oh boy). Even claimed she heard everything and knew what Hawke had done to Yuri. She threatened to sell him out to the "cockroaches at the police station" without realizing the club owned every fucking cockroach at the police station.

I had to pick my jaw off the ground when they finished telling me the story. Shay had lost her damn mind!

What she'd done would have normally earned her a death sentence, and Hector was already carrying his gun, about to pop her before Hawke intervened, telling him, "No more death under this roof." She was still in her bra and panties, standing her ground in the hallway and screaming like a banshee, when Hawke grabbed her banshee screaming ass by the arm, led her outside and chained her to the truck to teach her a lesson. By the time I'd showed up, she'd been chained to it for six whole hours.

And it was a hot day. I'm talking about the kind of hot day so motherfucking hot you could see time.

What she did was horrible. I got that. But...Christ, she was going to die of a heat stroke if she wasn't let go anytime soon.

I sought Hawke out and found him alone in the meeting room, seated and staring blankly ahead. His chest was rising and falling at an unnatural pace, and I paused in my step, wondering if it was the adrenaline over what he'd done that was still coursing through him.

I shut the door behind me and turned to him.

"Hawke," I started carefully, "you gotta let Shay go."

His eyes flickered to mine, and a moment of warmth flashed in his eyes before he hid it and retorted, "It ain't up to me."

"It is."

"She threatened the club. As far as I'm concerned, it's the club's decision."

"But you got to decide what happens to her in the first place."

"I didn't want another murder scene in the clubhouse."

"She's in really bad shape."

"I don't care, Tyler."

My eyes glistened as I stared at him in shock. "You would never have done something this like to a woman before! It's evil."

He chuckled dryly. "Are you fucking dense, Tyler? I'm letting her have her LIFE!" he roared on the last word.

"She won't have it for long out there in the heat!"

He suddenly shot out of the chair and moved to me, his anger strong in his eyes as he growled, "She was going to hurt Holly. She threatened the club's secrets. As far as I'm concerned, if she was a fucking man she'd have died the second she opened her fucking mouth."

"Hector has been stringing her along –"

"Stop defending her!"

"Would you do that to me, Hawke?" I asked him bitterly. "You know, I gave her water. So what're you gonna do? Chain me up to a truck and leave me to bake in the sun too? Are you all that *fucking* unfeeling?"

He jerked his chin around us. "Where do you think you are right now, Tyler? Because just as I'm convincing myself you're startin' to understand things, you ask me a really stupid question. Don't plead that girl's case like she did nothing wrong. If she had, she wouldn't be where she is right now. If you're looking for saints, you're in the wrong place, darlin'."

I glared at him, feeling my heart thump faster as I grated out, "I wish you weren't like this. You're so fucking dark."

"I've always been this, Tyler."

"No."

"I told you this is what I had to become to set this club right again. You want to see it go under? You want some other club to come strollin' in here and fucking up the streets? At least this club has a fucking code. We don't fuck with people unless we're fucked with first. Another club though? You don't know what they'll do. You don't know what they'll make *you* do for them. The only way to stay at the top is to become your own worst enemy."

I didn't have anything to say to that.

I felt truly lost.

Part of me was desensitized by the brutality the club possessed.

The other devastated that it had to be brutal in the first place.

The silence built between us, the tension thicker than it had ever been before.

Hawke tried his hardest to keep his walls up, but the look of hurt in my eyes made his breath run thinner. He shook his head and rubbed at his face. "Fuck, Tyler, you wanna know why I'm doin' all this?" His face looked tormented as he watched me and said, "I'm doin' all this for you. So I can be here…with you. I don't like it. I fucking hate it. That fucking adrenaline, darlin', is shootin' through me and I wanna fucking claw that monster inside of me that's feeding off the rage."

He moved back and collapsed in his chair, taking in deep breaths as his eyes glistened.

"I hate it," he repeated. "I fucking hate it. I want that money out of your account so we don't have to deal with all this…bullshit. Go clean and start over. That's what I want. What I've always wanted. But that takes time."

Hawke looked absolutely shattered, like he'd reached the end of his rope. Just as much as I'd hated him seeing what he had to do, he had hated it too.

I moved to him, drawn by his pain, wanting nothing more than to remove it. My hands immediately flew to his face, and he shut his eyes as I stroked his cheeks. The beard was starting to grow thicker again, and I combed through it with my fingers as I sat on his lap and pressed my forehead against his.

He breathed out longer than before, his eyes tightening as he shut them, his face breaking. His arms wrapped around me and he kept me coiled there, breathing in the same air as me.

"I'm sorry," he whispered. "I'm so sorry about everything, about the lie –"

"You lied to protect me," I interrupted, pressing my lips against his. "I understand."

"You hate me."

"I was trying to find a reason to hate you, but I could never truly hate you, Hawke."

He kissed me back slowly, and god, it felt nice to be reunited with his lips. His hands ran down my back and around my ass. He gripped it tightly as he slipped his tongue into my mouth and stroked mine gently.

"I know what you're doing," he muttered as he began to harden beneath me.

"What am I doing?" I breathed out, baring my throat to him.

"You're trying to distract me."

I nodded, not even bothering to hide it. "Yeah, Hawke, I am. Do you want me to stop?"

His hand ran back up my body and he gripped my breast, squeezing it in the palm of his hand. "Fuck no, Tyler."

We kissed for a while, and he tenderly felt every inch of me, telling me how much he missed it.

Afterwards, he slid me off and, looking heaps clearer and in control, he left the room and ordered the boys to let Shay go. Then he got Marshall to gather her things, put together some money in her wallet, and ordered her to leave town.

He understood her obsession with Hector had fucked with her head, and he also knew she didn't need to lose her head over it too.

Hector felt like shit, blaming himself for how far he'd pushed her.

That, in itself, was a miracle.

thirty-eight

Tyler

Later that night, Hawke took me for a ride.

The weather was cooler than usual, and the wind had picked up. I could smell the rain coming, a welcoming respite after such a hot, shitty day.

I should have been wary when he turned to the same creak he'd broken the news to me. After all, it was a place that would only remind me of the horrible truth.

Of what my father was.

But I was honestly too excited to spend quality time with Hawke to let the bad thoughts in. I jumped off his bike and hurried toward the creak, him following closely behind. This time I sat by the water, kicking off my shoes and socks to dip my feet in while staring up at the sky.

A lightning bolt flashed, and I counted the seconds before the thunder followed.

Three, four, five…

CRACK!

There it was.

I felt Hawke behind me dropping to the ground, his legs on either side of me. I leaned back, closing my eyes as I relaxed into his embrace, the smell of leather and his cologne surrounding me.

"We should do this often," I told him. "That way I don't see you acting like an ogre all the time."

He ran his hands down my arms. "Like I said, it's –"

"Necessary, I know."

"It won't be for much longer."

I nodded in understanding.

"Until then, Ty, stop putting me on a pedestal."

"Is that what you think I'm doing?"

"I haven't done great things."

"You keep forgetting how great you make *me* feel."

"When I'm not lyin'."

I laughed lightly and nodded. "Yeah, when you're not lying."

Another lightning bolt, and this time I counted out loud before the thunder cracked overhead. It was so beautiful being in this spot, secluded, with a man I cared about – loved – holding me.

The whole world disappeared. All the problems, the club's bullshit, the violence, the despair…all of it faded into white noise, and it was just Hawke and me.

"Can I ask you something?" I wondered sometime later.

"The fact you have to ask me if you can ask me is troubling as it is, Tyler."

I rolled my eyes. "Well, I mean, it's personal."

"What do you wanna know?"

I turned my head to look at him, his dark eyes meeting mine as I said, "Who was that beautiful woman that walked out of your bedroom all those years ago?"

His brows came together. "You're going to have to be more specific."

"The blonde with those really nice platform heels."

He let out a long breath, surprised. "Fuckin' hell, Tyler, that has to be the most random fuckin' question I could have expected from you."

"Oops."

"How do you even know about that?"

"I saw her."

"And how old were you, you little fuckin' creep?"

I let out a laugh and nudged my elbow into his stomach. "Not that young."

"How old?" he demanded.

"God, I don't know, eleven?"

He groaned, muttering a curse under his breath. "What is this? Honestly, when we have our own, the last place that kid will be is that fuckin' clubhouse."

I ignored the way my chest blazed at him talking about our nonexistent kids. “I grew up fine, remember?”

“You’re insane.”

I gasped, feigning shock. “How am I insane?”

“Because you’re asking me about a girl I took to bed ten years ago. And I thought Shay was unhinged.”

I elbowed him again, this time hard enough to knock the air out of his lungs. He laughed nonetheless, forcing my elbow away from his stomach. His amusement over my question made irritated, and I tried to elbow him again with my other arm. He gripped that elbow too and then pulled me flush against his chest, caging me with his arms around my front.

“That girl was meaningless,” he then whispered in my ear. “I’m flattered you’re jealous a decade after the fact, though.”

“I’m not jealous,” I argued.

“Liar.”

“I’m curious. You weren’t with a lot of girls after you took the gavel, and I wondered why.”

His arms loosened around me, allowing me to turn my body around so my arms wrapped around his neck. Hawke looked down at me, his smile relaxed as I waited for his response.

“Because I was tired of bedding fakes,” he finally said after a minute of silence. “It’s all the same after a while, Ty. I liked a bit of a connection.”

“Did you feel connected to her?”

He shook his head, running his teeth over his bottom lip. “Christ, Ty, what if I prodded you about your jock from high school?”

“You already did.”

“I didn’t stop to ask the specifics.”

“Well, if you’re curious about whether I gave him a blowjob, then I –”

His hand shot to my mouth, silencing me before giving me a very dark look. "I don't want to fuckin' know a thing about what you did to that boy, or what he did to you, Tyler. You understand? My blood's boilin' just thinking about it, and I don't want to have to hear something that'll make me responsible for putting him in his grave. Got it?"

I nodded, and when he dropped his hand he looked irritated to find me grinning like a fool. "Now who's jealous?" I said.

He was pissed now. "Fuck yeah, I'm jealous. Because I want your body for myself. I hate that you've been touched by some other dick. Part of me wishes I could turn back time and be the first inside you just so I can say all you had to experience was me, but that ain't going to happen anytime soon. Now strip so I can fuck you and forget what you just told me."

I giggled, trying to fight his hands but they were already grabbing at my shirt and throwing it off. He pushed us back and then turned me so that my back was flat against the earth and he was over me, undressing me as I stared up at the sky, catching another lightning bolt fork into the blackness overhead.

When the thunder rumbled seconds later, my body thundered along with it as Hawke's mouth worked my clit with his tongue.

*

We ended up naked in the grass, spent and pleasured, welcoming the cool drops of rain falling all around us.

I never knew peace like this.

Never felt so full of happiness in my life.

And then he had to break the moment by saying, "Ty, now that I fucked you, I need to tell you something."

My smile faded as I looked up at his face, guarded and afraid. "Is it bad?" I asked, hesitantly.

He searched my eyes and quietly replied, “It’s going to hurt. Again.”

Fuck.

He’d taken me out here with a motive yet again.

This time I braced myself, determined not to crumble and determined – beyond anything – not to hate him again.

thirty-nine

Hawke

When it was time to deal business with Abram, Hawke decided to round up Hector and Gus and ride out to him instead.

"I don't trust him after Yuri," he'd explained to Gus. "At least this time there won't be any surprises."

Gus agreed, and they rode out, armed in case anything happened.

Abram's estate was like before: filled with soulless girls and guards. Abram himself was outside in the courtyard behind his gargantuan house, sitting on a chair that overlooked his pool, staring at a lone girl swimming on her own. He appeared particularly invested in her as the guards approached, the bikers following a few feet behind.

Abram barely glanced in their direction as he said, "Your money will be out front in a few minutes. Have you considered my terms about you needing to stop supplying to my rivals?"

Hawke nodded, tearing his eyes away from the elegant swimmer feet from them. "I have, and I agree, so long as we get something else in return."

Abram turned his head to them, unreadable behind his shades and said, "And what would that be?"

Hawke took a moment to respond, glancing at a confused Gus and an angry Hector before replying, "You're the banker."

Abram's lips flinched upwards. "You got Borden to figure that out."

It wasn't a question. He knew.

Hawke nodded. "I did."

"And you're trying to get ahold of that girl's account. I'm afraid I'd need her here, and the last time I checked my calendar, we're still days from her birthday."

Hawke chuckled dryly. "I'm not here for the money today. How much is in there anyway? Seven million?"

"Eight."

"Right, well, I'll come back with Tyler another day. I'm here because of Yuri and the attacks on my clubhouse."

"*Your* clubhouse," Abram replied, smirking as he removed the shades. "Nice to see you wearing that patch, Hawke. But again, if you're here to accuse me of attacking that shithole, I'd rather just put a bullet in your head because I didn't fucking do it."

"I know you didn't," Hawke said calmly. "You said last time you wanted an eye for an eye, and I'm here to give you it."

"An eye for an eye?"

"We killed Yuri, you kill Gus."

Before Gus could react, Hector wrapped his arm around his neck and kept him in place.

"What the fuck are you doing?!" he wheezed out in disbelief, his face turning purple. "What the fuck is this, Hawke?"

Hawke didn't look at him. He kept his gaze level with Abram and said, "Your cousin was aware of the accounts, wasn't he?"

Abram looked between Hawke and Gus before nodding once. "He was aware of the banking I controlled, the many accounts I overlook for many dangerous people."

"And Dennis locked away the club's money."

"We don't ask where the money is from."

"But you knew."

Abram shrugged. "I had my suspicions, but I overlook too many accounts to really give a fuck. Plus, there was nothing I could do. I'm loyal to my word, to every contract I make with every person and every mob that's dumped their cash in my bank."

"Where is this bank?"

"Well, it's not really a fucking bank, Hawke. It's a place I horde their cash in. Several places, in fact."

"Did Yuri know about the locations?"

"No, but I knew he was aware of the girl, that perhaps he got into contact with someone in your club about it too."

Hawke nodded in understanding before pointing at Gus. "And that would be this fuck."

"I didn't tell Yuri to grab Tyler that night!" Gus screamed, his voice pleading. "He did it on his own, Hawke! He went behind my back. I never knew he was going to do it. It wasn't supposed to happen that way. He was fucking high off his shit! I told him we'd go halves once the money was returned to the club. We were never planning on taking her! Never! I would never have hurt Tyler!"

"Like you would never hurt Dennis before you fucking shot him in the back for being on to someone in the club stealing money?"

Gus went quiet, still trying to breathe through Hector's tight grip around his neck.

"You stole half a million dollars," Hawke explained, his voice cold. "Borden found your offshore account, acting as a major shareholder in some non-existent fucking business in Panama. It was the same half a million dollars that disappeared in cash right before Dennis took the rest of it and locked it up to protect the club from whatever thief was inside it. But you didn't know that the money was already out of his hands until you gunned him down, isn't that right?"

Gus didn't respond. His eyes went glossy with emotion, as he continued shaking his head.

"You were waiting for Tyler's birthday," Hawke carried on, taking a step toward him, wishing he had a gun so he could blow the old man away. "That's why you were adamant you needed to keep her with the club, telling me how many fucking times how important her safety was. I was a fucking idiot not seein' what was in front of me. A fucking snake that tried to pit us against Abram with your hired fucking muscle attacking our place so we could go to war and put him to ground and take every account from under him!"

"And then you turned your sights on my brother," Hector hissed in his ear, tightening his grip even further as his anger roared. "Sold him out, didn't you? Tried to get rid of him so he wasn't around to figure out the fucking truth."

Gus struggled in his grip, barely able to stand as oxygen depleted from his lungs.

Hawke narrowed his eyes, feeling pained by the betrayal as he stated sadly, "Once you figure out one thing, everything else starts to come together. You betrayed us, Gus, and Dennis tried so hard to tell me there was someone on the inside. He didn't even know it was you in the end, did he?"

Take care of Tyler.

Don't trust.

Don't trust.

Gus's eyes dimmed, tears falling his eyes as the truth came out, one by one collapsing years of trust. Years of love. Years of brotherhood. Over money.

Abram stood up, his focus now on Gus. He was furious, his own pain evident in his face as he icily said, "Let him go. I'll take your eye for an eye and kill this fucker. He took Yuri from me, and his family's still hungry for revenge." Then he stepped closer, looking Gus over before adding, "I'm going to remove your eyeballs first, like my cousin. Then I'm going to cut you up, but I won't give you a quick death like him. I'm going to make you bleed out slowly."

With that, Hector released him and he fell to the ground in a heap, gasping in air as he screamed for Hawke to stop and listen, to not do this, to not leave him.

But Hawke and Hector were already walking away.

"Please, Hawke! Just listen to me! Just listen!"

The old man didn't realize there was nothing left to listen to.

Their money was loaded into the back of a van that followed them all the way back to the clubhouse.

Back to Tyler, still shaken from the news that her father was innocent all along.

forty

Hawke

Being numb wasn't the answer.

Tyler.

Fuck, she grounded him; *she* was the answer.

He ran a bath for her that night, and together they sat in the large tub, her back resting against his chest as she ran her hands over the bubbles.

He thought to tell her about what happened with Gus. She knew he'd gone to take care of him, but she didn't know that he'd handed him over to Abram instead. He was going to have to break that news to the entire fucking club who were already questioning his whereabouts, and fuck, that was one of the hardships being president again, wasn't it? Dealing with the backlash that one of the members of the club had betrayed them.

Yeah, that shit could wait another day. He was determined not to ruin the moment he had with her. Not when he was aching to be inside her, filling her up with his seed.

Maybe he should tell her to put a stop to those birth control pills.

The thought of her belly round with his baby gave him satisfaction. It would be the ultimate marking, the caveman inside of him whispered.

"You ever thought about having kids?" he asked her as he ran kisses over her shoulders, eyes on her tits floating in the water. He wouldn't last very long not taking her at this rate.

"Once or twice," she answered, turning her flushed face to look at him. "But not for several years yet. I want to have some quality time with you first."

"What would kids do to sabotage that?"

She laughed. “Oh, my God. You didn’t just ask me that.”

“I did.”

“It’s not that they would sabotage your day. I think they’d just fill it. Don’t you want to have your cock inside me more? Because you wouldn’t be able to take me half as much with a screaming toddler.”

That was true.

“Okay, I’ll ask you in a few years then,” he said.

She smiled so wide at him. “You’re so convinced you’ll still want me then.”

He smiled back and her expression gentled at the look of it. “Babe, I’ve wanted you since you were fucking fifteen, I just didn’t know it.”

Tyler’s eyes glistened and she swallowed thickly, about to turn her face away. He took her chin before she could and turned her back to him. He ran his fingers under her eyes, wiping away her happy tears that’d fallen.

His heart felt so heavy with her in his arms. He felt like he was capable of anything with that look in her eye as she took him in like she fucking revered him.

And he revered her too.

He adored Tyler, adored every single beautiful inch of her.

He used to think that was a problem. Like caring for someone to this extent was a weakness. But how could it be a weakness when he felt so much strength coming out of that love?

Still stroking her face, he leaned in and kissed her, his other hand already running down her breasts and smooth abdomen. Once he found her clit, she jerked in his tight grip and moaned, shutting her eyes as her breathing began to change.

He rubbed her slowly, slipping his finger inside her warmth as he went, taking his time to build her up. Her head fell back against his shoulder as he continued, sucking at her bare neck as he fingered her to orgasm. Her mouth opened, panting out loud as it tore through her so strong he felt her muscles tensing around him.

Shit, he could never get tired of this.

He immediately withdrew his finger and turned her around. Grabbing at his cock, he nudged it at her opening and thrust inside her before she knew what was happening. Her hands shot to his shoulders, gripping him tightly as she gasped again.

Hawke thrust inside her a few times and water spilled from the top of the tub. The tight space was annoying. The fucking wave of water was even more annoying. He worked her slowly, his fingers digging into her hips as he brought her down on top of him.

It still wasn't hard enough.

He wanted to go deeper, faster, *harder.*

Still inside her, he stood up and led her out of the bathroom, leaving puddles on the floor, droplets of water falling all around them as he took her to his bed. Pulling out, he flopped her on her stomach and then brought her up on her knees. Running his hand down her spine and to the sexy curve of her ass, he rubbed himself against her folds, watching as she shook, fisting the sheets, waiting for him to take her.

He thought to fuck her from behind. A nice quick pounding to ease the two of them for an hour or so before he took her again.

Only…he wanted to see her face, wanted to go slow again just to watch her come undone.

"On your back, Ty," he told her softly.

She crawled up the bed and then turned on her back, her naked wet body gleaming under the light. She looked divine.

She's mine.

Mine.

He chanted that to himself, and it made him feel heady with pride that he had the sexiest woman he'd ever seen want him just as much.

He crawled in after her, kissing up her leg, along the curve of her hip, right above her belly button, between those gorgeous fucking breasts and then settling on her mouth.

She spread her legs for him, and he kissed her, doting on those succulent lips as he took her slowly, feeling the walls of her pussy squeeze around him as he went.

Unhurriedly, feeling every inch of himself filling her.

It drove her wild, the slowness.

Made her unusually needy.

"I'll have to fuck you like this more often," he promised her, chuckling in her mouth as she begged him not to step.

Her orgasm tore through her so strong, he barely needed to thrust as she squeezed his cock, making him come hard in her at the same time.

After an hour, he took her again, this time on her knees, pounding into her, drawing out more pleasure and leaving her limp in bed.

He should have stopped right there, but he didn't. This want for her was insatiable. He was obsessed with making her come, so he took her again, this time with his mouth between her legs.

She was exhausted afterwards, her head resting on his chest as he drew circles over the insignia tattoo on her back.

Only Tyler could make that fucking tattoo look feminine.

"Hawke?" she let out, barely conscious.

"Yeah, babe," he responded, shutting his eyes as well.

"Whose bed are you in?"

His mouth flinched upwards, his heart burst at the seams as he replied, "Yours, baby."

epilogue

Tyler

One year later…

We had a barbecue at Hawke's mother's house on my twenty-second birthday. Everyone was there, crowding her backyard and filling her home with noise after it'd been quiet and still for so long.

Since Hawke and I had come together, Adella had spent a ridiculous amount of time prodding us for a wedding, for grandchildren, for all the things I hadn't even had time to think about for myself.

Hawke had asked me to marry him months ago when he'd taken me to a resort and we'd spent the entire time either in bed having sex, or out in the pool getting a tan. It wasn't done in some romantic gesture. Hawke never got on his knee. He'd done something better: given me a wicked orgasm that had me collapsing on his chest and breathing harshly. He'd stroked my back and kissed me on the forehead before whispering, "Marry me."

Of course I said yes, and I was rocking a gorgeous opal wedding ring, but a date hadn't been set and I wasn't really thinking of having a fancy wedding.

I wanted something small.

Something personal.

I wasn't even sure I wanted any of the guys at the club to be there either.

In fact, I wasn't even sure I wanted it to be legally done. In my heart I was married to him. Wasn't that enough?

Hawke took me on many retreats over the year. It was always nice having time away from the club, from work, from the noise, and from constant obligations Hawke had to tend to.

He loved it though. His entire world was filled with purpose again. We'd gotten the money out of my hidden account and put it into the club. Hawke scaled back on their illegal activities, determined to run legit. It was a slow process, mostly because there were too many business partners dependent on the club's supply, but Hawke was aiming to be clean in at least five years' time, and by then, who knows? We could finally settle down, find a house and think about starting a family.

That wasn't set in stone, though, and life was exciting that way. Never planning, never knowing.

We took things one day at a time.

And then everything had been made better when Borden showed up one afternoon and handed Hawke a folder. Hawke looked at him questionably before Borden explained, "It's your new identity. Don't fucking hate me for the name. There weren't many options."

Hawke hated him for the name.

Richard Cox.

That was the name he'd been given, and I ended up laughing for hours. Hector teased him relentlessly, even Jesse had something to say. "Isn't Dick short for Richard? So you're Dick Cox now, bro. Nicely done."

That earned Jesse a punch across the face.

It was a totally legal identity though, and Borden had paid an absolute fortune for it, tapping into every source he had to make it happen for Hawke.

"I owe you," Hawke had said, their bromance alive as ever as he gave him a hard pat on the back.

"No, now we're even," Borden replied. "For everything you've done for me."

Borden had been invited to my birthday, but he hadn't showed up. Which wasn't a surprise. He had a family of his own, and I was secretly glad I didn't have to be around him. He was a very scary asshole, and he still hadn't warmed up to me.

"Your father would have been proud of you," Adella told me, touching my arm lightly as she looked at Hawke across the backyard, sitting and staring off into thought, those wheels once again spinning. "He would have been proud of both of you."

I smiled at her and swallowed back the emotion threatening to spill.

My father had been loyal to his brothers right to the end.

It meant everything when I learned that.

All the doubts I'd had washed away, and I knew wherever he was, he'd be happy that Hawke had kept to his word.

He had looked after me.

Killed men for me.

Loved me.

As if sensing my thoughts, his eyes found mine and he smiled softly, gesturing me to come to him.

I walked, never looking away, smiling back as I told him with my eyes rather than my lips, that I loved him too.

In the end, that was all that mattered.

THE END

thank you!

Thank you so much for reading! Reviews and ratings are welcome and so appreciated! For news of upcoming books and giveaways, you can find me here:
www.facebook.com/rj.lewis13

And I just wanted to say, I appreciate every single reader. All the ones that have reached out and sent messages of support, thank you so much! The encouragement it gives me is out of this world. It's always a strange feeling knowing people bother to read what I have to say.
This journey started out by chance, and now it's turned into something I can enjoy doing fulltime.
All because of you.
And your desire to read my craziness.

CPSIA information can be obtained
at www.ICGtesting.com
Printed in the USA
LVHW020337240321
682229LV00005BA/1222